Children of Sinai II:
The Sixth Fire
By
Clarke Nixon

Paperback Edition October 2021
ISBN: 979-8497787634
Copyright © Clarke Nixon 2021

Authors' Note

This story is entirely a work of fiction based on Biblical events, Native American stories of creation and prophecies, theories, historical finds and Clarke's imagination. It is an interpretation only and not intended to cause any offence; we hold the greatest respect for peoples' beliefs.

Children of Sinai is based on the Abrahamic religions; *The Sixth Fire* incorporates Native American beliefs. Although the story is fictional, the intent is to show we all have the same origins; that our stories may once have been the same – albeit changed by human migration and organised religions – and hopefully will be again, one day.

If you would like to read more about Children of Sinai please visit www.childrenofsinai.com

This book is dedicated to everyone who believed in
Children of Sinai.
Our heartfelt thanks for your support.

Contents

Children of Sinai II:
The Sixth Fire
By
Clarke Nixon

Prologue

Towaoc, Summer 1978

The floorboards slid back over the hiding place, blocking most of the light and leaving only the faint rectangle around the boards. The last thing they saw was her face, smiling at them, with the light of the kitchen behind her... Nita thought she looked like an angel.

When they could no longer see her, Billy curled into a ball and sucked his thumb, and Nita curved herself around his back and hugged him, although he was a whole year older than her. They had practiced this a few times, but they had only been left in here for a very short while before; it had been a game then, but things were different this time. As they lay together they could hear her washing clothes above them, and singing the songs she usually sang to them when they went to bed. It was comforting to hear her voice, but Nita didn't like being in the hole; it was smelly, small, and scary, but she had to be brave for Billy. She was a Ute warrior now.

When her eyes had adjusted to the dark, she moved quietly onto her knees. Billy turned to her and opened his mouth to say something, but Nita shook her head and put her finger to her lips. *As quiet as the snow and as still as the mountain.* He squeezed his mouth shut.

Nothing happened for a long time, and Nita could sense Billy getting more agitated; he had never liked the

1

dark. She took his hand and pulled him up onto his knees, and pointed to the small band of light that went around the edge of the hole. His wide eyes followed the trail of her finger as it traced the shape, and she felt his shivers subside.

Then came the loud knock on the cabin door, and they quickly lay down again; Billy shaking with fear, and Nita holding him tight. Although she could only hear two sets of muffled, angry, female voices, she sensed another presence... A man. Somehow she knew he was kind, but sad; she always knew when someone was sad. She remembered when *he* had found them, before the summer, and she had liked him, but he hadn't remembered anything; his spirit was lost between the white world and theirs. Nita didn't want to not remember any of the ones she loved, and she didn't want to be taken away... She was close to tears herself now, but held them back with all the strength she had.

The front door slammed at last, and it went quiet. Billy opened his mouth once more to speak, but Nita shook her head again, and he obediently put both his hands across his lips. *As quiet as the snow...* They waited, holding on tight to the promise that she would come and get them, and then everything would be okay.

It was hard being a warrior when you were only four years old.

Part One
Ute Mountain Ute Tribe Reservation, Colorado

'And Sinawav the Wolf, the creator of all things, called his younger brother Coyote to him. Coyote was tasked to carry a magical bag to a land that Sinawav had chosen for His children. He placed sticks of different sizes inside the bag and as he did so, the sticks became people. Coyote was told not to open the bag until he had reached his destination, but as he travelled over the land the people became noisy, and his curiosity grew.

With his flint knife, he cut a little hole in the bag, looked inside, and laughed at Sinawav's strange creations. Coyote threw the bag over his shoulder and carried on his way, but did not notice that people were jumping out of the hole. Those people ran away in different directions and started new lives, with new languages.

When he reached the sacred mountain he realised that the bag was almost empty. The people at the bottom were lifted out, and Coyote told them they were to be called 'Ute,' and they were to roam the beautiful mountains of the chosen land.

When Coyote returned, Sinawav knew what he had done. Coyote lied and told his brother that he'd tried to catch all the people who had escaped, but he couldn't understand what they were saying. Sinawav was furious, and explained that, because of Coyote's curiosity and stupidity, there would now be more than one tribe and that they would wage war against each other. But the Utes would be brave and strong, and the mightiest of them all.

Sinawav took the empty bag, and saw that the sticks he had placed inside had left marks in the material. He turned the bag inside out and gave it back to Coyote. He cursed his brother to wander the night on all fours, and tasked him to return the bag to His mountain children. The Utes were to keep the bag as a sacred reminder of their beginning, and a message for their future.'

Adaptation of The Ute Story of Creation

'At the time as a great sickness comes to our people, a skinwalker will rise from the burial grounds. Known by the mark of the bear, his boha (spirit) *will be defeated by a great warrior. A tainna wa'ippe (*two-spirit), *blood of aagwayq* (bear) *and pia-kwinaa* (eagle), *the blood of brothers, will re-unite the scattered tribes, and you will know him by his name.'*

The vision of Dakayivani, Shoshone shaman

Chapter One
Kuku

Towaoc, Summer 1961

The limp form of the girl was borne away to be prepared for the burial ground at the edge of the reservation; one slender arm hung down from the blanket in which she'd been wrapped, the fingers curled, never to know the touch of her new-born baby's skin.

Rose looked back down at the infant; at the pool of his mother's life-blood into which she, as midwife, had delivered him; at the angrily contorted face demanding attention now he'd been so rudely pushed into the world. But his world was gone now; carried away by someone who barely knew her name – there had been no father or mother to grieve over the girl, and this child would never know her either… the fact that it was all too common an occurrence didn't ease the sense of futility and sorrow.

Rose gathered up the screaming child, and took him to the one-roomed cabin her father had built. She bathed him, and fed him, wishing more than ever that her mother was there to tell her whether she was doing it right, but her parents had died last year. The grief was still strong, and it seemed to Rose that perhaps this child had come along now, needing her, to help her through that grief. So she lavished all her love on him, even though she knew it was a temporary arrangement, and that she would reap the pain of such devotion when he must, inevitably, leave her.

She named him Logan. So many of her people, including herself, had been forced to adopt so-called Christian names; it seemed pointless to fight it, and she wanted to give him the best chance of finding a home. Repeatedly, she sought help, but was met with refusal at every turn – perhaps those she asked were genuinely unable to afford to feed another hungry mouth, or maybe they felt the shame of the poor dead girl, who had not given up the name of the child's father.

Whatever the reason, Logan stayed with Rose, who gradually allowed herself to accept that, without the support of a husband, she was now his mother. When the people of Towaoc saw how she fostered the boy with generosity and kindness, they began to entrust care of their own children to her; sometimes only for a day or two, when sickness necessitated, sometimes longer, when a family went through a crisis that took time to conquer.

The town's population had only recently begun to grow, but even as the number of children increased, Rose knew them all by name. And they knew her. As an honorary grandmother she had told them they must call her Kaku, the Shoshone word her mother had used when she'd talked about her own mother, but Logan's infant tongue had turned it into Kuku, and the name had stuck. It sounded like the English word for the bird that placed its own offspring in another's nest... The irony had not been lost on her.

Rose continued to use her father's teachings to heal the townspeople; skills he had learned from his own father. Whilst Rose, her parents, and two of her grandparents, were Ute, her paternal grandfather had been Shoshone, and one of the last medicine men. Rose had strong memories of foraging on hillside, forest, and mountain, for herbs and plants, and, despite the availability of modern medicines, many on the reservation still trusted the old ways and so came to Rose for help. She would accept no payment, but food and hand-me-down clothes for Logan were always welcomed. As were odd jobs around her home, and wood for her fire. It meant she was always fighting for survival, but the fight was a good one. An honourable one.

Logan had grown into a happy, bright little boy who liked, more than anything, to build with his coloured blocks. Rose sat clapping and laughing with him, as the towers toppled and crashed to the rug, and marvelled at the patience with which he re-built. It reminded her of how her grandparents had had to do the same; as the last generation to live in tents it had been unbearably hard for them to give up their nomadic lifestyle, to settle on bone-dry land.

The initial affluence afforded by oil and gas revenue had too swiftly dwindled away, leaving them all struggling through poverty. Rose's father had tried desperately to hold on to what they had, believing in his skill as a gambler, but that too had forsaken him, and while others were buying homes, he had built this one with the little he'd had left.

Rose looked around it now. The single room served as their bedroom, lounge, kitchen and washroom; there was no plumbing. The modesty curtain, that separated the kitchen and washing area from the rest of the room, stayed pulled back now, and wherever Rose worked, either sewing on the sofa, preparing herbs at the table, or cooking their meals, she could see Logan.

The cabin wasn't perfect, but it was dry, warm, and clean. The walls were decorated with beaded tail bags, pouches, belts, and a knife case that her mother had sewn by hand. On her bed, in pride of place, was a beautiful red and black striped woollen blanket, woven by her Ute grandmother. In winter it kept her and Logan warm, in summer it lay on the ground where they sat and played in the sunshine.

Yes, it *was* a good fight, and with the best of rewards.

Logan climbed into her lap for a hug. 'Kuku … kahi!'

Rose held him tight, and kissed him. 'And what would you have me sing, my little one?'

He grinned at her around the wooden block he held up to his face, and she smiled and began to sing one of the songs she had learned as a child. He joined in where he could, singing the odd word, but mostly accompanying her with a happy, tuneless hum, until they were interrupted by a sharp rapping at the door.

'Rose Harrison, open up!'

Still holding Logan, Rose climbed stiffly to her feet and went to answer the door to find two white people in suits: a man and woman. They were looking distastefully down at the box that served as a step, and the moment Rose opened the door they stepped off it and into the house.

The woman spoke briskly, and the man translated. 'Child Protective Services.' His translation into Shoshonean wasn't perfect, but Rose understood them well enough and her blood chilled.

'We're caseworkers,' he went on. 'We have some reports about neglect.' He looked pointedly at Logan as he spoke, who beamed back at him, the picture of cheerful curiosity.

'You don't need to translate,' Rose said, surprised to hear her own voice coming across calmly. 'I speak very good English.'

They looked surprised, and glanced around the room as if someone living in such a small place had no business being intelligent and educated. 'Well… good.'

She shifted Logan higher in her arms. 'What reports?'

'Are you this child's mother?'

'No.'

'Aunt then? Sister?'

'No, I was his mother's midwife. I was there when she—'

'So you're not related in any way?'

'No, but—'

'Then you understand you have no legal right to raise this child.'

Rose caught her breath, and reflexively clutched Logan tighter. He wriggled, and his smile dropped away, causing the strangers to look at one another with a certain satisfaction.

'Is the child hurt, Miss Harrison?'

'No!'

The man stepped away to peer into the tiny washing area. 'No plumbing, I see.'

'We're still waiting for the water supply your government promised us.'

'No toilet facilities either.'

'We manage, like everyone else does.'

'And no private sleeping area for the child?'

'He's only little, he—'

'And what about when he's older?' The woman shook her head. 'Miss Harrison, you must see that this is no place to bring up a child.'

'It's his home!'

'Nevertheless, there are standards. Living standards. Safety standards.'

'He is perfectly safe, and very much loved here. Ask anyone.'

'We're talking to *you*. I'm afraid we're going to have to insist you hand the boy over.'

Rose stared at them, speechless. Surely they didn't mean it?

'If you don't comply,' the man said, returning to stand at his colleague's side, 'we have the power to order your arrest.'

'And the boy will come with us anyway,' the woman added. 'Do the sensible thing, and let us take him. It's best for him.'

'No!' Rose took a step back, but before she could turn to run the man had grasped her shoulders, and the woman plucked Logan from her arms. Logan let out an outraged wail, and then burst into frightened tears.

'Don't make a scene, Miss Harrison, it'll only upset him further.' The woman turned Logan to face her shoulder and as she turned to go Logan's chubby arms reached frantically for Rose, but she couldn't move. She felt as if her heart had been ripped from her chest, just as viciously as her child from her arms, and she let out an agonised wail, howling until there was no air left in her lungs, and when she couldn't breathe anymore she dropped to her knees.

'Kuku!' Logan's voice drifted across the yard and was cut off short as the car door slammed. It was a sound that would haunt her dreams forever.

Towaoc, Summer 1978
'Rose Harrison, open up!'
Dread filled Rose at the words, and swift, dark memory followed. It had been twenty years since the last time she had heard someone use her full birth name… for a moment her breath froze in her throat. There was no escape; the authority in that voice was unassailable.

She grasped the door handle with shaking fingers and pulled the door open a crack, and she almost collapsed as she saw two white people, a man and a woman, holding up identical, opened ID wallets. As she stood in stunned disbelief at the way it all seemed to be repeating itself, they pushed past her into her home. Just like before.

The man, kind-faced but sad looking, looked to be around fifteen or twenty years younger than the woman, who was clearly in charge. He took up a respectful

11

position by the door, and offered a sympathetic smile, but said nothing.

The woman was closer to Rose's own age: late forties, and her hair was scraped back into a tight bun that exaggerated the severity of her expression. As she looked at the two interlopers, Rose felt time disappear until she could almost swear she still held Logan's firm, warm little body in her arms. But as reality asserted itself she just felt emptier than ever. And angrier.

'How dare you come into my home? Get out!'

'Your English is very good,' the woman observed.

'I've had a long time in which to learn your harsh language,' Rose said bitterly. 'And I've also learned enough of your customs to know that, even for you, to enter a person's home uninvited is an act of trespass. Not to mention rude.'

'We are authorised, by this state, to enter the homes of people we suspect are fostering children unofficially. Which is illegal,' the woman stressed, and she fished in her pocket to produce a warrant.

Rose slapped it away. 'I stopped fostering years ago, after your people stole my Logan. And as you can see, there are no children here, so you can leave. Now.'

'*Your* Logan?' The woman raised an eyebrow. 'Our records show that Logan wasn't yours, *Miss* Harrison. The law states that children who cannot be raised by their own families, and under suitable conditions,' she glanced around her in undisguised disdain, 'must be given up for fostering or adoption.'

Rose could scarcely believe what she was hearing. 'Don't you look down on *me!* My people were fine until

12

you poked your noses into our affairs.' She shook her head, and her lip curled into a knowing grimace. 'Tell me, does this law apply to your people too? Would you take a white child, and place it with a Ute family?'

The woman ignored her, and checked her warrant. 'We're here about a... a Billy Walker, and a Nita Rogers. We believe you're currently harbouring them.'

'Your information is out of date,' Rose said. I *cared* for both children, yes, but only for a few months.' She lowered her voice. 'Billy's mother left him with his aunt here in Towaoc, but she couldn't cope. Nita's mother took her own life. Relatives for both children were found on the Uintah and Ouray Reservation in Utah. The children were taken there.'

'Do you have proof of this? Documentation?'

'Why would I need it? You're the ones who need paperwork!' Rose felt a grim flash of satisfaction at the look on the woman's face. 'Our people never needed everything to be written down, until you forced your laws on us. We had trust. Billy and Nita must be aged five and four now, so why have you waited so long to check on their welfare?' She managed a small, contemptuous laugh. 'You white folks running out of children? Is that it?'

The woman's face tightened further. 'Our aim is take children at risk of neglect. It's for their own good, their protection.'

'Protecting children is an admirable cause, but you take it upon yourself to do this without your... your *proof,* that you're so fond of. Logan was well cared for. He was neither neglected nor abused. He was a happy child, yet you took him from me and his own people.'

13

'Hmm.' The woman frowned and looked around. Rose followed her gaze, and her own eye lit upon something near the door that stopped her breath again; a little stone with windows and doors drawn on it. Before she could think of a way to draw the woman's attention back to her, the young man moved his foot, covering the stone. As the woman's attention focused on the kitchen area, the man stooped quickly and put the stone wordlessly in his pocket. He did not meet Rose's astonished eyes, but hope surged in her heart that all was not as desperate as she'd suspected. There were good people out there.

Taking courage from it, she stepped up to the woman until they were face to face and, without touching her, began herding her, backwards, towards the door. 'I'm not the naive girl I was back then, I'm aware of my rights. You will leave my home now. You will not come back unless you can show me *proof* of the reason for this violation of my privacy. And as there will be none, I don't ever expect the pleasure of seeing you again.'

The woman almost tripped backwards out of the door, but recovered herself in time and turned to walk away. But Rose's fire was up, and as the officer stumbled over the step she continued, in a rising voice that trailed the woman to her car.

'You come here quoting your laws to me, but where were your laws when Nita's mother was raped after the Spring Bear Dance? She was *sixteen years old!*' She hit the door jamb with her open hand, then followed the officers across the yard. 'The rapist was a white boy, so there should have been a federal investigation, but nothing was done about that was it! No, you were all too busy writing your paper laws in order to take *our babies!*

'We'll be checking with the Utah Child Welfare department,' the woman said, tight-lipped and clearly furious. She turned to put her key in the lock, and Rose was about to say something more, but was halted by the young man, who pressed something into her hand before joining his partner. She looked down; it was the stone. She slipped it into the back pocket of her shorts, and as he turned one last time she gave him a brief nod of bemused thanks. She watched the car pull away in a cloud of dust, and took deep breaths trying to calm her anger. The panic was over, but for how long?

She hurried into the kitchen area and picked up the knife from the counter, then knelt down, murmuring low words of comfort as she pulled back the grass mat and prised up two floorboards to reveal a hole, dug out herself over a few hot, back-breaking days. She had lined it with the discarded plastic sheeting from a neighbour's delivery of wood, and with the boards from the pallets on which the delivery had been left. The neighbour had never asked why she wanted it, but sensing the question anyway, and keen to dispel speculation, she had told him she was building a store room. And so she was, but not for supplies.

She lifted the floorboards away and peered down. Nita had her arms around Billy, whose hands were clamped across his mouth, his eyes huge and terrified. They climbed to their feet, and held out their arms for Rose's help.

'Are you two brave warriors okay?' Rose asked, lifting them out in turn, and brushing cobwebs and dust from their clothes and hair. She kissed them in turn. 'I'm so, so sorry. But everything's alright now, I promise.'

'I wasn't scared,' Nita declared, but the tears pooling in her dark eyes gave her away, and she held on tightly to Rose.

'I was,' Billy admitted. 'Like darktime, but we were quiet, like you said, Kuku.'

'Yes you were,' Rose said, fighting tears of her own. 'And I'm so very proud of you both.'

'Has the govern't gone?'

'They have, Billy. The government people have gone, and you're safe now.'

'Where's my car?'

'In Kuku's pocket,' Nita said promptly.

Rose frowned briefly at her, then handed the painted stone to Billy, who trotted off, dropped to his knees, and began playing as if nothing had happened. She turned back to Nita.

'How did you know I had that?'

Nita shrugged. 'I just did. The man gave it to you.'

'But…' The man hadn't even spoken, Rose was sure of that, she couldn't put a voice or an accent to him. 'You couldn't have seen him give it to me, so *how* did you know?'

Nita's brow puckered. 'I don't know. I'm thirsty, can I have a drink now?'

'I'll fix some juice from the berries we picked this morning. Then I think we all deserve some chocolate as a treat, don't you?'

Rose leaned down into the hole and retrieved the few belongings she'd hastily thrown down, and the blanket, then put everything back to where it belonged. She glanced at the clock as she made their juice. An hour. A whole hour they'd been down there, poor mites, and the day had started out so well – no hint of the terror to come.

Rose had taken the children for a walk along the gravel roads, to the edge of Ute Mountain. She'd been carrying her hand-woven baskets, and Billy and Nita had each carried a bottle of water and their gathering gloves, and they'd stopped at the edge of town to gather the sticky red berries from the squawbush growing along the path. Rose collected the long slender stems to strip later, to use for weaving, and the leaves to make tea, and after a while they travelled onwards, and up the slope into the base of the mountain, through the gnarled brush and sweet scented cedars and piñion pine.

Rose knew the route well; she pointed out the vultures flying overhead, and watched the children with pleasure as they reacted with awe to the echoing cry of an eagle. When they had arrived at the spot they were heading for, she took a jar from her basket to collect sap from a pine tree, then climbed the ladder her friend Joe had put there a few weeks ago. She pulled on her gloves, and began collecting green cones, dropping them for the children to collect up and put in two large baskets. By the time she climbed back down, Nita and Billy were covered in berry stains and sticky pine resin.

When they returned home, she put some water on to heat, then set the children to picking the tiny white pieces of dried resin from the squawbush while she prepared the berries for a healthy juice drink. In a few weeks the pine cones would open, and the nuts could be eaten. It had been a good morning's work, and, just as importantly, a time of companionship and freedom.

'Now then, Nita,' Rose said, wiping her hands on a rag. 'Do you remember how these berries can help someone who's poorly?'

Nita thought for a moment, then brightened. 'They help if you have a cold or a tummy ache.'

'Very good, child. And what about the leaves, once they're prepared?'

'They help sore mouths.'

'Excellent, well done.'

'Her's got the answers right, Kuku,' Billy chimed in, clearly feeling left out. 'Ask me some'ping.'

'Okay.' Rose considered something he would be likely to know. 'Those white bits you're picking off the stems, what are they for?'

'Gum!' he announced proudly. 'For Joe to chew!'

'Good boy,' Rose smiled. 'And… what's that animal called, with a big long nose and floppy ears?'

'A nelephan!' He spoke in English, since there was no Shoshonean word for it.

'Goodness, what clever children I have! And very dirty ones they are too,' Rose added. 'Go and get those sticky clothes off while I get your bath ready.'

She had placed a tin bath on the kitchen counter, and tipped some of the warmed water into it. She added some soap, then turned to see the children were ready. Once they were covered in soapy bubbles, she dripped water over their heads and narrow little shoulders, and started to tell them again about the Ute Mountain warrior. Nita's soapy finger traced the outline of the mountain they could see through the small kitchen window.

'Look, Kuku,' she exclaimed proudly, 'there's his toe, and there's a knee!'

'Can't see them,' Billy grumbled.

'What can you see then?' Rose asked.

'A car! See? A car!'

Rose smiled. 'There are no cars on the mountain,' she said gently. 'Only the sleeping Ute.' She pointed through the window. 'We can only see his toe and knee from here, but do you remember when we came home from that trip to Cortez? We saw the big yellow cliffs of the Mesa Verde wall on one side, and on the other we saw *all* of the warrior, lying on the top of our mountain.' Billy looked doubtful, so she went on, 'We saw his face and hair, and his arms folded across his chest too, remember? He was a great warrior who was badly wounded after fighting our enemies, so he lay down to rest and he's still there, but asleep. One day, when he's needed, he'll wake up and fight our enemies again.'

'I see a car,' Billy said stubbornly, and Rose stifled a sigh.

'Yes, of course there's a car. I see it now, too. It's very smart.'

'What colour is it, Billy?' Nita asked, trying as always to blow a soap bubble. It burst on her fingers, making her blink.

19

'Blue! It's blue!'

Nita leaned over and kissed his wet forehead. 'It's beautiful.'

Rose had felt a surge of pride. Nita was so much like her mother: clever, pretty, and, most of all, caring. One day Rose would have to tell her what had happened to her mother, but it would have to be done carefully. Likewise Billy's own mother.

Towaoc was supposed to be a dry town, but no one had been able to stop the alcohol being bought in. Along with drug abuse, it brought its own problems, by way of violence and health problems; this boy had come into the world with birth hypoxia, and the lack of oxygen to his little brain had deprived him of some of the sense he should have had.

His mother had given him to her sister when she'd left town, on a drunken spree with her latest boyfriend. She never returned. Billy's aunt had tried with him, but had taken to dropping him off with Rose with increasing frequency, until one day she had just not picked him up at all. His family kept in touch but it was tacitly understood that he was now Rose's responsibility. Billy was an uncomplicated boy, with a good heart, and Nita was very protective of him.

'Right, out you come,' Rose said briskly, feeling herself becoming emotional. 'Let's get you dried and dressed, then we'll play some games.'

'Don't like games.' Billy pulled a face.

Nita scooped up some soapy bubbles and blew them at him. 'Yes you do, silly!'

Rose had then wrapped them both in towels, and left them sitting on the rug while she picked up the dirty clothes to soak in the still-warm water. At this time of year water was in short supply, with the run-off from the spring melt being almost depleted. The water truck would be returning from another top-up from Cortez soon, and the queue would be ridiculously long before she found time to join it with her barrel.

'It's lucky I washed your spare clothes,' she said, fetching the only other set she had for each of them, from the small cupboard they all shared. She handed them dry t-shirts and shorts, and returned to the kitchen. As she stood by the window, absently swishing the sap-drenched clothes in the soapy water, a flash caught her eye. She peered more closely; there were some newer homes in the distance, but in this part of town they were more scarce, and often in disrepair, scattered over the gentle slopes below the mountain. If you wanted to catch your neighbour's attention you had to go to them… or shine a light.

Rose's gaze had travelled slowly, left to right over the sparse, dry ground, and there it was again. The flash of torchlight. A warning. Her heart stuttered, and it took vital seconds for her to move into action.

'Quickly,' she said, drying her hands. 'I have to get you into the hideaway! The government is coming. You know how we've practiced this.'

She seized her knife and peeled back the grass mat on the kitchen floor, and worked the blade into the loose floorboards. She heard the children in the other part of the room gathering up their few toys, and she took a blanket from the cupboard. She threw everything down into the hole, then hugged each of the children before lifting them carefully down after it all.

'Remember what you have to do,' she said in a low, urgent voice, trying not to look at the terror on their innocent faces. 'Just remember that I'm right here, even if you can't see me. You'll be able to hear my voice. I'll let you out the minute it's safe, I promise. Now, what must you do?'

'Be as quiet as the snow, and as still as the mountain,' Nita said in a small voice.

'Yes, good. You must not make a sound, or what will happen?'

'The bad people will take us away.' It was Billy's turn, and she could see he was trying to be brave, but his lips trembled and his hand sneaked into Nita's.

'And we'll never see you again,' Nita added.

Rose had knelt on the floor, and leaned down to kiss each of them. 'I love you,' she'd whispered. 'It will be alright. Now sit down and close your eyes.'

An hour. No child should live like this…

Rose poured the juice into two glasses, then braced her hands on the counter top to take a deep, calming breath. A bang on the window made her heart leap and race and, gasping, she looked up to see Joe's face grinning at her through the glass.

Angrily she banged back, and the face disappeared as Joe limped around to the door, leaning on his wooden crutch. Rose gave the children their drinks as she passed by, then yanked the door open and stepped out into the yard, hands on hips.

'Are you completely out of your mind, you stupid, thoughtless idiot?'

A lifelong friend, Joe didn't seem to take offence at her tirade, he merely held up a hand. 'Whoah! I thought you'd be happy!'

'Happy?'

'You beat the government this time, Rose! They've gone! You won!'

'Don't you realise how scared I was?' She dropped her voice, and now spoke from between gritted teeth, so as not to frighten Billy or Nita. 'My heart has only just started to calm down, and you do *that?*' She slapped his arm, hard, and he ducked another blow, almost losing his balance.

'Ow! You crazy woman,' he grumbled. 'If I fall and break the other leg it'll be your fault. I thought you'd be grateful for the warning!'

'Of course I'm grateful! I'm just… I don't know what I am…' The tears came at last, hot and helpless, and Rose felt herself pulled into Joe's clumsy one-armed embrace. She heard running feet, and then smaller hands wrapped themselves around her hips.

'Kuku okay?' Billy asked, sounding close to tears himself.

Rose pulled away from Joe, and drew the children to her. 'I'm fine,' she said. 'How could I not be, when I have you two, and Joe?'

'Hi, kids,' Joe said, his voice a little rough.

'Hi, Joe.' Nita smiled shyly at him. 'We've got something for you.'

'Is it a surprise?'

'Yes.' Nita pushed Billy ahead of her and the two of them vanished into the house, then Joe grabbed Rose's hand and led her to the step. He propped his crutch against the wall and sat down, one leg stuck awkwardly out in front of him.

Rose sat down next to him, grateful once again for his solid, unshakeable friendship. 'How's the leg?'

'I'm getting around, slowly, but I need these splints off. I can't work.'

'You're lucky you'll be able to work again, once it's healed,' she pointed out. 'You could've killed yourself.'

'I know.'

'Climbing a ladder drunk.' She shook her head. 'Those children have more sense than you do.'

'Yeah. But you fixed me up good.' He gave her a little smile. 'My arm's healing well, too, it's just itchy now.'

When she'd found him lying on the floor near his home, there had been a heart-stopping second when she'd thought he was dead. Then he'd twitched and groaned, and on examination she discovered he'd broken his leg, and caught his arm on a stone as he'd landed. She'd set his leg in splints first, then cleaned his wound and applied pine sap to it, while he'd held the gash together, cursing her to the ends of the earth while she did it.

'I have no sympathy for you,' she'd said then, and she said it again now, but then her tone softened and she kissed his cheek. 'Thank you for the warning.'

He seemed about to respond, then cocked his head as he listened to the children inside the house. 'Are they counting in English?'

'Yes. I'm teaching them our language *and* English, and when they can read and write I'll get them books, so they can learn about the world.'

'Well, they'd learn that in school, like the rest of us.'

Rose shook her head. 'You're forgetting not everyone had the chance to go to school in Cortez, like we did. We were the lucky ones.'

'You didn't think so at the time,' he grinned.

'Well, no. I wasn't happy that I had to travel fifteen miles every day to get there. If Billy's grandfather hadn't given us lifts on the water truck we'd still be struggling.'

'But they have that choice now, we didn't.'

'And how can I send them to school?' Rose sighed. 'All that paperwork… the authorities would discover they're not mine, and they'd be taken away after all. No,' she shook her head, 'I'll teach them myself, until I can figure something out.'

'Okay.' He put a hand over hers. 'You know I'll help in any way I can.'

'There is something,' Rose said hesitantly. 'It's Billy. I worry about him, about his future.'

'In what way?

'Well, he can read letters, but he can't string them together into words. And he doesn't pronounce his words properly.'

'I'm no teacher,' Joe said, frowning.

'He'll need to learn a trade, Joe. Something that he can do with his hands, and enjoy doing, or he won't learn.'

Rose gave him a hopeful look from beneath her lashes. 'He's car-obsessed. Would you teach him what you know? Take him for a few hours a week, make a game of it, and see what you think?'

Joe looked down at her for a long moment, then smiled. 'Of course I will,' he said softly, then added in a gloomy voice, 'as soon as this damned leg heals.' Then added 'There's another way I can help. When they're both old enough, I'll show them how to defend themselves.'

Rose smiled with him, then bumped him gently with her shoulder. 'Thank you. That means a lot.'

He opened his mouth, but before he could say anything the children reappeared. Nita handed Joe a leaf with little pieces of white resin on it.

Billy said proudly, 'There's twenteen-three pieces. That's lots.'

'And we picked them all ourselves,' Nita added.

Joe grinned at them. 'My favourite gum. Thanks!' He put it all into his mouth at once and made a great show of chewing, and Rose couldn't help smiling as she saw the children watching, goggle-eyed with fascination. After a minute or two the gum had softened admirably, and Joe opened his mouth to show strands of it sticking to his teeth; he roared at the children, who shrieked, and then dissolved into laughter as they ran back indoors.

Joe and Rose sat quietly for a moment after they'd gone, then Joe looked at her. 'What about Nita?'

'She'll be fine,' Rose said. 'She learns quickly, and has an amazing memory for a four-year-old…' She hesitated, then went on, 'She said something strange earlier.'

'Strange how?'

Rose told him about the car-stone they had left on the floor, and how Nita had known what had happened to it. It sounded fantastical to her own ears, and when she'd finished she could see Joe felt the same.

'It's probably just a one-off coincidence,' he said. 'Don't read too much into it.'

But Rose wasn't so sure. 'I can't help it,' she said quietly, and looked over her shoulder, towards the sound of laughter from indoors. 'I think she has the gift.'

Chapter Two
Logan

The desert sky was streaked dusky pink as the day drew to a close. Joe sat with Rose on the step of Rose's home, and gave her an admiring, sidelong glance, as she released her long black hair and raked her fingers through it with a sigh of relief and relaxation. For a while they sat in companionable silence as they stared at the mountains, sipping the cool mint tea Rose had made earlier.

'Kids okay?' Joe asked at length.

'I hope so, they've settled down well, at least. It's been quite a day.'

'And you?'

She smiled. 'I'll be fine. It's just nice to sit here with you. Actually, can I borrow your car tomorrow? I need to pick up more supplies in Mancos.'

'Of course. But you know you can order whatever you need over the phone now, don't you? You can have anything delivered.'

'I know, but postage costs, and this way I can trade my baskets at the market too. Besides, I want to check the quality of the plants I need myself. And it's safer,' she added. 'There was one time when I was looking through a stall that was supposed to be selling bear root, but it was actually hemlock!' She shook her head. 'A lot of people could've died if I hadn't pointed it out to the seller.'

'Your father taught you well,' he observed, not for the first time, and she nodded.

'He did, but it wasn't easy. Back then we had to go to the Rockies to collect the plants we needed, and he only allowed me to go to school if I continued to study medicine with him too. Mother agreed, but it meant there was little time for playing.'

'He was a hard task master,' Joe mused, remembering, 'but he was a good father. You were lucky, having parents like them.'

'Yes, I was. I miss them a lot.'

Sensing the lowering of her mood, at the turn the conversation had taken, he changed the subject. 'So, what are you after this time?

'More bear root,' she said. 'Lots of it. A few people have gone down with bronchitis, and it also comes in handy for arthritic pain. Billy's cousin has eczema, so I'll need some elk root for that. And a few other things.'

'No peyote, then? Joe teased. 'You don't fancy a magical trip somewhere?' He grinned and wiggled his eyebrows.

'No!' Rose rolled her eyes. 'It'll be many years before I acquire *that* again! I plan to give the cactus to Nita when she's older though, it'll open a pathway to the spirits if she's the natural shaman I think she is.'

'Well *I* might be a shaman,' Joe pointed out. 'How will I ever know, if you don't let me have any?' He laughed as Rose smacked his good leg. 'Ow! Why are you always hitting me, woman?'

'Because you deserve it,' she said archly. 'You say and do things you shouldn't, and you're always trying my patience.'

'Well, maybe you should be more patient, and perhaps try doing things you shouldn't, sometimes.' His voice softened. 'Try to live a little, Rose.'

'I have responsibilities,' she pointed out, but the mock annoyance had dropped away.

'That doesn't mean you can't have fun. I remember a certain beautiful, skinny young girl, who used to sneak out at night to meet a certain *very* handsome young boy, and they—'

'Hush! The children might hear!' But Rose was smiling as she looked at him. 'They were good times, Joe. You've always been there for me and for the children, and I'll always love you. Crazy as you are.'

'Then you should have married me when I asked you.' Joe tried to keep the tone light, teasing, but it was hard to hide the truth he felt in the words, and Rose must have heard it.

'It wasn't an easy decision to refuse you,' she said gently. 'But I was, and always will be, too independent for any man. I wouldn't make you happy. I'm too busy to care for anyone apart from the children, and,' she added with a wry smile, 'if we *had* lived together we'd probably have ended up killing one another.' She shrugged. 'At least this way we stay friends.'

Their eyes locked for a long, understanding moment, and when Joe put his arm around her and drew her close, she moved easily into the circle of his embrace and he dropped a kiss on the top of her head. She rested against his shoulder, and in companionable silence they watched the pink sky darken, until pinpricks of silver began twinkling against the deep blue it became. Joe knew that, for Rose at least, it was the first peace she'd felt that long, long day.

After a while he moved to get up. Rose passed him his crutch and he accepted her hand to get to his feet. 'How about I come with you tomorrow?' he suggested. 'We can have a picnic with the children on the way home.'

'That would be lovely.' Rose kissed him goodnight. 'See you tomorrow then.'

He started away, then turned. 'As soon as these splints are off, get Billy's aunt to watch over the kids… You're sneaking out to my place.'

The windows of Joe's battered Oldsmobile were wide open, and the radio blared as Rose and Joe sang along to the songs they knew, made up words to those they didn't, and the children jiggled in the back seat to all of it. The day had gone well; a successful trip to the markets had turned into a truly lovely day out, as they'd picnicked by the banks of the stony Mancos River, the children paddling in the cool water while the adults lazed under the aspen.

As she drove home, Rose's thoughts turned with some satisfaction to what she'd brought back with her. Aside from the plants and roots she'd gone for, she'd picked up a large ham hock and some lima beans; she already had a good stock of corn, onions and potatoes, so tonight they would have succotash for dinner. They turned into town, along the Mike Wash road, and she was about to ask Joe if he would stay and eat with them when a loud, high-pitched squeal stopped her and she grimaced. The children put their hands to their ears, and Joe winced and turned off the radio.

'Sorry. The fan belt's going. I'll fix it later.'

'It's awful,' Rose said. 'Thank goodness we don't have to listen to that for long.'

Billy piped up. 'What's a fan belt?'

'It's a rubber band,' Joe explained. 'It makes things go 'round, under the hood, and moves power from one place to another in the engine. I'll show you later.'

They passed the trailer park in Mountain Sage Road, and Rose was surprised to see a car parked outside her home. 'Who's that?'

They all leaned forward to look, and Joe whistled. 'That's a beauty. Billy, look, it's a—'

'Cadillac!' the boy shouted. 'A Cadillac!'

'Well done! A Cadillac convertible.'

'But whose?' Rose wondered, uneasy, especially after yesterday. 'It's too smart for around here.'

'Let's find out,' Joe said, and as Rose drove nearer she saw a man sitting on her step. Her fingers tensed on the wheel; visitors were not welcome. Then she gasped.

'It's Logan!'

'I'll watch the kids,' Joe said, 'It'll give you two chance to talk. Just drop us off at mine, and I'll bring them back in a while. I really want to see that Caddy.'

'If you're sure.' Rose pulled up and leaned out of the window. 'Logan! I'll just be a few minutes, I'm going to drop Joe and his car back.'

Logan waved back, smiling. 'Okay!'

Rose left the children with Joe, and collected her shopping to carry back home. During the short walk she thought about the first, and last, time Logan had visited. During his short stay she'd learned it had taken him a long time to find her, and he'd come to see where he'd been born, and to pay his respects; all he and his adoptive parents had been told was that he was Ute, and that he'd been orphaned... though that wasn't strictly true, Rose reflected, they just didn't know who his father was. Logan had been well cared for, and loved, but he had only found out about Rose when he'd begun questioning the people in Towaoc.

As glad as she was that Logan had had a safe and happy home, Rose had been saddened to see this poor lost soul, struggling so hard to discover where he belonged. So many Native American children had been taken from their homes, and after he'd gone again, promising to return, she had cried for those countless other children, and she had cried for Logan... And she had cried because he hadn't remembered her.

Logan rose now, as she approached, and walked to meet her. 'Let me carry that.'

She handed over the bags with a grateful smile, but an inward pang that there was no spontaneous embrace. Nothing had changed, it seemed; they were still friendly enough, but with no natural affection. 'Thank you.' she said. 'This is a lovely surprise, how are you?'

'I'm well,' he said, falling into step beside her. 'And you?'

'Yes, I am, thank you.'

'Where are the children?'

She told him, resisting the urge to put an arm around him. More than anything she wanted to draw him close and hold him tightly enough to banish the memory of that awful day when he'd been ripped from her arms... But she couldn't. To him, she was virtually a stranger. 'Let's get out of this heat,' she said instead, 'and I'll fetch some nice cool lemonade.'

While Rose poured the drinks, Logan vanished back out to the car and brought in a basket of fruit. 'I couldn't carry it all,' he said with a smile, and put the basket on the table. 'For you.'

'Thank you! And for the help, too. Here.' She passed him his drink and he took a long, appreciative swallow.

'This is delicious! It tastes like lemon, so why is it pink?'

'It's made from red squawbush berries.'

Logan drank more, and a faintly awkward silence settled over them, which hurt Rose's heart. Shouldn't they be talking over each other, with all they had to share? She blinked, and inwardly berated herself for the rising emotions; he was doing all he could, and she would have to accept that.

After a moment he lowered his glass to the table, and fixed her with a steady look, as if he'd been quietly forming the question in his mind. 'Rose, I'd like to learn these things from you,' he gestured to the glass, 'and... and all about my people. Would you teach me?'

Rose closed her eyes briefly in relief. 'Of course,' she said, and smiled. 'Let's go and sit down.'

They sat, close together, on the sofa, and Rose began to tell him about the Ute tribe, how they had roamed most of Colorado, Utah and Northern New Mexico, moving with the seasons to survive.

'There are several bands of Ute,' she told him. 'The one that settled in Ute Mountain Ute reservation was known as Weminuche, which means "the people who keep to the old ways." And they tried.'

'What happened to them?'

'First their land was taken. Then their tribal names were replaced with Christian ones, like ours. Their culture was being eroded, bit by bit. They'd had sheep, horses and cattle,' she went on, 'but had to give them up when they settled, because there wasn't the water to sustain them. Then,' Rose's voice grew hoarse, 'the children were taken from them.'

'The *children?*'

'All the Ute women were sisters. The men were brothers. The children belonged to them all.' Rose watched his face as she went on, 'The white folk started imposing their laws on them, which… which is how you were taken from me.'

His hand came out and found hers, and she grasped it tightly as she told him how Nita and Billy were at risk from the same fate.

'That's terrible,' he murmured, his fingers tightening around hers. For a moment they said nothing, though it was a thoughtful, respectful silence rather than the tense one of before.

Then Rose patted his hand and went to fetch the blanket from her bed. 'This is the kind of thing they used the sheeps' wool for,' she said, laying it over his knee. 'My grandmother was a weaver, and she made this.'

He fingered the exquisite cloth with awe. 'It's beautiful.'

'Yes, it is. And there's a story to it, too.' Rose told him the Ute story of creation, of Sinowav and Coyote, and how Coyote was made to return the empty bag to his mountain people. 'You see the lines woven into the blanket?' She pointed. 'They represent the marks that were left inside Sinowav's empty bag. It became a tradition in my family that each generation create something with those lines on, and they had to be copied exactly.'

Logan looked up, interest lighting his eyes. 'What did you make to follow your ancestors?'

Our ancestors, she almost corrected, but stopped herself. 'I'm afraid I've been remiss in that area, but it will be done, and I will then pass the responsibility on to Nita.'

Logan handed back the blanket. 'I'm sure you'll make something equally beautiful, and so will she.'

They chatted a little longer, but it was growing strained again, and Rose kept trying to find ways of getting closer to him, but forced herself not to rush things. There was time; now she knew he'd enjoyed her company enough to come back, he'd do it again.

'You will stay to dinner, won't you?' she asked. 'Since you helped carry half the ingredients!'

'I'd love to, but—'

He turned, startled, as the front door crashed open and two grease-covered children came in.

'What have you got all over you?' Rose asked, holding out her hands to keep them at bay, and remembering to revert to Shoshonean for their understanding.

'Engine oil.' Joe hobbled in behind them. 'Sorry.'

'What *have* you been doing?'

'We helped Joe take off the squeaky fan belt,' Nita explained.

'And it was a bitch!' Billy chimed in.

'Billy!' Rose shot a look at Joe, who winced, clearly knowing exactly what that look meant for him later on. She glanced apologetically at Logan before remembering, and relieved for the first time, that he didn't speak their language.

'What just happened?' he asked Joe.

Rose shook her head warningly, but Joe ignored her and translated Billy's declaration into English. Rose held her breath, fearful that Logan would think her a poor role model, but Logan laughed. Joe grinned too, and so did the children, and eventually Rose saw the funny side, though she flung another dark look at Joe.

Logan stood up and shook Joe's hand, ignoring the grease. 'I'll be happy to come back and help you fix that belt, if you haven't done it yet?'

'Great, but you're not leaving yet, are you?'

'Soon, yes. Rose has just invited me to dinner, but I have to return home, sadly. I very much look forward to visiting again.' He wiped his hand on his shirt, and grinned at Rose. 'There, now we're all mucky.'

'Not quite,' Joe advanced on Rose, who squealed and backed away, but there was nowhere to hide. Joe's bad arm snaked around her waist, and he slowly and deliberately wiped grease from his other hand on her cheek. Rose gasped, tempted to hit him, and all the rude words she'd ever heard were building up ready to let fly. She could have outmanoeuvred him, as disadvantaged as he was, but the light of humour in his eyes was too much, and once more she gave in and laughed instead.

'So,' Joe said, releasing her. 'What have you two been talking about?' He had reverted to English, so as not to be rude, and Rose saw Billy and Nita glance at one another, but this was precisely the kind of thing that would make them determined to learn faster, and it would be rude to exclude their guest, so she responded in English too.

'I've been telling him all about our ancestors, and our customs, and, before we were so rudely interrupted, I was just going to tell him what his name means.'

'Yes, I've been curious about that. Why Logan?'

'Once at the market, some white folks were very rude to me and tried to give me less than my baskets were worth. I got into an argument with them and it got a bit heated, but a kind Irish man came to my rescue. It turned out his name was Logan, and he told me that meant "Little Warrior" in his own language. I never forgot that.'

Logan smiled. 'So, I'm a little warrior, eh?'

'What are you saying?' Billy asked. Rose told him in Shoshonean, and his eyes opened wider. 'What does my name mean, then?'

'Your name is a short form of William. An English king.'

He frowned. 'What's a king?'

'It's like a chief. But of a whole country.'

'So I'm a chief?'

38

'Yes! But you and Nita are my little warriors, too.'

'But I'm a *chief!*' He began to dance around the room. 'A chief! Yeah!'

'Don't go getting any ideas, young man,' Rose cautioned, smiling, 'A chief still has to do what his Kuku tells him to do.'

She glanced over to see Nita sitting very quietly during this exchange, her eyes on Logan, who was smiling at their little family's antics even though he might not have known exactly what they were saying. She knew he was happy to be with them all, but felt there was a sadness about him that he was clearly trying very hard to hide. She guessed Nita felt that too, because the little girl suddenly got up and walked over to him, took his hand, and led him to the middle of the floor, where she gestured for him to sit down.

Mystified, he did so, and Nita went to the cupboard and pulled out a box. She dragged it over to where Logan sat, and tipped out all the wooden blocks in front of him, then proceeded to build. She looked up at him with solemn eyes, until he too began to stack the blocks, a little self-consciously. When the tower had reached her desired height, she laughed, poked at a block low down, and clapped as the tower collapsed. She looked around as Billy came over to join in, and they began again. Rose and Joe exchanged a silent question and response: *what are they doing?*

I don't know…

Nita began humming. Not the tuneless, absent kind of humming that often accompanies a monotonous task, but a very deliberate tune, and then began adding in the words

39

she knew. Rose's scalp tightened, and time spun back, back, back… the sense of déjà vu was almost overwhelming; *How did Nita know that's what we were doing that day?*

Nita handed a block to Logan, who took it and opened his mouth, perhaps to say a simple *thank you,* but stopped. His eyes widened slightly as he looked at the tower, at Rose, and then back to the block in his hand.

His voice was small, hesitant. 'Kuku… kahi.'

Rose's heart stopped, then raced. Her hand crept to her mouth, and she stumbled over to the cupboard and withdrew the treasured old blanket in which she'd wrapped the new-born infant and brought him home. The one he'd taken to bed with him every night until the day he'd been stolen from her.

She sank to the carpet in front of him, and held the blanket out. 'Moy.' *Blanket.*

Logan's hand rose, dreamlike, and brushed the woven cloth with shaking fingers. 'Yack-e-ack.'

Rose's composure broke. Tears poured unchecked down her cheeks as she handed Logan the blanket, as he'd requested. He rose and drew her to her feet, and his voice was choked with his own tears as he wrapped his arms around her and buried his face in her hair. 'I remember! Rose, I *remember…*'

Chapter Three
Surprises

Summers on the reservation were blisteringly hot, but the winters were correspondingly freezing, and snow had been falling steadily all morning. The light dusting that had greeted Rose that morning had become a thick covering, and on an icy ground that meant it wouldn't be melting anytime soon. Rose tucked her hair down inside her coat, for added warmth, and checked that the children's hand-me-down coats, from Billy's cousins, still fitted. Only just, but they'd be alright for this year. Their boots were a better fit, thankfully, and they each had new hats with pom-poms from Joe. Nita was helping Billy to pull on his gloves without getting his fingers stuck, when Joe and Logan came in.

Joe had been out of splints for a while, and was able to spend more time teaching Billy about cars, and Logan had become a regular visitor, helping him out and playing with both children. It was obvious Nita still held a fascination for him; the way she'd reached past the difficult moment and into his memories, easing them out into the open. It was wonderful to see them all getting along so well, and in particular to see how much happier Logan had become.

'Hi, Rose,' Joe said. 'Hi, Nita. You ready, chief?'

'Yup.' Billy gave him a big grin, and clapped his gloved hands together.

'Done your chores?'

He nodded. 'Filled a pan with snow for Kuku's cooking.'

'Great.'

'What are you boys up to today, then?' Rose asked, pulling on her own gloves.

'We're gonna fix a carallbetter,' Billy told her proudly.

'Good boy,' Rose said, exchanging an amused glance with Logan. 'I'm very proud of you, and I'm sure you'll do a great job of making a car all better.'

'No,' he said earnestly, 'a *carallbetter*.'

'He means a carburettor,' Joe said with a grin. 'Come on, champ.' He put a hand on the little boy's shoulder and guided him towards the door. 'See you girls later.'

The afternoon was almost over. Nita skipped ahead of Rose in the snow, and Rose couldn't help laughing as the movement sent the pom-poms on her hat dancing from side to side. She swapped her burdens over: the medicine basket, and the fresh chicken, which had been payment for arthritis medicine, and thought about how well Nita had helped her with administering Old Mary's treatment. *Old Mary? She's only ten years older than me, and I'm already past the average life expectancy for this place!*

Rose brushed the gloomy thought away, and instead looked forward to home, a blazing fire, and chicken and corn soup for dinner. She loved opening the front door and being met with the smells of herbs and plants, hanging from the ceiling to dry, and the clean washing drying by the fire. Joe had been busy lately, chopping firewood, and there was now a large pile outside the door, for which she was extremely grateful.

As they neared home she smiled at the welcome sight of the smoke curling out of the chimney and disappearing against the heavy grey sky. The snow was still coming down, and she blinked it off her lashes as she and Nita knocked their boots against the step, dislodging the caked-on snow before going indoors. Rose stoked the fire, listening to the hiss of melting snow in the fireplace, and put fresh logs on it. Then she set to work preparing the chicken. Nita didn't have to be asked to begin picking the corn off the cobs that had been dried and stored months earlier, and they worked and chatted as they readied the meal.

The pan of snow had melted, and Rose had just finished scraping the ingredients into the water, when a knock sounded at the door. Knowing Joe and the others would have simply walked in, Rose frowned and wiped her hands on her apron before crossing to the door. She didn't open it.

'Who is it?'

'Miss Harrison, it's Donny Ross, from Child Protective Services, we met in the summer. May I speak with you, please?'

Rose felt her entire body tighten up, and threw a panicked glance over her shoulder at Nita, but there was no time to hide her now. 'You're not welcome, Mr Ross,' she managed. 'This is not a convenient time.'

The voice lowered, became friendlier. 'I'm not here on official business, I've come with good news for you.'

Rose remembered how he'd stood on the stone to hide it, when he'd been here with his superior officer, but although she was grateful, she couldn't trust him. Not entirely. She twisted her apron between her fingers, knowing she shouldn't wish for Joe to ride up and save her, but wishing he would anyway. She jumped as she felt a small hand slip into hers, and Nita looked up at her with earnest eyes.

'It's alright, he's a good man. I know he is.'

For a moment Rose just looked back at her helplessly, then nodded. She might not trust this Ross man, but she trusted Nita. She opened the door to the shivering officer; his hands were wrapped across his chest, and his nose was blue although he could only have been standing there for a minute. His car had left shallow tyre marks in the snow, and if he didn't get back into it soon he'd be stranded here, so he wouldn't be here for long, at least.

'You'd better come in before you freeze,' she said, and stood reluctantly aside.

He brushed snow off his coat, and knocked it off his shoes. 'Thank you.' As before, he remained by the door, but Rose gestured towards the fire.

'Go and sit down, we can talk there.'

He must have seen the tautness in her features, because he spoke gently. 'Please, don't be afraid. I'm here to help.'

'I've only invited you into my home because you helped me once before. I have no trust to offer you.'

'I understand.' Ross sat on the sofa and stretched his hands out towards the crackling fire. Nita returned to corning the cobs, and Rose waited for Ross to speak again.

'Miss Harrison, the reason I didn't give you away before was because, unlike some of my co-workers, I trust in what I see, not what I read. I know you take good care of your charges.'

'I do. But how do *you* know this?'

'I'd been watching you, prior to our visit. I could see no evidence that these children are mistreated. In fact they seem like very happy, healthy children.'

Despite those words, the revelation sent a chill racing down Rose's spine. She'd thought she was being so careful, so how had this man come out here, unseen, and watched them for long enough to form an opinion? She felt a little sick at the thought of being spied upon, no matter how benevolently, and the feeling formed into a knot of anger in the pit of her stomach.

'Then why do your people insist on trying to take my children away from me? From my people? We take care of our own; Ute children belong to us all, but your laws say otherwise. Our tribal culture is given no consideration!'

'Believe me, we take the protection of children as our highest priority, and most of the caseworkers I know do act in the best interests of the child. But there are those that take their duties too far, and—'

'Mr Ross, are you aware that many children have been taken, and not even placed in foster or adoptive homes? Some go to boarding schools, where they're mistreated, and in some cases have *died!* Can you imagine how scared those poor children must have been? Can you imagine how I felt, not knowing where my Logan was, or how he was being treated?'

'I'm aware, yes.' He flushed and looked away. 'I'm ashamed to say that some of my superiors have admitted that, in the past, these were attempts to destroy your people, and your culture. That's why I take it upon myself to get the facts straight, before I condone the removal of a child from his or her home.'

'By *spying* on us?'

'What better way to see how things really are?'

Rose still felt queasy at the thought, but she was too anxious now, to dwell on it. 'What's this good news you have for me?'

Ross cleared his throat, on firmer ground now. 'The law's changed. Last month the Indian Child Welfare Act was passed, and this was brought about by good people who could not stand by and let this situation continue. Reports of abuse or neglect will still be looked into, of course, but the child's tribe will have exclusive jurisdiction over each case. Our laws will still have to be adhered to, but no Indian child will be taken and placed with a non-Indian family. Plus no child can be forcibly removed without notice.'

Rose refused to allow her hopes to be raised before she knew more, but she couldn't deny the sudden quickening of her pulse. 'How can this help me?'

'If you could obtain more suitable accommodation…' he held up a hand to forestall the contradiction he knew was coming, '…before you jump down my throat, by *suitable,* I mean *larger.* The children would need their own rooms. If you can do this, I think you have a good chance of obtaining legal custody of Billy and Nita.' He reached into the inside pocket of his jacket, and withdrew an envelope. 'There are some guidelines here, I'll leave them with you.'

'And then what?'

'Well, the decision on whether or not to apply for custody is yours, of course. It's not guaranteed, but I think you—'

'If I apply, they'll know I have the children.'

He shrugged. 'As I say, I think you have a strong chance. I strongly recommend you do, for the sake of the children and yourself.'

'How can I, when I can't find bigger accommodation? The gas and oil revenue shares are so small, and even with benefits I can't afford to buy another home.'

Ross chewed his lip. 'A loan, maybe?' he ventured.

She almost laughed. Would have, if it hadn't been so frustrating. 'That's impossible. Think about it! Your government is the trustee of our affairs, so none of us have any assets to use as collateral.' She shook her head. 'Mr Ross, no company will take the risk of loaning my people money, because they can't foreclose on tribal lands! We can't control our own resources, and,' she finished bitterly, 'we have no way to better ourselves.'

Ross climbed to his feet. He looked genuinely crestfallen, but could offer no solution. 'I'm sorry, Miss Harrison, I truly am. I hope you're able to work this out somehow.'

Rose felt the anger drain out of her, along with that flicker of hope she'd been foolish enough to allow herself. 'I'm sorry I shouted, Mr Ross,' she said. 'Life isn't easy here, but it's no fault of yours, and I know you tried to help.'

47

'I understand.' He held out a hand. 'You have the guidelines and the forms you need, and you have my name. Please, call on me personally if your circumstances change.'

'And you won't tell anyone? About… about the children?'

Ross clasped her hand in both of his. 'I hope that you have more trust to offer me than when I arrived,' he said quietly. 'I'm worthy of it, Miss Harrison. Remember that.'

She watched him trudge through the snow to his rapidly disappearing car, and as the lights cut through the gloom and he drove carefully away, she could only give thanks for the bad weather. It was the only time she and the children were truly safe.

***

April

Now, Rose, close your eyes,' Logan ordered.

'What? Why?'

The snows had melted away, and as the first tentative signs of spring appeared, Rose and the children had gone for a short walk with Joe and Logan, down Mountain Sage Road.

The men had been acting strangely all morning, and although it had been intriguing at first, it was getting old and irritating now. Rose hated surprises, and, used to being in control of her own life, she equally disliked being the only person who didn't know what was going on.

'Just do it,' Joe urged, grinning. He'd definitely been up to something, and she gave an exaggerated sigh, and complied.

Startled, she felt hands clasp around both her arms as Joe and Logan took hold of her and turned her in what felt like a full circle but she couldn't be sure. The temptation was strong to simply open her eyes again and tell them to stop their idiotic behaviour, but they began walking again, this time slowly so she didn't trip. They had only gone a short distance before they stopped again, and she heard a light, metallic jingling sound.

'You can open them now,' Logan said, and she heard the eagerness in his voice.

She opened her eyes, and jerked her head back as she encountered something shiny dangling right in front of her face. Then she focused and recognised a couple of keys on a ring. 'What are they for?'

Logan walked up to the nearest of the park trailers, and put a key in the door. Rose drew a pleased gasp. 'You're moving in? Oh, Logan, that's wonderful, but won't your parents mind— '

'*I'm* not moving in, you are.' Logan smiled at her confusion. 'It's for you and the children,' he added patiently.

Rose stared, uncomprehending. 'What… How?'

'I made a trade with the previous owner,' Logan explained. 'I know it's not new, and it needs a good clean, but it's solid, and roomy. It just needs a bit of fixing up here and there, but Joe and I can help with that.' He laughed. 'Okay, don't ask any more questions, just go and look around!'

The children had either understood a lot more quickly than Rose had, or they'd been in on the surprise, because they were already through the door and exploring, exclaiming in delight as they peered into rooms and out through windows. Rose was still stunned, robbed of speech, but she finally followed the children, and began walking around in something of a daze, muttering about which belongings from her little cabin home would fit where. It wasn't until she saw the children standing in the middle of the kitchen, staring at her with wide eyes and beaming smiles, that the penny finally dropped.

She went up to Logan, who had been watching her anxiously, and put her arms around him. 'I don't know how you've done this, but thank you.' When he returned the embrace she had to choke back tears. 'Thank you *so* much. I can never repay you, I have nothing to give.'

'You've given enough, Rose,' Logan said softly. He cleared his throat, and spoke more briskly. 'Right, well we'll leave you and the kids to look around, and we'll come over tomorrow to help you move your stuff in.'

He stepped outside, and Joe bent to kiss Rose gently, and then murmured, 'Now you can put in that custody application.'

She nodded, still unsure whether or not she was dreaming, and lifted a hand in a vague wave as Joe and Logan started out towards Joe's home.

Once out of earshot of the trailer park, Joe clapped Logan on the back. 'You did a good thing, my friend.' Then he grinned. 'I suppose you're gonna need a lift home now!'

Chapter Four

Nita

Rose carefully lifted the jug with both hands, and poured the infusion of lemongrass and ginger through the strainer into two waiting mugs.

'D'you want honey in yours, Joe?'

'I've been having honey in your teas for years, I'm not gonna change my habits now.'

Rose turned and placed her hands on her hips. 'If you're going to be tetchy you can fetch your own damn tea.'

'Sorry,' Joe muttered. 'I didn't sleep too well.' He gave her a wry look. 'These old joints just don't stop aching.'

Rose nodded. 'There's extra ginger in this, it should help us both with that.' She added the honey and took Joe's drink to him, carefully cradling the mug in both hands, before returning to fetch her own. She sat next to him with a little grunt and a sigh, and he smiled at her.

'How're your hands?'

'I can still manage simple things.' She flexed her fingers tentatively, eyeing the swollen knuckles and the way one finger had started to stick out at an angle from the others. 'They're getting stiffer with each winter that passes.'

Both of them tired so much more easily these days, and neither could remember a time that they'd been able to stand up, or sit, without some little exclamation.

Joe took her hands in his, and dropped an affectionate kiss on her knuckles. 'You'll always be my beautiful little scorpion.'

'Scorpion!' Rose raised an eyebrow as she added, 'You'd be a lot kinder to me if you remembered I could still whack you one!'

He chuckled softly. 'We've had hard times, Rose, but things are easier now. We're really lucky we have such good kids, Nita looks after us so well.'

'Yes, she does. I'm glad she talked you into moving in with us. We can take care of one another.' Joe had such trouble getting around; that broken leg of his had come back to haunt him in recent years.

'I think Billy got the best deal, moving into my old place,' he observed with a grin. 'Nita got the oldies, and he got a bachelor pad!'

'Bachelor pad!' Rose snorted. 'I don't know where you get your ideas from! Your place was a dump, it took the kids weeks to make it habitable!' She softened. 'We've got a lovely home here, and I'll forever be grateful to Logan. I'm so proud of all three of them.'

Rose put down her cup and picked up the pretty carved wooden box that sat on the coffee table. It had been a gift from Joe, two years ago for her sixtieth birthday, and she smiled as she brushed a finger across the carved rose on its lid before opening it. Inside lay a few treasured photographs, and she lifted them out one by one, holding them so Joe could see.

'Look at this. Logan and Carol on their wedding day – such a wonderful day.'

'It was,' Joe agreed, putting down his own drink so he could take the photos from her. 'I wasn't sure about going, but his parents made us so welcome.'

'You got drunk,' Rose reminded him, and he affected an affronted look.

'I was cheerful, is all.' He studied the picture, and turned to look at her. 'You looked beautiful that day.' He bent to kiss her, and she kissed him back, then smiled and went back to the photographs.

'Here's that one of Peter with Joseph, on his first day at school. I love this one.'

'Still blows me away that Logan called his boys after his father and me. Not that I didn't deserve the honour of course,' he added with a little grin, 'but I was still very proud.'

Rose rolled her eyes, but couldn't help smiling. 'Oh! Here's the photo Logan took of Nita and Billy when they put up the sign for their repair shop. *Weeminuche Auto Repairs*,' she read aloud, with a familiar surge of pride. 'Billy would never have come this far without your help, Joe.'

'He's a natural,' Joe said with a little shrug. 'The boy might not be good at much else, but he sure knows his way around a motor. He's working flat out right now.' Word was getting around, and now that the new casino and hotel were open, and tourism was on the rise, things were looking good for the shop.

'Nita works just as hard,' Rose said. 'I know she's only at the shop part time, but when you add the voluntary work at the health centre, *and* taking care of us—'

'We've got it made,' Joe said, settling back. 'Great kids; comfy home, with hot and cold running water; and beer. In a refrigerator!'

'I see you have your priorities straight,' Rose said with a laugh. She picked out the last picture and studied it, remembering the day as if it had been just last week. She and Joe were dressed in their best clothes, and standing behind an equally well-dressed Nita and Billy on the courtroom steps… The momentous day when Rose had finally been granted custody of the children. All four were smiling, and little Billy was waving at Logan, who'd been taking the picture.

'Look how small they were,' she said softly. 'I was so scared that day.'

'I remember. I was, too.'

'You never showed it.'

'I couldn't, for your sake.' He took her hand again. 'I love those children as much as you do, Rose.'

'I know.' She patted his hand and felt his fingers tighten on hers. 'It took you so long to find Billy's mother… I still find it hard to believe she'd sign over her child for the price of a bottle of whiskey.'

'I'm glad we lied to the boy,' Joe said. 'No child should go through life believing they're unwanted.'

'It was better for him to think she'd died,' Rose agreed. 'In the long run, anyway. I hope Nita can come to terms with what happened to her own mother, she's still so angry about it.'

'Yeah.' Joe's voice was quiet, regretful.

'She's twenty now, and there's still no man in her life.'

Joe gave a little laugh. 'Times are changing. She's gonna need a strong one; she's like you: independent and tough. Men are afraid of her.'

'You weren't afraid of me,' Rose pointed out.

'Ah, that's 'cos I knew the real you.'

Rose put the photos carefully back in the box and replaced the lid. Then she sat back and leaned against Joe, smiling at the way he casually kissed the top of her head. The way he always had done.

'Tomorrow's the big day, then?' he said.

Rose nodded. 'It's Nita's day off. It took me a long time to get the peyote, it's so hard to find now.'

'Will she need much?'

'I've only prepared a small amount, but I have no doubt she'll be following in her great-grandfather's footsteps.'

They fell silent, thinking about what might happen. 'How was it for you, when you did it?' Joe asked at length.

Rose paused, recalling it to mind clearly. 'At first I threw up,' she confessed. 'It tastes *horrible*. Then… well, after a while I just felt peaceful. Such an amazing sensation, and it lasted for hours. Everything was so pretty, the way the colours stood out.' It had been so vibrant, it was hard to put it into words. But the memory was strong. 'Anyway, like my father, I had no significant visions.' She twisted to look up at Joe a little wistfully. 'I guess we were destined to be healers of the body, not the spirit.'

May 10th

Nita had emptied and cleaned her room and put fresh sheets on the bed, and now she placed a bucket beside it, eyeing it with mild distaste. *A purging bucket.* While Rose made a fresh smudge stick from sage and pine, Nita washed and changed into clean clothes, then tied her damp hair back and sat on the bed, watching Rose ceremoniously wafting the lighted stick into every corner of the room.

'Call on Dakayivani to guide you,' Rose said. Nita's Shoshone great-grandfather had been a highly respected shaman, a *boha gande*, and his visions had been legendary. Rose had told her all this as they prepared the room, adding that, after one particular vision, Dakayivani's hair had turned white. Nita couldn't help wondering what her great-grandmother, Kimama, had thought of that.

Rose finished her preparations, and came to sit next to Nita. 'Joe and I will be here with you the whole time. Although there is nothing to fear.'

'I'm not afraid, Kuku,' Nita assured her, reverting to the childhood name without even thinking. 'I'm curious though, and I hope I can bring back something wonderful to share with you both.'

'Lie down,' Rose said.

Nita did so, and closed her eyes. Her breathing deepened, taking in the scent of sage and pine, and she concentrated on the rhythmic ticking of the clock beside her bed. After a while she felt a strange pulling sensation, and almost jerked awake again but forced herself to lie still, to feel the bed beneath her, and focus on the clock, and, as her body grew weightless, to follow the muted sound as it faded into the distance…

She opened her eyes.

She was standing beneath… no, *inside*, what looked like a hundred intermingling rainbows. She caught her breath and reached out, expecting her fingers to pass through, and stunned to find that not only could she touch each colour, but that each felt different against her skin. As the colours faded, so, so slowly, she realised she was high in the air, looking down on an unfamiliar land. It was a new and strange sensation, but neither unpleasant nor frightening. None of her day-to-day worries had followed her here, and she allowed herself to float, utterly at peace.

People below, perhaps as many as thirty of them, were moving east from a warm, dry climate, crossing a frozen wasteland and dressed in skins and hides against the chill. She drifted closer, fascinated, and saw they were not people as she knew them, after all. Human, but ape-like in appearance, and ahead of them was a herd of animals she'd never seen before. Not like the buffalo that had roamed her homeland, more like the pictures of elephants that Rose had shown her and Billy when they'd been little, but these creatures were covered with long, rich-looking fur. Perhaps the same as was worn by those who followed them.

Nita knew instinctively that this land was far from her own, and her fascination grew as she floated lower; some of the ape-people had moved ahead of their group, and she saw now that they carried spears. One of the lumbering beasts fell to the skill and determination of the hunters, who made short work of skinning and butchering, cutting the tusks away with a reverence that showed deep respect for their prey. As Nita watched, the people made their way to a mountain range, and there, in a cave at the base of one of the largest mountains, they made their home.

Time flowed differently here. Nita watched three more migrations, all different peoples, but following the same route. It was hard to fathom why they would risk leaving a temperate climate to travel through such icy wilderness, but it became clear that each group relied on those huge animals for food and warmth, and that they must follow them to survive.

The last of these groups looked more familiar, more like the species Nita knew and recognised as her own, and as she watched them she saw how all these different people were living together in peace, sharing skills and hearths, each helping the others in their own way. Their numbers grew, many children of combined heritage were born, and Nita watched, breathless with the speed of it all.

After a while she realised that none of this was happening now, in her time; what she was seeing had happened over several millennia. Somewhere along the way, the first three groups she'd seen had faded away, and she understood, with a sharp pang, that she had witnessed the death of the last of their kind.

Eventually, after many generations had come and gone, the people began to move again; farther north, but veering off to the east again, to live on a bridge of land where vegetation was lush, and food plentiful. When the glaciers started to melt, they were able to cross over into another land. Some remained there, but some left and travelled farther east, before turning to the south, and warmth.

Instead of using the hides they hunted as warm clothing, they now covered wooden frames with them, and these served as their homes. Nita recognised these as wickiups, the same type of tents in which her ancestors had lived in the summer months; in winter they had used the versatile, but more temporary teepees. Generations passed, and the people divided again, spreading out to claim that warm land, to hunt, grow, and live well, and these people began to look more and more familiar.

Nita could still feel the hardness of the bed frame beneath her, could still smell the sage and pine, and could hear Rose's and Joe's voices. Their words were indistinct, but it was a deep comfort to know they were close by, though she wasn't ready to return to them yet; there was more to see, and to experience... She left them, and slipped deeper into her visions.

Once again the swirling colours danced before her eyes, and, although entranced, she waited with growing impatience for them to fade and to show her what she knew she must see. As before, when the rainbows dissipated she found herself looking down, and on the same land. This time there were only five men, walking through the desert. The similarity in their looks led her to think this was an elder and his four sons; their vivid orange, red and yellow clothes billowed in the desert wind, making them look like a fire streaking across the barren landscape.

When they reached the lands of ice and snow their robes changed to furs, but they did not stop to find a home there, as the others had. Instead they followed the same path immediately, turning north and east, but this time there was no bridge of land; the glacier melt had covered it with freezing choppy water. It was summer. Nita watched, as they backtracked and struck camp to wait for winter, when the water would once again freeze hard enough to be crossed on foot. They felled and prepared small trees, and lashed the logs together with dried animal intestines to make a raft.

When the time was right they set off across it, using the raft to navigate the large channels of water in between the solid chunks of ice – a treacherous journey, but one that appeared in far more detail than the others to the watching Nita. She looked on in fascination as the travellers stopped to rest, on a small island between the two land masses, before continuing on the other side.

There they were met by villagers, out hunting with their dogs, and the old man was pulled along on the raft by his sons, while being guided to a fertile oasis in the middle of the icy land. They were accepted as guests while the increasingly frail older man rested and regained his strength – the long, long journey was taking its toll. After a few weeks the five men continued on their way.

They came upon another village with the familiar dome-shaped homes, and Nita abruptly became aware of a warm wind against her skin, and as her heartbeat sped up she realised she was dropping lower, and at speed. The voices that had anchored her to her physical self, and to her home, went the way of the rainbows, and for a moment a rising panic gripped her before understanding took its place; this was it. All that had gone before had been background, a layer of history to help her understand the path the old man and his ancestors had followed that had led to this, the true intent behind the vision. She must put fear aside and be the warrior Rose had always told her she was, and, more importantly, she must remember every detail.

There was no jarring landing, no bursting onto the scene that awaited; she was just there, among them, unseen and unheard. The hard-packed ground beneath her feet replaced the wooden bed frame, and instead of sage she smelled wood smoke and cooking meat. But there was no time to stand and gaze at her surroundings, she was swept along with the old man and his sons, and she realised she had next to no free will here; she was a passenger and an observer, and curiosity would have to wait. The villagers welcomed the visitors unreservedly.

'We are the Anishinaabe people,' the chief told them, in a language that Nita understood here, but knew would be alien to her otherwise. She realised that the men did not have the same understanding but communicated by way of actions. 'I would hear your stories, old man, I feel they will be of great interest. But first, we eat.'

Nita sat behind the old man, still unseen, and although the sight and smell of the food awakened a growling appetite, she only watched. She was not hungry in the way these people were, and did not attempt to take their food.

'We are travelling to a land promised to me in a visit by a holy spirit,' the old man told the eager listeners. 'In a dream. I have been directed to the path I and my sons now take. '

The old man removed a bag from his belongings and carefully extracted a small tablet covered in raised lines. He showed it to the chief, and told of another journey, made long ago, to a mountain of light.

'This was the message given by the Holy Spirit, for the future. But I cannot interpret it. I must take it to lands in the south.'

The chief sat forward, his meal forgotten, his eyes shining. 'Dreams are of great importance to us too. Our shaman had a similar vision. It foretold of a land where food grew on the water. We followed signs until we came here, to the rice fields. Life is good and we live in contentment.' He paused for a moment then asked, 'But tell me, why did your whole tribe not follow you?'

'We are many thousands, and too great a number to travel the distance. My instructions were to take only my sons. It was difficult to leave my people behind.'

The chief nodded, and an understanding of their responsibilities passed between them.

Nita wanted to know more, but the scene in front of her was shrinking, and an odd feeling bloomed in the pit of her stomach; she realised she was moving away again. The smells and noises faded, and time sped up again, and the next time she felt the warm wind on her face she was among a collection of adobe buildings; once more a ghost among mortals, aware of everything but passing unnoticed through their world.

As the men journeyed farther south, the temperatures climbed, and the travellers' furs had once again been replaced by their bright, lightweight robes. The old man's strength had been waning, the pain in his joints increasing, and they had travelled a long way in that time, but Nita knew he would not cease in his quest until he had completed it.

The buildings were built next to, and on top of, one another. Ladders were everywhere, allowing free movement between rooms, and this, alongside the squash blossom-design hair styles of most of the young women, told Nita that this was the home of the Hopi, old neighbours of her own people.

Once again they were welcomed without hesitation, and after a short while the old man was invited to attend the chief in a special meeting. Nita was drawn along with him, down a ladder into a hole in the ground, and into a room she understood to be sacred, a kiva. She felt uncomfortable to begin with; women were not allowed in kivas, until she remembered she was not truly there.

The chief gestured for the old man to sit, and poured some kind of drink into a cup, waiting until the old man was comfortable before he began.

'We are the Fire Clan of the Hopi, and our people were led here by the Creator. We are all now living in the Fourth World.'

'Fourth?'

'The first was destroyed by fire. The second by ice, and the third by floods.' The chief took some of his own drink, and eyed the old man keenly. 'One day, it is said, a lost brother, Pahana, will come. When he is recognised there will be a time of peace. That is when we will enter the Fifth World. But first, this world will be destroyed. We must follow the dictates of the Creator, and the people of the new world must cease their disregard for Mother Earth.'

The old man nodded, and in his turn he told the story of his own travels from his homeland, and of the dream given to him. 'We are to find a mountain in the shape of a great warrior, and have been led to these lands to prepare the way for the coming of a saviour, the final prophet.'

When, as before, he took the tablet and showed it to the chief, the chief studied it with deep interest, stroking the raised lines with great reverence. 'Do you believe your saviour, and our lost brother, to be one and the same?' he said at length.

The old man nodded. 'It is possible. Your *creator* and our *holy spirit* may also be one and the same.'

'We have been told that Pahana will come clothed in red, but how will we know who it is?'

The old man took back the tablet, and broke it in half. He passed half to the chief and replaced the other in his bag. 'I will take this to the mountain I have been shown. One day, when these two halves are brought back together we will know who Pahana is.'

'I know the mountain of which you speak,' the chief said, 'but you have come too far south. Rest awhile, you and your sons. Regain your strength, and when you are ready to leave I will show you the path you must take.'

It seemed to Nita that she had barely blinked, when she was racing above the land again, watching the old man and two of his sons leave the Hopi, while the two remaining sons stayed to begin a new life with the wives they had found. It must have been several weeks in the lives of the three men though mere minutes in her own, before she saw the group of wickiups nestled at the base of a mountain and realised they had arrived.

Arrived to the land she called home.

The old man barely had the strength to relay his story once more, and to give his half of the tablet to the chief, before he collapsed. Nita watched, with tears in her eyes as he was taken inside one of the dome-shaped dwellings to rest, and she knew he had nothing left to give. He was little more than a husk now, and Nita felt a great wave of respect and love wash over her; he had sacrificed everything for his belief, had persevered and fought through danger, hardship and hunger, and he had achieved his goal.

His sons sat on the floor watching over him lying on a bed of furs, talking to him and to each other in barely audible voices, and pressed his hands and smoothed his brow. There was a palpable grief in the room, and Nita felt it in the very roots of her being. She moved closer, hoping to somehow transcend the barriers that separated her from the old man by the force of her respect. To thank him, though he would never know it.

He was saying his goodbyes now, and as Nita reached the foot of his bed, he lifted his head and looked directly at her. She froze, her heart tripping, and moved back… he couldn't possibly have seen her! But, as she rose away from him, his gaze followed her, and he smiled.

The old man's sons buried him on Ute Mountain peak. Nita stood a little way back and watched the ceremony, feeling the wind tugging at her hair and her clothes, and wondering how all this could be only in her mind. She could hear the birds calling, and each blade of grass waved in its own pattern, fluttering, caught by the wind currents and falling still again. Such detail… she started as she saw a white-haired woman coming towards her. The first time someone had acknowledged her presence in what felt like a hundred lifetimes. The figure drew closer, and Nita realised it wasn't a woman at all, but a man dressed in an intricately beaded dress, the fringes on the hem and sleeves flowing like water in the breeze. His beautiful long hair hung loose, but parts of it were plaited with intertwined feathers and beads. He was a breathtaking sight.

All at once Nita knew him. 'Great-grandfather?' She paused. 'Dakayivani?'

He nodded. 'Haa'a.'

Nita bowed her head in return. 'I'm honoured to meet with you. Have you come to guide me further?'

'Tsaan ma nahate, Nita, you have done well to come this far, child.' Dakayivani gestured, encompassing all they could see spread out below the mountain. 'You have witnessed our ancestors, and how they came to this land. But the hardest part is yet to come.' He came closer, and drew her into a brief embrace, before holding her at arm's length, his strong hands warm on her shoulders. 'Are you ready?'

'I am, Great-grandfather.'

'Tsaan. You are a brave child, little bear, and I am proud. Do you have any questions, before I guide you onward?'

'Why am I here?'

'You have a destiny to fulfil.'

'What am I to do?'

'That is not for me to say.' There was regret in his voice. 'You must find your own way.'

Nita accepted his words, and remained quiet for a moment. Then she asked, a little shyly, 'Why do you wear the clothes of a woman?'

Dakayivani smiled. 'I am a tainna wa'ippe, a two-spirit. I, like others, was a man born to see the world through both a man's and a woman's eyes. Once we had high status, but when the white man came we were seen as abominations, and had to hide our spirits.'

Nita frowned. 'Will I see the coming of the white man, in my visions?'

'Why do you ask?'

'I have so much anger, for what they have done to our people, and to my mother.'

Her great-grandfather sighed. 'Do not keep anger in your heart, little bear, it will consume you. Never judge all by the deeds of the few.' Then he answered her question. 'You will see only what you do not already know.'

He squeezed her shoulders and turned to leave, and when she called her thanks he only looked back and smiled.

Soaring above the world once more, the swirling rainbows became a bright ring of light and Nita witnessed the births of many children. The rapid overlapping of images made her dizzy, but she realised after a short time that all the children were twins, and she understood this was happening in real time; these children were not part of her race's history as before, they were being born as she watched.

When her vision cleared she found she was swooping down, and with a feeling of relief and happiness she recognised her own home of Towaoc, and the area set aside for communal celebration. She was moving among them, people she knew, dancing to the beat of scraped bones against notched wood rasps, laughing together, and listening to the men singing the traditional Bear Dance song.

The women's hair was fashioned into different styles, but each was adorned with some form of hand-beaded ornament. Different coloured skirts and shirts were all finished off with their customary fringed shawls. The men were largely dressed in jeans, and cowboy hats, but some had made a special effort and wore beaded shirts, their long hair braided.

Nita looked down at herself, to see she was wearing a long skirt in bright flowery material, and the shawl onto which Rose had spent weeks sewing beads many years ago; gold, and with a yellow fringe. She wore Rose's mother's beaded earrings, and an exploratory hand at her head told her Rose had lent her the matching head band too. She twirled around, and shuffled into line with other women, facing the dance partners they had chosen by slapping them with the fringe of their shawls. Nita had no interest in any of the local men so she always chose Billy, and the two of them chuckled over his two left feet. It was a good time.

All at once Billy decided to do something different, and he grabbed her hand, raising it into the air, and spun her beneath his arm. Laughing, Nita lost her balance and stumbled to the ground, thankfully not hurting herself. Billy's hand was stretched out to pull her back up, and she took it, her mouth open to tell him off, but instead a scream tore from her throat; Billy's face was flushed red, bloated and bleeding, his lips drawn back in a hideous parody of a smile. She jerked her hand away and screamed again; all around her people had fallen to the ground, convulsing and writhing in agony.

She dug her heels into the ground and shoved herself away from Billy's still-outstretched hand, shock rendering her unable to stand. She screamed once more and squeezed her eyes tightly shut and then, to her relief she heard Rose's calm voice, and felt a hand on her forehead. Joe was speaking too, sounding worried, and Nita realised she was back in her own room. She forced her eyes open,

Rose was facing away, talking to Joe, but Joe wasn't there... Nita could hear him speaking, but she couldn't see him. She was about to ask where he was when Rose turned back, and Nita moaned in horror and pistoned herself away again, as far up the bed as she could; Rose's face looked just like Billy's had.

'Hush, Nita...'

Her vision cleared, and she saw Rose and Joe sitting on either side of her, their faces the same as always, but wreathed in fear for her. With an effort she put out her arms and pulled them both close, feeling the sweat cooling on her body and face. She was home, and her loved ones were safe... but she couldn't shake that horrific image.

***

69

Only when Rose was completely satisfied that Nita was calm and relaxed, did she and Joe return to the lounge. Exhaustion made her limbs tremble; a little over two hours of watching over her beloved girl as she endured who knew what, in the depths of her mind, and instead of relief when she'd woken there had only been more fear.

Joe held out his hand and drew her down to sit next to him, and he was shaking as much as she was. 'I thought you said these visions were pleasant?' His voice was low and frightened. 'That girl looks like she's been to Hell and back.'

'I know. I was terrified for her. I don't understand what just happened.'

'Me neither.' He shook his head. 'Damn it, just how much peyote did you give her? You said a small dose!'

Rose looked at him blankly for a moment, then pointed to the kitchen counter. 'It's still there, Joe. I didn't give her any.'

Chapter Five

News

November 2nd 2003

Nita clicked her tongue as she checked the clock yet again. Nearly ten o'clock, so where was he? She was about to get up to call him yet again, when the door to Rose's room burst open and a small, scruffy, black and tan mutt came hurtling out, her tail wagging fast enough to create its own breeze as she ran to the door and sniffed the bottom of it, whining in excitement.

'Who is it, Kimi?' But Nita had an idea, and she was right; Kimi backed away from the door as it opened, and Billy came sauntering in and knelt to let Kimi lick his face.

'Hello, girl.'

Nita stood up, her fists planted on her hips as she faced him. 'What time do you call this? You should've been here two hours ago and we're an hour late for opening already. Any customers who've bothered waiting for us will be mad as hell.'

Billy ignored the outburst, and gave her his disarming grin. 'You look just like Rose when you do that.' He went over to the cooker and put some water on to boil. 'Anyone else want coffee?'

'No!'

'Nor me, thanks.' Rose came out of her room and shuffled into the lounge, wiping at her bleary eyes. 'You know I can't stand the stuff, but I'll have herb tea, since you're brewing.' She sat down carefully, with a little sigh. 'What's all the noise about, anyway?'

'He's late,' Nita said, stabbing a finger in Billy's direction. 'Two hours! I was beginning to think he wasn't going to turn up at all, that I'd have to walk all the way and open up by myself.'

Rose frowned. 'Well, Billy?'

'I had a date last night, and overslept,' he confessed. 'But then I *am* the boss.'

Nita made a small derisive sound. 'You'll be the boss of an empty shop if you lose all your customers,' she pointed out. 'Did you think about that?'

'No, but I had a *date,*' he repeated, with exaggerated patience. 'A proper one. With a girl.'

'Must've gone well, 'cos he couldn't be bothered to turn up on time this morning. And now he's wasting even more time.' Seeing Billy would not be rushed, Nita dropped onto the sofa next to Rose, only to move aside when Kimi nuzzled her way between them. 'You might as well make me coffee then.'

'Well something's certainly up,' Rose observed. 'He's never offered to make coffee before, and he looks like he's won a million bucks.'

Billy's grin surfaced again. 'Lola's great, and knows about cars, too. Her dad's got a gas station and repair shop in Dolores, and Lola works there.' He brought the drinks over and started to sit down, but stopped to pull a folded newspaper out of his back pocket and drop it onto the coffee table. He threw Nita a sweet, conciliatory smile as he sat on Rose's other side. 'I'm sorry for being late, honest.'

Nita always found it hard to stay mad when he smiled like that; he looked so genuinely happy. Despite his height and undeniable good looks, his dates never seemed to last beyond a couple of hours, and although Nita had tried to train him to widen his conversational horizons, he found it hard. She often wondered if he'd ever find someone to share his interests, so this looked promising and she could hardly blame him for seizing the moment.

'It's okay,' she said grudgingly, 'but we go right after we've had our coffee, right? And next time make your dates for a Saturday, or at least get up earlier. We have a business to run.'

'So,' Rose patted Billy's leg. 'You talked about cars all night then?'

'Not *all* night.'

Nita spluttered coffee. 'I see!'

'No!' Billy flushed. 'Not what you're thinking. We talked about that stuff on the news.' He picked up the paper and tossed it to Nita. 'The man in the shop said it's all in there, everyone's talkin' about it.'

Nita gave the newspaper a cursory glance and put it back on the table. There was no time for reading now. 'Talking about what?'

'The new people, down by Glenwood Springs.'

'What *new people?*'

'The aliens!'

Nita groaned. 'Oh, for—'

'It's true!' Billy protested. 'He said so. Will you read it to me?' His voice turned pleading as he pointed to the paper again, and the usual frustration at his continued inability to read seemed almost desperate now. He'd tried so hard. Nita sighed, wishing she could help him, and put down her half-finished coffee.

'Later,' she promised. 'Come on, let's get to work.'

'Before you go…' Rose turned to Billy. 'That repair shop in Dolores that you mentioned, is that the one run by Esteban?'

'Yeah, that's Lola's father.'

Rose nodded approvingly and picked up her tea cup again. 'Good, he's a nice man.'

'Do I know him?' Nita asked, standing up and straightening her shirt.

'Yeah, sure you do. He's been in the shop a couple times for parts. Spanish. Short, with reclining hair.'

'Reclining hair!' Nita tried not to giggle but Rose was less restrained. She spat out a mouthful of tea on a hoot of laughter, and Nita seized a bemused Billy's sleeve and pulled him to the door.

'What?' he demanded, but Nita just grabbed her bag and shook her head, as they left Rose chuckling quietly to herself.

It was good to see Rose laugh. Losing Joe at the beginning of this year had left them all devastated of course, but Rose had become utterly withdrawn, and it would be a long time before she would come to terms with the loss of him. It was a blessing for Joe himself that he'd slipped away suddenly, and peacefully in his sleep, but for those left behind the pain was still sharp, and took them unawares at times.

Nita and Billy settled themselves in Billy's pick-up, and Nita leaned out of the open door and whistled. A moment later Kimi came bounding down the steps and scrabbled up onto Nita's lap before settling between them on the front seat; she'd been coming with them from the first day, and the customers loved her, and loved hearing how Nita had adopted her.

It had been a month after Joe's death, and Nita had been called to a nearby house where a child had somehow wedged a bead up his nose. Still feeling numbed, and reluctant to leave Rose's side, Nita's patience had been short, and when she'd seen four puppies running around the room where the child was playing, she'd told the child's mother to remove them, and advised her to keep her dog from roaming free when on heat. 'There are way too many dogs running loose in Towaoc already!'

'I will. Only hurry… I can't see the bead anymore! What if he breathes in and swallows it?'

Nita had softened, seeing the woman's panic-stricken face. 'Don't worry, you did the right thing calling me. Watch me carefully, so you'll know what to do next time. Which nostril is the bead in?'

The woman indicated the little boy's right nostril, and Nita knelt down and gently pressed the left one closed. 'Open your mouth, honey.'

The boy did, and Nita blew a quick puff of breath into his mouth. The bead flew out, striking her on the cheek and bouncing harmlessly onto the carpet, and the child's mother had stared in wide-eyed disbelief that her fears had been so easily laid to rest.

'I don't know how to thank you,' she'd breathed. 'I don't have any money just yet, but—'

'It's okay,' Nita told her. For those few minutes she had been able to think of something other than Rose and Joe, and it had been a welcome change. 'Just pay me by keeping those beads out of his way.'

'Here.' The woman had hurried into her kitchen, and returned with a wriggling puppy in her arms. 'You'd be doing us all a good turn if you gave this little one a home.'

Nita had opened her mouth to refuse, but the puppy strained up to lick her enthusiastically, and the refusal turned into a laugh. One look into those huge brown eyes and Nita had fallen in love, but Rose had been less easy to convince. Her disapproval, when Nita had brought the puppy home, had been palpable, but Kimi's insistence on sleeping on her bed eventually won her over, and Kimi quickly became part of the family.

She sat now, alert and ready on the front seat of the pick-up, as Billy reversed out of the parking spot and waved to Rose who'd come out to see them off. Rose's small figure dwindled into the distance as they headed off down Mountain Sage Road, and Nita settled back into her seat. 'So, what's this Lola like then? I don't think I know her.'

'Real cute!' Billy enthused. 'She likes the way I talk too, and calls me…' he hesitated, 'something Spanish. Kinda like… carryo?'

'Cariño?'

'Yeah! That's it, but she says it better. What's it mean?'

'It's like when we call someone *honey*. I think she really likes you.'

Billy's smile widened, and Nita's echoed it, and it was only when they drew up at the shop and saw the queue of waiting customers that those smiles faded. Billy sighed and turned off the engine.

'Well, looks like we'd better get these apologies over with.'

Rose finished her tea, and took the mugs to the sink. She could just about loop one arthritic finger through the handle, while she used a cloth with the other, but everything was becoming so difficult now. And not just with her hands. She was tired all the time, and everything seemed so much more of an effort; things she had taken for granted, and had done without thinking twice, now required careful preparation and thought, and she needed to brace herself for the inevitable twinges and aches.

She took a small breakfast back into the lounge, and as she sat down again to eat, her gaze fell on Billy's newspaper. She spread it out on the table and hunched forward to read.

'Are the Sinai Spawn really Alien Angels?'

During a special press conference held in Washington DC yesterday, the peace organisation known as Eagle *gave a statement that some have found hard to swallow. Following ancient prophecies discovered in and around Jericho (Palestinian Territories, not New York), events have transpired that supposedly prove they have been fulfilled. The tablets (see picture below) have been authenticated and handed over to the authorities for safe-keeping, having been stored in a specially-designed secret basement since their discovery.*

They tell of the story of Moses leading his people out of Egypt, but, contrary to universal understanding, he had a twin named

Maor, and they shared the journey to get their people, plus twenty-three special sets of twins, to safety.

At the mention of twins, Rose sat up a little straighter and pulled the newspaper closer, to help with her failing eyesight. Nita's vision danced in the forefront of her memory…

The message came from a "higher being" on Mt Hira, which is now believed to be the biblical Mt Sinai.

Another pair of twins, the Maliks, were evidently born to be new protectors of another twenty-three sets of twins, who were born all around the world on exactly the same date and time: during the annular eclipse of May 9th, 1994.

The date jumped out at Rose, and she felt her heart speed up, but she kept reading, though her attention was wavering towards something closer to home.

These children, now nine years old, along with their protectors and families, were moved to a secret location which has now been discovered to be on land near Glenwood Springs, under the hospitality of our own government. Why? Because not only are they here for some apparent higher purpose, but they all have a unique immunity to disease. They claim to be Nephilim, but there has been speculation that these 'people' are aliens, or are the result of an experiment that can no longer be hidden. Some have labelled it a 'cult,' and have claimed it's blasphemous, but above all else there is curiosity.

It was also reported that they have a special communication system, and that in the early hours of this Sunday morning, during another such eclipse, the twins will climb Mt Hira. How? It seems their bodies will remain asleep in their beds, but their alter egos, or spirits, as they call them, will ascend Mt Hira together in the hope of receiving another important message. This will occur at 3.40am our time, 12.40am Saudi time and will be reported on live TV worldwide.'

Rose, her breakfast left untouched, took the paper into her room and laid it almost reverently on the bed while she went to the bookcase and withdrew her journal. She held the leather bound volume briefly to her chest as she thought about the day Joe had given it to her—another treasured gift from a man she missed more with every passing day—and then took it over to the bed, where she sat with the newspaper open at her side, the date seeming to loom in larger print as she looked at it: *May 9th, 1994.*

Once she and Joe had recognised Nita's talents for what they were, Rose had begun to keep a record of every event that had held some kind of meaning or question. Her fingers shook more than usual as she turned to the page now, remembering how she'd suspected, even back then, that Nita hadn't been telling her everything.

And there it was. *Nita's vision: May 9th, 1994.*

***

Nita cleared away the dishes after their evening meal, and, when Rose had scraped the leftovers into Kimi's bowl, she put the plates into the sink ready for washing. It had been a long and tiring day, but a good one; Billy had smiled all day and she'd even heard him trying to whistle a tune as he drove away after he'd dropped her and Kimi off home. Rose had cooked a beautiful dinner, with the ingredients Nita had helped her prepare the evening before, but throughout their meal Nita hadn't been able to shake the sense that she was distracted in some way.

Quieter. Subdued. It was worrying, and as soon as they sat down for the evening she asked if Rose was alright.

'I'm fine, child.' Rose picked up the book she'd brought in. But Nita waited, unconvinced, and finally Rose sighed and turned to her. 'I do need to ask you something though.'

'Sure.'

'When you had your vision, nine years back, you knew something bad was going to happen in the future, didn't you?'

'You know I did. I told you.'

'But what you didn't tell me was that you couldn't see Joe there, at the time it was going to happen. You couldn't, could you? You knew he was going to die.'

Nita lowered her eyes, feeling them prickle with fresh grief and remorse. 'Yes, I knew, but I didn't know when. I never told you, because I didn't want to upset you. There wasn't anything we could have done about it. I'm so sorry, Rose.'

'Silly girl.' Rose put an arm around her. 'I'm not upset because I didn't know, I'm just upset that you felt you had to carry that burden alone all this time.' She smiled and brushed a finger down Nita's cheek, as she had when Nita had been a child. Nita's throat tightened and she fought back more tears.

'You didn't go to the Bear Dance this year,' Rose went on. Her voice was gentle. 'Honey, you can't avoid the future, you said it yourself. Visions are not always clear, because they haven't happened yet. You may have sensed a future catastrophe, but that doesn't mean it'll happen just as you saw it. That's why prophecies can seem ambiguous, they're explained as the seer interprets them. Like Tarot cards.'

Nita nodded. 'Why are you asking about this now?'

Rose picked up a newspaper from the table, and Nita recognised it as the one Billy had left that morning. 'Because of this.' She handed it to Nita, and sat quietly while Nita read the story in growing fear and wonder. When she'd finished, she lowered it and met Rose's calm gaze, unable to speak.

'I believe you witnessed the birth of these children,' Rose said quietly. 'I don't believe the ridiculous notion that any of them are aliens, but I do believe they're special, and that they're here for a reason. Why else would you have been shown them?'

Nita shook her head. 'I… I don't know,' she managed.

'Well, we need to find out more about them,' Rose said. 'Right now I'm going to take a nap, and I suggest you do the same. We're going to stay up and watch them on TV tonight, and see if we can make any sense of this.'

She pressed Nita's hand and went to her room, and Nita picked up the book she'd left. It was a journal she recognised as a gift from Joe, but when she opened it she saw that Rose had been using it for recording details of everything Nita had done over the years; everything, at least, that had given rise to questions. She read the scribbled notes about her vision, feeling her stomach start to churn as she recalled the vivid images, and the horror. More than once she was tempted to put it down, as if the pages themselves could infect her mind and draw her into that shocking place once more, but she persevered.

81

When she reached the end, she found her great grandfather's prophetic vision and read the words: *At the time a great sickness comes to our people.* Forcing herself to remember that part of her own vision, she picked up the newspaper again and re-read the part about the twins having a unique immunity to disease. The way everything was slotting into place was dizzying, and the sick feeling increased; she recognised it now as raw fear.

Just before 3:30am, Rose came into the living room and Nita switched on the TV, expecting to have to search around for the channel covering the twins' story, but it was on every single one. She and Rose sat together, fighting infectious yawns, but soon the tension had them both alert and waiting, and their hands found one another and held tight.

The female reporter at the foot of Mount Hira was being jostled by a huge crowd as she tried to speak directly to camera, and now and again her voice was drowned out by helicopters flying overhead. As the shadow of the eclipse began to touch the mountain Nita strained to hear what she was saying.

'Twelve-thirty-eight. The cameras are trained on the summit, zoomed in, we hope to see… Look! Oh, my word, just look! Shapes. Figures… are they real? I'm counting…ten, twenty, forty, forty four… forty six. And two others, much larger. Are those the children then, and two adults?'

Nita focused so hard on the words that it was a minute before she acknowledged the new, heavy sensation in her body. Something told her to go with it, and she closed her eyes, feeling the weight shift suddenly until it was all beneath and around her, but she herself was free and floating... the rainbows were there again, and she drifted among them until they faded, and she found herself in a room with two women. A lounge, in someone's private home, and the women slept awkwardly, on a sofa not dissimilar to the one she and Rose occupied. One of the women, the younger of the two, jerked awake as the door opened and two small girls came in. Twins, of course...

Nita listened while the conversation buzzed around her, though she couldn't understand it all; they had been on the mountain. The one on the television. They must have been among the children the reporter had spoken about in tones of such reverence, but how could that be? She tried to think past the confusion; perhaps what had happened to the twins was similar to what she herself was experiencing right now?

The girls were dismissed back to their beds, and the younger woman quietly opened the door to another room. Nita could see past her to where two men lay; alike enough to be twins themselves, though one had longer hair. What was more shocking was that both men's bodies were rigid and trembling, and their eyes were wide open, staring blindly upward.

The woman's hand went to her mouth as she clearly tried to stifle a cry of fear or alarm, but the older woman drew her gently back into the lounge. Nita couldn't shake the image of the men and their obvious distress, and wondered if she too had looked like that when she'd had her vision – it must have been heart-breaking and frightening for Rose and Joe to have seen her like that.

A moment later she was outside what appeared to be that same home, and the property was surrounded by children; a chain of protection formed entirely of sets of twins… Protection from whom? Then Nita's gaze found the approaching mob, and she could see anger, built from fear, and heard it in their voices as they demanded access to the men inside.

A stone flew out of somewhere in that crowd, and as the children stood strong, something shimmered in front of them, white amorphous forms that took shape as Nita watched, and the crowd fell back, but the forms did not attack. The crowd simply fell silent and began to disperse, and even as Nita tried to understand what had happened she found herself lifted again, and this time she was taken right into the room where the men lay. One of them, the one with the longer hair, sat up and spoke to the younger of the two women.

'We know why we're here now, Jen. And part of it's not good. There's a virus coming.'

His brother also rose, and he laid a hand on the woman's cheek, with a familiarity that told Nita these two were close. 'And it's going to wipe out everyone who doesn't have this immunity gene.'

Chapter Six
Goodbyes

December 2003

Everyone had either watched the TV report in November, or heard about it. The Malik twins and their German friend, the geneticist Otto Fischer, had spoken of a global virus that was set to wipe almost all of humanity from the face of the Earth, but had initially been met with a degree of scepticism; where was the official announcement from the government? As much as people mistrusted them, *they* were the ones in the know. Who were these twins to sow such fear and go unchallenged?

Nita, however, deeply troubled, had gone to the tribal elders and told them of her vision.

'We cannot risk causing a public panic,' they told her, after listening to her story. 'There has been no timescale after all – it might be years away. Centuries.'

But the first official warning came soon after, and the chiefs and elders of all the Ute bands held a meeting, attended by the staff of their health centres, and all their traditional healers. It was held an hour and a half away, on the Southern Ute reservation, and Nita drove through the snow to Ignacio, with Rose at her side, neither of them speaking much.

The reports were disturbing. The virus was moving fast now, and isolation could not prevent the inevitable; the infected droplets were evaporating, and becoming so light that they remained airborne for several hours, travelling long distances. There was no cure that had worked, either natural or man-made.

The twins who had appeared on that talk show evidently carried total immunity, but it seemed there were some who were likely to possess a weaker version. Those who did would become sick, perhaps dangerously so, but could ultimately survive.

'Go home,' Chief Robert Coyote advised gravely. 'Stay with your families, make all you can of the time you have left together, and perhaps some of you will be among the fortunate ones. I will call a town meeting tomorrow.'

The town gathered the following morning, in Little Bear Gardens. There had been more snowfall during the night, and the town had an almost fairytale white blanket; sharp edges were softened, and it seemed absurd to believe it could be touched by death and disease. The concrete area in front of the lawns had been brushed free of snow, and those gathered in the gardens watched with narrowed eyes as speakers and a PA system were hastily set up.

The sky was a clear, deep blue, but the air was frigid and the townspeople, in their heaviest coats, stamped their feet, tucked chins into scarves, and rubbed their gloved hands together to keep warm.

Billy had brought a chair for Rose, and an extra blanket which he draped over her knees and tucked in at either side. 'You okay? Warm enough?'

She nodded and touched his hand. 'Thank you, Billy.'

The crowd fell silent as Chief Coyote mounted the block behind the microphone, and looked over the people gathered there. They stared back, and Nita saw fear and hope on their faces in equal measure; they weren't fools, they knew what was going on, and now here was the official line they'd both dreaded and needed. As Coyote spoke, his words hung in the air before him, a white mist that drifted away and disappeared.

'My people, Mother Earth has been crying for too long now. For thousands of years we only took what we needed and the spirits were respected. Our ways have been forgotten and man has become greedy and disrespectful.'

The crowd shuffled in discomfiture, and glanced at one another, but Coyote continued, 'Forests have been destroyed to make room for more homes and roads, and the expansion of agriculture and ranching and timber supply. Man has destroyed natural habitats, coming into contact with contaminated animals. It is these that have given us this virus. The animals are immune. This sickness is Mother Earth's punishment on us all.'

Nita thought this a harsh opening salvo, but he was a revered chief, and his words would be respected by all.

A lone voice spoke up from somewhere near the front. 'Is there *no* cure?'

'There is no man-made prevention or cure,' Coyote said grimly, 'And Mother Earth Herself has not provided one. The newcomers to our lands have spoken of an ancient spirit named the Fathers who, over millions of years, has given some a survival gene but we don't know which of us have been blessed with it.'

'So… we *might* survive?'

'How do we know?'

More voices joined in, and the noise level rose. Nita and Billy glanced at one another and each laid a hand on Rose's shoulder as they waited silently for order to be restored. Coyote wisely let the questions run their course for a minute or two, before raising his hand, and the shouts gradually died away.

'I can't answer all your questions,' he said quietly, into the new, tense silence. 'My advice to those who have families elsewhere is to leave now while you can. To the rest of you, go home and stay with your loved ones, spend quality time together until the inevitable happens.'

Nita's hand tightened convulsively on Rose's shoulder, but the older woman merely patted it and remained facing their chief.

'You will need to store your food carefully,' Coyote went on. 'Soon it will be too dangerous to leave town. Marta will empty the local store, and share the tinned and dried stock with those of you who choose to stay. It's too early in the year to harvest the corn, but some fresh vegetables will be available. Cattle will be slaughtered and shared amongst you all, and when the sickness comes, all the remaining livestock will be set free to give them a chance of survival.'

'What about medicine?' a voice called out.

Coyote shook his head. 'As I have said, there is no cure nor medicine for this. But since the staff from the health centre have all left to join their own families, Nita has offered to collect any pain relief drugs that are in stock there.' Several faces turned towards Nita, who nodded.

'She will share them out, along with her own stock of analgesic plants,' Coyote said, 'and will advise on how to cope with the sickness. Marta and Nita will stay behind today and organise the distribution. For today, only those families with young children will be seen, the rest of you will receive your share over the next few days.'

'How long do we have?' This voice shook with fear, and Nita felt the sudden sting of tears as the reality finally sank home. Her neighbour, her friends…

'We don't know,' Coyote said gently. 'My only advice is for you to stockpile your wood, gather as much food as you can, and only eat fresh food. Keep your tinned food for emergency rations.'

Another outburst was quelled, instantly this time, as Coyote raised his arm once more. 'My people, we are the Weeminuche, the Utes of the sacred Ute Mountain and we *must* stay strong. We and our ancestors have suffered many hardships, and have overcome them all with dignity.' Now his own voice trembled, and for Nita that was the most frightening thing of all. 'Be proud of who you are, help one another, and pray that the spirits have seen fit to bless us with survival as the Mother has done in the past.'

He stepped down, and the people turned to one another instead, their questions now directionless, angry. Desperate, and frantically seeking solace in one another, as if they held the answers between them. Others simply wept quietly, alone. Very young children found themselves seized by their mothers in panicky hugs, and wriggled to get down, mercifully not understanding; older children stared at their parents, eyes wide in disbelief that their protectors had let them fall like this.

After a while those with children seemed to remember the single hopeful part of Chief Coyote's speech, and broke away to find Marta and Nita, and the only source of comfort they could offer: medicine. The rest clung together for a while longer, trying to wring some answers from one another, before breaking away and going to their homes to try and make some sense of it all. Billy touched Nita's arm and indicated that he would drive Rose home, and she nodded and turned back to the people who now looked to her for a miracle. A miracle she could not perform.

The long, emotional day drew to a close, and an exhausted Nita picked up her bags of supplies and locked up the health centre, looking forward to home. She turned into Rustling Willow Street, and even found a tired smile for the name she had always loved, reflecting on times when her own ancestors would have gone by such names. The sidewalk-less roads, usually just dry dirt and sparse bushes, were softened by the fresh snowfall, and Nita trudged through it and along Mountain Sage Road, and as she walked a memory struck her; herself as a child, running along the road through snow just like this, flipping her head from side to side to make the pom poms on her hat dance. The hat Joe had given her.

As she drew level with the two small trees she recognised, her feet slowed and she stopped to look on the space where their old home had once stood. Her heart ached with a sudden and unexpected pang of homesickness, and for a moment she stood still, letting more memories seep through her. Memories of a lifetime: all those terrifying times she had slid into the hollowed out space beneath the kitchen floor, holding Billy close and telling herself she was a Ute Warrior, protecting and strong; then later, standing at the table slicing roots and vegetables, and learning all the wisdom Rose had been able to give her… if only it had been enough to help them all now.

She quickened her pace, relieved to see the trailer coming into view, and the moment she'd placed her bags on the floor Kimi bounded over, barely letting Nita shed her coat and tug her boots off her icy feet before attempting to clamber up her legs.

Nita sat on the floor and let Kimi lick her face, as she stroked her and rubbed her ears. Kimi rolled onto her back, proudly displaying her soft belly and waiting for it to be rubbed, and Nita picked her up and took her to the sofa where she huddled close to the heater. The heat from the electric bars, and Kimi's warm body, soon took away the chill that had crept through her bones, and when Billy brought her a mug of hot coffee she took it with a sigh of pleasure and wrapped her cold hands around it.

Rose came over and sat next to her. 'How'd it go?' she asked, petting Kimi's head.

'I expected there to be a lot of pushing and shoving,' Nita confessed. 'Panic, you know? But it was harder to deal with than that, the families who came to me were more tearful and worried than anything else.'

Rose took her hand, and squeezed it in sympathy. 'I can imagine.'

'It's so cruel,' Nita went on, remembering. 'If Mother Earth has decided to cull the blight in Her world, She could have seen fit to spare the children, couldn't She?'

'If She had a soul,' Rose agreed. 'But this is purely a survival response. Nature is beautiful, but you know She can be cruel too, and shows no favouritism.' She gave a soft, regretful sigh. 'This might be the only way to save Her world, and stop it destroying itself completely.'

Billy turned to them, from where he was heating more water in the kitchen. 'So, these Fathers in the mountain you heard about, they can't help us?

'We've been told they warned us,' Nita said. 'Tried to help by giving some of us a special gene, so at least those could survive… I don't think there's anything else they *can* do.'

Billy frowned. 'Why's this spirit called the Fathers? I don't understand why *they* tried to help us, but Mother Earth abandoned us. Mothers and fathers should take care of their children, shouldn't they?'

Nita and Rose exchanged a glance; Billy's simple soul had gone straight to the heart of the matter and asked the only pertinent question.

'Maybe this is the only way the Mother *could* help us,' Nita ventured at last. 'Mankind has lost respect for our world, and if it died we would all die with it. This way some will survive, and we can start again.'

Rose's hand tightened on hers, and her voice sounded old for the first time. 'I'm so sorry, children. I've lived longer than I should have, but you—'

'Don't!' Nita cried, distressed. 'Don't talk like that.' She lifted Rose's hand to her lips.

'You two are only halfway through your lives,' Rose went on quietly. 'I wished for so much more for you both. The times ahead are going to be hard, especially for you, Nita. There will be so much work for you, and you're going to have to go on being so strong.'

'I don't feel strong at the moment,' Nita said, her throat thickening with tears. 'I'm exhausted. I wish Joe were here, he'd somehow find something to laugh about, even in all this. What would he be doing now?'

Rose gave a tiny smile. 'He'd be breaking out the beers, and making us all do something crazy.'

'Hold that coffee, Billy,' Nita said. 'We're having beer.'

Billy reached into the refrigerator and took out three bottles. Levering the caps off as he crossed the room, he passed two of them over and sat on Rose's other side, then he raised his.

'To Joe.'

The three bottles clinked together, and they drank.

Rose saluted them again. 'To us.'

'Yeah,' Billy chimed in. 'We're awesome!'

'Always have been, and always will be,' Rose agreed.

They shared a smile, and for a while no-one spoke as they sipped on their beer, each lost in their own thoughts. When Billy spoke up, it was in a suddenly lost, bewildered voice that stripped the moment of its peace, and Nita felt her heart crack.

'I don't want to die,' he said. 'I've just got a girlfriend.'

Nita swallowed past a lump in her throat. 'None of us wants to die,' she said quietly, 'but at least we'll all be together.'

Billy wouldn't meet her eyes. 'Uh, yeah. About that…' He took a deep breath. 'I'm leaving, to be with Lola.'

Nita could see he was wary at telling them, but she didn't think he realised just how devastating an impact his words had. 'What do you mean you're leaving?' She jumped up. 'You *can't* leave! We're a family!'

'Nita—'

'No! We've been together over thirty years, you've known Lola for seconds!'

'Hardly seconds!' Billy sounded defensive now. 'Look, you had me for thirty years, she gets weeks, if that.'

'Oh, so I'm supposed to be grateful now?' Nita heard the bitterness in her own voice. 'Well fine. Thanks a lot. You can just fuck off and leave us then.' She saw Rose flinch at the uncharacteristic language, but she didn't care. She backed away, still staring at Billy and seeing genuine puzzlement in his face, then she turned and went into her room, slamming the door behind her.

From the lounge she could hear Billy's voice. 'I don't understand!'

'She loves you, honey,' Rose's muffled voice came through, and Nita felt the tears start as she imagined the old lady taking Billy's hands in hers, the way she always did. 'She's just upset that she's not going to see you anymore. We both are. Look, it's been a hard day for all of us, and this has all been a terrible shock. Of course you must go and be with your woman, but you can't leave like this. Wait here, I'll go talk to Nita.'

A moment later the door creaked cautiously open, and Rose came in. By now Nita was lying curled up on her bed, feeling very much the child again, and Rose sat wordlessly next to her and stroked her hair. After a little while Nita felt some of the betrayed anger fade, and she sat up, swinging her legs over the side of the bed so she could lean on Rose's shoulder.

'There's only going to be you and me left,' she said in a small voice. 'My mother left, then Joe, and now Billy.' Another realisation hit, and she caught her breath. 'The way things are, we won't even get a chance to say goodbye to Logan. Carol. The boys.' She looked up to see her pain mirrored on Rose's face, but also the familiar strength with which Rose always shored up others, and it made her heart ache even more fiercely.

'You're a strong woman, Nita,' Rose said gently, 'And you're going to have to use that to get through the coming weeks, or however long we have. I know it's hard letting go of those you love...' her voice caught, and it was a moment before she continued, 'but we've been so fortunate to have had them in our lives for so long.'

Nita nodded, understanding the truth of the words, though the impending loss still twisted inside her. 'But Billy—'

'Billy finally has the chance to feel the love of a woman, and the happiness he's missed out on all his life. Who are we to deny him that in the short time he has left?'

'Don't say that. He might be immune.'

'He might,' Rose agreed, 'but we both know it's more likely he's not. And, honey, if that's the case you can't let your last moments with him be ones of anger.'

'I know you're right,' Nita said. 'I shouldn't have yelled at him, I know that. But with everything that's going on… And my emotions are all over the place. I'm so tired, and I haven't a clue what I'm supposed to do. People are looking at me as if *I* can save them but—'

'I know.'

'You always know what to do in any situation,' Nita said, almost pleading, as if she hoped Rose might suddenly have all the answers.

But Rose shook her head. 'You think so? I'll let you into a secret, shall I? I winged it every time. We all do. I just put on a good show, so you do the same and you'll be fine.'

Nita found a shaky smile for her, and Rose patted her hand. 'Now, go and speak with Billy. He'll be leaving soon.'

Nita wiped her eyes on her sleeve, and walked slowly back into the lounge. Billy was waiting for her, leaning against the back of the sofa. He was already wearing his coat, and she wondered how she hadn't noticed the large bag that now sat at his feet.

She raised her eyes from the bag to his face, and saw the deep sorrow there, and when he straightened and opened his arms she went into them and gave way to the sobs she had been trying so hard to hold in check.

He held her while she wept against his shoulder, then dropped a kiss on her head. 'I have to go to her, Nita.' He sounded older now; gone was the light, boyish humour, the innocence, the gentle teasing. In its place was the grief of a man who finally understood what he was leaving behind, but who knows he must do it anyway.

Nita nodded, still held tight within the circle of his arms. 'I know. I'm sorry I yelled, I had no right. I just can't believe I might never see you again.' She felt the warm trickle of his tears in her hair.

'I love Lola. And I love you, too. You're my sister, and my best ever friend.'

Nita sniffed and pulled back so she could look up into his face. His brown eyes swam with tears and she put a hand either side of his face and looked into them. 'I love you too. Now go, and be happy.'

Billy pulled a set of keys from his pocket and gave them to her. 'Some of the others are going to Dolores, and I'm getting a lift. They're outside waiting for me. You can have my wheels, you'll need them to get around and help everyone.'

Nita's fingers closed over the keys, they felt hard and all too real, banishing the last of her light-headed sense of unreality. 'It's all happening so fast.'

A horn beeped outside, and Rose came back into the lounge. Billy went over to embrace her, and Nita swallowed hard as she heard the muffled sobs between them.

'Lola's a lucky girl to have you,' Rose said as they drew apart.

'I know.'

Nita felt the ghost of a smile touch her lips at Billy's typically unselfconscious and honest response. She moved to stand next to Rose as Billy slung his bag over his shoulder, and together they watched him walk out of their lives. He climbed into the back of the car, and as she raised her hand to send him on his way with a wave, Nita felt a little piece of her heart go with him.

In January the airports had closed. Road blocks were put in place, in a futile attempt to halt the spread of infection, and by this time Towaoc's population had halved to around four hundred. Fear kept its people huddled within the town; fear of both infection and the marauding looters who emptied food halls and liquor stores in other places. In Towaoc itself the chaos had been admirably kept to a minimum, although many had turned to drink to dull the terror and the hopelessness, which had, in turn, led to a few brawls and some theft.

But for the most part the community had drawn together, and Nita's pride in her people had never been stronger. She visited everyone when she could, and rallied groups of the younger ones to collect vegetables and forage for edible roots, to provide for their families.

Every year, when the snows melted and the first signs of spring appeared, there was rejoicing for the passing of another winter and the promise of new life. This year there was none, only a cautious hope that they had been spared the sickness, that the spirits were showing them mercy for the way they had helped one another. Maybe, on a more prosaic level it was simply their isolation that had protected them. Nita didn't have the heart to tell them otherwise, that she had been shown their fate and she knew there was no escape from it.

It wasn't just the new buds sprouting, or the hatching of birds' eggs that heralded the coming of new life; Nita became vaguely aware that Kimi had taken to wandering off alone for longer periods of time. But the dog otherwise seemed quite well, and Nita's time and attention was on the people of the town who, by April, had begun to develop fevers, sore throats, aches and pains. The virus had finally found them.

The symptoms also brought waves of weakness, and if they hadn't known better the victims might have attributed it all to the simple flu. But then came more severe symptoms: stomach cramps, internal and external bleeding, diarrhoea and vomiting, and it spread through the community like a wildfire. Some developed rashes and had reddened eyes, and finally there was catastrophic organ failure.

Nita worked constantly, always waiting for the first harsh cough, the first flush of fever, the first sense that her body was failing her. At first she had help, but as the townspeople fell away into their own worlds of pain and suffering she struggled on alone, administering whatever medication she could find that would temporarily ease them. The worst part was watching the little ones suffer; the pain of seeing the light fade from their eyes, and their little bodies weaken and die, would stay with her for whatever time she had left.

When Rose became ill, Nita spent more time at home tending to her needs. Her heart broke to see this strong, capable woman bed-ridden and weak, and she spent long hours at her bedside, holding water for her to sip, and spoon-feeding her soup. Whenever Rose slept, Nita ventured out to help the children who still clung feebly to life, but when the fever struck, and Rose became delirious, Nita did not dare stray from her side. Rose called out, incoherently for much of the time, but now and again a clear cry for her lost Joe would tear from her dry lips, and Nita would hold her and weep for what they had all lost.

Then, early one morning and to Nita's joy, Rose's fever broke. None of the worst of the now-familiar symptoms had materialised, and despite the dreadful cough, and a difficulty in drawing breath, the worst was over. Almost giddy with relief they spoke about what might have happened to Billy and the others, and Rose hesitantly suggested that, since she had been lucky then perhaps they might be too. Nita kissed the dry cheek and nodded. Who could tell if the most harrowing part of her visions would come true?

When the power went down, Nita used what little remained of the fuel in Billy's truck to drive to Beardance Street, and the downtown store. The shelves had been emptied long ago; in line with Chief Coyote's instructions the rations had been distributed early on, and as fairly as possible. Still, there must be other supplies somewhere. She jammed her ignition key into the drawer of the cash register and, after some effort, managed to lever it open and found what she was looking for: a small set of keys, one of which had to be for the dry-goods store room.

She tried them, and after a moment found the right key and pushed open the door, allowing her eyes a moment to adjust, then stepped in. Using the thin light from the late April afternoon that spilled through the large front window of the shop, she scanned the shelves, and

100

eventually selected a few boxes of candles, and the batteries she needed for her torch.

It was warm for April, and it had been a bright, sunny day, but the afternoon was creeping on and soon it would be dark. Nevertheless she had every intention of walking the short distance to the health centre, but as she stepped out of the store, her arms full of the last supplies she needed, a leaden weight seemed to drop over her. It suddenly felt like too much effort to place one foot in front of the other, and the candles and batteries pulled at her arms until she felt certain she would drop them if she didn't put them down quickly.

Somehow she made it to Billy's truck and shoved her burden through the open window, watching the batteries roll onto the floor. She didn't care. A headache was starting to push behind her eyes and creep across her forehead... when had she last slept? Properly, for more than a stolen hour or so? She rested her forehead against the truck for a moment, then dragged open the door and slid behind the wheel.

At the health centre she found the nebuliser she'd been looking for, to help Rose's breathing, and dropped it onto the passenger seat next to the candles. She scrabbled in the footwell for the batteries, then sat for a while, staring out of the window and waiting for her lost energy to return. *This is it... it's my turn now...*

Outside nothing moved, except a few dogs – thin through neglect, and scavenging in bins – and a flock of birds wheeling in the sky. It was eerily quiet, and Nita's sorrow redoubled at the thought that she would never again see her beloved town swelled with life and laughter, even the mild annoyances like drunks, and boisterous teens, now seemed infused with the glow of fond memories that would never be re-lived. Not by her. Maybe not by anyone.

She could feel a light coating of sweat all over her body, and the headache throbbed with increasing ferocity; perhaps she ought to go back into the health centre and see if there were any stronger painkillers that she hadn't yet harvested? But the thought of dragging her feet back inside the building made her shudder, and besides, what would be the point? After a moment she summoned the strength to twist the key in the ignition, and backed out of the parking lot to head for home.

Kimi was waiting for her outside. Nita thought back to the one and only time Kimi had slipped her collar to chase a rabbit, and hadn't returned until the next day. She felt bad that it had taken her so long to work out what was going on with her; Kimi had started to get fussy with her food, and clingy, and then had begun to put on weight. Eventually Nita had realised, and had put an extra block of wood down by the front door, to help Kimi in and out as her belly had swelled. Now the dog stood up, her tail wagging, as Nita climbed wearily out of the truck.

'Hi, Kimi.' She sat down and Kimi climbed into her lap so that Nita could ruffle her fur and scratch behind her ears. 'Yes, yes… I love you too, girl.' Usually Kimi would roll ponderously over to let Nita rub her busy belly, but this time she seemed eager to go indoors so Nita went back to pick up what she'd brought home, while Kimi waddled up the rough ramp. Finding a thread of humour at the sight, Nita smiled.

'That'll teach you to go playing with the boys, huh?'

Kimi ran right through the lounge instead of waiting, and straight up to the door of Rose's bedroom. When Nita didn't immediately follow, she ran back to her, whining, and then returned to stand anxiously at Rose's door.

'What's up, girl?' Nita began, then her blood froze. She crossed the lounge, feeling distant and removed from reality, and opened the door.

Rose lay quietly in her bed, just as Nita had left her, and the heavy rasping had stopped. But everything else had stopped too. Nita stretched out a trembling hand, one that seemed to belong to someone else, and touched the back of it to Rose's forehead. The skin was cool.

'No…' Nita moaned. It was a soft sound, but it cut through the unearthly stillness of the room like a shout and it broke Nita's paralysis. Barely aware of the tears that coursed down her cheeks, she lay down on the bed and wrapped her arms around the woman who had been mother, sister, and life itself to her. 'Kuku…'

She lay like that for an unknowable time, not even realising she had almost fallen asleep until a sudden jerk brought her back to reality, and the understanding of what she must do now. Reluctantly she sat up and kissed Rose goodbye, then made herself walk into the kitchen, swiping at her streaming eyes and trying to think straight.

Her head pounded fiercely and she was suddenly overcome by a bout of dizziness. She steadied herself, holding on to the counter, and waited until the feeling passed; she couldn't give in just yet. Somehow she had to prepare everything so that Kimi would be alright. She took out two large bags of dried dog food and placed them on the floor, then slit them open. She hoped that would be enough, until the pups were old enough for Kimi to leave them alone.

She began to fill a large bowl with water from the tap, then had a better idea; she took a spanner from the kitchen drawer, opened the cupboard beneath the sink, and leaned in to loosen the nut to the cold tap. She placed the bowl underneath it to catch the drips, and sat still for a moment, breathing hard with exertion and willing her legs to propel her to her feet so she could finish her work.

Finally she was able to stand, and rummaging once more in the kitchen drawer she found a ball of string, and used it to tie open the door, securing it against the side of the trailer so Kimi and her pups would be able to come and go as they needed. Finally she went into her room and piled her dirty laundry on the floor beside her bed, and arranged it into a nest where Kimi could have her babies.

Kimi looked up at her questioningly, her head on one side, her tail wagging.

'I'm so sorry I won't be able to help you, girl.' There were no tears now, Nita was too exhausted to cry. She coaxed the dog onto the pile, to help her grow used to it, and Kimi went willingly, the smell of her beloved mistress the only enticement she needed.

Nita went to the kitchen for the last time, and gathered the analgesics, along with a glass of water and her torch. She looked around the room, much as she had stood and remembered a life well lived, out on Mountain Sage Road where her old home had been, and said her silent goodbyes. To Billy, to Logan and his family, to Rose and Joe, and now, finally, to herself.

She collapsed onto her bed fully clothed, and felt the scramble and thump as Kimi tried to join her. With the last of her waning strength Nita leaned over to pull her up, and as she closed her eyes she took comfort from the solid warmth of the dog as she snuggled as close as she could get.

The last thing she heard, as she closed her eyes, was the haunting cry of a mother eagle on her way back to her nest.

Part Two
Hope Meadows, Colorado

Passing from the second world into the third, there were four holy people who lived in the mountains and travelled the way of the rainbow and the sun. The holy people transformed First Man and First Woman from spirits into human beings, and they had great powers. They had many twins, the first of which were neither male nor female, and when the twins found mates many people came into being.

Part of the Navajo creation story

'When the iron bird flies, the red-robed people of the east who have lost their land will appear, and the two brothers from across the great ocean will be reunited.'

A sacred tablet was given to the Fire Clan of the Hopi people as the lost white brother (Pahana) began his journey east. A portion of the tablet was taken by Pahana and it was said that when he returned, he would be known to his people by his red clothing, and would carry the missing piece of the tablet. When he comes it will be a time of choice.

The Hopi were given nine signs. They prophesised the weapons and wagons of the white man coming, railroad tracks and power lines. The signs also told of oil spills in the oceans, the time of the hippies and the falling of the US Space Station Skylab. After the signs were shown to them, the ceremonies of their people would end.

Parts of the Hopi Prophecy

A monster with white eyes will cross the oceans and have powers that will damage Mother Earth. It will kill many children of Turtle Island (America) and those that survive will lose their ancestral connections.

One day the spirits of the lost children will be reborn, and restore Mother Earth, and all races will live together peacefully.

Parts of the Cherokee prophecy of The Monster With The White Eyes

Chapter Seven
The Singer

August 2PV (August 2005, Post Virus)
From Hope Meadows, the views were breathtaking. Mount Sopris stood proud, devoid of the winter snow that had long since melted and flowed into the lower rivers and lakes, creating the lush forests and meadows below. The forests were a deep, dark green, and the trees nearer Hope Meadows equally beautiful shades of greens, golds and yellows.

But there was not much time to appreciate it during harvest. Sinead dragged off her gloves and sun hat, and joined Jen and Clare on her veranda. She gratefully accepted a cup of cool mint tea, and used her hat to fan her face, sighing at the meagre relief it provided.

'Chicken coop's coming along,' she observed, listening to the ring of hammer against nail. 'That bloody fox'll have a job getting any more of our birds, that's for sure.'

Jen grinned. 'Who'd have believed somewhere so famous for being packed with bears and mountain lions, and so on, would offer up a red fox as its most annoying predator?'

'Should be grateful, I suppose.' Sinead squinted around. 'Where are the little ones?'

'Todd's playing hide-and-seek with Karl and Emily, and my two are making themselves useful with the blood sample queue.' Jen gestured to the open door of the meeting hall, and a canopy-covered desk, where Holly was busy at her laptop, and Hannah was keeping the waiting people cool with cups of iced water. Their friends, Ruhi and Alima sat at their own desk just inside.

The resilience of children was staggering, Sinead thought. Discovering that your dream companions were real, and that you were at the heart of the biggest, most mind-blowing development in human history, would have driven most adults into a decline... But then, they came from strong stock, particularly Holly and Hannah, whose own father had been through exactly that.

She blinked sweat out of her eyes, and looked across to where Todd was making the younger children giggle by hiding behind various things that were clearly too small to shield his adult frame. 'Todd's a natural with them, isn't he?' she said. It still surprised her, even now. 'I love watching him with them.'

'Me too,' Clare said, and it was easy to hear the maternal pride in her voice. 'I wish he'd had this from his own father when he was little.'

'Richard's loss,' Sinead said bluntly, and got no argument from the others.

'How are they doing anyway?' Jen asked, reaching up to adjust one of the hanging bundles of herbs that were drying in the sun.

'Considering what they've been through, the wee mites are doing very well. Karl's a brave lad, and very protective of Emily.'

'She's still not speaking?' Clare asked.

'Not since that time with you, when she asked Ron to make Mooshy better.' Sinead couldn't help an inward shudder, as she remembered what had happened the night she'd found the girl's teddy bear in the grass. The horrific and terrifying events had played out many times in her mind ever since, with a different outcome, but somehow in reality they'd all come out of it alive. Even Mooshy.

'It's been over a year now,' Jen said. 'I can't quite believe that. And look how far we've come. Especially Todd.'

Sinead watched Emily, as she searched for a place to hide while Todd and Karl dutifully closed their eyes. The three-year-old clutched Mooshy tightly in her right hand as she clambered underneath a neighbouring veranda, and although her little face was peeking out, the boys pretended not to see her.

'I was always used to having children around me, but he wasn't and I'm so proud of him. The kids love him to bits.'

Jen grinned. 'He's certainly come a long way from that smart-arse Cambridge toff.' She softened. 'He found the right woman, Sinead, and neither John nor I have ever seen him so happy. Tired, but happy!'

'We're all tired,' Clare said, 'I don't mind admitting I'd forgotten what hard work was.' She looked at her cracked nails and stained fingers. 'Still, it's rewarding to see the result, even if the crops are a bit meagre at the moment. Is it just me, or do things taste better when you've grown them yourself?'

'I know what you mean.' Sinead stretched out her legs and studied them critically. 'I don't know if I'm suntanned or just filthy. And my back's killing me.' The others murmured in agreement. 'And once we've finished this harvest,' she added, 'it's time to start planting again. It's never ending.'

'Well,' Jen said, in her usual pragmatic way, 'considering we only started a year ago we've done pretty well. And it'll stand us in good stead for years to come; tinned food can't last forever.'

'True.' Clare looked over at the twins. 'What details are they taking, exactly? I wasn't at that meeting.'

'Now that we have so many more people coming in, we've had to devise some kind of record system,' Jen said. 'Holly and Hannah have developed a database so that when they feed in each newcomer's names, personal details, family connections and so on, it'll trigger an alarm for any matches. It's also a way of keeping track of who's survived and who they might be related to, and helps when people arrive searching for lost loved ones.'

'Skill sets too,' Sinead put in. 'It tells us who we can call on if we need someone with a particular expertise. Then, when Holly and Hannah have those details, Ruhi and Alima take a pin-prick sample to check blood type, which Otto can investigate for the single immunity gene.'

Clare frowned. 'But the virus has gone now. Is that part still really necessary?'

'I don't know, but it's a good precaution to take. And Otto still lives in hope he can find a way to give the immunity to everyone, so—'

A loud squawking cut her off, and they all turned to see a pair of twins chasing a protesting chicken away from

111

the queue of newcomers, and guiding her back to the run behind the hall.

Clare smiled. 'That Betty definitely rules the roost! She's a character alright.' She shielded her eyes and shifted her attention. 'What's your mother-in-law up to, Jen?'

The others followed her pointing finger. Rena was on her hands and knees on the ground outside her cabin, pulling carefully on a length of rope.

'Oh, that's her experiment,' Jen said with a laugh. 'Ron has put together a sort of box on wheels, like a go-kart, I suppose, and she got the kids to fill it with cow dung and earth. She's hoping to grow mushrooms. The rope is so she can keep it under the house, and pull it out when she needs it.'

'Great idea,' Sinead said. 'I want one. I've been worried about picking the wild ones, since I can't even tell a wasp from a bee, never mind separating mushrooms from toadstools.'

'Well, we're in a strange land,' Jen said charitably, but Sinead grinned.

'I wish I could use that as an excuse. I could never tell a weed from a flower, even back home. Ma was always moaning at me when I tried to help and ended up pulling up all the wrong plants.' Her grin faded, and she fell silent, as a wash of sadness swept over her. She knew she wasn't the only one missing family, or wondering if her loved ones were even still alive. She changed the subject quickly, though she could see her moment of sorrow hadn't gone unnoticed.

'This tea's delicious. Anyone else want a re-fill?' She stood up, ready to take Jen's cup, but stopped. 'What's that? I can hear singing.'

They all twisted in the direction of the sound, and Sinead saw a tall, burly, bearded man, his long hair tied back in a tail. He had just joined the end of the queue and begun singing, presumably to himself at first, but as his audience grew he sang louder. Sinead recognised the song: *Mustang Sally*.

'I love that song!' Her foot was already tapping along. 'Just what we need, a good, old-fashioned sing-song to lift our spirits!' She started to sing too, and as they reached the familiar chorus, and everyone joined in, she was surprised to see little Emily emerging from her hiding place on all fours, her eyes wide.

Emily stood up and approached the newcomer, heedless of the bits of mud and grass clinging to her hands and knees, and as he finished his song and accepted his applause with a beaming smile, she reached out and tugged at his trouser leg.

He glanced down, and his towering height, compared to the child, made Sinead tense protectively, but she needn't have worried. He knelt on the ground in front of her and held out a hand, and addressed her solemnly in a soft Highlands accent.

'Hello, lass. My name's Ian, what's yours?'

'Emily.'

'Well, I'm very pleased to meet ye, Emily.' He looked taken aback as she ignored his proffered hand, but when she instead crawled into his lap his smile broadened and he put his arm around her. He looked up, as if suddenly worried he might be acting inappropriately, but seemed reassured to note that Todd and Karl, clearly her family, merely stood by and watched. Curious but not worried.

Ian looked back down at Emily. 'Did ye like my song then?'

She nodded, and then, to everyone's astonishment, said, 'Sing *Dreamer?* Please.'

He looked at Todd, who looked questioningly over at Sinead. She shook her head, also puzzled, but Karl moved closer to his sister.

'She means *Awaken, Little Dreamer.* It's the song our Mommy used to sing.'

'Used to?' Ian looked over at Todd, who gave a tiny shake of his head, and Ian clearly understood. A shadow crossed his features. 'I know the one. I used to sing it to my own lass, many years ago.'

Karl leaned down, and whispered something, and Ian winked, and began to sing.

'Awaken little dreamer, another new day is born.
Arise little dreamer to find your troubles—'
Emily sang, '*… all gone.'*
'Show a smile for your mummy, yawn the dark clouds away,
For today the sun is shining bright and gay.'

Karl stayed close to Ian while he sang, and Ian stretched out his arm in a gesture he didn't seem to think would be accepted, but the five-year-old moved towards him, and Ian wrapped his arm around the boy's waist as he finished the song.

'There's your… Mooshy bear… and dollies too, all waiting for your fun.'

Now Sinead understood what Karl had whispered, and unexpected tears started to her eyes as Ian completed the song,

'So it's up to you to show them now, that a new day has begun.
Awaken little dreamer, to show those bright eyes of blue.
For today the sun is shining just for you.'

Emily had joined in where she could, with the odd word, and seemed utterly enchanted by the newcomer. She gave him a huge smile, and Sinead saw her own emotion reflected in Todd as he held out his hand to the Scot. 'I'm Todd Hampton. Thank you, Mr...?'

'Sloan.' Ian shook his hand. 'Ian Sloan. Pleased to meet you.'

Todd turned to the children. 'Off you go for a bit, while I talk to this nice gentleman.' When they'd scampered off he turned back to Ian. 'You're from Scotland then?'

'Aye, Aberdeen. Born and raised there. And there's no need to thank me, by the way, I love to sing. And people need a bit of cheer at the moment, do you not think?'

'I do think... I mean yes, I agree.' He indicated Sinead. 'Sinead and I are Emily's and Karl's guardians, their parents died during the outbreak.'

'Poor bairns.'

'It's been hard for them,' Todd agreed. 'Emily hasn't spoken since, not really, and to hear her speak to you was... Well, it was pretty damned wonderful.'

'You're welcome. I've always had a way with women,' he winked, 'but now it seems with the wee yins too.' He raised a hand. 'I'd better step back into line with my adoring fans. I'm also a modest man, as you can tell.'

115

Todd laughed, and as Ian turned to walk away, he called out, 'What plans do you have, once you've registered?'

Ian considered. 'None, to tell the truth. I've been travelling around trying to make up my mind.'

'Well I'd be happy if you could join Sinead and me for dinner tonight?' Todd gestured Sinead closer, and she lifted her hand in greeting. 'She's going to be making Irish lager stew, and we have a few beers in the fridge.'

'I'd be glad to join you, thanks.' Ian returned Sinead's wave. 'It's been a while since I've had a home-cooked meal. I'll finish up here, then come and introduce myself properly to your good lady. And I'll be ready to help you for the rest of the day in the fields, too.'

'An extra pair of hands would be a massive help,' Todd agreed. 'Thanks. Oh, and there's a small cabin you can use to freshen up before dinner, if you like. The lady who lived there moved out last year. It's small, but it's kept empty in case Ron has a patient who needs overnight care.'

'Ron?'

'Doron Malik, one of the twins. You've heard of him?'

'Aye, of course. The doctor.' Ian nodded. 'A scrub-up would be great. It's been a while, you can probably tell!' he gave a loud guffaw, and his humour was infectious. 'I'll take you up on that offer, with thanks.' He turned away yet again, but was evidently struck by an afterthought. 'Will I get to meet the famous twins then?'

'You should have met them today, they usually like to welcome all new arrivals. Unfortunately though, John was

116

called to a council meeting, and Ron had an emergency to attend to.'

'Nothing serious, I hope?'

Todd pulled a face. 'We warn all newcomers not to drink straight from the rivers, even though they may look clean. They're supposed to boil the water first, but some just don't listen.' He sighed. 'It's suspected giardiasis.'

'Nasty!'

'Yes, it is. Ron'll sort them out though. Water's been a problem for everyone. We're okay here, with our own well, but even that needs regular checks.'

'I'll bet.'

'It was really hard last year,' Todd said, 'but the other twins discovered that Carbondale had its own water source. They've purified it, and now everyone has safe water to drink. They're working on hydropower now.'

Ian looked surprised. 'But they're just children!'

'They may look and act like children, but they're mini-geniuses. Hydropower is nothing in comparison to their other projects.' Todd clapped him on the shoulder. 'Come to the newcomers' meeting tomorrow. You can meet the Malik twins, and they'll tell you all about our progress.'

'I'd like that.' Ian squared his shoulders. 'Now, I'd *really* best be off, and give those lasses my details.'

'Looks like you're too late, I've kept you talking too long.' Todd pointed to where Holly had just slammed down the lid of her laptop.

'Battery's died *again!* Just when we'd reached the end of the line, too.' She looked up as Ian approached. 'I'm sorry, you'll have to wait awhile, I need to re-charge.'

'I know the feeling!' he grinned. 'Never mind, hen. Just means I can get stuck into work sooner.'

All the windows were open, as was the front door, to admit the faint evening breeze. Sinead looked out of the window to see a bunch of wild flowers advancing up the steps, and she smiled and gave the dining table one last check. They had borrowed an extra chair from Rena, to accommodate their guest, and Sinead had placed Emily's cushioned seat next to it, remembering how the girl had taken to the big Scotsman. The children, bathed and already in their pyjamas, were sitting on the floor surrounded by colouring pencils and paper, and they looked up eagerly as footsteps sounded on the wooden steps.

Sinead greeted Ian warmly, and as he lowered the flowers she gave an exclamation. 'Oh, my word, you've shaved! I nearly didn't recognise you, you look so much younger.'

'Aye,' he rubbed his chin as he passed her the flowers, 'feels good, too. Much cooler, for starters!'

She wiped her hands on the cloth at her shoulder. 'Thank you, they're lovely. Please come and sit while I put them in a jar, I'll be with you in a bit.' She gestured to the sofa that had been placed against the open front window, and went to find a jar.

When she came back, Ian was hunched over, looking at the children's drawings. They were looking at his new appearance with frank curiosity, and he grinned as he pointed at their wet hair.

118

'We all look better wi'out the dust and dirt, eh?'

'Here.' Todd passed him a bottle of cold beer, and he took it with a little sigh of bliss and drank it in one go. Todd laughed and passed him another, and he took this one more slowly.

'Have you travelled far?' Todd asked.

'Initially aye, from North Carolina.'

'Wow.' Todd saw the children's blank looks, and added, 'That's about fifteen hundred miles by road.'

'It's a long way,' Ian agreed. 'I was stationed at Fort Bragg, and lived there with my daughter Becky. When I heard about the virus, I loaded up the wagon and brought Becky down here. I took her all over the state, but no one could help when we got ill. I survived but...' he broke off for a moment, then said simply, 'she didn't.' He cleared his throat. 'Anyway, since then I've just been driving around, trying to get my head in gear.'

'Most people here have lost loved ones too,' Todd said quietly. 'The twins all tried to give as much of their blood as they could, but there just wasn't enough. I'm so sorry.'

Sinead turned, from where she was stirring the stew on the hob. 'I'm sorry too, Ian, it must be unbearably hard to lose a child. I can't imagine.'

He shook his head. 'It's not your fault. I heard you had a supply of blood stolen.'

'Yes, unfortunately, along with Otto Schmidt's work. He's our resident geneticist,' Todd explained. 'Louise Miller, the lady who provided crucial evidence and testified against my father—'

'Your *father?*' Ian looked surprised. 'Your father's Richard Hampton?'

119

'I'm afraid so.'

'You have my sympathies.' Ian shook his head grimly. 'Still we have no choosing over our family eh?' He waved a hand. 'Sorry, I interrupted.'

'Well, Louise was duped into believing if she helped with the theft, safe passage would be arranged from England for her mother.'

'Was this before or after the virus warning?'

'Before.'

'And d'ye think if this Otto's work hadn't been stolen, he might've found a cure?'

'I don't think so,' Todd admitted. 'Everything happened so fast, he didn't have enough time. The blood bank would only have helped a handful of people.'

They were silent for a while, as they drank their cooling beer, and Sinead put plates out ready for dinner.

'Ah well,' Ian said at length. 'Who's to say any one of us wouldn't have done the same thing for someone we love?'

'That's not the point,' Todd said, his voice grim.

'Miller couldn't have known that her actions would take away someone's chance of survival.'

'That's true, but it did. Her case went before the Eagle council, and because of the circumstances they ruled that her punishment would be to have to live with her guilt. She came back to Hope Meadows for a while, but it didn't work out.'

'Ah, hence the spare cabin?'

'Yes.'

'Can't think of any other reason someone would leave,' Ian said, evidently seeing his surprise. 'Where'd she go?'

'She got herself a camper van, and set up home on Morrison Farm, near Carbondale. She and several other families are helping the farmer take care of his livestock and crops.'

'And what is the Eagle council?'

Todd blinked. 'You seem to know a fair bit about us here already, but there's so much more. We'll keep that for another time, shall we?'

Sinead came over to join them, and spoke hesitantly. 'You never mentioned your wife, Ian, did you lose her too?'

'Aye, but not to the virus. I moved from Scotland to America for the love of Linda. She was visiting friends in Aberdeen, who happened to be my friends too, and we got matched.' He gave her a cocky, somehow endearing little grin. 'There were a lot of lasses after me back then, I was like a god, ye ken. I had my fun. But, when I met my Linda, I only had eyes for her.'

'Just as it should be,' Sinead said with a smile, and exchanged a knowing glance with Todd.

'I moved here to be with her,' Ian went on. 'We married, and I joined the army.' His voice broke suddenly. 'I lost my bonnie Linda, when our Becky was a baby.'

Sinead put her hand on his shoulder, and he patted it but didn't look at her. 'When the bairns came to me for a song … Well, it filled a big hole.' To lighten the mood, he said, 'I tried for days to get a date with Linda, but she was a stubborn one. I won her over with a love song.' Looking at Sinead at last, he asked, 'So what was the chat up line this man used to win a beauty like you?'

121

Sinead laughed. 'He said, "That dress looks great. But you know what would look better on you? Me!"'

'And that worked?'

'The hell it did! But it made me laugh, as he was usually the perfect gentleman. To be fair, he *was* drunk at the time.'

Todd made a sound of protest. 'I was not... very!'

'I told him he was a cheeky little gobshite,' Sinead went on, 'and he was mortified and kept trying to make up for it. I knew he was a good bloke, and I fancied him like mad, but kept him running around for a while.'

'Good girl.'

'Now, I think that stew is ready and it won't serve itself.' She turned to Todd. 'Remember to keep some back for Otto, won't you?' Seeing their guest's raised eyebrow, she explained, 'We have a rule here: the cook doesn't serve, or clean the dishes. All the chores are shared. Those who have other business to attend to get their meals cooked for them, and we cook for Otto.'

'I don't care who does what,' Ian said happily, 'I'm so hungry, ye could put it on the floor and I'd eat it like a dog.'

Everyone took their places around the table, and no-one seemed to mind being squashed up against their neighbour; there were a few murmured apologies when elbows got in the way, but they soon got used to it, and after an active and busy day, the crock pot was soon emptied.

Ian mopped the last of the broth with his bread. 'That was the best meat-free meal I've ever eaten. You're a good cook.'

Sinead accepted the compliment with a smile.

'The Commandments from the Fathers specify that no living creature should be killed, or be made to suffer,' Todd explained, 'except in self-defence or self-preservation. Anyone wanting to live here or in the surrounding areas has to live by those rules. Hopefully one day everyone will.'

Sinead nodded. 'It's a change in life-style for sure, but when you really think about it, it's just not right to kill for food, we all have a right to be here. The only exception we have allowed is tinned meat, but that's only until the supplies are gone. Newcomers are hungry, and don't have the resources we have. Not yet, anyway.'

'So what other rules are there?'

'We expect everyone to learn Hally, so that we can all communicate.'

'That's it?' Ian shrugged. 'Fair enough. Now, let me help with the dishes, and maybe I'll be rewarded with a couple more bevvies?' He shot Todd a cheeky grin.

'I'm up for that,' Todd said. 'You know, we could use the help of another strong man around here, and you worked well in the fields this afternoon. Would you consider staying on for a bit? You'd be welcome to stay in the cabin.'

'I can sort out some linen for you,' Sinead added, and the children both looked at Ian hopefully.

He looked around at them all, then nodded. 'Aye, I'd like that. For a wee while, then I'll be moving on.'

'The children will be going to bed soon,' Sinead said, 'would you sing them another song?'

'Yes please' said Karl, while Emily just nodded, but her eyes shone in anticipation.

'Well, I might be persuaded, but only if I hear these scalliwags say goodnight to you both first.'

Karl went over to Todd and Sinead in turn and hugged them. 'G'night.'

Emily gave them both a kiss, and Karl nudged her. She took a quick breath, and said, 'Nite, Todd, nite Shinny!' before hurrying from the room.

Sinead and Todd looked at one another in shared surprise and pleasure. 'Shinny?' Sinead repeated slowly. 'Oh I *love* it!'

Her emotions were in danger of getting the better of her, and she was glad when Ian stopped in the doorway and said, with the impish smile she was already coming to recognise, 'If it's not too much trouble, a couple more beers would go down nicely. The last ones just, sort of, evaporated.'

Chapter Eight
A Few Surprises

John parked the jeep in the dusty gravelled parking area, at the edge of what had become, almost unnoticed, a real town. Was it really only just over two years since the dreams had begun? He switched off the engine, but although it was good to be home he rested on the steering wheel for a while, bathed in the blissful silence and thinking about how far they'd all come in that short time.

The thought that all this, and even the future of mankind itself, had hinged on such a brittle series of *what ifs*, was sometimes chilling, sometimes exhilarating, always terrifying. What if his parents had declined their friends' invitation to Jericho? They'd never have found the prophecies that his mother had been able to decipher. What if he'd never met Jen? Would fate have found another way for the twins to be born? If Todd's father hadn't orchestrated the boys' friendship, what then? Who would have helped him understand what was happening? And Aunt May's death, the catalyst for it all... What if she hadn't kept his parents' paperwork? If it hadn't been for Eagle, and the encounter with the Fathers, humanity might even now be nothing but a scrap of memory lost in the wind.

John and Doron had worked hard to keep up with their responsibilities to the community, but it had become too much for just the two of them, particularly with the almost daily influx of new arrivals, and when the Eagle council members had finally left quarantine in Denver and moved to Carbondale, the relief had been immense for everyone. Each member had taken responsibility for a particular area of management: water; power; communication; transport and housing, along with their judicial services, freeing Doron to take charge of health care, John and Jen able to concentrate on education, and Ana and Diego Garcia on supplies.

Doron was still the town's only doctor, but Ruhi and Alima were doing well under his and Otto's wings and tutelage; John had little doubt they would be fine doctors themselves, and soon too, at the rate they were learning. The other twins, including his own, were all working hard to make life easier and safer for everyone.

He watched the harvesters now, carrying the last of their bounty from the fields, and turned his thoughts to his old life. He didn't miss it, but he did miss the simplicity of it; this new life was hard, sometimes brutal, and always in the back of his mind was the biggest *what if* of all... *What if next time he made the wrong choice?*

A growling in his stomach brought him out of those disturbing thoughts, and he climbed from the jeep and stretched, wondering what was for dinner. As always, whenever he walked this gravel road towards home, he found his tension easing, and knew it was in no small part thanks to Jen; she had put everything on hold for their family, had put her unquestioning trust in him when everything had fallen apart, and had been at his side ever

126

since. As long as they were together they could conquer anything.

He wasn't sure when the custom had started, but at some point he'd begun whistling a few notes every time he climbed the steps to their home, and he did so again now. The front door stood open, and he smelled the remnants of an earlier evening meal, presumably the others had eaten earlier. But where were they? He looked around the still, quiet room, and his gaze fell on Jen, curled up on the sofa and fast asleep. He watched her for a while, her breathing slow and steady, one hand cupping her cheek, the other hanging off the sofa, her fingertips brushing the floor.

Out of nowhere he thought of those fingers touching his arm last night, when he'd removed his shirt. Her voice had been half amused, half admiring. 'You've certainly been working hard.' She had let her fingers drift lightly down across his forearm, before returning to trace the curve of his bicep as he raised his arm to slip his hand around the back of her neck. What had followed had been... He shook his head to clear that thought, but dropped a light kiss on Jen's clear brow, meaning to ask her later tonight what she thought of his pectorals. He grinned to himself and retraced his steps, ignoring his meal in favour of the chance to catch up with Doron for a while.

He started up the road towards his brother's cabin, but before he reached it he saw Holly and Hannah emerging from the hall. They were distracted, and arguing, and he listened with interest; they rarely had much to say these days that wasn't worth listening to. Hannah was clearly the more aggrieved.

'It was my turn to record the newcomers today!'

Holly was grumbling, defensive. 'Well you should've turned up on time then.'

'I'm the one who always does the backup, you forget every single time! The one who records, backs up! So *have* you?'

'That's not the point. You were late! You're always late.'

'And you're always—'

'Hi!' John broke in. The girls neither saw nor heard him, so wrapped up were they in their argument, so he stepped directly in front of them. 'Girls! What are you arguing about this time?'

'Hi, Dad.' Holly said. 'It's nothing.'

'Didn't sound like nothing.' He softened his voice. 'Neither of you seems very happy lately, what's up?' He held up a hand. 'And don't go giving me some lame answer. Come on, what's really bugging you?'

The girls looked at one another, and shrugged. 'We're bored,' Hannah said.

'Bored?' John stared at them, genuinely baffled. 'How can you be? You're working as hard as anyone, harder than some. Do you need a break, is that it?'

'No.'

'Then what?'

Holly looked at her sister again, and sighed. 'It's our database. It's so... *basic.*'

'Basic?'

'It's just so simple!' Hannah clarified.

'Maybe to you and me,' John conceded, 'but not to everyone else. That database will help hundreds of people. Maybe thousands, and we're all very proud of you for building it.' He smiled. 'I heard you reunited two best friends the other week, and thanks to your data we discovered another teacher amongst us. Do you realise how amazing that is?'

'Yes,' Holly said, 'but we have *ideas*, Dad.'

'We can do so much more.' Hannah added.

John looked at them for a moment, torn between wanting to make them happy, and needing them to understand. 'Let's sit here for a minute.' He gestured to the steps of the nearest cabin, and they obediently sat down either side of him, looking up at him expectantly.

'I know you're capable of so much, and that's really hard to keep in check, but for now you have to be patient.' He sensed the slump in their shoulders, and pressed on. 'Look, our priority for the time being is to survive, isn't it? You understand that.'

'Yes, but—'

'The small hydropower plant in Carbondale will be finished soon, but that's not going to be anywhere near enough power for everyone. The Shoshone hydroelectric plant is looking like a good bet, but there's lots of work to be done there too.' Appealing to something he knew was close to everyone's heart, he added, 'Whatever we do, we have to ensure the wildlife doesn't suffer, there are repairs to be made, and there needs to be some re-arranging of power distribution. This all takes time, you know that.'

He tried to the sting out of his words by taking a small hand in each of his. 'Whatever brilliant ideas you have will have to wait just a little bit longer, okay? At least until we have more power and more manpower. For now, record your ideas, and plan for them.'

'I suppose,' Hannah said, in a small voice.

'It's not just us, Dad,' Holly added. 'The others feel the same way. Leon and Luca have ideas for a solar sky mesh. They're drawing up the plans for that, but they can't do anything about it.'

'It's alright for Ruhi and Alima,' Hannah put in. 'They're using their gifts. They're working on a vaccine and stem cell stuff.'

'Never mind them, did you say a *solar sky mesh?*'

Holly nodded. 'Yeah, it's a special net that floats in the sky, and acts like a huge solar panel. Takes away the need for generating electricity on the Earth.'

John shook his head. 'Wow. You kids amaze me, and I know your own ideas will be just as wonderful.' He shook at their hands. 'Your time will come, girls. In the meantime, carry on what you're doing, but remember to have fun too. You're still so young. There's our big celebration party to look forward to when the harvesting's done, and we have so many more people to join in this year.'

Both girls brightened. 'I'd actually forgotten about that,' Holly said.

'Me too! We need to get some new clothes ready for it.'

'Well, there you go.' John dropped their hands and slapped his raised knees. 'We'll organise a trip into town, see what we can find.'

'Thanks! That'll be great!'

'Right, off you go home then, but mind you go in quietly, your mum's asleep on the sofa and I don't want her disturbed. When she wakes up you can tell her I'll be home soon, I'm just nipping up to speak to Uncle Ron.'

They leapt up. 'We will, Dad!'

'See you later!'

With their still childlike voices chiming in his ear, John watched them go, wondering when they'd stopped calling him "Daddy." They were growing up so fast... Not too long ago they'd been playing dress-up, and singing in front of Top of the Pops; now they were bemoaning their "basic database" and talking about solar sky meshes. He tried not to feel the wrench as a negative thing, after all weren't they growing into exactly what he and Jen had always dreamed of?

He watched them wandering up the road for a while, then turned to continue on his way to Doron's cabin. As he drew close he saw Doron sitting on the verandah, eating, and he waved. Doron waved back, calling out a greeting around a mouthful of food, and as John climbed the steps his stomach growled again.

'I heard that from here,' Doron grinned. 'Aren't they feeding you at home?'

'Jen's asleep and I didn't want to wake her. I'm starving!'

'What, you can't fix your own dinner?'

'I mean I didn't want to make a noise,' John began, before seeing the glint of teasing humour in his brother's eyes. 'Okay. You got me.'

Rena came out of the cabin and opened her arms to embrace him. 'Alex has made a curry,' she said, 'there's plenty more in the pot.'

'I don't want to put you to any trouble.'

'It's no trouble. Sit down, I'll fetch you some.'

'Thanks, Mum.'

Rena smiled. 'I love the way you boys call me Mum and Mom.' She disappeared back into the house, and John sat down next to his brother and took a deep, relaxing breath. It felt good.

Doron scooped up another spoonful of curry. 'How did the meeting go, then?'

'Very well, as it goes. I've got a fair bit to tell you, too.'

'Go on.'

John tried not to watch as his brother shovelled down his meal, it smelled too good. 'The council needs a replacement for their American counterpart, to bring the numbers back to five.'

'Sure. Mike Ford went missing, right?'

'Right. Well Todd's mum Clare was nominated, and voted in.'

'Great news. I can't think of a better replacement for Mike.'

'Nor can I. But she doesn't know yet, so keep quiet about it, okay?'

'Of course. She'll be really happy about it though.' Doron stirred his meal thoughtfully. 'Speaking of Mike, is there any news yet?'

'That's the other thing.' Everyone had believed Mike Ford to have been behind the bribing of Louise Miller to steal the twins' blood, hence his disappearance. 'It wasn't him who betrayed Eagle.'

'What?' Doron put down his spoon. 'How do they know that?'

'The council decided to find out for sure what had happened, so Jimmy and Andrei went to his home and found him.'

'They knew where he lived? Before, I mean?'

'When the outbreak was imminent, the council got in touch with one another for the first time, to organise a meeting once all their members arrived in the US. Mike's home was the arranged meeting place.'

'So,' Doron urged, 'what did he have to say for himself?'

'That's just it. He couldn't say anything. They found his skeleton lying on a bullet.'

'No way,' Doron breathed. 'Murder or suicide?'

'More than likely murder, from the position of the bullet.'

'By whom?'

'They don't know, but they suspect a Veritas member. The feeling is that some of them are still very much alive and kicking. That would explain why the blood was stolen, and it would have been fairly easy for one of them to impersonate Mike, and fool poor Louise.'

'Bastards.'

'My thoughts exactly.'

Rena came back out, this time with a steaming bowl of curry on a tray. 'Who are bastards?' she asked. John rose to take the tray, and reiterated what he'd told Doron.

'It doesn't surprise me,' she said, 'and it does make sense. If Veritas are still operational we might have to be a bit more alert. We know how clever they are. Although I can't see any reason they'd still want to cause harm to any of you twins now, their plans would have died along with the virus.'

'The council would agree with you,' John said, and blew on a spooonful of curry. 'Even so, we should warn the community to be on their guard. Just as a precaution.' He tasted the food, and made a thumbs-up sign. His mother smiled.

'Maybe we should organise the Eagle security members to re-assemble,' Doron suggested.

Rena nodded. 'We could ask that new fella to help out. Todd tells me he was in the army. I went around to say hello just before you got back, but he was saying goodnight to the children.'

'What new fella's this?' John asked.

'His name's Sloan. Scottish. Lovely singing voice.'

'And you just... *went around*, huh?' Doron gave her a knowing look, which she primly ignored.

'He helped out with the harvest today,' she said, 'and even got little Emily talking.'

'That's good news. Where did he come from?'

'I told you, Scotland.'

'Mom! I mean recently.'

'Oh! Um, from Fort Bragg.'

Ron blinked. 'That's Special Forces!'

'Well that clinches it then,' John said. 'Maybe he'd help out with security.'

'Another member would be good,' Doron agreed. 'We'd be a man down at the moment. The original chief of security is one of the people I visited today, with his wife and her best friend.'

'Oh, that must be the friends my girls re-connected,' John said, pleased. 'How'd you get on?'

'Right, I'll leave you to it,' Rena said, turning to go. 'I've heard all this before.'

'Thank you for this meal,' John said, 'it's delicious.'

Rena looked back and smiled. 'Alex loves to cook, and this is one of Farrah's recipes. Did you know dried rice can last up to five years? Thirty even, in the freezer. That's what Farrah says. We've got that long to enjoy it. Glad you like it, John. I'll see you boys later.'

John turned back to his brother. 'So, how'd you get on?' he repeated.

'Fine.'

'You don't say that with much conviction.'

Doron considered. 'Well, all three definitely have giardiasis, but the married couple are more sick than I'd have expected. I've given them all antibiotics, and left plenty of bottled water for them, along with some soup Mom made. I'll check up on them again soon.'

'I'm sure they'll be fine.'

Rena came back out. 'I forgot to tell you. Ana says she and Diego went into Glenwood Springs today with some of the others. They were looking for more suppplies, and wanted to check out the Shoshone plant, and they met a bunch of newcomers. Native Americans. Seems they've settled in the lodge at the Springs, and best of all, they've got a doctor.'

'Really?' Doron looked delighted. 'That's great news! I'll go introduce myself first thing tomorrow. It'd be such a relief to get some help around here. Want to come?'

'I'd love to,' John said, 'but there's still a lot of work to do around here. We could invite him over for tomorrow's meeting though?'

'Will do.' Doron waited until Rena had gone back inside, then leaned closer to John. 'Mom certainly has a way of finding out information.' He winked. 'She should've been in the CIA.'

***

The following morning Doron drove the half hour to Glenwood Springs. The Roaring Fork River ran adjacent to the highway, though he couldn't see it, but he would soon be crossing the Colorado River. This was one of his favourite drives, cruising comfortably along the Grand Avenue, never tiring of the beauty of the mountains that rose on either side of the road, though the pretty, tree-lined streets were eerily quiet. He didn't think he'd ever get used to the once thriving community becoming this ghost town.

Once over the bridge, he took the exit to Glenwood Hot Springs, and within minutes he was pulling into a space in the parking lot behind the lodge. He plucked the key from the ignition, and looked out at the sandstone cliffs and steep green mountainsides that surrounded him, and then at the SUVs in the lot next to him. Any sign of new people was a welcome one, but he couldn't help being glad he had not stumbled on this group alone, and

136

without prior notice that they were decent people; there was no guarantee in this post-virus world that they would be.

He walked around the building to the front entrance, and when he pushed open the door he saw what looked to be about a dozen people sitting at various tables, chatting. The room fell silent when he stepped in, and faces swivelled towards him, open and curious. Doron went to the nearest and held out his hand.

'Hi, I'm Ron Malik.'

A man around the same age as himself, with a warm, friendly smile, rose and took the hand he offered. 'Nice to meet you, Ron. I'm Beau, and these people here are my friends. We've all heard about you and your brother, up there at Hope Meadows.'

Doron nodded around at everyone, and returned their smiles. 'What brings you here to the Springs?'

Beau dragged a chair over and beckoned for Doron to sit. He did so, with thanks, and Beau re-seated himself. 'We're a mixed group here. Mostly Ute, Shoshone and Hopi, but some Navajo too, and a few Anishaabe down from Canada.'

'That sounds similar to our own community,' Doron said. 'We're a mixture of races and old religions, and we're all learning to compromise so we can live together peacefully.'

'I hope it's working out for you. I think it will for us too, in time. But,' he gave a rueful shake of his head, 'we can be a stubborn bunch. Anyway, to answer your question, we're here for a few reasons. For us, meaning the Utes, the Springs were a sacred place before the white

137

man, pardon the expression, took it from us. We named it Yampah, which means Big Medicine. No Ute actually lived here, but it was ours to travel to for healing.'

'I see.' Doron looked around. 'So how many of you are there in your group?'

An elderly woman seated next to Beau spoke up. 'There are around a hundred of us here. After the virus had taken its toll we went searching for survivors, and this is all we've found so far. I'm Belle, by the way.'

'My mother,' Beau added.

'It's nice to meet you, ma'am,' Doron said, shaking the woman's hand and smiling at the firm grip. 'It's good to see so many more survivors. Would you and your people be interested in joining us? There are around four hundred of us now, and more arriving every week.'

Beau exchanged a look with his mother, and the silence stretched, then he responded, carefully. 'That's a generous offer, and we thank you, but it's not so easy to answer.' Seeing Doron's questioning look he went on, 'We're curious though, of course.'

'Well, we're having a newcomers' meeting tonight, at Hope Meadows at around 7 o'clock. Perhaps some of you would like to come along?'

Beau inclined his head, still non-committal. 'Thank you. I'll ask around.'

'So... do you intend to settle here and reclaim your land?' Seeing people shifting in their seats, and looking uncomfortably at one another, Doron held up a hand. 'Please, don't worry about your answer. No-one owns this land anymore, and if you wish to settle here it's your right. You'll find no argument from us. However, if you wish to join our community we'll need to discuss that at a later date.'

'We may stay for a while,' Beau said, 'but don't intend to settle just yet. So anyway,' he turned it around, 'what brings *you* here to us?'

'I came to introduce myself, and to invite you to the meeting of course, but mostly I wanted to meet with your doctor. I'm the only one around here, and I'd love to speak with him, compare notes... even ask for his help.'

A murmur of amusement ran around the room, and Doron frowned; he hadn't said anything funny, had he?

'Our doctor is down at Yampah vapor caves,' Beau said, pointing behind him. 'It's only a two minute walk along the river. Perhaps you'd like to meet there?'

'Thanks, I'll head down there now.' He stood up. 'It was nice to meet you all, and I hope some of you will come along tonight. Should you want fresh water we have plenty in Carbondale, so please take what you need.'

'That's kind of you, Ron, thank you.'

'Enjoy your meeting.' He nodded around at everyone, and as the door closed behind him another faint ripple of laughter followed him out into the parking lot.

The spa was easy to find, and even as Doron went in through the front door his throat protested the rich, sulphurous smell of dissolving rock minerals; he breathed deeply a few times, to acclimatise himself to it, then followed the signs that directed him to a stairway. He emerged into a stone corridor, and felt his shirt sticking to his back with the increasing heat. The smell was also stronger, and the way ahead pitch black, and he hesitated, remembering that laughter. Was he being mocked? But the newcomers hadn't seemed malicious in their intent, though who could blame them for enjoying the thought of what he'd find here? There had been little enough to laugh about for years.

The heat though, and the *smell...* He swallowed hard and stared ahead through the darkness, feeling sweat trickling down from his hairline and stinging his eyes. Every movement seemed to result in a fresh rivulet, plastering his shirt to his skin and his hair to his brow. He looked behind him, recalling the fresh, fragrant, early evening air he had left behind, and had even half-turned back towards it when a flashlight flickered down the corridor.

He sighed, plucked his soaked shirt free from the skin of his chest, and started towards the light. In the faint glow, he could see small channels of flowing water – *that must be over 100 degrees Farenheit...* but he kept going.

'Who's there?' A female voice bounced off the stone throat of the corridor, and flashlight rose to shine full in his face.

He lifted both hands to shield his eyes. 'It's okay, ma'am, I mean you no harm. Beau sent me, I'm here to see the doctor. Do you know where he is?'

'Yes I do, but if you're going to survive in here you're going to have to undress, and stop moving around so much.'

There was no way he was doing any such thing. 'Perhaps you'd been so kind as to let him know I'd like to see him? My name's Ron Malik, and I've come from Hope Meadows. I'll, uh, I'll wait upstairs.'

A wave of relief carried him back up the stairs and into daylight. He recalled how his throat had clenched when he'd first come in, but the air up here smelled daisy-fresh now, compared to the stench down there. How had that woman stood it? It was still warm outside, but he went out and gulped some clean air before returning to wait indoors, resisting the urge to see if he could actually wring out his shirt.

After around ten minutes, a young woman appeared at the top of the staircase, rubbing her long black hair with a towel. Ron tried not to stare, but as she came towards him, barefoot and clad only in a blue swimsuit, he realised he'd never seen anyone quite so heartbreakingly beautiful before.

She looked less than happy, however. 'Mr Malik?'

'Yes. Hi. I've come to meet the doctor. The lady inside the cave said... Oh.' He immediately felt foolish for not realising. 'That must have been you.'

'Yes it was. You startled me, and interrupted my meditation.'

'I'm so sorry. I was told...' A second realisation: that laughter hadn't been about the smell and general discomfort he was going to find after all. 'You're the doctor, right?'

'Obviously. What do you want?'

A little taken aback by her abruptness, he nevertheless smiled, eager to redeem himself.

'I truly am sorry. I came here to introduce myself to you, and if you and your people plan to settle around here I was hoping you and I could join forces. I'm a doctor too, and could sure use the help.'

'So this is all about you, then?'

'Not at all!' He could feel the flush creeping across his face. 'I also came to invite you and some of your friends to our newcomers' meeting tonight at Hope Meadows. I thought we could all get to know one another, we might even be able to help each other.'

There was a long pause, while he once again tried not to fasten his eyes on any particular part of her glowing perfection, then she spoke again. 'Do you like dogs, Mr Malik?'

'I... What?' Bemused by the swift change in subject, he was at a loss. Was she going to tell him she was actually a vet?

'I said, do you like dogs?'

'Yes. Very much. Why?'

'Well, if you leave me to enjoy some peace now, I'll come to your meeting, and maybe others will come with me. But I don't go anywhere without my dogs.' She saw him looking around, and gave a little sigh. 'Obviously I don't bring them here,' she said patiently, 'it would be too uncomfortable for them.'

'Of course. Great. I'm really pleased. I'll leave you in peace then, and look forward to seeing you this evening.' Doron gave her a little smile. 'With your dogs, of course.'

She turned to go, raising a hand in either dismissal or farewell, he couldn't work out which.

'Miss,' he called out, 'Uh, I mean, Doctor? What's your name?'

'Nita.'

Chapter Nine
A Change of Heart

'Kimi, Boss, Echo! Up!' Nita waited until all three dogs were settled on the folded tents in the back of the truck, next to the two small sacks nestled there, and then closed the tailgate. She waited at the wheel, while Beau helped his mother into the back seat, and when he'd pulled his own door closed she started the engine and they rolled slowly out of the parking lot. She turned towards Hope Meadows, and settled down for the drive.

'I wonder what this evening will be like,' Belle said, raising her voice over the rattle of the truck's engine.

Nita glanced at her in the rear view mirror. 'I wouldn't get your hopes up, it's just a welcome meeting for newcomers.'

'Aren't you curious, then?'

'Vaguely.' Nita negotiated a turn. 'If we decided to settle here, though I don't think we will, we'd need to know what our neighbours are like.'

'They seem friendly enough to me. And generous, don't forget, they offered us unlimited use of their water. That's got to count for something, don't you think?'

Nita shrugged. 'I'll reserve my judgement for when I know them better. It might not have been totally altruistic, after all – they want to use the hydro-power plant that stands right in the middle of the Springs and the caves. It could just have been a gesture to keep us happy and compliant.'

'Oh, Nita!' Belle said, clearly irritated. 'We have no interest in that plant! We don't have the skills to work it, and if we do settle here we're going to need electricity!'

Nita felt her jaw tightening. '*They* don't know that though, do they?'

'Wow,' Beau piped up dryly, 'ever the sceptic, aren't you? If you looked for the good in people for a change, you might just get a nice surprise.'

Nita favoured him with a brief scowl. 'If you look for the bad,' she returned, 'you don't get disappointed when you find it.'

'Young lady,' Belle said, her tone becoming haughty now, 'we've been invited to meet with our neighbours. Your attitude could be better. If you keep this up while we're there you're going to shame us all.'

Nita was about to say something snappish back, but caught a glimpse of Belle in the mirror again and sighed. 'I won't let you down, Belle. But,' she added, 'I don't give my trust lightly, you know that.'

After a few minutes of tense silence as the road sped by beneath them, Beau spoke up again, his voice deliberately light. 'So, what did you think of that Ron Malik? He's a good looking guy.'

'I didn't think of him at all, certainly didn't notice.' Nita frowned again. 'He disturbed my meditation, scared me half to death in the dark, and then fell over himself in his introduction. I agreed to this invitation out of curiosity, nothing more.'

Beau laughed. 'Scared? You? I don't think so.' He paused, and added in a playful tone, 'I think you liked him.'

'I most certainly did not!' Nita flicked out her right hand blindly, and felt it connect with his arm.

'Ow!'

'I agreed to go,' she went on, 'because I want to find out more about the twins. I want to know if what they experienced is true. I mean, I saw Ron Malik on the TV before I ever saw him in my vision, with his family, and I need to see it with my own eyes now. The truth of it.'

'Have you ever doubted your visions before?' Belle asked.

'No, never.'

'Then why doubt that one?'

Nita hissed in exasperation. 'I... I don't know!'

'Nita,' Belle said with infuriating calm, 'you have Rose's temper, and that's tolerable, but your anger is your own. That's been getting worse since we left our home.'

Nita stamped on the brake, and the truck slewed to a stop. She clenched her fingers on the steering wheel, then felt the frustration drain out of her, leaving her tired, but calm. She turned off the engine and sat back in her seat, and saw Beau glance into the back, an unspoken question behind his eyes as he shrugged.

Nita remained silent for a moment, gathering her thoughts, then twisted to look at Belle. 'In my first vision, Dakayivani said to me, *"Do not keep anger in your heart, little bear, it will consume you. Never judge all by the deeds of the few."* I try to remember, Belle, but it's hard.' She shook her head. 'And that's only a small part of how I feel. My latest vision showed me the Springs, and I'm grateful that you all put your trust in me to come here, but it also showed me fields of corn. Corn that we can no longer grow at home, not without water.'

She turned back to Beau. 'I know you were joking, but I *do* get scared. I want control of my life, but the visions are taking me somewhere I've never been, and I can't plan for what I don't know.' She gave him a tentative smile. 'I'm sorry I hit you, you're a good friend.'

'No I'm not.' He grinned suddenly. 'I'm an awesome friend.' He looked somewhat plaintively at his arm, and added, 'An awesome friend with bruises.'

She smiled back, and was gratified as Belle leaned awkwardly forward and pressed her shoulder. 'You are not only our healer, but our shaman. Though that does not mean the fate of our people is on these shoulders, Nita, we all share in that responsibility.' She squeezed lightly. 'You must stop fighting your destiny. Embrace it, and just let be what will be.'

Nita's eyes prickled as she reached back and covered Belle's wrinkled hand with hers. 'Thank you. You've been like a mother to me this past year, and you don't deserve my sharp tongue. I'm sorry.'

Belle nodded, then sat back, and when Nita didn't move, she raised an eyebrow. 'Well, what are we waiting for then?'

Nita rolled her eyes, turned back to the front, and twisted the ignition key.

The little town was buzzing with activity. Nita had deliberately arrived early, in order to observe the people before the meeting began. She pulled the truck to a stop outside the perimeter fence, and watched. Most of those she saw were busy carrying chairs from a large cabin to an area at the rear, others bore heavy bags, and some were laden with trays or baskets.

'Looks like they're providing food for their guests,' Belle observed. 'Kind of them.'

'Great,' Beau enthused. 'I'm real hungry.'

Belle snorted gently. 'You're always hungry, boy.' She prodded Nita's shoulder. 'Are we going to join them, then?'

'I just want to watch for a moment, if that's okay?'

'Of course.'

Nita hadn't really prepared herself for how strange it would be to see so many sets of twins in one place. A couple of much younger children were running around, getting under feet and hampering progress, but no one seemed to mind, and tolerated them quite happily. In fact they were looked on with indulgence and even fondness. An elderly woman's basket slipped in her fingers, and the contents spilled to the ground, but before she had time to ask for help, it was given.

Nita saw someone she thought she recognised as Ron Malik at first, and almost tooted on the truck's horn, but checked herself as she noted the shorter hair, and realised it must be his brother John. He had his arms around twin girls, presumably his daughters, and was talking earnestly to them. All three were smiling.

'Everyone's working hard,' she mused, to no one in particular, 'but they all look so happy and relaxed about it. Friendly too.'

Belle's voice was amused, but kind. 'Why so surprised?'

'I don't really know.' Nita unclipped her seat belt. 'Come on, let's go meet everyone. Maybe we should help too. But as she let the dogs out of the back she was irritated to find herself looking around for Ron.

Beau helped his mother climb down, then took out the two small sacks while the dogs, freed from constraint, made straight for the fence and relieved themselves before returning obediently to their mistress's side.

The three of them, and the dogs, walked around the edge of the town and in through the parking area. They were greeted with nods and smiles, but no one stopped them to ask who they were, they just carried on with their tasks. Ahead, three women saw them, looked at one another, and began to walk towards them, waving a greeting.

Without warning, two children of around four or five broke away from the women and began running towards Nita and the dogs.

'Doggies!' the little girl yelled in excitement, and Nita held out her hand quickly, appalled.

'Stop!'

The children skidded to a halt, and blinked in surprise at her.

'Never run towards a dog you don't know,' Nita admonished. 'You might frighten them, and a frightened dog will bite!' The children's faces fell, and she added, more gently, 'It's okay, mine won't bite you. But you should ask your mom if it's okay to pet them.'

'Can we?' They begged in unison, looking back at the women. In answer to a look from one of them Nita nodded encouragingly, and the children advanced again, more slowly this time.

'Well done. My name's Nita.' She smiled, and indicated the smallest of the dogs. 'This one's Kimi.' She pointed to the other two. 'This is Boss, and this one's Echo. What are your names?'

'I'm Karl, ma'am,' the boy said.

'Emily,' the little girl chimed in.

'Well, it's nice to meet you both. Do you want to sit down over there? I'll send them over to say hello properly.'

The children sat, and Nita looked down at the three dogs, who panted up at her, waiting as she raised a hand in the air. Holding off just long enough to make them start shifting their front paws impatiently, Nita finally swept her hand towards the children.

'Go!'

They leapt forward as one, but Nita was proud to note how they slowed down to approach the children carefully, before jumping up and covering the eagerly grinning faces with slobbery kisses. The children squealed with delight, and Nita saw the three women smiling too as they approached, and she relaxed a little. She introduced herself and they shook hands.

'I'm Jen,' one of the younger women said. Nita recognised her as the one she'd seen approaching the two men in her vision.

149

'Sinead,' the other said, in a soft Irish accent. 'Lovely to meet you. She indicated the slightly older woman. 'This is Rena.'

'Ron and John's mother,' Nita explained to her friends, then turned back. 'This is Belle, and her son Beau.'

Beau stepped forward and gestured a little shyly to the sacks. 'At our home in Towaoc we grew corn, but we can't do that anymore. We saved what crop we could, and made cornmeal. It's highly nutritious and keeps well, and we would like to gift this to you.'

'That's so kind of you!' Jen said, and Sinead echoed her thanks.

Rena looked pleased too, but eyed the sacks doubtfully. 'What's best to do with it?'

'Do you have eggs, milk and salt?' Belle asked. Rena nodded. 'Then perhaps if you'd take me to your kitchen I can show you how to make corn bread. I have the other things we'll need here.' She patted her pocket. 'It doesn't take long, and we can put it with the other food you've brought to feed your guests. I'd have made it myself, to bring with me,' she added, 'but I didn't have all the ingredients.'

'Of course,' Rena said. 'I'm cooking jacket potatoes, and I can easily make room for cornbread. I've heard of it, of course, but never had it before. I look forward to tasting it.'

Belle beamed at her, and Rena offered her arm. The two waved a brief farewell and walked off like old friends, with Beau trailing behind carrying the sacks. Nita watched them go, a little smile tugging at her lips.

Rena's voice drifted back. 'How did she know I was John and Ron's mother?'

Nita's smile slipped as she realised her error, but Belle glanced back at her. 'It's the likeness,' she said.

Discomfited that she should have slipped up so carelessly, Nita whistled to the dogs, who came straight back and sat at her feet.

'Those dogs are so well behaved,' Sinead said admiringly.

'Thank you, and so are… I guess, your children…?' Sinead filled in the details of how they came to be a family.

'We've all lost people close to us,' Nita said quietly, and they were all caught up in their own thoughts for a moment, before Jen smiled to lift the mood.

'Come with us,' she said, 'we'll show you around our little town.'

'I'd like that a lot, thank you.' Nita joined the two women, and as they walked into town she made sure she didn't give any hint that she'd seen the place before. The children walked alongside her and the dogs, bending now and again to pet one of them, and Karl occasionally scuffed his foot to send a pebble shooting a few metres away, grinning as one of the dogs scampered after it.

As they neared the town hall, Jen explained a little of their system. 'We hold these meetings once a fortnight for all newcomers. We tell them how we came to be here, and what we're doing to make life easier. We also tell them what's expected of those who want to join us.'

'Does everyone join?'

'Almost everyone, so far at least. There've been a few who decided they want time to think everything through, first. Which is understandable.'

'So no one has to stay, if they don't want to?'

'Of course not!' Jen gave a little laugh. 'I mean, we have certain rules, for the good of all, and we expect people to follow them, but we'd never ask anyone to give up their own traditions.'

'We try to compromise on any issues that come up,' Sinead added. 'We used to hold meetings in this hall, but it's warm tonight, and we're expecting quite a few. Sure, it'd be too cramped, so we're all going to sit in the field.'

Nita was about to reply, but was stopped by the tug of a small hand on her fringed skirt. She looked down to see Emily's face turned up to hers. 'Is Kimi a girl?'

Nita crouched, and drew Kimi close. 'Yes, she is. She's the mother of those two.' She nodded at the other dogs. 'Both boys. I named her after my great grandmother, who was called Kimama. It means butterfly.'

'That's a pretty name.'

'It is, isn't it? So's yours. Boss is called that because he's bossy, and Echo? Well, he just copies everything Boss does. Like an echo.'

'My name means princess,' Emily said firmly.

Nita looked over at Sinead, not sure whether to correct the girl, and grinned when she saw Sinead rolling her eyes as she shook her head. 'Does it?' she said instead. She turned to Karl. 'I met a man once whose name was Karl, so I know it means a strong man, like a warrior.'

A lance of pain went through her as her own words reminded her of those times she and Billy were squashed

152

into their tiny hiding places; she'd been the warrior then, protecting him, but she hadn't been able to protect him for long enough. She blinked the image away. 'Are you a warrior, Karl?'

'No, ma'm,' he said solemnly. 'I'm a knight of Haverhill.'

Jen and Sinead laughed, and Nita felt some of her sadness peel away at the seriousness of the little boy's reply.

'I'm going to have words with Todd later,' Sinead said. She saw Nita's questioning look, and shook her head, still smiling. 'I'll explain later,' she promised.

Nita looked down at the children, and adopted a gruff voice. 'Well, my name means... bear!' she growled, and they jumped, but soon dissolved into giggles as she tickled them with her hooked fingers.

'Ian!' Karl shouted.

Emily followed his pointing finger and she shouted too, and a moment later both of them had forgotten the dogs, and Nita's bear-tickling, and ran to greet two men who'd clearly just returned from the field.

'He's new too,' Sinead said, nodding at the burlier of the two men, and she told Nita how the hitherto shy children had immediately taken to him, particularly Emily. Nita was beginning to get a real sense of peace here, and that these people actually were as nice as they seemed.

The men reached them, slowed a little by the two children hanging onto their hands, and introductions began all over again.

'Welcome to our town,' the man introduced as Todd said. 'Ron will be so pleased you came. As are we of course.'

'This is one of the other knights of Haverhill,' Sinead supplied. 'He and John have been best friends since school, it's one of their private jokes. One of many, I might add.' She turned to Todd, who Nita realised was her partner. 'I understand the knighthood has a new recruit?'

Todd looked sheepish, but put his hand secretively behind his back, whereupon Karl delivered a perfect low-five. This went unnoticed by Sinead, and Nita couldn't help grinning.

Ian proffered his hand, and Nita shook it, but dropped it almost immediately, hoping it wasn't too obviously hurried. She rubbed her hand thoughtfully.

'Are you alright, lass?' Ian asked.

Nita recovered herself. 'I'm fine. Sorry, I'm just a little on edge.'

'Well,' he smiled, 'there's nae need to worry, these are good people, very welcoming, and I'm sure the meeting will be fine. It'll be my first, too,' he added.

Before anyone could mention her reaction, two girls came around the corner of the hall, and she recognised them as the twins she'd seen with John. They came over to join the small group and the dogs.

'Girls, come and say hi to Nita,' Jen said. 'She and her friends have settled for a while in the Springs. Nita, these are my daughters, Holly and Hannah.'

'Hi, girls,' Nita said.

'Hi, Nita,' they chorused.

'I love your hair,' Hannah said. 'Is it *all* plaited with ribbons and beads? She ducked around Nita to look at the back.

'Thank you,' Nita said, amused, 'and yes, it is.'

'Would you show us how to do that with ours?' Holly chipped in.

'Of course. Another time, perhaps, but it would be my pleasure.'

The girls were examining her quite openly, and Jen flushed. 'Girls, don't be rude.'

'Sorry, mum,' Hannah said. She and her sister knelt, to make a fuss of the dogs. 'Uncle Ron said you might be coming, with your dogs, so we made something for them just in case.'

'But we thought there would only be two,' Holly added, 'and we thought they'd be bigger. Wait here, I'll be back in a mo.' She ran into the hall, and emerged a minute later carrying something. She trotted up to Nita, puffing with exertion and pride. 'Me and Hannah got two collars from the pet shop in Carbondale, and we decorated them ourselves.'

Hannah pointed out the embellishments. 'See? We stitched little hearts on.'

Nita was deeply touched; after all she was a stranger to these girls. 'They're beautiful, thank you so much. What a wonderful, thoughtful gift.' She brushed a finger across the stitching. 'But, just so there's no jealousy, and because the mama dog deserves it most, do you mind if I only put one on Kimi?'

'Of course not.' The girls beamed with pride at the way their gift had been received, and looked on with interest as

155

Nita fastened the collar around Kimi's neck. Their interest grew to awe as, realising the collar was too big, Nita took her knife, from an attached sheath inside her boot, and made an extra hole. She caught them looking at one another in delight; clearly a blade in your boot was a pretty cool thing to have, in their eyes.

'There,' she announced, running her finger around the collar to check she hadn't misjudged and made it too tight. 'A perfect fit, and I think Kimi likes it too.'

Nita helped carry chairs to the field while the dogs were happily exploring, but made sure she never let them out of her sight; this might be a friendly place, but it was also a new one to them, and she had no idea what might take their interest. As she placed the chair she was carrying alongside the next in the row, her attention was caught by Doron, who was helping move a table into place.

As if feeling her eyes on him, he looked over at almost the same moment, and muttered something to his partner. He came over, dusting off his hands and looking a little less uneasy than she'd expected; he was on his home ground now, though.

'Hi,' he said, 'glad you could make it.'

'Hi. Uh, listen,' she began, then tried again. 'I'm sorry about my behaviour earlier today.' She looked at him directly, and, to balance her conciliatory words, she kept her stare clear and direct, and didn't attempt to soften it.

Doron was silent for a moment, was he waiting for an explanation? Well she wasn't going to give him one, she didn't owe him, after all.

'Don't worry about it,' he said at length. 'I'm sorry I startled you, it was...thoughtless of me. Did you come alone?' He looked around.

'Belle and Beau are here too. Beau's around here somewhere, and Belle is helping your mom with the cooking.'

'Wow. Didn't take them long to make friends, then. I'm glad.' He smiled at last, and it was such a warm, genuine smile that she found herself returning it. 'I do have a favour to ask, if you don't mind,' he went on. 'I'm making a call to see some patients tomorrow, and I wondered if you'd come with me. I'd like a second opinion.'

'On what? What's the problem?'

'Giardiasis, but with unexpected factors.' At Nita's frown, he realised he'd used an unfamiliar term, so he described the symptoms and watched her expression clear.

'Oh yeah,' she said. 'Beaver fever. I've treated that in the past, but you're right, I think a re-assessment is the right way forward.' She saw he was getting ready to thank her, and broke in, before he could. 'I'll meet you here at 8 o'clock tomorrow morning.'

Before he had time to either agree or argue, she walked away. She wasn't ready to surrender all her qualms just yet; this place had to prove itself before they started thinking she and the rest of those at the Springs were part of their little community. Despite telling herself this, she saw Beau coming into the field, and she couldn't deny the flicker of pleasure it gave her to see him and Doron greet each other like old friends.

More people had started to arrive by now, and after they'd been greeted by John and Doron they stood in little groups, chatting. When it became evident that everyone who was expected was there, John called out to ask everyone to take their seats. Nita naturally gravitated to the back, where she saw Belle and Rena placing more food on the tables. They came over to where she sat, and joined her, and Nita whistled for the dogs, who trotted up obediently and lay at her feet.

The brothers waited until the shuffling had stopped, and John smiled around at the assembled group. '*Sannu*...Welcome, everyone, it's nice to see so many of you here, although I'm sure there are more inhabitants of Hope Meadows than this. I guess they're bored of hearing our voices and the same old speech.' People smiled at this. 'We usually start by telling you all how we came to be here, and Ron is a better storyteller than I am, so over to you, bro.'

He stepped back and Doron moved to the centre and began to tell them the now-familiar story of their foretold birth, how they had been separated in order to keep them both safe, and the extraordinary circumstances that had led to them being reunited.

Although most had heard the story, hearing it from the twins themselves gave it a different feel altogether, and Doron held the field spellbound. He explained, in detail, how he and the others had collected the twins and brought them here, to receive the message from the Fathers.

John then took his part, explaining the tale of Moses and Maor, and how their own story held so many similarities. 'And we are all descendants of Moses and Maor,' he finished, 'so we all carry the same genetic code given to them, and their ancestors, by the Fathers.'

Nita put up her hand and was invited to speak. She rose to her feet, feeling very exposed but needing to know it all. 'You say that there are records of Moses' descendants, but what of those of Maor?'

'I'm afraid there are no records,' John said. 'The wisdom passed to Moses on Mount Sinai was recorded on a tablet by Amnon, a trained scribe. Maor wasn't with them at the time, he'd been sent back to the Nubian people who raised him, and his story would almost certainly have been only a verbal one since he wouldn't have been able to write.'

Nita nodded her thanks, and sat down again, but remained thoughtful. Something about what he'd said had struck a chord with her, but she couldn't work out what it was.

Doron then explained about the commandments. 'We all follow these rules,' he finished. 'They're simple enough, but the one that most people have difficulty with is giving up meat.'

Nita noticed there was some nodding in the crowd. John indicated a couple among them. 'Farrah and Ravi here have been vegetarian all their lives, and can advise you on how to eat a healthy diet.'

This time it was Belle who raised her hand. 'I would be happy to show you all the plants, herbs, berries and nuts that grow wild in this region,' she said. 'There are some you may not yet be aware of, which have supplemented our diets, and those of our ancestors, for hundreds of years. There are many that are used as medicine too, but Nita here can show you those.'

Doron nodded to Belle, and then to Nita. 'Thank you both, that would be a great help.'

A woman in the front row spoke up, without raising her hand, but neither Doron nor his brother seemed to mind. 'Is it always so... so peaceful and friendly like this?' she asked, in faintly wondering tones.

The brothers exchanged a glance and a grin. 'Unfortunately not,' John said. 'We're all on our best behaviour today.' A ripple of laughter ran around the gathering, and Nita smiled too. 'This actually brings us pretty neatly to the next part of our talk,' John went on. 'Occasionally people get out of line, though thankfully nothing serious yet. Just in case you were getting ideas though,' he paused for more good-natured chuckles, 'we have a council of five respected people, who judge each case on evidence and testimonials, then decide on the length of punishment.'

'What punishment?' a man called out.

'Well, the length of time is different for each case, but the punishment is usually to respectfully remove any human remains that are left in their homes, and to deep clean the houses ready for newcomers as they arrive.'

That had the effect of quelling any further laughter, and an uneasy silence fell as the newcomers no doubt recalled their own experiences of doing just that, for their lost loved ones.

Doron spoke up. 'Any of you who wish to become part of our community, and of course we hope that you *all* do, will be expected to do their share of work in order for the community to survive.'

'And we ask you all to learn Hally, the twins' language,' John added. 'Over time, people from other countries will find the means to travel here, and it's the one way we can all communicate with each other.' He gave them an easy, friendly smile that eased the tension again. 'We'll end now, with *cibu jahi*… Food is ready!' People twisted in their seats to follow his gesture towards the back of the room. 'Dig in! There's not a lot, but please help yourselves. The end table has bags of fresh vegetables for you to take home.'

'Once again,' Doron added, 'thank you for coming. It's nice to get to know one another, and if you have any questions or concerns, we're here to help.'

The brothers left their place at the front of the group, and mingled with the participants of the meeting as they rose and made their way to the back, and the tables of food. They shook hands with several people who stopped them to thank them, and as the atmosphere became one of bustling friendliness and camaraderie, Nita dismissed the dogs to their play once more. The younger two fell into one of their tag-style games, while Kimi was content to sniff the ground. Making herself at home already, Nita thought with a little smile. She, Belle and Beau went over to take their turn thanking the twins.

'What happened to the cornbread, ma?' Beau asked, scanning the table.

'There wasn't enough time, or room, to make enough for everyone, so I just showed Rena how it's done. It was good to see it—'

The sound of yelping and barking cut her short, and everyone turned to see what was happening. A second later a heart-stopping squeal drifted across the field, and Nita's blood ran ice-cold as she realised that the tawny shadow flashing through the long grass had Kimi gripped in its jaws... a mountain lion.

'NO!' Nita felt the scream rip from her throat, but it sounded as if it came from someone else. Her food fell from her suddenly slack fingers and she began to run, her legs trembling. Someone grabbed her around the waist and dragged her to a halt, though in her mind she was still running. 'Let me go!' she pulled and twisted to get out of the grasp of whoever had her, then she heard Doron's voice, urgent in her ear.

'Stop struggling! Be still, trust me!'

'I said let me go!' She kicked back, feeling her boot connecting with his shin, but his grip on her did not slacken. 'Kimi!' she screamed, and doubled forward before jerking upright again, bringing her head up and back. She heard a sickening crunch from behind her and then she was free, but she could already tell it was too late; the lioness, with Kimi swinging limply from her mouth, was loping away.

Defeated, she fell to her knees, and felt a hand on her arm. She turned to see Doron, his other hand clasped to his face and blood soaking into his sleeve.

'Watch,' he managed, sounding thick and muffled. 'Just watch.'

Numbly, she obeyed, and saw Holly, Hannah, and their friends Ruhi and Alima holding hands. She stared, and felt a cold fear seeping through her veins as their eyes turned white.

As one, they held out their arms, and from their little frames came wisps of white smoke, wraiths that floated forward... Their arms moved in an eerie beckoning motion.

Seconds passed that felt like minutes, and Nita saw a speck in the distance, now moving towards them; the lioness, with Kimi still between her jaws. In dry-mouthed terror, she watched as it drew nearer.

She tried to get up, but Doron pushed her back down. 'Just do as you're told and watch,' he repeated, sounding even more muffled now.

As the lioness moved nearer to the crowd there were first murmurs of disquiet, then cries of alarm. People started to move backwards in panic, one or two tripped over themselves, and others began shoving to get through.

'Please!' Doron held up a bloodied hand. 'You have to *trust* them!'

The wraiths, detached from their hosts, now moved out to greet the lion, and as Nita watched in growing disbelief, two settled on each side of the animal, caressing it, urging silently, persuading with wordless motions, then, once again as one entity they moved back a few steps. The lioness hesitated, her head low, and for a moment it was as if the world itself had stopped; Nita was aware of every blade of grass that lay between herself and the beast, and of every breath that huffed from its mouth.

Then, just when she thought she could bear it no longer, the cat dropped Kimi, turned away without another glance at the silent humans, and sauntered back

163

off towards the forest. The saunter turned to a lope as it reached the edge of the field, and Nita could hear the low grunting sound it made with each step; it was only that which convinced her what she'd seen was real.

The girls' spirits returned to their bodies, and their eyes once more looked normal, but by then Nita was running out to Kimi, who lay whimpering on the ground. Sobbing, Nita scooped her into her arms, uttering meaningless but soothing sounds as she removed her collar and checked the wounds beneath. She parted the fur, wincing as she saw the amount of blood matting it, then peered closer in hesitant relief.

Boss and Echo crept over, bellies low to the ground, and sniffed their mother where she lay in Nita's arms. Nita heard Holly and Hannah calling to one another, as they ran over to where she knelt in the grass.

'Is she okay?'

'Were we quick enough?'

The young twins' voices were absurdly young, and worried, considering what she'd just seen them do, and Nita held up the collar, smiling through her tears.

'She's traumatised, but the bite marks aren't deep thanks to this. The collar saved her, I'm sure of it. I thank you Holly and Hannah for that. But mostly I thank all four of you. I don't know what you did just then, or how you did it, but you...' her voice choked off, and she swallowed hard. 'You saved my Kimi's life, and I will be eternally grateful. If there is anything I can do for you, *anything,* just say the word.'

Holly grinned. 'Well, showing us all how to do ribbon and bead plaits would be nice.'

Nita was surprised into a laugh that she just managed to stop becoming a sob. 'I'll do it for you myself!'

'And you should be kinder to Uncle Ron,' Hannah added. 'You made him all bloody and he was only trying to help.'

Nita closed her eyes momentarily and nodded. She should have realised. Should have trusted, as he'd asked.

Beau had arrived now, and helped Nita stand up with Kimi in her arms. Belle was following more slowly, her face anxious but relieved as she saw the smile on Nita's face.

'I need to speak to Ron,' Nita said, nodding her thanks to Beau. She walked over to where Doron was standing with a cloth held against his face. 'She's going to be okay, thanks to you and the girls. I can't thank you enough, and I'm truly sorry about your nose.'

Doron raised a quizzical eyebrow above the cloth, then nodded. 'I'm glad to hear it. On both counts.'

'When we meet next, please explain to me what happened just now.'

He carefully removed the cloth, and dabbed at his swollen nose, evidently satisfied that the bleeding had stopped. 'Did it shock you?' he asked, and he seemed genuinely curious, not taking her answer for granted.

'No, but it amazed me. I...' she hesitated. *Trust me!* he'd said, and his eyes said the same thing now. She took a deep breath. 'I have a gift of my own that... that I would now be happy to share with you.'

A slow smile spread across his battered face. 'In that case I hope our next meeting will be more pleasant. You don't appear to be very good for my health.'

Chapter Ten
Connections

Nita held her flashlight steady as she approached the door on the first floor of the lodge, but the beam still shook a little as her thoughts tumbled over one another. She had to master them, take her time over ordering them before she presented them, but it was difficult...

She knocked at the door. The dogs clustered around her as if they already knew there would be treats on the far side, and she spared them an indulgent little smile; they knew what was truly important.

'It's Nita,' she called softly through the door.

'Come on in!'

The room was softly lit by a couple of camping lamps, the curtains were open, and the smell of a late supper drifted in from the barbecue on the balcony. A middle-aged man, comfortably attired in pyjamas, put down his coffee cup next to a pair of binoculars on the coffee table, and held out his hands.

'Nita.'

'Thank you for seeing me so late, Moki,' Nita said, embracing him. 'I would've called earlier, but it's been a busy, and strange, day.'

'So I heard from Belle.' Moki indicated the seat next to where he'd been sitting on the sofa. 'Sit.' Never one for unnecessary words, he was nevertheless a good listener, and Nita knew he wouldn't probe the reason for her visit until she volunteered it. 'We caught rainbow trout this afternoon,' he went on, and pointed to the barbecue. 'There's some left, if you'd like it.'

She shook her head. 'I'm good, thanks.' She could feel herself tensing up again, and Moki seemed to sense it, and sought to distract her.

'Then the pups are in for a treat.' He fondled Kimi as he rose, mindful of the bandage around her neck. He went out onto the balcony and returned with a foil packet, which he opened on his lap when he'd sat back down. 'Smells good, huh?'

The dogs, ranged before him with open, laughing mouths, seemed to agree, and each gently took the piece he offered.

'Oh, that's great, thank you,' Nita said. 'Kimi wouldn't eat when we got back from Hope Meadows, she was still kind of traumatised.'

'In that case she gets the largest portion.' Moki fed Kimi an extra piece, and when the two younger dogs had eaten and gone to explore, Kimi settled contentedly on the sofa between Nita and Moki, her head on her paws.

Moki passed Nita the binoculars. 'Go look at the stars.'

She went out onto the balcony and raised the glasses, catching her breath at the sight. 'They're so beautiful tonight. And there are so many!'

'No more than usual,' he reminded her. 'But it's been a long time since the skies were so clear.' After a pause, he asked, with deceptive casualness, 'Are you here to talk to me as a friend, or because I'm on our council of elders?'

Nita lowered the glasses, and returned to the main room. 'Both,' she confessed.

'Good.' He leaned across the sleeping dog, and patted Nita's knee as she took her seat again. 'Now tell me, how is Kimi?'

'Dogs are quite resilient. I've put a bear root salve on her wounds, so they shouldn't be painful, and that should hold back any infection. The bandage will stop her scratching them as they heal. She'll be okay, thanks to the twins.'

'Ah yes,' Moki said, giving her a sidelong look. 'The twins. They have an extraordinary talent.'

Nita nodded. 'I'd seen their spirits before, in a vision, but it was quite something to see them in person.' She paused, recalling the incident, then said quietly, 'They're good people, Moki.'

'I never doubted it.'

'Then why are you so against joining them?'

'No more so than you.'

Nita conceded this. 'But some things have happened that have made me realise we, or at least I, need to stay a while longer. I'd like the elders to consider offering to help Hope Meadows with the labour on the hydro plant, and in turn they could help us get settled further downstream. It's good land for growing corn. If we were to decide at a later date, to join their community, we don't need to be close by do we?'

Moki inclined his head. 'It could be considered. There are many more people out there, who will have started their own communities.' He hesitated and shifted slightly in his seat, and Nita knew this wouldn't be as easy as she'd

168

hoped. 'The people of Hope Meadows may be good people,' he went on, his tone cautionary, 'and hopeful of a change for the good, but the virus did not distinguish between good and bad. We have yet to meet the bad. We have very different cultures, and I'm not yet ready to accept theirs. Or to be more accurate, I am not ready to compromise the Hopi beliefs. The others may be more flexible, but I am not.'

Nita tried not to let his bluntness put her off. 'I was surprised that the Hope Meadows community is such a mixture of race and religion,' she said, 'they're managing to compromise on their traditions. It impressed me. By talking together, they've discovered many similarities within their beliefs, and it's given me reason to compare everything.'

After another pause, Moki replied. 'As I said, there will be others out there not so ready to compromise. Like me. But unlike me they might not be tolerant of differences.'

'But the comparisons I've made are between their beliefs and those of the tribes... I haven't just found similarities, I've found parallels!' Nita felt the tension return, and saw Moki had noticed it by the way his eyes lingered on her hands, clenched on her knees.

'Alright,' he said at length. 'Whatever it is, let's hear it. Just remember our prophecies pre-date their religions.'

'I know.'

'Come on, then.'

Nita took a deep breath, and searched for the right place to start. 'I remember you telling me that the Hopi deity, the great Massau'u of the Fire Clan, sent your people in four directions to become the colours of Hopi corn: black, yellow, red, and white. Those people are supposed to someday come back together. The only colour missing from their community is red. Us. At some point we will become one people.'

He nodded. 'The Great Spirit Massau'u told us that would only happen when the lost brother Pahana returns. We know he will be white but will have black hair like us. He'll be wearing red, and his coming will be at the start of the fifth world. Pahana will have the missing piece of the sacred tablet he gave to the Fire Clan, and its meaning will be revealed to us all then. At the time of his coming, a spirit in the form of the Blue Star Kachina, will be seen in the heavens.' Moki's fingers brushed the binoculars. 'I watch for it, but my belief is that we're still in the fourth world, and will remain so until that time comes.'

'Wasn't another coming prophesised by a great star?'

Moki's voice was quiet, but firm. 'Our prophecies were given thousands of years before any of the Christian stories, Nita.'

'The Anishinaabeg believe we are now living in their Sixth Fire prophecy, and they predicted that a great sickness would come. We were all warned about the white man coming, and that he would ruin the lands that we took care of and respected. I think Mother Earth has had a hand in this. Everything was out of balance; she was dying and has taken extreme measures to ensure the world can be repaired.' Nita sat forward her hands linked on her knees as she ordered her thoughts again. 'With regards to timing, their Seventh Fire prophecy equates to the Hopi and the Navajo fifth world. When we've all discussed this together it gets confusing, but the main gist is that... well, *all* the prophecies have come true.'

'Yes they have, so I see no reason to doubt that the final one will also come true.'

'I can't argue that fact.' Nita gave him a wry smile. 'Even if I could, you wouldn't budge. You're the most stubborn person I know.'

'After yourself, of course.' He returned her smile briefly, then sighed. 'But we've gone over all this before. You've had a hard day, and it's late... there's something else bothering you.'

How well he knew her. She chewed her lip for a moment, then nodded. 'It's the parallels between our beliefs and the Christian beliefs, and what we now know about the Fathers and the twins. And some other stuff too.'

'Well let's start with one thing at a time.'

Nita was unable to sit still any longer, and rose to stand near the balcony door; the clear evening sky helped her think. 'The Navajo believe that once there were four holy people living in mountains, who travelled the way of the rainbow and the sun,' she began. 'I've travelled the way of the rainbow when I've had my visions. I've never been sick in my whole life, even this virus didn't touch me...' she broke off as she thought of Billy, and of Rose, then blinked the pain away and continued, 'I thought it had, in Towaoc. I thought I was dying, but when I awoke I was just ill from exhaustion. Only the twins have full immunity from illnesses, so how come I've been blessed with it? How come *I'm* the only one? And where does my gift of visions come from?'

171

No response came from Moki, and she hadn't expected one. She turned away from the balcony and started pacing the room. 'I know my great grandfather was blessed with visions, as have been many of our people in the past, but I seem to have gifts from both sides.'

'Could it be because your mother was Ute and your father white?'

'Hmm. That's what I've been thinking, but I couldn't make sense of it. Then something was said at the meeting this evening that got me thinking further.' She threw him a quick glance, hoping to see an open, interested expression, but his face was unreadable. She went on, 'The Jewish people kept records of Moses' descendants, but there are none for Maor. He was sent back to Africa, to the people who raised him.'

Nita stopped, and propped herself on the back of the sofa, idly fondling Kimi's ears as she thought it all through yet again.

'Go on,' Moki prompted.

'Okay. The old man in my first vision travelled from Africa, with his four sons, because of a vision. He brought the tablet that you have placed alongside the one that Massau'u gave your people. His twin, Moses, gave a tablet to *his* people; the tablet of the Ten Commandments. Which has been lost.'

'I think I see where you're going with this,' Moki said. 'You think the tablet that I have was given to Maor, and passed down to his descendants?'

'Exactly. But he had no access to a scribe, so I've no idea how such a tablet could have been made.' Nita stood straight again and resumed her pacing. 'Plus, it's different.

172

It's not like the petroglyph one from Massau'u, that's indented like the Commandments would have been. His is full of raised lines. Just lines, that make no sense to anyone.'

'Well, it doesn't really matter, because when Pahana comes he will decipher the one from Massau'u.'

'But how can you be so sure *that's* the one to be deciphered?' Nita pressed. 'Both have a missing piece. You know how oral stories can get jumbled up.'

'Pahana cannot bring what no longer exists,' Moki said. 'The other half of the tablet was destroyed years after the old man died. One of his sons was careless, and it broke into so many pieces it became dust.'

Nita drew a quick breath. 'No! You never told me that before.' After a moment's silence she shook her head. 'Well it doesn't change the fact that it could still have come from Maor.'

'It's possible,' he conceded. 'Continue with your thoughts.'

'If the old man was a descendant of Maor, he and his sons would have passed their genes onto our people. I think my mother had the inherited gene from Maor, and my unknown white father donated the one from Moses. It could explain my immunity.'

'Then why don't you have the same talents as the twins?'

'Because I'm *not* a twin. And in any case the Fathers had a hand in their conception, but not mine. The visions that our people and myself have been blessed with could be a separate gift from Massau'u.' She gave him a wry smile. 'I'm a freak of nature.'

173

'A fortunate one, if so,' he allowed.

'Thank you. Alright, going back to the Navajo story of the four holy people, living in the mountains. They transformed spirits into human beings with great powers. The First Man and First Woman produced twins that were neither male nor female... that's how Ron and John described the Fathers, when they met them on the mountain. And when the younger twins eventually die, their spirits will become the new Fathers. This has happened before, so I think they may need to regenerate.'

'But the Fathers you speak of are just one being. You said there were four.'

'What if...' Nita took a deep breath. 'Moki, what if there were *four Fathers?* What if each one created their own First Man and First Woman?' She heard her own words almost running together in her haste to get them out. 'I saw four different human-like creations at the beginning of my first vision, even after interbreeding, three creations died out. If they had no replacement spirits, the other three Fathers could have died out themselves. What if the Fathers are your Massau'u?'

Moki frowned but was silent, and Nita continued, 'You, like many others, believe our ancestors were spiritual sky people from the Pleiades. Their visit to earth is even recorded on many petroglyphs. Could they have come here from the stars and lost their way home?' She stopped pacing and looked over at Moki, who was still silent. 'Have I totally lost it?'

He looked at her steadily, then gently eased the snoozing Kimi from her place on the sofa. 'Come and sit back down with me, Nita. Be calm, and breathe.'

174

Nita did so, and he put a hand over hers and spoke gently. 'I think you have an active imagination, and needed to clear your thoughts, but I'm glad you decided to disturb my peace with them.' He patted her hand, and sat back. 'You have some interesting theories, I need to think on them. Then I will discuss them with the elders.' He raised one eyebrow slightly. 'I must be honest, if anyone else had come to me with these thoughts I might've been offended.'

Nita slumped against the cushions, feeling a weight lift a little. 'Thank you. My head is just fit to burst. Moki, I have the greatest respect for your beliefs and everyone else's, and I would be mortified if I ever said anything to upset you.' She shook her head. 'I just have this feeling that we're all connected, that we all may have once had the same story to tell, but it's like the game of Rumours... The story has become many different ones.'

'These are not bad thoughts, Nita, but they are still not what's really troubling you. What is it?'

Nita swallowed hard. 'It's my visions,' she said in a low voice. 'Something is coming. Something is about to happen. The troubles we've been through are not over yet.'

He grew still and looked at her seriously. 'What makes you say that?'

'Dakayivani's vision prophecy mentions an evil man with the mark of the bear. When I touched hands with Ian Sloan, a newcomer to Hope Meadows, I saw it.'

'What? The newcomer?'

'No, not him. I didn't see his face, just the mark. I saw him through the eyes of Sloan, *he's* seen him. Now I know

175

why I have been led here, and it's bothering me that I don't know what to do.' She heard the helplessness in her own voice, and it frightened her a little, so she took another breath and spoke firmly. 'If I can work out everything else, it might help me with what's to come. If the elders decide our people must move on now, I'll have to stay on my own. I have to see this through.'

Hope Meadows

The town looked very different this morning. Gone was the infectious hum of activity as residents prepared to greet their new neighbours, and in its place a few early risers were sleepily greeting one another as they headed out into the fields to continue the harvesting.

Nita had arrived early, as was her custom, and she was glad she had; it gave her the chance to take in her surroundings as they would be on any normal day, and to enjoy the surprising sense of peace and tranquility she found here. Doron would be a while yet, so she looked around for somewhere to sit, and saw the table and chairs, where the young twins had greeted newcomers the day before, still set out in front of the hall.

She crossed over to them, her jaw cracking in a yawn as she slipped off her backpack and sat down. It had taken her quite some time to fall asleep last night, after her conversation with Moki, but she'd felt the weight of her thoughts lift as she'd shared them, and it felt good.

She settled back to wait, her gaze drifting over the cabins that so many people now called home, and passed the time by wondering what kinds of houses those people had come from originally; some of them would have been used to much grander, she was prepared to bet, but a good many would feel they had been granted luxury in these simple cabins. She remembered how it had been to move into the trailer on Mountain Sage Road, it had felt like a palace, compared to the little house she, Rose and Billy had been used to.

Her attention was caught by a movement on the veranda of one of the cabins, and she looked over to see a couple, of quite advanced years, picking up baskets before carefully descending the steps, their arms linked to support one another. They turned towards the end of town, but the man's gaze passed over Nita, and he spoke a few words to the woman, who turned and followed his eye-line. Both started towards Nita, who could see now that the woman was walking slowly, and that her grip was loose on the handle of her basket. The years had not stolen her beauty, however, and the long hair tied back from her fine-boned face was still black and glossy. She reminded Nita powerfully of Rose, and Nita swallowed a pang of sadness as she thought about the woman she had loved as a mother.

As the couple drew closer they smiled, and Nita rose to greet them. The man spoke first.

'Hello, young lady. Are you here to register?'

'Register?' Nita frowned, puzzled.

'As a newcomer,' he clarified, and she smiled in understanding.

'Oh, I see. No, I'm here to meet with Ron Malik. He asked me to attend some of his patients with him, but I'm a bit early.' She held out her hand and he took it in a firm grasp. 'My name's Nita. Pleased to meet you.'

'Likewise,' the man said. 'I'm Uri, and this is my wife, Maya.'

Nita shook Maya's hand, making sure her own grip was gentle. 'It's an honour and a pleasure.'

'Ah, Nita!' Maya said, 'We heard you were at the meeting yesterday. And of course we heard what happened. An awful thing.'

Nita felt a fresh wave of guilt. 'I regret it more than I can say. I hope Ron hasn't been in too much pain.'

'No, dear,' Maya soothed, 'I meant with your dog. How is she?'

Nita smiled at her concern. 'Thank you for asking, and thanks to the girls she'll be fine. I don't remember seeing you there last night?'

Uri gave her a wink. 'We were playing hookey, I'm afraid. In fact I feel like doing the same now, shall we sit for a while?'

Nita laughed and sat back down, while Uri pulled out a chair for Maya. The woman eased herself into it without complaint, but Nita noted the tension in her fingers as she gripped the arm of the chair.

'I hope you don't mind me asking, Maya,' she said, 'but are you suffering with arthritis?'

Maya nodded. 'It started last year. It's not too bad, generally, but it is getting worse. Mostly my knees and my hands. We've been put on light duties,' she added, pointing to the baskets. 'One of our choices is to collect the eggs each morning. Uri does most of the collecting though.'

Nita bent and picked up her satchel, and after rummaging for a minute she brought out a packet. 'I have some ginger root you can have,' she said, 'but no lemongrass. I'll find some for you though, and you can grow it here too. If you steep them both in a tea, it will help. And it's safe to take with any other medication you might have.'

Maya took the ginger. 'That's very kind of you,' she said with a warm smile. 'Thank you. So, you're a healer?'

Nita nodded. 'What modern doctors provide with synthetic drugs, I provide with natural resources.'

'Well, you'd better get teaching here then,' Uri put in, 'synthetic drugs won't be effective forever. What a find you are!'

Nita flushed slightly at the compliment, and by way of thanking him she said, 'I understand that everyone might not even be here, if it hadn't been for your help and hard work. I heard about you both at the meeting.'

'It was our life's work,' Uri said, 'but we couldn't have done it either, without the help of John's parents, Karen and George. And of course their friends, Mark and Denise. They're the ones who found Amnon's tablets, and the six of us worked out the prophecies together. We're retired from active work now, but we're still members of Eagle.'

Maya was looking at her closely. 'We're Palestinian Jews,' she said. 'What do you call yourself?'

'I'm Ute.'

Maya blinked and looked at her husband. 'Mute?'

'Ute,' Nita repeated, smiling. 'I come from Towaoc, on the Ute Mountain Ute Reservation. There aren't many of

179

us left though. We joined with some Hopi, Shoshone, Navajo and Anishinaabe, and I'm sure there will be others joining us. Just as you have new people joining your community.'

Uri nodded. 'I hope it won't remain *us* and *them,'* he said.

'It's a work in progress,' Nita assured him. 'I have a question to ask you, if you don't mind?'

'Go ahead.'

'Well, at the meeting they mentioned that there's no record of Maor's descendants, nor any details about Maor himself.' Nita looked at them both hopefully. 'I was wondering if you knew anything?'

Uri raised an eyebrow. 'That's an interesting question, no one has asked that before. Why do you ask?'

'I'm only half Ute,' Nita said, 'I believe I might be descended from both Moses and Maor. I have an idea that, although Moses may be *your* ancestor, Maor may be the ancestor of my people.'

'How interesting!' Maya leaned closer in fascination. 'But I'm afraid the boys are right, my dear, there's no record of his descendants.'

'Then again,' Uri added, 'It's not strictly true that we know nothing about him.'

Nita sat up straighter, but he added quickly, 'Don't get excited though, it's very little, and I doubt it will help you.'

'Nevertheless,' Nita urged, 'please go on.'

'Before we met our dear English friends, we found some small sections of tablets that recorded part of Maor's life, didn't we Maya?'

'That's right,' Maya affirmed, 'but until Amnon's story was discovered, we had no idea who he was. You see, the small pieces we found were written about a man named Noor. Karen told us that the Hebrew equivalent of the Nubian name *Noor* was Maor.' She frowned. 'Did we tell our friends about this, Uri?'

'Yes we did, but we were concentrating on the prophecy found at Shiloh, and I think it just got put aside.' Uri shrugged. 'It didn't seem important at the time, though I'm not sure what we knew *would* be important, to be honest.'

'Please tell me,' Nita said eagerly. 'Anything would be a help.'

'Very well,' Uri said. 'The fragments told of a long journey, where Maor helped his lost brother. He dreamed that he climbed a mountain with his brother and heard the word of God.'

'We believe that he climbed Mount Sinai in spirit form with Moses,' Maya added, 'as Amnon recorded seeing a second figure on the mount. Maor was miles away at that time, and we now know that all the twins here in our town can do the same thing.'

'He was found wandering around, talking in a strange language that might actually have been what we now call Hally,' Uri went on. 'We worked on this a long time ago, but I think that's all there was, apart from him being exiled back to Nubia. I believe that region is now split between Egypt and Sudan...' He sat up suddenly, and his eyes were sharper, though still staring somewhere into the past. 'There was only one other thing: Maor wandered around until he came to an Acacia tree and—'

181

'Yes!' Maya interrupted. 'I remember now too! He sat down, cut off some bark, and carved a line of grooves in the trunk. He told his people it was a message from God. But he wouldn't have been able to write... and of course we have no idea what he carved there.'

'So, he wouldn't have had access to a scribe?' Nita pressed.

'No, I'm afraid not. Even after everything he had done for those people, they still didn't trust him. After his strange behaviour, they actually feared him, that's why they sent him away.'

'Why would he carve grooves?' Nita mused.

'We couldn't work that out, even back then,' Uri said. 'No known language is composed of just lines.'

'Lines...' Nita felt the stirring of excitement. 'Uri, would he have had access to clay?'

'Possibly.'

'That's it, then! He must have put clay against the tree as a casting. That would explain why the tablet had raised lines!'

'What tablet?' Uri exchanged a puzzled look with Maya. 'You've lost me.'

'Oh I'm sorry,' Nita said. 'It's a long story, but I believe Maor made a tablet, and a descendent gave half of it to the Hopi and half to the Ute. I've seen one half, but it can't be deciphered. My great grandfather had a vision about something that was to happen in the future, and... well, I think there might be a connection.'

Maya and Uri looked at each other again, then back at Nita.

'You must tell us more about this,' Uri said, 'it's intriguing.'

'I'd love to,' Nita said, with real regret, 'but there's not enough time right now. Perhaps I could meet with you and the others, and we could all put our heads together.'

'That would be wonderful,' Maya said, and she looked as if years had peeled away from her. 'I haven't heard anything so exciting for ages. Please come back, and soon.'

'I will, and I'll bring the lemongrass with me.' Nita looked up. 'But now I see Ron's on his way over, so I'll have to leave you. It's been great meeting you, and I look forward to seeing you again.'

'As do we,' Uri said, and held out a hand to his wife. 'And now, reluctantly, we must get on with the egg collecting.'

Nita got up, and was slightly taken aback when she was drawn into a hug from each of them in turn. Then she relaxed and enjoyed their embrace, even feeling a little tearful at their display of easy affection.

Doron had now reached the group, carrying a water container and a large flask, and with a bag slung over his shoulder. Nita could see the puffy blackness under his eyes, and was struck by another pang of guilt. As he spoke she realised that he was having trouble breathing through his swollen nose.

'Hi,' he said. 'Thanks for coming. I wasn't sure if you'd still come, after what happened, but I'm very pleased you made it. I see you've met my aunt and uncle.'

'I said I'd be here,' Nita reminded him. 'I came early, and was lucky enough to meet with Uri and Maya. We've been chatting.'

'So I see.' He turned to the couple, looking a bit sheepish. 'How are you both? I've been meaning to pop by, but I've been so busy, sorry.'

Maya put a hand on his arm. 'Don't you worry about that. We'll catch up soon, and I think you'll find we'll have a lot to discuss.' She winked at Nita, and Doron frowned as they walked away, with Nita waving them off as if she'd known them for years. He opened his mouth to ask what it was all about, but Nita spoke first.

'How's your nose?'

'It's fine, no worries. I'll be as handsome as my brother again in a few weeks.'

He gave an uncomfortable smile, as he put everything he was carrying down on the table, and Nita knew he must be in pain, and appreciated his chivalrous humour. But she knew another apology would only make things awkward again, so she touched his hand briefly instead, and smiled at him.

He smiled back. 'Ready? You can carry the flask.'

'Sure. We can leave as soon as you fetch your keys.'

'Fetch them?' Doron patted the pockets of his jeans, and a blank look came over his face. He checked the table, and frowned again. 'Huh. I'll be back in a sec.'

'They're on your sofa,' Nita said helpfully.

He gave her a distracted smile. 'Thanks.' He started in the direction of his home, then stopped and turned back. 'How did you—'

'Look.' Nita nodded to where Rena was standing on the veranda, jiggling a set of keys on her finger.

'You left these on the sofa,' Rena called.

Doron looked back at Nita, who smiled and shrugged, then picked up the flask.

'Let's go.'

Chapter Eleven
Ruth

'It's not too far,' Doron said, as they turned onto the main road. 'About a fifteen-minute drive along Highway 82. They're camped alongside the Roaring Fork, between Basalt and Snowmass.' He looked across at Nita, who was sitting forward and looking out of the windows with interest. 'If I wasn't in a hurry to get to my patients I'd have liked to have taken you down the Rio Grande Trail instead,' he added, 'now that vehicle restrictions don't apply anymore. The river's almost level with the road there, it's beautiful.'

'My people used to roam all over this area,' Nita said. 'They called it Thunder River, because of the sound it makes after the snows melt and the level rises. I've never seen it myself.'

'Well unfortunately you'll only catch a few glimpses of it from the highway. We'll cross it twice at Basalt though, so you'll get to see it pretty well then.' He glanced at her again. 'Thanks again for agreeing to come with me.'

She acknowledged it with a nod. 'Why didn't you ask Uri for a second opinion?' she asked. 'He was a doctor.'

'If I'd asked him, he'd have insisted on coming with me, and at his age I can't risk him picking anything up. He's more frail than he looks.' Doron smiled, as he remembered the looks on their faces when he'd arrived. 'I assumed you were discussing medical matters with them both,' he said, 'they had a spark in their eyes I haven't seen for far too long.'

'Actually neither of them mentioned their professions,' Nita said.

'Oh? That's not like them. Well, whatever it was, it's good to see the old Uri and Maya.' He didn't want to ask, outright, what they had been discussing, but the fact that Nita didn't venture the information only increased his curiosity.

'They may both be frail,' Nita said after a few minutes, as if she'd been considering whether to speak up, 'but they still have active minds. I think they may be feeling a bit...'

'Left out?' he suggested, when she trailed off.

'More like useless.' Her blunt words surprised him, but she went on, 'It must be frustrating for them, after so many years of research and problem-solving, to be relegated to collecting eggs.'

Doron winced. 'I hadn't thought of it like that,' he confessed. 'We were just trying to take care of them. I'll have to do something about it, perhaps—'

'Look out!'

Even as her shout cut across his words, Doron saw a pack of rangy-looking dogs, seemingly from nowhere, loping across the road directly ahead. He stamped on the brake and jerked the steering wheel, sending the jeep slewing in the road to face the direction in which they'd come. He and Nita were flung forward and then back into their seats, and sat breathing heavily as the oblivious hounds disappeared off the other side of the road.

'Are you okay?' Doron asked after a moment, stunned at the nearness of the miss. His skin crawled as he considered what might have happened, especially out here, alone and with no hope of help.

'I'm fine,' Nita said, though her voice was very quiet. 'You?'

He nodded, and carefully turned the jeep around again, but the sick feeling remained; what might have been a minor bump in the 'before days' could all too easily be fatal now.

'I've seen a few packs like that lately,' Nita said, as they resumed their journey, more slowly and both carefully watching the sides of the road ahead. 'They must be the strong ones, most domestic pets wouldn't have survived this long.'

'You'll have to be careful with your Kimi,' Doron said. 'If she comes on heat, these wild dogs could turn dangerous, sniffing around. She could be badly hurt.'

Nita nodded. 'I'd already thought of that, plus the fact that her own sons would take an interest too. So before we left Towaoc, me and Beau took her in to the vets' office in Cortez, and spayed her.'

'Who taught you how to do that?'

'I taught myself, from a text book, and Beau already had some veterinary experience. The main thing that worried me really was giving her the wrong dose of anaesthetic, but luckily it went very well.'

'Wow, impressive!' Even more so was the fact that she didn't seem at all aware of it. 'Who taught you your healing skills?'

'Rose. She was my guardian. My mother died giving birth to me, and we never knew who my father was, only that he was white. Rose cared for me from that day on, along with a little boy called Billy. He was older than me, but he was like a little brother. Rose and her partner, Joe, raised us both, and Rose started training me when I was about three years old.'

'You didn't go to college then?'

There was a surprised silence, then Nita gave a short, rather bitter laugh. 'I'm a Native American, Ron. We lived in a one-room shack, with no running water and very little health care.' She shook her head. 'This country did everything it could to wipe us out, you must know that. If it hadn't been for Rose, Billy and I would've been taken away and given to a white family, like Logan, the first child she tried to help. Or even worse, placed in a boarding school, and more than likely abused. So no. I didn't get to go to college.'

Doron flushed, chastened. 'I'm sorry,' he said quietly. 'I had no idea things were so bad on the reservations.'

'Most people don't.' She sounded as if she might be sorry she'd rounded on him, so he felt safer asking more about her life.

'Did Rose have any children of her own?'

'Rose was *Kaku,*' Nita said, pride creeping into her voice now. 'Grandmother to all children. She had none of her own, and she never talked about it so I thought it was by choice, until Belle told me she suspected Rose might have been one of the thousands of Native American women who were sterilised without their consent.

'What?' Doron took his eyes off the road again, in his shock. 'That's appalling! How could it be allowed to happen?'

'It was their law.' The hardness had returned to Nita's voice, and she almost spat the words out. 'It's one reason why we have trust issues.'

He didn't respond, there was nothing he could say, and the road passed beneath the jeep's wheels as the awkward silence stretched.

At length, Doron ventured his own story. 'I never knew my biological father, either. My mother was also abandoned when she got pregnant, then she had to give up one of her sons because of a prophecy. She moved to Chicago, and, after a few years of struggling she met Alex.' He remembered that time, and the years that came after, almost as if he were seeing them as happening to someone else. Those *before times*, again. 'Mom never got over losing one of her boys,' he went on, 'so it was wonderful for her to see us reunited.'

'I can imagine.'

'Unlike you, John and I both had comfortable lives, but many of our people certainly didn't. Our whole community has its stories, of abuse, war, torture, and slavery... your people aren't unique on that score.' Aware he was sounding a little defensive, he added, 'We *all* have to forget the hurt of the past, Nita. We have a chance to make a new world. This is a new beginning.'

'You're right, of course,' she said, 'except that the new world hasn't begun yet.'

He frowned. 'What do you mean?'

'The prophecies given to *us* have all come true, but there's one more to be fulfilled. It tells of an evil to be defeated, and of a saviour who will come to lead us to the final world.'

He felt his eyes widen. 'Now *that* sounds like something that would get my aunt and uncle excited. So that's what you were talking about?'

'Only briefly,' she said. 'I want to talk about it with all of you. Soon. Rose recorded it, along with other stuff, in her journal.'

'You have it?'

'It's in my truck back at Hope Meadows, I'll show you when we get back.'

'You've got my curiosity going now,' he admitted, 'but I guess I can wait a while.' He paused for a moment. 'Shall we talk about something lighter?'

'Like what?'

He considered. 'Like… Okay, tell me a story of when you laughed so much it hurt.'

'That's silly.' Nita sounded uncomfortable, but he persisted.

'So what? It's no sin to laugh, silly or not. Go ahead, try it.'

Nita smiled, and he guessed memories were coming back to her of happier times. She gave him a sidelong look, and shrugged, but the smile still lurked around the corners of her eyes.

'When we were little,' she began, 'me and Billy used to help Rose pick squawbush, she used it for medicine and flavourings,' she added, in response to his puzzled look. 'It had little white pieces of resin on, that we'd pick for

Joe to chew. He loved that stuff. So, anyway, one time, Rose had managed to get hold of some hot root... you call it horseradish,' she clarified again. 'She used it for back pains and toothache. I took some small pieces, and mixed it with the resin... Joe's face was a picture when he chewed it! He chased me for ages, and when he caught me he made *me* chew some. It was awful! But we laughed *so* hard.' Nita started laughing again now, at the memory. 'Rose told us off of course, but she was always telling us off, and we all knew she was laughing inside.' Her own laughter faded into a sad little smile. 'I miss them so much.' She took a deep breath, and tapped his arm. 'Okay, your turn.'

'For what?'

'To tell a silly story. Fair's fair.'

'I never said I was going to tell one,' he pointed out.

'But—'

'No time now,' he interrupted, 'I want to go over everything with you, before I take you to meet everyone.'

'Fool me once,' Nita said with a sigh. 'But you're right, patients are the priority. Go ahead then.'

'Pete was head of Eagle security,' Doron said. 'Then, when things settled down, he and his wife Ellie wanted to travel, but they never got any further than Basalt. I guess they realised that travelling alone now would be too dangerous, and this is the farthest they were comfortable settling.'

'Sensible.'

He guessed she too was thinking about their close-run thing with the wild dogs. 'I'd gone to see Pete about security issues,' he went on, 'and to see if Ellie's friend

Ruth had found them okay. When I got there, the three of them were all suffering from diarrhoea, vomiting, headaches and fatigue. They'd got their boiled and unboiled water cannisters confused, and once I'd established that, it made sense they'd taken a giardia parasite on board.'

'Scarily easy to do.' Nita shuddered, and Doron nodded grimly.

'I returned later that day with clean water, and Mom's soup for them, and gave them one dose each of Tinidazole, which is more than enough to get rid of the parasite. When I checked up on them two days later, which was yesterday, Ruth was weak but much better. But Pete and Ellie hadn't improved at all. Ruth assured me she had been giving them plenty of water, and some soup where she could, but they couldn't keep anything down.'

Nita frowned. 'Could the antibiotic have taken longer to work on them for some reason?'

'I'm hoping that's the case. If not, I'm considering trying a different drug, in case they've got a bad case of food poisoning or possibly another parasite. I assumed all three had the same thing.'

'I would have, too.'

Doron pointed. 'There's Wingo Junction up ahead, and the iron bridge. Once we've gone underneath, there's an exit off the highway that'll take us straight down to the river.'

Soon they were headed down what had probably once been a private road, that wound down towards the Roaring Fork.

193

'Here we are,' Doron said, pulling off the road. 'Pete's Winnebago.'

Nita looked nonplussed. 'I've seen some real nice houses along the way, and the one we just passed looks amazing! Why would anyone choose to live in a camper van?'

'Each to their own.' He shrugged. 'It's cosy, and Pete's rigged up portable solar panels for its roof, so at least they have some power. They wouldn't have that in the houses I saw along the way.' He glanced into the back seat. 'Before we grab the gear, there's some masks there. You'd better put one on, in case whatever they have is contagious.'

'I won't need it,' she said, loosening her safety belt, 'I have the same immunity as you.'

He stared, not sure he'd heard correctly. 'You what?'

'I have the same immunity as you,' she repeated, preparing to climb down from the jeep.

'That's not possible,' he began patiently, and as she turned to look at him, one eyebrow raised, he heard himself adopting a rare, sarcastic tone. 'I suppose you were born under an eclipse, and have a secret twin hiding somewhere, too?'

Her anger visibly kindled. 'Yes I was, and no I don't! And it most certainly *is* possible!' She gave him a thin, humourless smile. 'You twins aren't unique on that score.'

Hearing his own careless comment thrown back at him, Doron couldn't think of anything to say except, 'Okay, I'll take your word for it.' He slammed the driver's door. 'On your head be it.'

They shared the job of carrying supplies over to Pete's home, and to Doron's relief the tension between them

194

melted away during the task. He thought she looked equally glad, and reminded himself that they hardly knew each other, and that he shouldn't presume they would automatically become friends, simply because they shared a vocation.

'What's that for?' Nita nodded at a fire pit and some fishing nets, hanging upside down from a frame with buckets underneath.

'It's a simple way of catching dew if you don't have access to water. The Israeli twins came up with the idea of how to construct a simple, quick way to do it, and it works, but it only produces a small amount of water.'

As they put down the supplies, the door was opened by a woman in her forties, of athletic build, and with her hair in a wild tangle as if she'd constantly been running her fingers through it. She looked as if she hadn't slept in days, and was clearly distraught.

Doron straightened. 'Ruth—'

'Oh thank goodness you're here,' she blurted. 'they've gotten so much worse! I've tried to help, but nothing's working, and they're in such pain... Come quick, *please!*'

Doron and Nita hurried up the steps and followed her inside, where Pete and Ellie were both making soft moaning sounds with each breath; it was immediately obvious they were delirious with fever, and to Doron's dismay there was blood all over the sheet under which they lay. More was dripping from their eyes and noses.

'How long have they been like this?' he asked in a hollow voice.

Ruth sniffed. 'Since yesterday. They got worse in the night. I'm so worried for them.'

Nita spoke quietly. 'It's the virus, Ron. It's back.'

'How can that be? It ran its course last year.' Doron turned to Ruth. 'How are you feeling?'

'I don't have much energy, but I'm feeling better than I did, thanks to you. I don't have any of the symptoms they have. *Please* help them.'

While Doron took his medical bag over to the bed, Nita took Ruth to the other end of the camper and sat down with her. Doron could hear her ask in the same low, careful voice, 'Did you catch the virus last year?'

'No, I was one of the lucky ones. I didn't get sick at all.'

'So you were given a blood transfusion then?'

'No I wasn't, why?'

Doron glanced over at her as he prepared a sedative for his patients, and saw she had a different kind of worry on her face now.

'Am I going to catch it?' she asked, her voice trembling.

'I don't think so,' Nita soothed, 'you would be showing symptoms already. I'm sorry to say this, but I think you may be a carrier. Someone who has an illness but doesn't get sick from it.'

Ruth paled even further. 'You mean poor Pete and Ellie… I *gave* it to them? This is my fault?' She covered her face with her hands, and Doron heard her breath catch as she gave in to the sobs she'd clearly been holding in check.

'No!' Nita said quickly. 'This is *not* your fault, Ruth. If you *are* a carrier, the virus is to blame, not you.'

196

Doron finished administering to Pete and Ellie, and joined Nita and Ruth. 'I've given them a strong painkiller, and something to make them sleep. Do you have clean bedding, Ruth? We'll make them comfortable, and then we'll discuss what's to be done for them.'

Ruth nodded, and gestured to the sliding doors of an under-bed cupboard. 'There's some in there. I'll help you with it.' And as if she'd only just noticed, she asked, 'What happened to your face, are you okay?'

Doron didn't look at Nita. 'I'm fine,' he said, 'just an accident at home. But thanks for asking.'

Once Pete and Ellie were clean and settled once more, Doron turned to Nita. 'Would you come outside for a moment?' Seeing Ruth's look of sudden panic, he touched her arm. 'It's okay, we're not leaving you. We just need to discuss what we can do, and then we'll come back. Okay?' Ruth nodded, and fumbled a handkerchief from her pocket. 'Okay.'

Doron descended the steps and started towards the jeep, his jaw so tight it ached. 'If only I'd known—'

'Then what?' She joined him, keeping pace with his furious strides.

'Maybe I could have saved them.' He aimed a kick at the tyre of the jeep. 'I could have at least *tried*, dammit!'

'Listen to me!' Nita pulled him around to face her. 'I nursed so many people through that virus, I couldn't remember when I last slept. I had to leave them after a while, to nurse Rose. When she died, I felt so ill I thought it was my time, but it wasn't. I was exhausted, and went to bed, thinking it would be the last time.' She took a deep breath, and he could see the memories unfolding.

197

'When I awoke,' she went on, 'Kimi had had her pups, Boss and Echo. She also had a little girl pup, who died, and I wrapped her up with Rose, for her to take care of in the next world. Once I'd recovered my energy, I looked back on my life and realised I'd never been ill at all, and was immune. I felt such anger... like you. Had *I* known before, I could've given my blood, and saved my whole family.'

'But you weren't to know,' Doron said, incredulous. 'You can't blame yourself.'

'Exactly!' Nita shook her head. 'I understand your anger, of course I do. But the next time you think you might've been able to save your friends, remember what you just said.'

Doron leaned on the jeep, his hands shoved into his pockets. 'I don't... I mean, after all this time, it's just not possible. A person *can't* be a carrier of a virus for that long.'

'You've got to stop saying things like that! After everything that's happened over the last couple of years, we both know anything's possible. Their symptoms were the same as beav… giardiasis, whether they had it or not, there's no way you could have known.'

'I was taught that, scientifically speaking, a virus is not considered to be alive,' Doron said. 'I never understood that. Has this one been waiting? Sleeping, if you like, inside Ruth, until it could be passed onto another host to survive?'

'Seems like it, huh? If it kills its host before it infects anyone else, it'll disappear. It's a matter of survival.'

Doron pursed his lips. 'Which means that, at some point, the symptoms could show in Ruth if the virus thinks it's safe. And if you're wrong about your immunity, you're in great danger too.'

'I'm not wrong.' She sounded calm and certain, but Doron was taking no chances.

'I'm going to take blood samples from all of them, for Otto to check. I'd like to take yours too. Plus a swab. I need this confirmed, Nita,' he added, before she could argue, 'and I can't risk taking you back to Hope Meadows until I know for sure.'

'I understand.'

'A lot of our people had blood transfusions that kept them safe at the time, but the protection will have worn off long ago.'

'Of course, I get it.' She put a hand on his arm. 'Really.'

He nodded. 'Okay. Look, I'm going to go back home and get the small cabin ready to quarantine Ruth, and get some other things organised. Pete won't be able to deal with the security now, so I might ask Ian if he could take over for a while.'

This time Nita shook her head, and he looked at her questioningly.

'I don't trust him,' she said, with characteristic bluntness.

'You don't know him.'

'Neither do you,' she pointed out. 'I sense things sometimes though, and...' She paused, and he could see she was searching for the right words. 'He's not a bad person,' she said at length, 'but at the same time he's not what he seems, and I don't think you should trust him either, until you find out what that is.'

'You *sense* things. Is this another of your talents? Like knowing where my keys were?'

She shrugged. 'Yeah.' The look she gave him was part defiance, as if she expected him to argue, and part hope that he wouldn't. He had the feeling she didn't know where that certainty came from either, but would defend it to the last.

He smiled. 'Okay. Would you mind hanging on here until I get back? I'll be about an hour.'

'Of course not.' She sobered and looked back towards the Winnebago. 'There's no hope for your friends is there?'

'No,' he said quietly. 'But we can keep them comfortable. Can you explain to Ruth?'

'Sure, of course.' Nita began walking back to the van. 'Come on then. Let's get those samples done.'

Hope Meadows

Doron saw John heading towards his jeep, and got out, holding up his hand to stay his brother's approach. 'Not too close, not until I've scrubbed up.'

John's welcoming smile faltered. 'Scrubbed up?'

'I've come to ask you to do some things for me, then I'm heading back to Basalt. Nita's looking after everyone until I get there.'

'What's going on?' John's brow creased in concern.

Doron gave him a brief description of what he and Nita had found at the river, and his brother's concern turned to dismay.

'Christ... Has Ruth been in contact with anyone else?'

'Recently only us, here, when she registered.'

'That was, what, two weeks ago?' John looked around reflexively. 'If she'd passed it on to anyone here we would've known by now, wouldn't we?'

'Yeah. Luckily a carrier is less likely to pass it on than an infected person. She has no cough or sneezes, so it must have been passed on by bodily fluids.' In answer to John's slightly widened eyes, he clarified, 'They shared drinks together.'

John nodded. 'Okay. What can I do?'

'Get hold of Ian first, and ask him to remove his personal effects from the small cabin. Then get fresh sheets on the bed and clean it through. I'm going to have to put Ruth in there until we can figure something out.'

'Are you mad?' John looked aghast. 'You can't bring her here!'

'What other choice do I have?' Doron shrugged. 'If I leave her there, she could come into contact with someone else. If she's here we can at least keep an eye on her - she'll be house-bound, with a guard at the door.' He reached in through the passenger window of the jeep, and brought out the bag of samples. 'Providing no one shares a drink or food with her, or comes too close, everyone will be safe. Strict rules will be put in place, and everyone has to be made aware of the situation.'

John still looked doubtful. 'I don't like it, but I trust your judgement.'

Doron placed the bag carefully on the floor, and stepped away from it. 'In there are three blood samples, one taken from an infected patient, one from Ruth, and the other from Nita. I want you to get them to Otto urgently for analysis, and while you're there, find out how his research is coming on.'

John nodded. 'Got it.'

'There's also Nita's keys,' Doron added, 'give them to Ian. She has a tent in the back of her truck, tell him he can use that until we sort something else out for him. I've wiped everything down, but do it again yourself before passing them on.'

'Okay. But why a sample of Nita's blood?'

'She's certain she has the same immunity as us.'

'But you're not?' John guessed, looking at him shrewdly.

'For safety's sake I want to make absolutely sure. If she's right, Otto might just have the answer to his prayers, and a way out of this mess.'

'I certainly hope so, but... Nita? How's that possible?'

'Not sure. I'm also going to need Holly or Hannah to access their database, and print off a list of everyone who has no immunity gene. They'll be the ones at risk.'

His brother seemed to sense he didn't want to talk in too much detail. 'Will do,' he said. 'And I was thinking, at some point I'll get the girls to add the details of everyone at the Springs.'

'Good plan. Look, I have more requests for you, if you have time.'

'Fire away.'

'Can you let everyone know what's happening, without causing a panic? Send someone to the Springs, to let Belle know Nita will be here for a while so she doesn't worry.'

'No problem.'

'Then we need to organise a guard detail for Ruth and the town, particularly in light of what happened to Mike Ford. I don't want Veritas anywhere near our people... What is it?'

John's frown had returned. 'I've already organised the Eagle guards, they'll be in place later today.' He hesitated, staring at the ground, then raised his eyes to meet Doron's. 'Louise Miller's been murdered too.'

Doron stared at him, stunned. 'What?'

'I've just come back from Morrison Farm,' John said, his voice subdued. 'We were going to organise an investigation.'

'Damn it! And everything had just started going so well. What's going on?'

John just shook his head, and Doron ran his hands through his hair while he thought it through. 'Right. The investigation will have to wait, this takes priority over anything.'

'Understood.'

'How did it happen?'

'She'd been shot at close range. No one heard a thing.' John's frown deepened. 'We think Veritas might be targeting those who gave evidence against them.'

'Sounds like a hit, for sure,' Doron said grimly. 'Even more reason to raise our security, and it may be prudent to put a watch on Otto, Clare, and the rest of the council too.' He sighed. 'I'm sorry to lay all this on your shoulders bro, but I'll help where I can when I get back…. Oh, and one last thing?'

'Shoot.'

'Try to find out how the *hell* Ruth slipped through the net at registration.'

Part Three
Veritas

Of the great migration, those that settled in north east America were known as the Anishinaabe. Seven prophets gave predictions of their future and each prediction was known as a fire. The first three fires were instructions on how to reach a land chosen for them. At some point in their journey they became lost. The dream of a young boy pointed them back in the right direction and they found their promised land.

The fourth fire was a warning about the white man; that he will be filled with greed for their lands. During the fifth fire there will come promises of a new way of life, when their people will be told to abandon the old ways. The people will be warned not to trust the white man but some will not listen.

At the time of the sixth fire it will be known that the promises were false, there will be much suffering and the people will almost be destroyed. There will come a time of great struggle, and a new sickness will come to them.

The seventh fire will be a time of a new people. If they continue to follow the road to the material world it will cause their destruction. A new age of peace will follow if they travel the road to the spiritual world and live in harmony with the earth, then the seventh fire will light the eighth and final fire.

Parts of The Seven Fires Prophecy of the Anishinaabe

205

People crowded the earth; they killed the animals for their meat, and when they got in their way. The animals punished them by creating diseases. But for every disease, the plants made sure they provided a cure. Each plant has a purpose; it just has to be discovered.

Part of the Cherokee spiritual beliefs

Chapter Twelve
Discord

Doron returned before noon, and as he parked up in his usual place it seemed the whole town was watching; people had stopped whatever they were doing, and stood in silence as he climbed out of the jeep, their eyes not on him, but on the woman in the passenger seat. He walked around to open her door, and was struck by how timid she suddenly looked, clutching at her belongings as if they were part of her.

She looked up at him, her eyes troubled above the surgical mask she wore. 'I feel like a pariah, Ron. No-one wants me here, you should have left me where I was.'

'That's not true. People are scared, of course they are. But once they know the situation they'll understand. They're good people.' He took her hand and helped her down from the jeep. 'You'll be safe here,' he said in a low, comforting voice. 'Otto can find a way to help you. Come on, let's get you settled.'

He put a protective arm around her shoulders, feeling her frame trembling beneath his hand, and led her through the town to the little cabin that would be her home for a while. He knew she was avoiding looking at the people they passed, and felt her flinch at the sight of the guard they had posted outside the cabin; he sensed her relief as they went inside.

'Don't worry about him,' he said, 'he's there in case you need anything. His name's Matt, and you can call to him from your window, or your door. You don't have to keep them closed.' He knew she deserved the truth, and added, 'He's also there to help others feel more relaxed.' He looked around, and noted, with satisfaction, the fine job the others had done in his absence. 'Make yourself comfortable, you'll find food, toiletries, books... And it looks like some extra clothes have been provided for you too. I'll come back later to check in on you, okay?'

Ruth took off her mask and looked at the boxes on the lounge floor. She nodded. 'That's very kind, thank you.' But the last word disappeared in a catch of breath as the tears she had clearly been holding tightly in check broke free. She lifted both hands to her face, and Doron put his arm around her.

'I can't pretend it won't be hard for a while,' he said quietly, 'but it's for the best. You'll be safe here at least, it'll all be fine.' He felt her nod, and drew back a little. 'All the things in those boxes have been donated by the residents of Hope Meadows. The people might seem distant, but they do care.' He waited until he was certain she'd gathered herself again, then touched her arm gently. 'I have to leave now, I need to scrub down, and then check on things. Will you be alright?'

She nodded, and he left her to go to his own cabin. Several times he had to ask people who approached him to keep back, and told them to put the word out that no-one was to go near his jeep. No-one spoke, they just watched him pass by. When he reached his home he saw the door was open, and that his parents were there.

'How can we help?' Rena asked, the moment he drew close enough.

'I need a bowl of hot water, and something to clean the jeep with.'

His stepfather frowned, concerned. 'Is that necessary?'

'Probably not, but better to be safe than sorry. Once I'm done with that I'll be able to shower and change, so you'd both better stay back until then. Mom, I'll need a bag to put these clothes in, and then I'll put them straight in the washer myself, okay?'

Rena nodded and went indoors to find what he'd asked for, while Alex studied him, concerned. 'Are you sure about all of this?'

Doron nodded. 'While I'm getting all this done, would you mind organising a town meeting for tomorrow evening?'

'Of course.'

'Thanks.' Doron looked over his shoulder, at the curious onlookers straining to hear what they were saying. 'I think it's best to try and put everyone's minds at ease.'

***

Jen moved away from the window, where she'd been watching Ruth's arrival. The sight of the woman, and what she represented, was worrying, but she couldn't deny the deep sympathy she felt for her; she must be feeling lost, alone, and terrified... Jen remembered how that felt all too well, thinking back to that awful night when John had taken off in pursuit of Sinead's captors, along with his brother and Todd.

She crossed to the sofa, but had only just sat down when she heard thundering footsteps, and Holly and Hannah ran into the house, both in tears. They went straight to their room, and Jen was shocked heard the bedsprings squeak as they flung themselves down. The memories of those early days at Hope Meadows vanished, and Jen seized a box of tissues from the table and followed.

'What on earth's wrong?' This was so unlike them it was frightening, but she kept her voice as calm as she could.

Both girls began talking at once, through hiccupping sobs, and Jen held up her hand. 'Wait.' She sat on Hannah's bed and beckoned Holly to sit on her other side, and gave them each a tissue. 'Now take deep breaths and start again, I can't make head or tail of what you're saying.'

She put an arm around each of her daughters and after a moment their sobs tapered off, and Holly began again.

'That woman, Ruth, has the virus and she didn't get tested at registration.'

'Uncle Ron thinks it's our fault,' Hannah put in.

'We let her go before she had a blood sample taken—'

'If she had, they'd've known to not let her go.'

Holly sniffed. 'Now Pete and Ellie are going to die, and—'

'And everyone's scared again.'

'And it's our fault!' Holly bowed her head as her tears flowed once more.

Jen gave the girls a squeeze, then turned to kneel on the floor so she could see them both properly. 'Listen,

210

none of this is your fault. How can it be? Tell me what happened on that day.'

Again, Holly was the one to start. 'Ruth gave us her details—'

'And our database pinged up a match to her best friend, Ellie,' Hannah added.

'We told her, and she was *so* happy! Wasn't she, Hannah?'

'Yeah. She asked where Pete and Ellie lived, and we gave her directions.'

'Then she just ran off,' Holly said, still mystified.

Hannah nodded. 'We called after her, Mum, honest, but she didn't come back.'

'We didn't really think it was important, it's just a registration.'

Jen felt for them. 'Of course it is,' she soothed. 'Your job is to record people's details, not to go chasing after them. You're not the FBI... or are you?' she added with mock awe, and the girls gave her watery smiles, and shook their heads.

She smiled back, and took a hand each. 'Phew. Now see here, your database did a wonderful thing finding Ruth's friend, and it'll link up other people too. What if you *hadn't* helped Ruth? What do you think might've happened?'

'We don't know,' Hannah admitted.

'What?' Holly asked, wide-eyed

'Well here's a scenario for you,' Jen said, her smile fading a little. 'Ruth gets her blood taken, and decides to hang around Hope Meadows or Carbondale for a while, chatting to people. Maybe sharing a drink with them.

Now, Otto wouldn't get the results of that day's tests until the next day, right?'

The twins glanced at one another and nodded. 'Right.'

'So it's possible Ruth could have infected someone here, or in Carbondale, and then many other people, like Sinead, Todd and the children, Clare, Maya, the council... All of them could have become very ill, or even died.' She shook at their hands for emphasis. 'You've actually *saved* all the people we care about, if you think about it.'

Holly wiped her eyes and looked at her sister. 'We didn't think about it like that.'

'No, we didn't. Thanks, Mum.' Hannah leaned in for a hug, and Jen drew them both close.

'Now I want you to stop worrying about it,' she said gently. 'Promise?'

She heard John come in, and, looking at her girls' reddened eyes, her scalp suddenly tightened with anger. She stood up, trying not to show it, and went out into the lounge.

'What the *hell* has your brother been saying to them?' she demanded, before he could voice a greeting.

He blinked. 'What? What are you talking about?'

'They've been breaking their hearts thinking they're responsible for what happened to Pete and Ellie! They're *children,* John! No matter what else they are, they're—'

'That's ridiculous,' John broke in. 'Where did they get that notion from? Ron hasn't even seen them, he's been with Nita in Basalt, and only just got back. I asked Otto... Ah.' He frowned. 'I went to see Otto, and told him Ron was mad that Ruth had slipped through the registration net, and wanted to know how. We worked out how it

212

happened, and Ruhi and Alima heard our conversation.' His frown deepened into a scowl. 'I bet those girls have spun a drama to Holly and Hannah, and they've added two and two together to make five.'

Jen subsided. 'That would explain it.' She sighed and sat on the sofa. 'I'm sorry for pouncing on you as soon as you came home, but what with everything else going on, the last thing I needed was to see the girls so heartbroken.'

'I know.'

'All the twins may be mini geniuses, but people seem to forget they're still only children.' She gave him a wry smile. 'They're also beginning puberty, which makes them more moody and sensitive.'

'Puberty? Already?' John sat down next to her and shook his head. 'Where's that time gone, Jen?'

'I know. On top of teenage twins all over the place, now we've got this virus thing to contend with, the murder of poor Louise, and guards all round town.' Jen leaned against him, and welcomed his arm around her. 'We're all getting stressed out,' she said sadly. 'Tempers and emotions are only going to get worse, too.'

She felt him take a breath to reply, but a knock on the door halted whatever he'd been going to say. 'It's Todd,' he said instead.

'Can I come in for a minute, or am I interrupting something?' Todd asked, looking pointedly at John's arm around Jen's shoulder.

'You are, but it's okay, mate. Come in.' John moved away. 'What's up?'

'I need to know if I've done something wrong,' Todd said, 'or whether Sinead's being unreasonable.'

213

'Oh.' Jen and John said together. Jen shrugged. 'Well, we've just had our own drama here, so we might as well hear yours too.'

Todd took the chair opposite and sat forward, staring at his own linked hands while he ordered his thoughts. 'Okay. So you know Ian had to give up the little cabin? Well, I suggested to Sinead that he stayed with us. Temporarily, of course.'

'Reasonable,' John ventured, getting up to fetch them all a drink.

'Exactly! But Sinead pointed out, pretty angrily I might add, that our cabin's too small. She didn't want him on the couch, it would be something else to worry about, and he's been offered a perfectly good tent to stay in.' He sat back, perplexed. 'She wouldn't budge, ended up in tears, and told me to get lost. So I thought I'd better do so for a bit.'

John patted his shoulder as he passed him. 'Don't worry, you haven't done anything wrong. Ordinarily I'm sure Sinead would've been fine helping Ian out, but this new uncertainty is frightening people, and causing upsets.' He gave Jen a pointed look. 'Eh, Jen?'

She rolled her eyes and nodded. 'Look, Todd. Sinead has more to worry about than most of us. Neither she, you or the children have any immunity to the virus, and it's back.'

'Yes,' Todd said, with his customary optimism, 'but it's contained.'

'It may well be,' Jen pointed out, 'but that doesn't stop the worry.' She gave him a sympathetic look, to take the sting from her stern words. 'You'll have to be a bit more patient with her for a while. Don't forget she lost her whole family back home, she doesn't want to lose the one she has with you.'

Todd's face clouded. 'No, of course. I didn't think about it like that.' He pondered, then brightened a little. 'Would a bit of a snuggle help, d'ya think?'

Jen nodded approval. 'Go back and tell her you understand.'

'Thanks, you two. Forget the drink, John, I'll go now.' He kissed Jen and said his goodbyes, and as he left he met Doron at the door, and slid sideways past him in his haste. 'Gotta go, Ron, see you later!'

'Yeah... Okay, bye.'

'Come in, Ron,' Jen said. 'It's open house today.'

Doron looked bemused as he came into the room, and twisted to stare after the swiftly departing Todd. 'What was that all about?'

'Oh, just a minor domestic with Sinead. They couldn't agree on letting Ian stay with them, rather than in a tent.'

'Well, it may be for the better that he doesn't,' Ron said. 'Nita has a hunch that guy can't be trusted.'

'What? But he's so nice.'

Doron pulled a face. 'He may well be, but I've seen evidence of her hunches, and it wouldn't hurt to be a little cautious. I've seen evidence of her temper too,' he added.

'That's true,' John said. 'Where is she, anyway?'

'She offered to stay with Pete and Ellie tonight. I'm going back in the morning to check on things, and hopefully bring her back here. Then I'll take the next shift. But it won't be for long I'm afraid.'

Jen felt a pang of sadness for the couple. 'I'm so sorry to hear that.'

'*Hopefully*?' John prompted. 'Why?'

'It all depends on the results of her blood test, as I said this morning. Otto will have them tomorrow, and then we'll have a town meeting to discuss it all. Can you help out?'

'Of course.'

A commotion in the doorway revealed Holly and Hannah, who went straight to their uncle and clearly caught him by surprise by flinging their arms around him.

'What's this?' He hugged them back, looking at Jen with raised eyebrows.

Haltingly, the girls apologised for letting Ruth run off, and he ruffled their hair as if they were still little children.

'Don't be sorry, kids, there's no way it was your fault.'

'So you're not angry with us?'

'Why on earth would I be? You're doing a wonderful job.' He looked quizzically at Jen and John, and Jen explained about the overheard conversation.

'Guess us grown-ups need to be more aware of what we're saying, and who's listening,' Doron mused, as his relieved nieces went outside. 'They seem resilient on the surface, but it just goes to show.'

***

Ian had been briefed by John on the circumstances that required him to leave the small cabin, and had accepted them graciously. He packed up his meagre belongings and put them outside, then took the time to clean the cabin

216

through before carrying his things to Nita's truck, where he found the tent that had been offered for his use.

Lifting it out, he noticed what looked like a small, embroidered cushion, on the rear seat, and was momentarily entranced by the beautiful needlework; intricate and colourful, with designs that drew the eye and begged a closer look. He opened the door and picked it up, and by the heft of it he realised it was in fact a wrapping and, feeling slightly guilty, he looked around him before he unfolded the material to expose a notebook with an obviously well-used cover. A journal.

He flicked through some of the pages, and noted there were two sets of handwriting. For a few minutes he became absorbed reading some of the entries, then, coming to his senses again he re-wrapped it, put it inside his holdall and closed the truck door. Once everything was packed away in his jeep, he looked around at the small town that had been his home for the last month, and gave an inward sigh, surprised at the depth of his sudden sadness, after being here such a short time.

He sent the community a silent farewell, and drove to the edge of town where he stopped, and smiled at the newly-placed guard.

'Hi, Paul. Nice day for it.'

Paul grinned. 'Not working today?'

'I've got time off for good behaviour.'

'Always the joker,' Paul replied, rolling his eyes. 'Lucky you.'

Ian put on his best smile, and jerked his head towards the back of his jeep. 'There's nae room for me here for a wee while, so I'll be setting up this canvas home over yonder. I'll be back for supper, mind.'

Paul ducked his head to see the folded tent in the trunk, and nodded. 'Yeah, things are hotting up around here, huh? I just might join you for some peace and quiet. Catch you later, man.'

Ian handed him a set of keys. 'Look after these for Nita, would you?'

He stayed carefully within Paul's sight, parked the jeep behind a clump of trees, and set to work putting up the tent. When it was done he gave a thumbs up to Paul, who returned the gesture.

He sat inside the tent for a while, reading the journal he'd found in Nita's truck. *The lass is gifted,* he thought*, but has different talents to the twins.* This would be of interest to the colonel, but just how much could Ian tell him, without putting everyone at risk?

He jotted down Nita's great-grandfather's prophecy, and made some notes of his own, then re-wrapped the journal and drove back to town. He collected Nita's keys again from a bemused Paul, and placed the journal back in her vehicle, then returned the keys with a little shake of his head.

'Always forgetting stuff. I'd forget my head if it wasnae screwed on tight! Back in a bit.'

He drove back to his tent, but left his engine running while he rummaged around it, and when he was sure Pete was checking elsewhere, he climbed back into the jeep and drove slowly away. He kept out of sight, driving through the fields for a while, then turned onto Interstate 70 towards Denver International Airport.

The three-hour drive gave him plenty of time to think things through, and he acknowledged that the last year or so had been little more than a blur of survival. After Becky had died he'd been filled with an anger even more intense than when he had lost Linda; all he wanted to do was fight something. Anything. In a last ditch attempt to salvage something of himself he had decided to return to North Carolina, to see if anyone he knew had survived; if there was anyone left that could stop him from becoming nothing but a wild man, filled with a directionless fury.

On the journey he had been hailed down by an army truck. He'd listened with rising disbelief to the driver, who said he was recruiting personnel to join an organisation called Veritas, and was promising shelter, safety, food and companionship. It had sounded good. Better than good: miraculous, and skirting the realm of absurdity... But he'd gradually realised the offer was a real one, and even the Veritas motto appealed to him: *Power, Profit, and Purity.* He could see nothing wrong with a bit of power and profit, and he wasn't bothered about the purity of heart bit; he'd learned through bitter experience that that didn't get you anywhere in this world. So, in the absence of anything better to do, and deeply curious, he'd followed the truck back the way he'd come, and into the airport.

All the signs there indicated six levels, with five lower than the main terminal, but he was shown a way down to a subterranean level. Following a security check, and quarantine period, he'd been permitted to join the rest of the community; around two hundred forces personnel, all of whom lived on the base.

219

He'd found himself in an immense, startlingly well-equipped bunker, comprising living quarters, kitchens, a medical centre, sports and training facilities, and with its own power and water supply – the latter two being something he knew he would not have found above ground. He'd heard the conspiracy stories about the place of course, but no one had really believed them. Yet there it was. And here *he* was.

It had been built nine years ago, at the same time as the rest of the airport, so its construction, funded by Veritas members, had gone virtually unnoticed. Most of the residents had been there before the virus had taken hold, and so had no immunity to it; this was their haven and, although built for a different purpose, it was now the new Veritas HQ. Ian later learned that the only ones who'd been natural survivors were Steve – the truck driver – along with the colonel's bodyguard and himself. He and Steve had become friends, and they often secretly shared their misgivings about the whole operation.

It had been months after he'd become a member of Veritas that it finally dawned on Ian; the *purity* part of the motto was nothing to do with the heart, but referred to purity of race. The ethos was against everything he believed in, but by then it was too late... it was clear that anyone who voiced disapproval tended to leave under strange circumstances. He was locked into Veritas now, and worse, he was good at his job. He must have been, or he wouldn't still be here.

Hope Meadows had been his first assignment. He'd been ecstatic to see the sky and breathe fresh air again, and he hadn't realised just how much he'd missed a home-cooked meal until Sinead and Todd had invited him into their home. After over a year of surviving on tinned food and field rations it had tasted like pure heaven. And then there were the children. Emily and Karl had stolen his heart, and he felt a pang of guilt at leaving them without a goodbye, or even a note.

As he turned into Peña Boulevard he realised he was missing them already. But he had a job to do. The colonel was to be obeyed; he was second in command only to the new president, who was also the head of Veritas. Ian had even taken an oath: …*and that I will obey the orders of the President of the United States, and the orders of the officers appointed…* But what if those orders went against humanity? This was an order that sat heavy in his heart. If he didn't return, they'd find him and he'd disappear like the others, so he had no choice but to play along. For now.

He saw the front range of the Rockies, and the peaked fabric roof of the Jeppesen Terminal in the distance, constructed to resemble the snow-capped mountains. Veritas said they wanted a new world, as did everyone else, but not a restrictive one… Ian couldn't help wondering how they intended to accomplish their goal, but there was no question that, whatever their plans, they would not be pleasant.

As he drove towards the entrance to the west parking garages, he could see the Boeing VC-25A on one of taxiways, with its burned-out fuselage, and remembered what Steve had told him: President Joan Philips and her closest members of staff had been in the jet under the call of Air Force One. Ordinarily they would have been

221

contained in the Presidential Emergency Operations Centre, below the east wing of the White House, but the blood supply set aside for them had not been delivered. The president's Chief of Staff had contacted Vice-President Max Holloway, who was already secured at Denver airport, to find out what was going on.

Holloway let them know the supply was safe with him and that they should land at Denver, but before they could, he had informed the captain that someone on the jet was infected. His orders were to land the plane, and secure everyone inside. No-one was to leave. There was an outcry on board of course, but no-one could take the risk of an infected person being allowed into Veritas HQ.

Ian had only found out recently that there had actually been two survivors of the virus, but they'd been executed on board by Holloway's staff, and the plane set alight... making Holloway the new president. Two questions remained unanswered: how had Holloway known about the infected member of staff? And why wasn't the location queried? Ian had his own theories on those. The more he'd learned about Veritas, the more he'd wanted out.

As he parked the jeep at the far end of Level 1, his thoughts turned to what he was going to report. He switched off the engine, picked up his flashlight, and headed towards the stairwell that would take him down below the airport. Minutes later he was walking along Level 1, towards the two guards who stood against what looked like a plain concrete wall; all there was to see here were wall lights, ceiling piping, and concrete. The guards raised their guns and demanded identification.

'Sloan V-198,' Ian responded as he placed his flashlight into his carryall.

'Ian! Welcome home, brother.' The guns were lowered and the guards smiled at him.

'Hi, guys.'

'Well look at you with your suntan! We never got your postcard.'

Ian chuckled. 'How's things?'

'Oh, same-old same-old. Catch up later, okay?'

'Sounds good to me.'

'Right let's get you sorted, and through the shower and into a clean kit. The colonel is gonna want to see you like yesterday. Raise your arms and rotate slowly.'

Ian put down his carryall and did as he was asked, and one of the guards lifted what looked like a small fire extinguisher, and sprayed the contents over him and his bag. As he endured the familiar precautions Ian wondered just how these people could be so ordinary and pleasant, yet at the flick of a switch become hate-filled, monstrous racists. He often looked at them and wondered if any of them were just like him, deep down. Playing the game.

'That's you sanitised and ready to enter.' The guard raised his arm and swiped his wrist in a downward motion in front of the wall. A remote-controlled door behind him slid open with a grating sound.

Ian walked through, and as the concrete door closed, he faced an inner steel door which he knew also contained a tiny monitor, barely visible to the naked eye. He took off his watch, raised his arm, swiped his wrist down in the same manner as the guard, and the microchip implanted there activated the steel door. As he entered the complex, the door closed with a hiss and the internal corridor became airtight once again. He knew the routine: he went down the narrow corridor, stripped off, and entered a sanitising shower, exiting at the opposite end where clean clothes awaited him. After ten minutes, his now sanitised paperwork was returned to him, but his other belongings were kept to be cleaned.

Dressed now in combat trousers and black T-shirt, Ian walked along the cool, barren corridor, with a clipboard under his arm. He didn't need to knock on the heavy metal door to the president's suite; it was open already, and Holloway's bodyguard showed him in. It always surprised him that the president and the colonel weren't worried about open doors, yet they each had a bodyguard... To guard them from what, Ian didn't know. He marched in and stood to attention, noting the presence of both his superiors as he saluted.

'At ease, Sergeant.' Holloway was sitting at his desk, and the colonel was turned away from him, hands behind his back, watching the sanity screen. There were a few around the base; live feeds of the outside world many miles away. All you could see were trees and wildlife, and the seasons as they changed, but it gave the impression of having a window. Ian slipped into the formal *at ease* position, facing square ahead.

'Stand easy.'

Ian relaxed. 'Sir.'

'You're looking healthy, Sloan. The fresh air and sunshine have done you good.'

'Yes, sir.' He kept his answers short; he knew neither man liked small talk.

'So, what have you got for me?'

'Sir, Hope Meadows is a thriving community. They have power and a good water supply, and they're farming and managing to provide for themselves. The community's growing on a daily basis, all races and the old religions are being catered for. A recent development has been the arrival of a large number of Native Americans.'

The president's face twisted with disgust. 'And soon they'll all be interbreeding, and they won't even know who they are anymore.' He shook his head. 'What of the unnaturals?'

'Sir?'

'The twins.'

'Ah. I saw first-hand the power they have, and it's remarkable.' Ian heard the awe in his own voice, and hurriedly reverted to the facts. 'They seem to be part supernatural spirit, and that part of them is the one with the power. The human side is also gifted, sir, they're super intelligent, and, as you are aware, are fully immune to pathogens.'

'And did you see any evidence of the virus?'

'Aye, sir. I'm sorry to report that it's still out there. Two people have caught it recently.'

'Fuck it!' Holloway's fist came down on his desk, hard enough to spill his coffee and rattle his pens. Although the colonel still had his back to him, Ian could see his hands tighten and the veins in his neck pulse; he was furious with the news too, but unlike Holloway he kept the impression of calm.

'*Eight* months we should have been in this rabbit hole, not eighteen!' Holloway's voice was tight with rage. 'Eight months was plenty of time for the virus and a quarantine period to pass. How much longer are we going to be stuck down here?'

The colonel turned his attention away from the screen. 'Once everyone has been infected with a virus and has either died or survived, it should die too. When we sent out a scout after eight months, we were sure we'd get the all clear to leave here and take up base at Peterson Air Force base. Our mistake was to not give him a transfusion, and he became infected whilst outside. *How* is that possible? How is it possible it's still transmitting?'

Ian kept his own voice steady. 'The problem, sir, is that there are carriers out there. I don't understand how, but that's the reality.'

'That's unprecedented.'

It was on the tip of Ian's tongue to point out that everything now, from the moment this particular virus had hit, was unprecedented, but he'd learned long ago to hold his peace.

The colonel continued, 'So we come to the most important question, under the circumstances. How far along is Fischer with developing a vaccine?'

'I cannae confirm success, sir,' Ian said. 'Trials were made to incorporate the double immunity gene, and all have failed. It's believed that part of their immunity is supernaturally donated, and therefore cannot be replicated or donated permanently by that method. Ott...Fischer is working on a vaccine that can also donate the single gene, but it's far from being ready. It's possible a simple vaccine could be made ready, but it's not known how long the effects would last.'

226

'So, we still need to keep that traitorous little shit alive, unless we find another geneticist or bio-chemist. Our medics are neither. If they had been, Fischer would have gone the same way as Miss Miller.'

The bodyguard smirked, and Ian immediately realised who the assassin had been.

'His time will come, Colonel,' Holloway said.

'Thank you, sir,' the colonel said, with evidently forced calm. 'So what now?'

'We move onto plan B, which we'll discuss later.' Holloway looked at Ian. 'Anything else to report?'

'Aye, sir. Nita Rogers, a woman of Ute descent, also has a gift but she's neither a twin nor Nephilim. She has visions, and it seems she's able to travel out of body.' Ian had already decided not to tell them about her possible immunity; any delay to their plans could only be a good thing.

'That's nothing new,' Holloway said dismissively. 'The Stargate Project had people practicing remote travel, but was declassified in 1995. It was deemed to have had no intelligence benefits whatsoever, so it's of no—'

'Could they travel through time, sir?'

'What? No, only to present locations. Why?'

Ian had the attention of both men now. 'Miss Rogers has the ability to "travel," both in the present and back in time, and see events as they happened.' As with her immunity, he declined to mention any of her visions of the future.

'That's very interesting,' Holloway conceded. 'We may have to find out more about this woman.'

227

'She also has details of her great-grandfather's prophecy, a man named Dakayivani, who had the same gift.'

'Another damn prophecy!' Holloway grunted. 'I thought we were done with them, they just seem to keep popping out of the woodwork. Colonel, you looked into Native American prophecies, didn't you?'

'Yes, sir I did, and there was nothing significant that could affect us. Most of them have already come to pass. The one exception is of Hopi origin, regarding the coming of a saviour called Pahana, who is supposed to take them into the next world. But there's been no evidence to support it.'

Ian stepped forward and put his clipboard down on the desk. 'This is what I've copied from Nita's journal, sir. I'll leave it with you.'

'Thank you, Sloan,' Holloway said. 'Good work. Dismissed.' As an afterthought, he added, 'And get your hair cut.'

'Yes sir.' Ian saluted both men and turned to leave but heard the colonel murmur that it might be prudent to keep the hair, the same as his bodyguard, just in case a further mission was necessary.

'Belay that last order,' Holloway amended.

'Yes sir.' Ian left the office, wondering grimly what plan B entailed.

Chapter Thirteen
Plan B

Hope Meadows

Rena greeted Nita warmly on her return. 'Come on in, I've put out some clothes that should fit you, they're on the chair in our room. The shower's through there.' She pointed. 'There's a bag you can put your own clothes in, too.'

'Thank you.' Though Nita felt like hugging the woman for her easy kindness, she kept her distance. 'It's really good of you.'

'It's the least I can do, you must be worn out. It's good to have someone to fuss around again. And,' Rena added with an emotional catch in her voice, 'I'm grateful for the help you've given Ron.'

'He's a fine doctor, but this has been a difficult situation, and I'm glad to be able to help.' Nita lowered her voice slightly. 'I don't think Pete and Ellie will last another day.'

Rena winced. 'Those poor people.'

'It's truly sad. But at least they're being kept comfortable, and pain-free, which is more than can be said for most others.'

Rena nodded, still distracted by her sorrow, then visibly pulled herself out of it; something they were all becoming too accustomed to now. 'Once you're sorted, come through to the kitchen,' she said, more brightly, 'I'm going to make us a nice omelette for breakfast before you go, with some freshly laid eggs Maya has brought over, and my own, home-grown mushrooms.'

Nita could have spent all day beneath the hot shower, feeling it first strip away the sweat and grime, and then needle freshness into her skin, but she kept it brief out of respect for her hosts, and was soon changing into the clothes Rena had left on the bed. They fit surprisingly well, with a turn-up to the trouser legs and a fold to the cuffs on the shirt, and she was soon pushing her old, soiled clothes into the bag, glad to see the back of them for a while.

She went to put the bag outside the front door, and on her way down the hall she passed an open doorway and automatically glanced in. The room reminded her so strongly of Billy's organised chaos that it gave her a little jolt of pain, but that was tempered by a surprising flicker of affection as she realised the room was Ron's.

Billy had always known where everything was in his room, despite the mess, and she suspected Ron would be the same. There was a scent lingering in the air that increased the unexpected pleasure she took from standing there, and, unwilling to probe too deeply into what that might mean, she hurried down the hall to put her bag outside.

When she returned to the kitchen, Rena was busily beating eggs, with rich, orange yolks, in a glass bowl. She looked up as Nita came in, and smiled approvingly.

'Well, my clothes look better on you than on me!'

Nita grinned, relaxing again. 'Hardly! Can I help?'

'You could chop the mushrooms if you like,' Rena said, resuming her whisking. 'I'm rather proud of my porcini, they've grown beautifully. Except those two.' She nodded to a couple of spindly-looking specimens. 'Don't worry, I'll put those in my omelette not yours.'

Nita came alongside her in preparation for chopping, then looked again at the two undergrown mushrooms and gave Rena a sidelong look. 'You're right about the others,' she said, 'they're fine examples. But these two?' She picked them up. 'The reason they haven't grown the same is because they're not porcini.'

'Oh?'

'And it's a good job you didn't eat them,' Nita added.

Rena looked horrified. 'Please tell me they're not poisonous? I was so careful!'

'No, not poisonous,' Nita assured her, 'but if you'd eaten them both you'd have been ill for some time. If you'd eaten just a bit, well... who knows?' She gave Rena a little smile. 'They're magic mushrooms.'

Rena's eyes widened. 'Thank goodness you spotted them!'

'They're similar, but smaller, and they have a little nipple right in the middle of the cap, see?'

'How on earth would I have lived *that* down?'

'I won't tell anyone, if you won't.' Nita pocketed the mushrooms. 'I can take them away, if you've no objections?'

Rena nodded earnestly. 'Please do. Come on, let's get these omelettes cooking.'

231

'At least we'll be on the same planet while we eat them,' Nita said, and her grin finally broke through Rena's embarrassment and she returned it, still looking mortified, but finally seeing the funny side.

'Is Alex not joining us?' Nita asked, using the knife to push the now-chopped mushrooms across to Rena, who dropped them into the pan.

'No, he's out spreading the word about the meeting this evening. It's going to be an early one, as I understand a few of you are having your own gathering afterwards?'

Nita nodded. 'Ron's coming back for them, then going back to his patients.' She couldn't help wondering at how natural it felt to mention him so casually, but she quite liked it.

'How about you?' Rena carried cutlery across to the table. 'What are you doing today?'

'I'll be going back to the Springs after breakfast. I miss the dogs, and I think Belle will probably be fretting. I'll be back later though.'

Rena emptied the eggs from the bowl into the pan, and was quiet for a moment, thoughtful. Nita did not prompt conversation; she knew the value of quiet contemplation.

'It's been very odd around here lately,' Rena said at length. 'So many things happening, and now that lovely Scotsman, Ian, has disappeared, too.'

Nita looked at her, startled. 'Disappeared? But the tent I offered him has gone from my truck, and it's been put up outside of town. He's not there, then?'

'No, we did check, but his jeep's gone too.' Rena tipped the pan to let the uncooked egg run. 'Todd and Sinead said he never arrived back for supper, and of course the kids are quite upset. They've taken a strong liking to him.'

'So what happened when he didn't turn up?'

'A few people went out to see if they could find him, in case he'd had an accident, but he wasn't there. As far as they could tell, the tent hadn't been slept in either, and it was empty.'

'How strange,' Nita mused. 'Maybe he'll turn up again soon.'

But she remained thoughtful. And doubtful.

The town's population had grown too large to make it feasible that everyone should attend every meeting now, and Nita learned they had necessarily become tailored to any particular current issue; tonight's was obvious, and most attendees were those whose lives were potentially at risk.

It was a nervous group, therefore, that gathered in the town hall that evening, but as Nita took her seat at the back, with Belle and Moki, she realised the dogs were proving to be an unintentional crowd-calmer. Kimi was on Nita's knee, and the younger dogs were obediently sitting at the end of the row, where they were the happy recipients of much distracted petting as the worried townsfolk passed by to their seats.

It was another warm evening, but even though it was still early, a cooling breeze drifted in through the open windows, which helped ease the heat created by the fidgeting crowd as everyone waited to hear the latest news. Otto was in the front row, and he was clearly excited about something; he kept twisting in his seat, and smiling and nodding at people; it gave the room an air of hope, and Nita was sure she wasn't the only one to feel it.

Doron and John were at the front, leaning against the small table rather than sitting at it, in what Nita was already recognising as their usual stance. Doron's long hair was still wet from what must have been a hurried shower, but he still looked immaculate; she thought back to the chaos of his room, and couldn't help smiling at the contrast.

Once everyone was seated, Doron pushed himself upright, and an expectant hush fell over the room as everyone's attention swivelled to him.

'Welcome, all,' he said, but his eyes found Nita immediately, and she only realised she must still have been smiling when his mouth lifted slightly in response.

When the murmured greetings had died down, he went on, 'I know you're all anxious about our newcomer, Ruth, and this meeting has been called to put your minds at ease. But first, we have some great news to tell you.'

The crowd shuffled as people glanced at one another, and leaned eagerly forward.

'As you know,' Doron said, 'Otto here had managed to make a vaccine for the virus, but not with the intention of using it as such.' He held up a hand to forestall the questions he clearly knew would be forthcoming. 'It wouldn't have been a permanent solution anyway, so he's been trying to find a way of giving you the same protection that others here have.' Now his smile widened. 'Well, some new information has come to light which I think you'll be very happy with.' He gestured to the front row. 'Otto, if you would like to explain to everyone please?'

Otto rose, almost before Doron had finished speaking, and turned to face his audience. 'I'd like to ask Ruhi and Alima to help me explain this,' he said, 'as without them we might never have come up with the idea. Girls?' He beckoned them forward. 'In addition to that, I'd like to publicly thank Nita here for graciously agreeing to donate some of her blood, so that we can begin trials right away.'

Nita was mildly discomfited when every face in the room turned to look at her with puzzled curiosity. She nodded, embarrassed, and was relieved when their attention returned to Otto, who was clearly bursting to continue.

'I'll try to keep this straightforward—'

'That'll be a first,' a voice called out, and a ripple of laughter ran around the room, which Otto ignored.

'Well, as you already know, the experiments I've been conducting in search of a way to pass on the double immunity, have failed. But Ruhi and Alima here,' he indicated them in turn, with an almost paternal pride, 'have come up with the brilliant idea of transferring the single UEP1 gene to a host, via a live vaccine. I'll let them explain.'

The twins were visibly nervous, and the one he'd introduced as Alima was fiddling with her hair, but after looking at her sister for support, she spoke up, in a surprisingly strong, assured voice.

'Well, what we did was, we grew the genetic material of the virus at a lower than normal body temperature. So it could survive, the virus adapted to the new temperature, which meant it lost its ability to cause harm to you.' She looked at Ruhi again, who picked up the story.

'When it's used in a vaccine, it would still cause an immune response, but not enough to make you ill. So we think that the vaccine should travel to every cell in your body, and if we add UEP1 to it, the vaccine would...' She hesitated, and Nita could see her mind working to find the easiest explanation. '...give it a sort of piggy-back ride,' she finished.

The first question was inevitable, and instant. 'So, does it work?'

'I see no reason to doubt it,' Otto said, 'but we haven't performed any trials yet. However, new information has come to light that would generate even better results. Before I ask Nita to explain, I think the twins deserve a round of applause, don't you? They've worked extremely hard on all their projects.'

The appreciative clapping broke through the girls' nervousness, and they smiled. Nita saw them turn to a couple who were clapping louder than everyone else, their faces alight with love and pride, and guessed these were their parents.

As the applause began to die away, Otto gestured to Nita, who rose and spoke from where she was, rather than coming forward. Her opening statement, drawing on what Otto had told her, was as blunt as ever.

'I have the same immunity as the twins.'

For a moment there was a stunned silence, and then the barrage of questions, which she allowed to wash over her for a moment before continuing. 'I thought it was caused by a genetic mutation, but I was wrong. Otto

236

tested my blood and saliva, and he discovered that I have two sets of DNA, and two different blood groups. I'm what's known as a *chimera*. My mother must have been carrying fraternal twins, each one with a different single immunity gene, and when the other embryo died I absorbed its cells.'

She sat down, and Otto nodded his thanks. 'This happens very rarely,' he told the room at large, who had turned back to him as soon as they realised Nita had said all she was going to say. 'It's perfectly normal, and natural, without any *super*natural intervention. Now, given the world population as it currently stands, it's possible Nita is the only one with this remarkable genetic make-up. With her help, we should be able to pass on the double UEP1 gene to you all.'

Again, a brief silence met these words, but gradually realisation began to sink in that there wasn't a huge black caveat attached, and there was relieved laughter, and a rising buzz in conversation.

'So... does this mean we could all be safe soon?'

Nita recognised the speaker as Paul Morgan.

'Yes it does,' Otto said, his old beaming smile returning. 'Safe from *all* pathogens,' he added. I just need to do a few more trials, and I think we'll be ready to go.'

He sat down, and Doron stepped forward again. 'Thanks, Otto. This leads us into the main reason we're gathered,' he said, looking around the room. 'We want to make sure that you have no more worries about Ruth staying with us. She may be a carrier, but that makes her less likely to be able to pass on the virus than someone who's showing symptoms. She has no cough, or sneezes,

237

so unless you get really close, or share anything that might contain her saliva, you won't be at risk.'

John nodded, straightening up to stand next to his brother. 'The poor woman has suffered enough,' he said quietly, 'she's lonely, and she's frightened. So we ask that you stop staring, and maybe smile or wave to her once in a while. Once Otto and the girls have the vaccine ready, we'll be able to help her too, so her confinement will only be a temporary measure. In the meantime, let's all be kind, okay?'

Nita could see people relaxing, and began to understand the hold these two brothers had over Hope Springs; they worked together so naturally. Doron had the authority of his calling, and his brother had the down-to-earth attitude of a born communicator. Between them they had created a community of people who trusted them, and trust was the single most important factor in this new world of theirs.

Paul Morgan raised his hand this time, instead of shouting out, and Doron nodded to him to speak.

'Is there any news about this Miller woman's murder?'

'Unfortunately not,' John said. 'We've been busy with safety issues, but first inspection showed no trace of her murderer, no fingerprints, footprints, or any other signs that someone had been in her trailer.'

'What does that mean for the rest of us?'

'Because of all that, we believe it to have been a professional hit, which is the reason we've placed extra guards around town.'

'We think Veritas may be behind it,' Doron added, 'so we're just being extra cautious. We should all go about our normal activities within the compound, but if you have to travel outside, don't go anywhere alone. The same goes for Morrison Farm and Carbondale, until we get to the bottom of it.'

'We heard you're having an additional meeting after this,' Diego Garcia called out. 'A closed one.'

'That's correct.'

'Why?'

'It's a private matter, concerning Nita and her family,' John said. 'It *might* have relevance to all the twins, and if it does, rest assured you'll all be informed right away. Any further questions?'

There were none, and Nita watched every face that passed her as they filed out of the town hall, relieved to see the overwhelming majority were smiling. She nodded to everyone who acknowledged her, and braced herself for the second meeting of the evening, wondering if the attendants would still be smiling when it was over.

***

The room emptied quite quickly, and Doron took stock of who was left: John of course, Todd and Sinead, Maya and Uri, Nita, Belle, and an elderly gentleman Nita introduced as Moki.

'He's a Hopi elder,' she said. 'Belle is Ute, like me, and she and Moki are my dear friends. They're on our own council, in the Springs.'

There was a chorus of welcomes, which Moki acknowledged with a friendly nod, but he remained silent as she introduced the Hope Meadows founders.

'Where's Jen?' Sinead asked, dragging a couple of extra chairs over.

'Gone to get us all coffee,' John said. 'Can you and Todd stay for the whole meeting?'

'Wouldn't miss it.' Sinead said with a grin, 'It'll be like old times. Clare's babysitting, so we don't need to rush back.'

'Alex has left paper and enough pens for us all... ah, here's Jen, now.'

Sinead went to hold the door for her, and the others took their seats. Belle produced a plastic container from her bag, and prised off the lid.

'Cornbread, cooked with sliced apples,' she said, as she offered it around. 'Rena helped me.'

'This is delicious,' Todd said, with real appreciation, and Sinead grinned.

'Leave some for the rest of us then!'

The cornbread was declared a success, and Doron noted the quietly pleased smile with which Belle watched them all eat, washing it down with Jen's good, strong coffee. When they had all settled at the table, with their paper and pens at the ready, he started the meeting.

'You all know by now that Nita is very special indeed.' He wondered, briefly, if his own personal regard for her was starting to show, and hurried on, 'With her help, everyone will be safe. I have to be honest, I was dubious at first, but I'm pleased with the results. Nita also has certain special... talents. We'll hear from her exactly what they are, along with her great-grandfather's prophecy.' He looked at Nita, and nodded for her to start.

'Thanks, Ron. First of all, I'd like to point out that my talents are completely different to the twins', and although they're genetic within my bloodline, I believe they were also passed on thousands of years ago by the Fathers. You've told me that most of you are descended from Moses, but no one's mentioned Maor's descendants, and that may be because they were not recorded.' She took a deep breath. 'I believe that all Native American survivors are descended from Maor.'

'Really?' Todd stared at her, fascinated. 'How did you come up with that theory?'

She explained about her visions; the four different species of Man, and how some of the fourth and final species made it across the Bering Strait, at that time known as Beringia; a land bridge from Russia to Alaska before the ice melt.

'They eventually settled in the Americas,' she said, and went on to tell them about the old man who walked from Africa to Colorado with his four sons, and how two of them stayed with the Hopi, and one half of a sacred tablet, while the other two joined the Ute people, with the other half. 'At some point, that one broke,' she finished.

Moki spoke for the first time, his face expressionless. 'This man is known among my people as the Man of Sin.'

Everyone looked to him for clarification, which didn't come. Doron was about to try and prompt an explanation, but a clearly incredulous Nita beat him to it.

'I've never heard of this, Moki, I never even knew he had a name. What sin did he commit?'

'It was no sinful deed, but was the land of his ancestors.'

'Why haven't you told me this before?'

He gave the tiniest shrug. 'The Hopi are a private people, our stories are sacred. There's a time and place for such things, and now is not the time.'

'You've told me some of your stories, so may I share our recent conversation with our friends here?' She spoke in a suitably reverent voice, and Doron realised she held this man in high regard, but he also noted a hint of irritation, and the slight emphasis she put on the word *friends,* as if to gently remind him they were all working together. She waited until Moki had nodded, and then focused on the paper in front of her as she began to tell the story.

'The Hopi believe that our ancestors came from the stars, as do many others, and that their creator was the Great Spirit Massau'u.'

Doron saw that some of those around the table were scribbling notes, and that Nita looked pleased about it, as if she knew they would need them. He took up his own pen and concentrated on her words.

'There are ancient petroglyphs all around this area,' she went on, 'that show the story of the star people's arrival, and even the Cherokee call us *star seeds*. My great-grandfather was Shoshone, and they believe that Sinav was their creator. My great-grandmother was Ute, and the creation story *we* were told was about Sinawav.'

She told the story of Sinawav, his brother wolf, and the bag of sticks, and once again Moki broke in.

'Your *Sinawav* is our Man of Sin.'

Nita blinked, and focused on him. 'How can that be?'

242

His voice was maddeningly calm as he raised a dismissive hand. 'Another time.'

Doron noted first of all that Nita was close to losing her temper, and secondly that Belle had seen this, and had touched Moki's knee.

'You're talking in riddles,' she said, 'and it's not helping Nita explain everything. We all know that Sinawav is a myth.'

'There are truths in all myths.'

'Moki,' Belle asked gently, 'why did you come?'

'To observe.'

'Then … observe.'

Nita was clearly grateful for Belle's interjection, but was distracted now by Todd, who had taken another piece of cornbread and was bending down.

'Do *not* feed my dogs!' she snapped.

Todd drew back, startled. 'I'm sorry,' he began, 'I didn't mean to—'

'No,' Nita said on a little sigh. 'I'm the one who should apologise. I'm too abrupt sometimes, forgive me. You may give them each a piece, but not until we've all finished eating.'

He nodded, but still looked wary as he replaced the bread on the table. Sinead dug him in the thigh with one finger, and when he poked out his tongue Doron saw the teasing grin she gave him. Their evident affection for one another was both warming and enviable.

Nita brought him back to the matter at hand. 'I'm finding this difficult, but I hope I've given you enough information to consider. I also have a confession.' They all looked at her expectantly, and she flushed. 'Before you

243

showed me around your town, and introduced me to your community, I had been here before.'

'But, you've only just arrived here,' Jen pointed out, puzzled.

Nita turned to her. 'The night your husband and his brother met with the Fathers, I had another vision. I have no control over them and I found myself here. I saw you, Jen, with Rena, watching over Ron and John as they awoke. I also saw your daughter hit by a stone thrown by the angry crowd. I'm sorry I never mentioned it before.'

A tense silence fell over them all as they considered this, until John broke it with a laugh. 'Well, I hope we looked our best, Ron's such a slob!'

'Hark at Mr Best-Dressed,' Jen said smartly. The laughter dispelled the last of the tension, and Nita smiled in relief.

Uri spoke up. 'Nita, Maya and I were intrigued with the sacred tablet that the… the *Man of Sin* carried here. It seems as though Maor made a casting of lines that no one can decipher, and that it was given to him while Moses was on Mount Sinai. He then passed it down to his descendants.'

'Sinai!' Sinead exclaimed, sitting upright.

'Uh oh, here she goes,' Todd said, and gave her an impish grin. 'Stand by your beds, something's clicked.'

'There seem to be quite a few *sin*s here,' Sinead said, ignoring him. 'I suppose with my name I was bound to notice, if anyone was.' In response to the interested looks all round, she went on, twiddling her pen as she concentrated. 'It all started with Sinai, right? Go with me on this a minute. If the tablet was from Maor, and the old

244

man was his descendant, he could originally have been referred to as the Man of Sinai, but over time the 'ai' got dropped. Sinai, Man of Sin, Sinav and Sinowav. Get it?'

'Yes indeed!' Maya said, and Doron saw a spark of her old self as her eyes took on a familiar gleam. It reminded him of their time in Jericho, and it gave him a pang to compare it to their lives here, in relative safety but with all that knowledge and experience wasting away.

'In Hebrew, *chait* has often been mistranslated as *sin* but it really means a failure,' she was saying, 'and *ai* means ruins, although Ai was also a city in Biblical times, located in The West Bank, Palestinian Territories.' She waved it away. 'That may have some bearing, although I don't know what.'

'I think it's more likely to have come from an Akkadian deity,' Uri said. 'Sin was their moon god. The world's first empire was Akkadian, and they conquered and merged with the Sumerians. To the Sumerians, Sin was known as Nanna, the father of Utu, who was the sun god. Sin was the father of *all* the gods, creator of all things. The moon and sun have featured a lot in the past, and especially in our lives, with the eclipses.'

'Of course!' Nita was making her own notes now, and the light in her own eyes matched that in Maya's. 'My people used to live in bands of different names but were given the collective name Ute, which means *land of the sun*. You've just said the sun god was named Utu, and that can't be a coincidence surely? It's all got to be connected.'

John pursed his lips. 'So we have the father of the sun, and the four Navajo holy spirits that produced the first set of twins—'

245

'Wait!' Doron interjected, his heartbeat suddenly racing. 'Say that again, slowly.'

John got as far as *Navajo*, and as his mind leapt ahead, he stopped. 'Oh my word,' he murmured. 'The father, the son and the holy spirits...'

'Another coincidence?' Doron said. 'I don't think so.'

'I've missed these brainstorming sessions,' Sinead said with a smile. 'This is getting interesting! Confusing, but interesting. I do agree with Nita though, that somehow it's all linked, and I like her theories. They make sense.'

'Thank you, Sinead,' Nita said warmly, 'that means a lot to me.'

She reached into her bag and pulled out a photograph, which she handed to Uri. 'This is the Man of Sin's tablet... well, the half that survived. No one has been able to decipher it, but I have hopes that it's possible, even if we have to wait for Moki's Pahana to do so. You may keep it to look at later.'

Doron turned to her. 'Nita, could you explain your other talent?'

Nita told them how she often sensed things. 'Sometimes the feeling is linked to a brief vision,' she explained, 'like when I touched Ian Sloan's hand. Through his eyes, I saw the skinwalker with the mark of the bear. He's known to him.'

'Now you've lost me,' Uri said, and it seemed the others agreed.

'I'm sorry, Uri, I'm getting ahead of myself.' She recounted Dakayivani's prophecy, and gradually his expression cleared.

246

'Ah I see. Well, the sickness he prophesied has happened, so this creature's the next part, yes?'

Nita nodded. 'I assume so.'

'Who is he, and what's a... a *skinwalker?*' John asked. 'Sounds horrible.'

'It's a sort of boogieman,' Nita said. 'Someone who basically possesses someone else's skin, and is evil personified. I don't know who he is though, I never saw his face, only the mark on his neck.'

'On his neck?' Todd visibly tensed, and looked briefly over at John before turning back to Nita. 'What does the mark look like?'

'Like a bear claw scratch.' She held up her hand, fingers curled into a claw, and scratched the air along her neck.

Todd rose, eluding Sinead's reaching hand, and knocking his chair over as he stumbled away from the table. 'No, no, no,' he muttered. 'It can't be...'

Nita's startled gaze met Doron's, and her eyes were wide. She turned to the others. 'What? You think you know who it is? Who?'

John looked over at his distressed friend, and his voice was weary and heavy. 'It's Todd's father, Richard Hampton.'

***

Denver International Airport
'Dismissed. And shut the door behind you.'

The colonel waited until his bodyguard had done as he was commanded, then sat down opposite the president, formalities dropped. 'I want Sloan to think we might still

247

use him for another mission, but I'm not sure it's a good idea.'

'Why not? He's obedient, and his report's been informative.'

'He omitted a couple of very important factors.' The colonel linked his hands on the desk. 'Rom completed his orders with regards to disposing of Miller, and the information he provided was limited, due to the small amount of time he spent there, but it substantiates what Sloan has told us.'

'Then—'

'However, he also reported that the Nasir twins are as competent as Fischer, possibly inherently more so.'

'Don't be ridiculous, they're eleven years old!'

'That's my point. They're not encumbered by doubt, or years of questioning every little breakthrough. Anything's possible as far as they're concerned.' The colonel gave a tight smile. 'I believe they'd be able to deliver some sort of vaccine to all our personnel. They've also developed, theoretically, a fast and safe procedure for stem cell transplants. Sloan spent a far longer time there than Rom, so I don't see how he couldn't have known about that. Yet he's not said a word.'

Holloway's eyes narrowed, despite the good news. 'That's astounding. But *you* didn't report that information to me either. Why not?'

'My apologies,' the colonel said, 'I needed to hear Sloan's report first. I played along, and I wanted you to have a natural reaction, just in case.'

'Ah, I see.' Holloway sat back, eyeing him shrewdly. 'You have concerns about his loyalty then?'

'I'm not sure, Max, but I think we need to keep an eye on him.' The colonel shook his head. 'He may have developed an attachment over there, and is protecting them. We haven't come this far in our respective careers by trusting everyone, have we?'

'You seem to have trust in your man Rom,' Holloway pointed out.

'It suits me to do so, for now.' The colonel got up, and walked to the sanity screen once more. 'Rom has been a faithful aide, and without him I wouldn't be here now. I owe him my freedom and my life. His skin's pale enough, yet he's still an Arab, and I wonder how he'll fare in the purity stakes once we get organised outside.' He turned back for Holloway's response.

Holloway spoke firmly. 'Until we organise ourselves externally, and form our own government, the current laws of this great country will be adhered to. Under American law, Rom's deemed to be white.'

'But surely that law was passed so we could get our hands on Saudi oil?'

'Nevertheless, it's the law and will remain so until I... *we,* decide to change it. Once that's done, and our power is irrefutable, then the New World begins.'

It didn't really answer the question, but the colonel let it go for now. He wasn't overly bothered about any adverse decision, but he wanted to know where his bodyguard stood in the future; he'd been loyal, yes, and unquestioning, and he had earned the colonel's gratitude. But, like everyone else, he was ultimately expendable.

He came back to the desk, but remained standing; it helped him think. 'So, going back to the beginning of our conversation,' he said, 'we'd already decided we couldn't snatch Fischer and bring him here. I mean, he'd be perfectly able to carry out his work here, certainly, but who's to say he wouldn't sabotage it, or, worst case scenario, make a "vaccine" that gives us all the virus? We'd be none the wiser.'

'Exactly. So, plan B?'

'We take the Nasir twins,' the colonel said, 'and get them to do the work instead. If their new procedure works, we'd need them anyway. They might be *wunderkind,* but they're still children, they'll be frightened, and will do as we tell them. For that reason we could be reasonably assured they wouldn't contemplate any form of sabotage.'

'As sure as we could be.'

'Rom would ensure they arrive with all the necessary components. We're not getting any younger, Max, plus our water and diesel reserves are almost depleted. We need to act quickly.'

'Okay. We'll put it to the cabinet, such as it is, but I'm sure agreement will be unanimous. If not...' he shrugged and smiled, 'I'll authorise it anyway. But we'll keep the twins' research development to ourselves for the time being, shall we? The same way you and Charles Whyte kept the details of the twins' immunity quiet, before the shit hit the fan.'

Hampton flashed him an irritated smile back, and wondered if Max was ever going to let that one drop. 'It worked out well in the end though, didn't it? If you hadn't found out, you wouldn't have agreed to Senator Morgan's request to bring all the twins here for research. The end result is still the same. We may have lost Whyte and Braun during the trials, and a couple of others to the virus, but there are five senior members here to serve on your cabinet.'

'Five majors and one colonel,' Holloway said. 'No-one can dispute your ranking, my friend.'

'And I am most grateful for that.'

'If all works out well, you may even be able to have Fischer disposed of sooner.' Hampton smiled, and Holloway continued, 'So, what do we do about the Ute woman?'

'She's of no use or interest to us at the moment.' Hampton dismissed the subject with a flick of his hand. 'We have bigger fish to fry. We'll file any ideas away until we're free of this place.'

'Agreed. Meantime, I believe we have some notes and a prophecy to read?'

He picked up Sloan's clipboard and read in silence, and then passed it over to let Hampton do the same.

Hampton replaced the clipboard on the table when he'd finished, and raised an eyebrow. 'Your thoughts?'

'She certainly does seem to have a talent,' Holloway conceded, 'although I don't think her visions are accurate. She states that we all come from the same African ancestors? Well that's a crock, to start with. No-one here would ever believe that. And that part about the old man bringing a tablet to the Hopi, that's nothing we don't already know is it? They've been harping on about a sacred tablet for centuries. And this prophecy is just like all the others, annoyingly ambiguous. Why the hell can't they be written in plain English?'

251

Hampton smiled at the irritation in the President's voice, and kept his own tones smooth and calm; it made him feel a little superior, having his emotions under control. 'I believe that's because, at the time the visions are experienced, the seer doesn't understand everything he or she is seeing. So they explain it the only way they know how. Also,' he pointed out, 'if every detail was included, it would be open to manipulation.'

'Hmmm, good point. The only thing there that makes sense to me is the "great sickness". Could the two-spirit that's supposed to come and re-unite the tribes be the Pahana the Hopi talk about?'

Hampton shook his head. 'Highly unlikely. Dakayivani was Shoshone, and although they have their myths, as far as I'm aware they, like the Ute, have no prophecies of their own. This is the first I've heard of it, and if he hadn't been this Nita's great-grandfather, we would have been none the wiser.'

'Okay. File it all away, we have more important matters at hand.'

'Of course. I'd like to gauge Sloan's reaction, when we tell him he won't be returning to Hope Meadows.'

'Fine. Look, Richard, Rom's tolerated here, but two little brown girls?' Holloway tapped the desk thoughtfully. 'Regardless of their benefit to us, once they arrive I think it would be wise to keep them away from the general population. Right,' he added, more briskly, 'set up a cabinet meeting, and prepare Rom for his new assignment.'

'Sir.'

252

'Oh, and once we can confirm the twins' research is viable, can I leave it with you to choose a volunteer guinea pig?'

Hampton hesitated halfway to the door; the President would be sure to kick against his next suggestion, but he could kick back. Harder, if necessary.

'I've been thinking about that,' he said slowly. 'Look, as I've said before, we're running out of time. I'm in my mid-sixties, and... well the fact is, I don't want to be an old man when our new world kicks off.'

The President frowned. 'And?'

'These twins live twice as long as we do, we know that much, so any recipient of their DNA, via a stem cell transplant, could potentially live a much longer and healthier life. They may even receive some of their talents.' Hampton eyed the President keenly. 'Do we really want to empower someone else with this?'

'So, your point is?'

Hampton took a deep breath. 'I will be the first recipient.'

Chapter Fourteen
Unwelcome Welcome

'You have a lovely home.' Nita gave Jen a grateful smile as she accepted a glass of lemonade, and a bowl of water for the dogs.

'Thank you.' Jen sat down and picked up a magazine to fan herself, and the dogs drank greedily from the bowl before retiring to the shade beneath the chairs. 'It's comfortable, but small, like the other cabins. Our house in England was a lot bigger, and it's been hard to get used to just one storey.'

'I shared a one-room shack with Rose and Billy for most of my life,' Nita said, 'this is large in comparison.' She'd meant it to sound comforting rather than harsh, but Jen flushed and looked mortified.

'I'm so sorry, I didn't mean to brag, or complain. That couldn't have been easy for you.'

'It's fine,' Nita said. 'It was all we knew until we moved into the trailer. Life was hard, sure, but Rose and Joe made sure we were happy.' She squinted up at the sky, and smiled. 'I don't miss the winters, though.'

Jen pulled a face. 'I wouldn't mind a bit of cold right now, to be honest, I'm melting.' She closed her eyes against the glare of the sun. 'I don't envy John and Ron's job right now either. If it wasn't wildfire season they could

254

at least have given Pete and Ellie a cremation, instead of a burial.'

They fell silent for a while, listening to the buzz of activity from the cabins around them, from the short queue of newcomers, lining up to have their details taken, and, beneath it all, the contented breathing of the dogs slumbering beneath their chairs. Nita had almost dozed off, when Jen spoke again.

'So, after what proved to be a very enlightening meeting, what did your friend Moki think of us? He's difficult to read.'

'He is, isn't he?' Nita smiled. 'Moki's a great man, and a good one. But he's proud, and can be secretive too. He liked you all, though.'

'Really?' Jen looked relieved.

Nita nodded. 'So much so, in fact, that he's suggested a meeting between our council of elders, and your own council, to discuss the help we might give each other in settling here.'

Jen gave her a delighted smile. 'It would be wonderful to have you as neighbours. I don't see any reason it wouldn't work.'

'We could help get your power up and running,' Nita went on, 'and you could do the same for us. Here, you're on the edge of Eagle County, with everyone else in Garfield, and the next county along is Mesa. It looks to be good land for growing corn, and it has a hydroelectric plant nearby. Yes,' she nodded, 'neighbours would be a good start.'

'Start?'

'Our council isn't ready to fully accept your way of life yet,' Nita said gently, hoping it didn't sound judgemental, 'but is happy for us to be mutually beneficial neighbours.'

'Ah, then yes,' Jen said, 'it *is* a good start. Trading crops, and building a strong relationship. A lot of people, including me, would miss you and Belle if you had to leave.'

'And it's not just food,' Nita went on, 'that same cornmeal you enjoy as bread can also be made into ethanol.'

Jen's eyes widened. 'Really?'

'Sooner or later we're going to run out of gas, and ethanol makes a good substitute.' Jen's earlier words sank in then, and Nita fell silent for a moment, touched.

'I'd miss you all, too,' she said at length. 'You've made me, *us*, so welcome.'

Jen reached out and squeezed her hand. 'I can't wait for this special vaccine,' she said, 'life can go on again as normal. It'll be all thanks to you, you know.'

Nita laughed. 'With just a little help from Otto and the girls,' she pointed out. 'Speaking of which, where are they?'

'In Otto's lab, working. Ross and Tommy, the American boys, are helping Clare with newcomers' blood tests for the time being.'

'Ah.' Nita shrugged. 'I'd hoped Ruhi and Alima might take instruction from me about natural medicine, but I understand they've gone in another direction. Still, Ross and Tommy have shown an interest, so I'll start teaching them soon.' She sipped her drink, enjoying the cool, sharp taste. 'Oh, and I want to propose a joint medical centre,' she said, 'modern and traditional, working together.'

'Great idea.' Jen gave Nita a sly look, and the hint of a grin touched her eyes. 'It would also mean you and Ron working together.'

'Huh?' Nita gave her a puzzled look that she could see was cutting no ice.

'Oh, come on, we've all noticed the attraction between you two.'

'I don't know what you're talking about,' Nita began, then subsided. 'Is it that obvious?'

''Fraid so.'

Nita flushed. 'I tend to scare men off,' she confessed. 'But Ron just seems to take my...' she trailed away, unsure how to say it.

'Temper? Anger? Jen supplied, but there was humour in her voice, and Nita smiled.

'Yes, both of those. He just...accepts them.'

'He's a good man,' Jen said. 'And you're a strong woman, but...' she gave a faint shrug, then her eyes met Nita's, and held them for a long moment. 'The people you're angry with are long gone,' she said quietly. 'Don't let them win.'

Nita nodded slowly. 'Thank you.'

Another silence fell between them, but it was comfortable now, and after a moment Jen changed the subject. 'The girls are so excited about having their hair done. Is it the way your people decorated their hair?'

'Well, we did plait it, and used beads sometimes too, but what I did was my own style. I'll show the girls how to do it, and let them create something original for

257

themselves.' She saw a strange look cross Jen's face; part fondness, part aching regret. 'What is it?'

'I was just remembering the last time the girls did something crazy to their hair,' Jen said. 'They were trying to be Christina Aguilera. It all seems so long ago. Another life.'

'You miss that time?'

'In some ways. But it's...' Jen faltered, searching for the words. 'It's a bit like missing a film, or a book, in a weird sort of way.' She visibly shook herself. 'Like I said, another life.'

It was Nita's turn to offer a touch of understanding, and Jen smiled her thanks. Across the way, the queue of newcomers had dwindled away to nothing, and Holly and Hannah were closing the laptop and tidying their table.

'Looks like they've finished for the day,' Jen said. 'They'll be over to see you soon, no doubt. Oh, and Ruhi and Alima will be here too, in a bit. Clare's picking them up from Otto's when she delivers today's samples.' She settled back in her chair. 'Better enjoy the peace, before they all descend on us.'

***

Carbondale
Ruhi Nasir stood quietly with her sister, while Otto peered into his microscope. He was silent for a long time, and while Alima stared fixedly at him, awaiting a verdict, Ruhi's attention wandered to the equipment with which Otto had stocked his home-made laboratory; all had been transported here, the moment it was safe to move from

258

Hope Meadows, from the closest state hospitals and universities.

The rest of Otto's living arrangements were sparse, almost an afterthought. He barely used any power anywhere else, in order to keep a good supply for what had once been a large master bedroom, so it was always a treat to step in here, into light and warmth, and the promise of new discoveries at every turn.

On the other side of his bent form, Alima was still staring, unblinking, as if worried she'd miss something if she moved, and Ruhi was about to say something when Otto at last straightened and pressed the heels of his hands against his eyes.

'It's still too early to tell, girls.' They both started to voice disappointment, but he held up a hand. 'We *have* to get the timing right here; we don't want UEP1 to kill off the weakened virus before it's had the chance to circulate in the host. We need to form a timescale for effectiveness, but...' he smiled, then, 'it's looking good.'

Alima beamed. 'That's brilliant—'

'Did you hear that?' Ruhi frowned, turning, her heartbeat picking up a little. 'I thought I heard something.'

'I didn't,' Alima said, and Otto inclined his head, then shrugged.

Ruhi subsided, but as the three of them turned back to the microscope, the door crashed open and she uttered a breathless little cry. A heavily-built man stood there, and as her terrified gaze dropped to his hand Ruhi saw he held a gun, and that there was something strange attached to it that made the barrel longer and thicker. He brought it up and let its awful black eye travel between the three of

259

them, and, almost worst of all, he was smiling. A horrible, sick sort of grin.

Otto pushed himself in front of Ruhi and her sister, but his voice was shaking. 'Who are you? What do you want?'

'Doesn't matter who I am. But luckily for you, little man, I haven't come for you. Yet.'

'What, then?'

'Them.' The intruder gestured at Ruhi and Alima with the gun. 'And all the... ingredients, or whatever, that they need to make a vaccine.'

'You can't—'

'So,' the man went on, the smile dropping away as impatience took its place, 'I suggest you help them pack it all up. We have our own equipment, we just need everything else.'

'Who's *we?*'

'People you don't want to piss off. So let's move it.'

Ruhi and Alima exchanged looks of horror, but it seemed Otto was not going to stand by and do nothing. He pushed the girls further behind him, and though his voice still trembled he spoke up clearly.

'I won't let you take these children! You can take me, instead... surely I'm—'

'Yeah, you'd think. But my orders are to get the freak twins here. Now no more talking. Move!'

Otto turned to the girls, his face white, and desperation written all over it. 'I promise you I'll think of something... I'm sorry.'

He carried a vaccine porter over to the freezer, and they began packing samples while the gunman waited, making impatient huffing sounds, and pacing by the door. Alima reached for a sample marked with Nita's details, but Otto spared a quick glance at the man by the door, and gently moved her hand away, using one finger to gesture *no*, out of the intruder's sight. He removed the vial and slid it into his pocket, then put the last two samples into their slots.

'We're finished,' he said, his voice low and angry, and the man, who'd been listening intently at the door, turned back.

'Good. Now move away from the kids.' When Otto hesitated, the man raised the gun so it was levelled at Otto's chest. 'I don't always obey orders,' he said, almost conversationally, 'so if you want to live you ought to move away. Now!'

Otto did, with evident reluctance, but as the man took a step towards them, they heard a knock at the front door. The man held a finger to his lips, and brought the gun around to bear on Alima, who was nearest. Alima almost cried out, but Ruhi seized her hand and gripped it hard; any sound now might make this crazy man pull the trigger.

Alima bit back her shriek, but Ruhi saw tears of terror in her eyes, and her own vision was blurred too... they remained breathlessly silent, at the same time praying for whoever it was to somehow realise there was trouble here, to find someone, and tell them. It had always happened like that on the TV.

There were no more knocks, but just as the man started to relax and lower his gun again they heard footsteps in the passageway downstairs, and then in the kitchen. A glance at the clock showed Ruhi it was around the time Clare was due to pick them up, and her heart sank as she realised it wasn't someone who would just give up and walk away after all.

A moment later the footsteps sounded on the stairs, and Clare's voice drifted up to them. 'Otto? I've put your dinner from Sinead in the kitchen. Are the girls ready?'

Otto shot a look at the intruder, who shook his head in warning.

'Not yet,' Otto called, then cleared his throat and tried again, more strongly. 'We're in the middle of something important. I'll bring the girls over in a little while.'

'No you won't,' Clare said. 'Look, I've got your samples here and they need to go in the fridge. I'd do it for you,' she added, 'but it would have been more helpful if you hadn't moved half the kitchen white goods up here.' They heard the amusement in her voice; it jarred with the tight sense of fear that permeated the lab.

'Just put them on the floor,' Otto called desperately. 'I'll collect them later. Please, Clare, just go... we're busy.'

'Oh, for heaven's sake, you have to stop work sometime,' Clare said, laughing. 'Your dinner's getting cold, and the girls are expected home for theirs. You can't expect them to keep the same crazy hours you do!'

The intruder leaned close to Otto. 'Clare who?'

'Hampton,' Otto said, through tight lips.

The man's eyes widened a fraction. 'Richard Hampton's wife?' Otto nodded, and the man's thin smile returned. 'Well, why didn't you say so?' He stepped up so that he stood directly beside Otto, and now the gun was aimed at the door. 'Ask her in.'

Otto's face went utterly white, and he choked out, 'Clare, go!' A second later the gun swung against the side of his head, sending him crashing against the desk. Through glazed eyes Ruhi saw his head bounce off the polished wood, and before she or Alima could move, or cry out, the door had opened.

'What was that?' Clare had taken two steps into the room before she realised what she had walked into, and she stopped dead, her mouth half-open to speak, but no words came out. Her gaze went to the sprawled, motionless form of Otto, and then to the girls, and finally the gun that rose in front of her.

There was a hollow, muffled popping sound, and a crash as Clare dropped the samples she'd been carrying. A growing red stain appeared on her shirt, and the look of astonishment froze as her knees buckled, and then she dropped, her head hitting the polished floor with a sickening crack.

Breathless with terror and unable to utter a sound, Ruhi and Alima reached out blindly to one another and clung together. Ruhi's eyes were closed tight, but the image of what she'd just seen burned as if she still saw it. As she breathed hard to try and calm the shaking in her limbs, she felt herself grow lighter. A familiar and pacific feeling stole through her, and she sensed the same thing happening to Alima as her sister's grip eased and they began to separate, to lean less on one another. For a single, blissful moment, she felt everything would, strangely, be alright, but a voice barked out.

'You can stop that hocus pocus shit *right now!* Or someone will come and do to your parents what I just did to the Hampton bitch!'

The jolt back to reality was sudden and devastating, but the intruder's voice was calm again as he rummaged in his jeans pocket. 'Now, where's that list? Right, yes. We'll also need your notes, and all the items to do with your stem cell research, okay? Hurry it up.'

Both girls remained frozen in place as he shoved the paper back in his pocket, and he returned their stare for a moment before yelling, *'Now!'*

The man, who'd irritably told them to call him 'Rom,' instead of 'Mister,' pulled Ruhi out of the car first, and as she stood on trembling legs she felt the plastic rub painfully at her wrists where zip ties kept them bound tightly. The blindfold was itching, and sticking to her skin with the heat, and she found herself longing for nothing so much as a breath of cool air and a drink of water.

She heard Alima whimper as she too was dragged out of the car, and wished she could go to her and offer some comfort, but there was no time; Rom had seized her elbow and, presumably Alima's too, and was marching them across what felt like concrete.

They heard the clanging of a metal door, and then they were inside, where it was at least blessedly cool. Ruhi heard Alima give a gasp, and her own echoed it as her wrists were released, and her blindfold removed. She blinked and rubbed her eyes, then looked around to see they were in a dark stairwell, lit only by the beam of a flashlight. Rom had a Medpac tucked beneath his free arm, and the vaccine porter in that hand, and was clearly in no mood for waiting around while his captives tried to get their bearings. There was a painted *Level 1* on the wall at the bottom of the stairwell, and Ruhi moved towards the stairs, her hand out ready to grasp the metal railing.

'Not that way,' Rom said sharply.

Ruhi and Alima glanced at one another, puzzled, but Rom swiped the air with his wrist, just in front of the adjacent wall and they watched, briefly mesmerised, as an opening appeared to reveal another stairway leading away into blackness. At an impatient nod, Ruhi once more led the way. Their feet clattered on untreated concrete, and Rom's torchlight flickered wildly as he came down behind them, every now and again disappearing entirely as he shifted his grip on his burdens.

At the bottom of the stairwell, the sign read *Level -1* and they stood in front of yet another door. Ruhi wiped her sweating palms on her jeans and swallowed a renewed feeling of unease, and on Rom's instructions she took hold of the door and pulled. The jumping shadows retreated, and they began walking along a huge, and thankfully well-lit, corridor.

Once inside, after they'd been cleared by the guards, they were taken to a large, tiled room, that smelled of chemicals and echoed with every footstep. It reminded her of the swimming baths back in Brighton, where they'd lived before, but there was no sense here of the anticipation of fun splashing about with friends. It just seemed to make everything worse, remembering those days.

265

Rom left them, with instructions to strip down, shower thoroughly, and put on the clothes that had been left on the chairs. Alone at last, the girls embraced until they could feel their shaking easing away, and then spoke for the first time, in low, horrified voices, about Clare's death and their worry for Otto. It seemed unthinkable that such a thing could have happened, yet here they were... And what would happen to them now?

At length they realised someone would be waiting for them, and reluctantly undressed, working out how the shower worked between them, and standing beneath the hot spray for as long as they dared, as if it could wipe away the memories.

They pulled on the clothes they found draped across the backs of the chairs in the changing cubicles. Ruhi folded the dangling sleeves back, and turned up the cuffs of the trousers, seeing Alima doing the same as she pulled back the plastic curtain. Coming out of the room they met Rom going in, wearing only a towel around his waist and clearly having just undergone the same rigorous cleansing.

Across the way a door opened, and a woman in a white coat beckoned them closer, with a smile that looked too wide. As if she were dealing with toddlers. Ruhi felt a flash of anger, and gave the woman a belligerent stare, deliberately letting her sleeves unravel, and flapping them pointedly.

The woman coughed. 'We didn't have anything in your size,' she said, 'but once your own clothes are laundered you'll be able to have them back.' She held out two white rectangles with metal clips. 'Put these on, so we don't get you muddled, and follow me.'

Ruhi and Alima took the name tags and fastened them to the pockets of their over-large shirts as they hurried after the woman, who called back over her shoulder, as if she couldn't even spare the time to stop and talk to them properly.

'My name's Julie Parker, and I'll be working with you in the medical centre. Keep up, we're going to see the President.'

'Of what company?' Ruhi asked, and Julie threw a prideful little smile back to her.

'Of the United States.'

'She's alive?' Alima asked, her eyes wide.

'No. Sadly President Philips contracted the virus and died. Vice-President Holloway has naturally stepped into the role.'

Ruhi walked close to Alima, and began to speak quietly in Hally; *'don't tell her anything that might help them—'*

'Girls!' Julie stopped at last, and swung around. 'No twin-speak allowed. English only. Understand?'

They nodded, but at least Ruhi had managed to get the message across, and for the rest of the time they remained quiet, but held hands. It helped. She tried to memorise the way they were going, in case an opportunity came for them to run, but she soon gave up; it seemed to her that they were walking in circles, and they had both completely lost their bearings within a few minutes. Each corridor into which they turned looked exactly like the others, and there were no door markings to help, but eventually Julie stopped by one that stood open.

'Wait here,' she said, and went inside. Ruhi and Alima looked at one another, and back down the corridor...

267

surely it was worth taking the chance? But before they could do any more than think of it, Julie had returned and was ushering them into the office.

There was a man sitting behind a large desk, who they vaguely recognised from way back on the TV, but he introduced himself anyway. 'Welcome Ruhi, and Alima,' he said, reading the names from their tags and addressing each in turn. 'I'm Max Holloway, and I'm so glad you accepted our invitation to join us. Please, do sit down.'

Invitation? Ruhi and Alima scowled at one another in shared disgust, but they took the seats Holloway indicated. He pointed to the other man in the room.

'This is Colonel Hampton, and... ah.' He looked up as someone else came into the room behind them. 'Rom, you've already met.'

They glanced back and shuddered at the sight of him. At the showers he had seemed almost normal. Even harmless. But now they remembered the frightening, indestructible man in the lab and the stairwell; the man who had shot dead Clare Hampton without a moment's thought. Hands clasped across the gap between their chairs, they turned to the front again as Holloway carried on talking.

'You're probably wondering where you are, and why you're here.' They nodded. 'Well you're in a top secret complex, and you're here to help us. Does that make you feel better?' They didn't respond, and Holloway went on, 'You're here to give us all immunity from the virus—'

'Our family and friends will come looking for us,' Ruhi blurted, trying to sound strong and certain.

268

The President smiled kindly, but there was an edge to it. 'I've no doubt they will, young lady, but they won't find you. After all, *you* don't even know where you are.' He seemed to relent, then. 'Look, all you have to do is complete your work here, and then we'll send you home. You won't be harmed, so there's no need to be afraid.' He gestured to the woman. 'Julie here will take you to the medical centre, and show you your lodgings. You won't be staying in the barracks with the others, don't worry.' His practiced smile widened. 'And she'll fetch you a meal too. I'll bet you're starving, right? It's getting late now.'

'Barracks?' Ruhi asked. 'How many people are there?'

'Getting on for 200 serving personnel,' he said. '185, to be exact.' He looked satisfied as the girls' eyes widened. 'This is a huge complex, but we can't stay here forever. We need your vaccine to be able to rejoin the world. For me to take up my presidential duties properly. So, you see, you have a most important role to play in ensuring the return to order of this great country.'

Now he sounded more like the politicians did on TV, but when neither girl responded, he cleared his throat and went on in a more normal voice, 'Julie will attend to your needs, and she'll also be your assistant.'

Julie stepped forward. 'Sir, will they need to be chipped?'

'That won't be necessary, they'll only require access to the medical centre and their lodgings, and you'll be in charge of their comings and goings from there.'

'Yes, sir.'

Hampton spoke up for the first time. 'So. We know you can provide vaccinations, but I'd like to hear about your stem cell research.' They remained silent, and he went on, with some impatience, 'I understand, for instance, that you've discovered a method of bone marrow transplantation without the need of a perfect-match donor, or the need of chemotherapy or radiation to prepare the recipient. Is that true?'

'How did you...' Alima looked at Rom, and frowned. 'Oh. Of course. Yes, we have, and it'll work. Although we haven't trialled it yet.'

'We developed an enzyme that will destroy recipient bone marrow cells without the need of harmful procedures,' Ruhi added quietly. 'We also found a way to prepare donor cells, so that they'll be accepted safely by a host.'

'And how long would this treatment take?'

'Normally it would take months until a patient is fully recovered, but with our method it should take less than a week.' They had been so proud of their discovery, but now there was neither pride nor excitement in sharing the details.

'That's amazing,' Hampton said. 'I'm *actually* impressed, and that doesn't happen often.

Well, girls,' Holloway said, 'you're going to get your chance at putting your work into practice.' He and Hampton smiled at one another, but Ruhi didn't like that smile one little bit.

'Well,' he went on, slapping his hands down on the arms of his chair, 'I think it's time Parker showed you to your room. It was nice to meet you both. Thank you, Parker V-30... Julie.'

'Sir.' Julie saluted the officers and gestured for Ruhi and Alima to follow her. The girls stood up but remained sullenly silent, and didn't so much as glance back at the President as they followed Julie from the office.

The medical centre was impressive. It even had its own theatre, and, under different circumstances, they'd have been happy to have been shown around. But now they merely followed Julie wordlessly as she walked them through it. Normal medical procedures were going on as they passed through the ward; here, someone was removing stitches from an arm, and there someone was tending to a head wound. Ruhi wondered how these people were coming by such injuries in a place like this, but her silent question was answered as Julie tutted at the men.

'Maintenance. Again. You boys should take better care of yourselves.'

No-one replied, and no-one spoke to either Julie or the girls as they passed by, but everyone stopped to look, and to follow their progress in a way that both Ruhi and Alima found frightening; Alima's hand stole out again and found Ruhi's, and they both held on tight.

The ward had looked huge, but Ruhi soon realised that ahead of them was a mirrored wall, and that three of the figures she could see walking towards them were in fact Julie and themselves; they reached the end of the ward far more quickly than she'd expected.

Julie swiped them in through another door, and they found themselves in a lab with a door at the far end. They

271

turned to see the whole of the wall behind them was a window, looking out onto the ward they'd just come through.

'It's a two-way mirror,' Julie said, seeing them blink in surprise. 'You can see out, but no-one out there can see in. Just as you couldn't.' She pointed to the other door. 'A room has been set up for you through there. Have a look around and get yourselves acquainted with everything, and I'll be back in a bit with your evening meal.'

'We're… we're vegetarians,' Alima ventured timidly.

'Yes,' Julie said on a sigh, and rolled her eyes. 'You would be.'

As soon as she'd gone, Ruhi and Alima walked slowly through the lab to the room at the far end. Alima pushed open the door, and they looked at one another before they went in, dry-mouthed and frightened; it was all so horribly real now they were alone.

There were two single beds, upon each of which lay a white coat; bedside tables; a desk with two plastic chairs and some writing materials; and a chest of drawers. There was a bookcase too, with a few books, some games, and a couple of decks of cards. Another door led into what looked like a bathroom, and, no doubt, a shower or bath.

It took a moment for Ruhi to figure out what was missing from what looked, otherwise, like a perfectly acceptable bedroom for two, then she realised there were no windows. Of course, there wouldn't be. She remembered how far below ground they were, and the misery that had so far been suppressed by angry fear, finally swept over her. A glance at her sister showed her the same reaction had set in, and they sank, as one, onto the closest of the two beds, and wept.

What was happening back at Hope Meadows? Had someone found Clare yet? Had Otto recovered and fetched help, or had he died too, on the floor of the lab he loved so much? What about their parents? They hugged each other, and sobbed until exhaustion took over, and when they parted Alima dabbed at her sore and reddened eyes with her sleeve.

'Don't trust anyone,' Ruhi said, her voice thick with the tears that still choked her.

'I won't.' Alima sniffed, and gave a final, sad-sounding little hiccup. 'Why is everyone so unfriendly?'

Ruhi shook her head helplessly. 'Let's just get the work done, so we can go home.'

'D'you think they really will send us home after?' Alima sounded desolate, and Ruhi put her arm around her again.

'Of course they will,' she said resolutely, not believing a word of it, and she knew she'd not fooled her sister either. She looked around the walls, especially at where they met the ceiling, and couldn't see any obvious cameras, so she got up as if to explore, and took some writing paper and a pen from the desk. She sat down to write for a moment, then passed the sheet to her sister.

Just in case they're listening to us we should write down private stuff. Tonight when we're asleep, we'll try and contact the others like we used to. Now let's pretend to settle in. She waited quietly until Alima looked up and nodded, then took the paper back and went into the bathroom, where she tore the note to shreds and flushed the pieces away.

When Julie returned, they were at the table, giving a fair performance of being engrossed in a card game. Julie was pushing a trolley with their meals on it, and some fresh water for drinking. Ruhi wasn't hungry, but eyed the water with a fresh realisation of how hot and thirsty she was. She wouldn't give the woman the satisfaction of seeing it though, and made herself wait.

'When you're done,' Julie said, 'put your trolley by the lab door. I'll collect it later. You can relax for tonight, we start work in the morning.'

'Doing what?' Alima asked, also gazing at the tantalising condensation on the water jug.

'The bone marrow transplant.'

All thoughts of ice-cold water were banished, and Ruhi and Alima stared at her.

'But... it's never been done before,' Alima stammered.

Julie shrugged. 'Well I guess you'd better get it right then, huh?'

'Who will be the recipient?'

'Recipi*ents*,' Julie corrected her. First you'll work your miracle on the colonel, and, if all goes well, then it's the President. Then you'll be working on the vaccine.' She crossed to the door. 'The colonel will see you tomorrow morning, for tests.'

'Wait,' Ruhi called out, as Julie started to open the door, 'We'll need to meet the donor, too.'

Julie turned back, and a strange, cold smile crossed her face. 'I'm looking at her.'

Chapter Fifteen
Nita's Vision

Hope Meadows

John heard the sound of his daughters' laughter as he walked up the steps to his cabin, and stopped, feeling a smile creep cross his face. He couldn't resist taking a step to the side and peeking through the window, where he saw Holly and Hannah swishing newly beaded and plaited hair, and each exclaiming over the way the other looked.

He heard them thanking someone, and angled his vision so he could see the rest of the room; Jen sat on the floor smiling up at them and petting two of Nita's dogs, and Nita herself had the older dog on her lap as she sat on the sofa.

'We're going for a walk,' Hannah said, and Jen and Nita lifted their hands in farewell; John stepped aside as the twins came past him, accepting his compliments with studied graciousness, and then went indoors.

'Walk!' Jen was laughing. 'Gone to show off their hair, more likely.'

'Hi, girls,' John said. 'And boys,' he added, as Boss and Echo turned their grinning faces to him.

'Hi, love,' Jen said, her smile fading in concern. 'All okay?'

'Yeah, it's done.' He grimaced down at his muddy jeans. 'I'm going for a shower, stick the kettle on?'

By the time he returned, Jen was alone. 'Nita's gone to drop some lemongrass to Maya,' she said. 'She'll have a chat with Ruth too, while she's waiting for Ruhi and Alima to get back. I called Otto's radio to ask when they'd be ready, but he didn't answer.'

'He'll have his head over a microscope,' John said. 'He wouldn't hear if Motörhead were playing in the next room.'

They made the most of the peace, sitting close together while John told her how the burial had gone, and then their talk gradually moved to brighter things; to Nita's explanation of how her people saw their relationship developing, and then to the girls' pleasure when Nita had showed them how to do their hair.

'It's good to see them being children again,' Jen said quietly. 'It seems such a long time since we saw them have real, innocent fun. We forget they're so young, still.'

John squeezed her hand, and was about to reply when Nita knocked at the door. He realised it had been an hour since he'd got home, time which had passed so quickly in the simple but rare pleasure of just sitting and talking to Jen.

'They're not back yet,' Jen said, as Nita came in.

'Have you tried Otto's radio?' Nita asked, a little frown appearing.

'Just after you left. You know what they're like when they get stuck into their work, and Otto's just as bad, if not worse. It's times like this I miss having a phone.'

John shook his head. 'It's like you said though, Jen, they're children. They shouldn't be working this hard.' He checked his watch again. 'Give them half an hour, then I'll go and fetch them myself. Could be a car problem.'

Nita nodded, then glanced out of the window. 'You're popular today,' she said, 'more visitors.'

John followed her gaze to see Todd approaching, accompanied by Farrah Nasir. The girls' mother hurried up the steps ahead of Todd, but John had already crossed to the door and opened it.

'Come in, both of you. The girls aren't back yet though.'

'Ah. I thought maybe they were excited, and had come to see your girls first,' Farrah said. She was clearly doing her best not to look too concerned, but there was an edge to her smile as she came into the cabin.

'Mum's gone off without me, to get them,' Todd put in. 'She was supposed to wait, but I was a bit late back from the Springs. She *knows* no-one's meant to go anywhere alone at the moment.' He too sounded concerned, but was covering it well with a show of affectionate exasperation. 'She'll be the death of me, that woman.'

'John was just saying he'd go out in half an hour and check on them,' Jen said, 'in case they've got car trouble.'

'Thank you, John,' Farrah said. 'Would you mind if Ravi went with you? He's on his way over.'

'Not at all,' John said. 'Tell you what, no need to give it the half hour. We'll just wait for him to get here, and then go.'

***

277

The evening crept on, and Jen was disturbed to note how a small crowd had gathered nearby, as if unease were as virulent as the disease itself; it even transmitted itself to her, and she glanced at the clock yet again. Where were they? Car trouble or not, someone should have radioed back by now... Farrah had also picked up on it, but neither of them spoke as they waited. Todd and Sinead were among the group over by the perimeter fence, and, by unspoken agreement, she and Farrah went to join them.

After a short while, someone said they could hear engines, and they all turned to stare up the road, where John's jeep and Otto's car were slowly approaching.

Jen exchanged a relieved smile with Farrah. 'There they are!'

'Not before time,' Farrah said, a sheen of emotion in her eyes showing her relief.

But as the vehicles parked up, that unease returned. No-one moved for a moment, and the girls didn't spill from the back seat with their usual shouts of excitement at the revelations their work had afforded them that day. Holly and Hannah looked at one another in consternation, which made Jen even more nervous.

Ravi climbed out of Otto's car, and stood with one hand braced on the roof, his head bowed. Farrah took a step forward, trying to peer through the car's windows. 'Ravi? Where are the girls?'

He didn't respond. Jen's attention was caught by John as he helped Otto down from the jeep's passenger side, and she realised why the little scientist hadn't been able to drive for himself; congealed blood sealed his right eye shut, and the left side of his face was swollen and grazed.

278

She could see his legs were shaking as his feet touched the ground, and John had a supporting arm around him. *What had happened?*

Todd was talking to Sinead, laughing about something, and only now looked back at the little tableau by the two vehicles, realising his mother had not yet climbed out of either. He started at the grim sight of Otto, and Jen saw him press Sinead's arm as he made his way to the fence.

'Ravi!' Farrah shouted, the sudden panic in her voice finally reaching her husband, who lifted his head as if it weighed the world. 'Where *are* they?'

His eyes found hers as she stumbled towards him, and his voice was as blank as his expression. 'Taken,' he managed at last. 'They're...gone.'

Farrah stopped dead, and Jen saw her hands go to her chest, as if the words had stilled the breath in her body. She wanted to move, to help her, but Ravi had come to life and reached her first. He caught her before her legs gave out, and pulled her close, and then, his eyes suddenly wild and furious, he pointed at Otto.

'And *he* did nothing!'

'I'm so sorry,' Otto mumbled, his good eye was flooded with tears, and he looked ready to fall, despite the grip John had on him.

'Leave him, Ravi,' John said, and he sounded exhausted both physically and emotionally. 'There was nothing he could do, you know that, he was already unconscious.'

Jen and Doron joined him, and he looked over at Todd, who had reached into the jeep for the keys John had left in the ignition, and was going to the back to help his mother climb down.

279

He lowered his voice so that only Jen, Otto and Doron could hear. 'Listen... it was Veritas. They took the vaccines too, and...' he spared Todd a brief glance, 'and they shot Clare. She's dead.'

Jen wasn't sure she'd heard correctly, but the grim expressions around her told her she had. Doron's eyes had closed briefly, and John's face was white and strained as he turned to him. 'Can you take Otto—'

'Sure,' Doron said quickly. 'I'll take him to my place, he might have concussion. Will you tell Todd?'

John nodded. 'And we'll have to keep an eye on Ravi, too. I couldn't let him travel in the same car as Otto; you can understand why.'

Todd came over, as Ravi started to lead his wife away from the crowd. He looked mildly puzzled not to see his mother, but not overly concerned, and Jen realised he'd simply assumed she was busy elsewhere. Her heart twisted.

'I'm so sorry to hear about the girls,' he said to the Nasirs, his eyes showing his deep concern. 'We'll work something out and find them, okay?'

Ravi gave a curt nod, then, to Jen's dismay he patted Todd's arm. 'And I'm sorry about Clare.'

'Mum?' Todd blinked in surprise. 'Why, what's happened?'

Ravi opened his mouth, then merely shook his head, and led Farrah away, and Todd turned bemused eyes on John. 'What?'

Sinead joined them, and she must have read the truth in John's face; she reached for Todd's hand. He looked down at her, and Jen saw a muscle flex in his jaw as realisation hit.

'Where is she?' he asked, in a stony voice. 'Why didn't you bring her back?'

'There wasn't time,' John said gently. 'There was nothing we could do for her, and we had to get back, to begin a proper search for the girls. Besides that, Otto might have collapsed at any moment, and keeping Ravi off him was—'

'Crap!'

Todd tore his hand from Sinead's and ran to the jeep, and before anyone could stop him he had jammed the keys back into the ignition and twisted them. John's shout was drowned first in the crazily-revving engine, and then in the roar of tyres on dry, dusty ground as the jeep screeched around in a semi-circle and set off in the direction of Carbondale.

Sinead watched it in despair, and Jen went over to her and pulled her close, unable to think of anything to say. Farrah, realising what had happened, returned as well, to add her broken condolences amid her own anguish, and Ravi immediately snapped into angry action. He soon managed to persuade a few men to join him on a search party, but his unreasoning anger caused most to step back warily, realising he was not in a rational frame of mind. He cast disgusted looks at them, and signalled to those he had convinced, and as they came towards John, clearly hell-bent on taking Otto's car, John held up a hand.

'Wait, what are you doing?'

'To look for my girls,' Ravi said, as if he were speaking to a dullard. 'What else?' His hands were curled into fists, and he was evidently ready to use them against anyone who stood in his way, and Jen tensed, sensing little could be done to stop him once his mind was made up. She watched, a little fearfully, but felt a little flicker of pride as John didn't raise his voice above the angry murmurs, instead cutting beneath it, speaking only to the distraught man in front of him.

'Which direction are you going to look in, Ravi?' he said. 'You were there when we spoke to Otto's neighbours, you know no-one saw anything. They've been gone too long to find any trace just by looking for tracks.'

'Oh, but it's alright for *him* to go shooting off after his mother,' Ravi snapped, jabbing a finger after the direction Todd had taken, but he instantly subsided. 'I'm sorry. That was uncalled for.'

'Look, I get it,' John said, as the erstwhile search party broke up, realising they wouldn't be heading out yet. 'It's understandable that you're angry, I've been the same when my family's been at risk. But I've also learned that hitting out at others doesn't help.'

'But I can't just stay here and do nothing.' Ravi's voice dropped into a desperate, harsh whisper, and he visibly sagged. 'We've already lost our son, John! We can't lose our daughters too.'

'I know.' John put a hand on the man's shoulder. 'But we're not going to just be doing nothing. Look, right now your wife needs you. Be there for her. Remember, Ruhi and Alima have been taken for a reason, and that's to produce vaccines... they won't be harmed.' He glanced at Jen, then turned back to the stricken father and raised his voice slightly, to speak to everyone nearby. 'Tonight all the twins will be primed to contact them, to find out where they are.'

Ravi nodded. 'And then?'

John's voice hardened. 'As soon as we have that information, you have my word that we'll *all* go, together, to bring them home. No matter what.'

***

It had been a long time since Ruhi and Alima had visited the mountain; since the Fathers had delivered their message there had been no reason to do so. Tonight though, there was a fresh urgency as their sleeping steps took them to where John and Doron waited.

'We weren't sure we could still get here,' Alima said, as they accepted the warm, relieved hugs of the waiting brothers.

'Neither were we,' Doron confessed, 'but here we are, thankfully.'

'How are you?' John asked, looking them over anxiously as they all sat down by the mouth of the cave. 'Are you okay?'

'Our others are safe, but scared,' Ruhi said. '*We're* fine, for now.'

'For now?'

Between them, the girls explained Veritas's plan, watching the brothers' aghast expressions as they laid it out before them.

'It'll be uncomfortable to go through, for whichever one of us donates our bone marrow,' Ruhi said, 'but physically safe. The thing is...' she faltered, searching for a way to explain properly. 'This is different again from passing on a gene through a blood transfusion,' she said at length. 'That was temporary, and it faded. This is our actual DNA, and it's different to others. It contains the Fathers' DNA too, and it's permanent. No-one knows how, or even if, it will affect the spirit.'

John's voice was grim. 'We need to get you out of there. But we don't even know where *there* is. Can you tell us anything to help?'

'We timed the journey,' Ruhi said, 'it took about three hours, but don't know in which direction.'

'We were blindfolded,' Alima added.

John and Doron looked at one another, and, while it was impossible for their spirit forms to feel anger up here, it was clear they were deeply concerned for the way she and her sister had been treated. It gave Ruhi hope that they wouldn't give up looking for them. An awful memory surfaced, and she touched Doron's arm.

'Is Otto alright? Rom killed Clare...'

'Yeah,' Doron began, but John broke in.

'Rom?' Again there was no anger in his voice, but they saw he'd certainly recognised the name, and it had a nasty sound to him. He looked at his brother. 'That's one of Hampton's top men, the one who almost got me deported back to England after we arrived in Israel.'

Doron nodded, and turned back to the girls. 'I looked Otto over when he got back. He's suffering from concussion, his memory's a bit foggy, and he'll have a headache for a while, but he should start feeling better in a few days.'

'I'm glad,' Alima said. 'He tried to help us, you know.'

284

'We never doubted it,' Doron assured her with a smile. 'What can you tell us about where you are?'

'Only that we're somewhere below the ground,' Ruhi said, 'and that the people in charge are, like, soldiers and stuff.' She started to explain all she could remember about the President, and the colonel, but broke off and stood up as she saw Holly and Hannah appear a short distance away. She and Alima went to meet them, and the four friends hugged.

'I like your hair,' Alima commented, giving one of Hannah's plaits a little flick.

'Your turn next,' Hannah told her with a smile. 'Nita's waiting to show you how.'

Other shadowy shapes emerged, as more sets of twins found their way to the cave to offer whatever help they could, and Ruhi and Alima turned back to the grown-up twins, to tell them the rest of what they knew.

'Everyone in the complex, which is huge by the way,' Ruhi added, 'has a microchip in their wrist, which they use to open certain doors.'

'*In* their wrist?' Holly gave a shudder.

'Julie, that's the lady who's looking after us, said each member has access to different parts of the complex, and the people in charge know each time they open one of those doors. She thought we might've been given one too.'

'So all their movements are followed then,' John mused.

'They must have GPS trackers too,' Doron added.

'No.'

They all looked around, to see who had spoken. Leon and Luca, the Israeli twins the girls had first met on Mount Sinai, took a step closer, and explained.

'No-one's been able to place a tracker in a microchip yet,' Leon said, 'but we're working on that, too.'

'And in any case,' Luca put in, 'the GPS would have failed pretty quickly last year; there was no-one to monitor or calibrate it. The solar powered satellites will all be charged, but any readings would be totally inaccurate.'

Leon was frowning in thought. 'It sounds to me like all those doors must be wired to a main computer. The thing about microchips, is that they all have their own IDs, so when someone uses them to get in somewhere, that ID is registered. It's one way to know for sure where anyone is.'

'I'd guess in a place like that, they'd also have security cameras everywhere too,' Luca added.

'Thanks, guys,' Doron said. 'That information'll be really useful when we go to get the girls. We just need to find out where they are.'

Holly spoke up. 'If we can get inside, me and Hannah could disable that main computer.'

'You two won't be going anywhere,' John said firmly, prompting a chorus of protest from his daughters. 'No,' he said. 'You'll have to come up with something else.' He turned back to Ruhi and Alima, who couldn't help smiling at their friends' mutinous expressions; it had fleetingly made them feel better to see something so normal, amid so much strangeness and uncertainty.

'We'll keep in touch like this every night, okay?' John said. 'It might take some time, but we'll do everything we possibly can to get you out of there, and back home where you belong.'

As the comforting spirits around them slowly faded from sight, Ruhi and Alima reached for one another's hands; it was time to rejoin the fearful existence that awaited their sleeping selves, in their unknown prison far, far below.

***

Todd rose early, after a fitful night, and after an equally puffy-eyed Sinead had given the children their breakfast they sat quietly at the table, the steaming coffee in front of them untouched. Todd rubbed his face viciously hard, trying to drive some feeling into himself, to banish the numbness that had set in the moment he'd found his mother's lifeless form on the bed in Otto's house.

He'd stepped in, his breath locked, still not believing, even then, that this strong, capable woman was no longer part of his world. Her graceful white hand, which had no doubt been placed carefully at her side, had slipped off the low bed and now brushed the floor beside it. There was a sticky, deep red stain on the front of her shirt; it seemed that, at least, her death must have been quick, hopefully before she'd had time to register fear.

Swallowing a sob, Todd had knelt beside her and reached out to replace her hand, intending to wrap her carefully in Otto's bedding and carry her down to John's jeep. He'd braced himself for the cold, but the stiffness of her fingers made him cry out and withdraw. Then he looked at her face, at the eyes, fixed wide and staring

287

forever into nothing, and he remembered her calm voice when she'd taken Karl and Emily into her home, offering up her own immunity booster to protect them. She didn't deserve this.

He'd taken a deep breath then, remembering something he'd once read, and begun to gently massage his mother's shoulder and arm, loosening the effects of rigor just enough to allow him to replace her arm at her side, before wrapping her in the lightweight duvet beneath which Otto had slept. Who could ever have believed that today it would be put to such a use?

He had managed to make himself cover her face, but not before he'd pressed a final kiss to the cool, smooth skin, and somehow got her down the stairs and into the jeep. The drive back to Hope Springs had been a single mindless blur of rage and tears, and it wasn't until he'd parked by the fence that he'd come out of himself to find he'd been driving without thought or care; it was a miracle he hadn't ploughed John's jeep into a tree, or a stalled vehicle on the road.

She lay now, his courageous, selfless mother, beneath a fresh white sheet on her own bed, in a room she had left that morning never suspecting she wouldn't see again. Sinead had washed and dressed her quickly, before full rigor would have made it too difficult. Now all they could do was wait, and grieve, and question themselves, endlessly but without hope of satisfactory answer.

'She shouldn't have gone alone,' Todd said, for the hundredth time. 'What was she thinking?'

'She was a strong woman, love,' Sinead said, putting her hand on his knee. 'She can't have thought there was any danger to herself.'

'I wasn't *that* late,' he went on, 'and someone could have gone with her. *I* should have gone with her.' He could feel his feet jumping, alive with nervous energy and impatience to be doing something. Anything. 'The three main witnesses who convicted my... Richard Hampton, were Louise, Otto and Mum. She *should* have realised.' He let out a groan. 'If only I'd gone with her, none of this would have happened.'

'You don't know that, Todd.' Sinead squeezed his leg and let go, clearly accepting that she wasn't going to calm him by the gentle pressure. 'The man's a trained killer. If you'd gone too, he might have...' She broke off, and he looked up to see her blink away tears, but she couldn't finish the sentence. 'We might have lost you both,' she said instead, and lifted her coffee cup to disguise her emotions. 'If it wasn't for Otto's work,' she went on, 'he'd be dead as well. Veritas are keeping him alive as a back-up, so lay the blame on them, where it belongs.'

'If I find out my father had anything to do with this...' He trailed away as his gaze fell on the children, and knowing he shouldn't finish that sentence within their earshot, he got up and went to the front door. He pulled it open and stood looking out at the town, the formless anger burning its way through him, seeking an outlet and not finding one. Christ, it hurt...

'Todd?'

He focused again, to see Doron walking towards him. He found he was unable to share the greeting, nor even to extend a welcome; he just waited until Ron came closer, to see what the man had to say.

Doron put a hand on his shoulder. 'The others will be here soon,' he said, 'they're going to help you with the... the burial. I'm so sorry.'

'Thanks.' Todd knew his expression was still blank, and he forced the words out through numb lips. He gathered himself, and tried again. 'Any news on the girls?'

Doron seemed to relax a little. 'We managed to make contact,' he said, 'they know they're around three hours away, but not in which direction.'

'No help, then.'

'Well, they were able to figure out they're in some kind of military complex, or one that's military now, anyway. There are several possibilities within that time range, so there's a group heading out to check them today. The only one that seems feasible, with its own water and power supply, is the Cheyenne Mountain Complex.'

'Sounds like you need more information,' Todd said, 'that's a big area to cover.'

'I know. They're holding off until I get back from the Springs.'

'Why are you going there?'

'Nita's going to try and bring on one of her visions, to find the girls' location.' Doron gave him an awkward look. 'Listen, I'm sorry I won't make the funeral, but it's imperative we—'

'Yeah, of course.' Todd waved a hand that looked airy, but felt like a lead weight. 'I get it, you have to find them. Keep me updated, yeah?'

'Will do.' Doron clasped his shoulder again, and seemed to be struggling with his next words, but took a deep breath. 'You should know, it was Rom who took the girls, and who... who killed your mom.'

He studied Todd for a moment, for a reaction. He didn't get one, but as Todd watched him go, his hands once more formed into fists at his sides.

***

Glenwood Springs
Belle called Doron in to Nita's room, where he saw Nita had now changed into clean clothes and was sitting on her freshly made bed, waiting to begin. She had used his shower before they'd left Hope Meadows, since there was still no running water at the Springs, but her long hair had been dried by the warm breeze blowing through the open windows of his jeep; she smiled at him, a little nervously now, as she flicked it back over her shoulders so it hung neatly down her back. Belle moved around the room, straightening things here and there; the dogs were safe in Beau's care and wouldn't disturb them. There were no more distractions. No further tasks. Nothing to be done now, except face the reason they were here.

'My thanks to both of you for being here,' Nita said. She looked at Doron. 'I need Belle, since she understands the procedure, and what might happen.' She seemed to sense Doron about to express concern, and shook her head. 'Beau offered to stay too, but I think you're more likely to understand anything I might say. You're more familiar with the area, and with the twins.' She flushed

291

lightly, as she added, 'You'll also need to guide me, or... or lead me back to my bed, if I go wandering.'

Belle had brought a bucket over, and Doron thought he saw the twitch of a knowing smile at the corner of her mouth as she placed it in front of the bedside table; she must have seen the faint colour in Nita's cheeks, too. There was a clock on the table, along with a water tumbler, and, beside that, a small packet.

Belle poured fresh water into the glass. 'I found some white sage,' she told Nita, showing her a wide bundle, bound together with twine, 'but I couldn't get any pine so I've substituted it with lavender. Most relaxing.'

'Thank you, that's perfect.'

'What's all that for?' Doron asked, feeling like a clueless bystander.

'It's a smudge stick,' Belle said. 'To purify the room.' She took out her lighter and touched it to the ends, and when it began to smoke she moved around the room, wafting it gently. Soon the room was filled with the comforting and evocative scents of wood smoke and camphor, and of the joss sticks he had burned at college.

Nita leaned over and wound the clock. 'The ticking helped me concentrate on my first vision,' she explained, seeing his raised eyebrow, 'so I'm hoping it will do the same this time.' She replaced it, and touched the packet beside it. 'And these are two dried magic mushrooms that I... uh, found. They'll hopefully induce a vision. It might not be enough, but it's all we have.'

The doctor in him vied with the fascinated onlooker, but the doctor won. 'I'd rather you didn't have to do that.'

292

'So do I,' she said, 'but I've tried to force these visions before and it just doesn't work. All my previous ones have come of their own accord, I have no control over them. But it's so important that we find where those poor girls are being held.'

'And dare I ask what that's for?' He nodded at the bucket, and Nita gave him a rueful smile.

'I regret to say, you're likely to see me at my worst. It can take a little while to kick in, and the effects, although weakened, can last for hours. During that time, I might *just* throw up.'

It was his turn to smile. 'I'm a doctor,' he reminded her, 'I've seen a lot worse than upchuck.' He spoke more quietly. 'Is there anything I can do? You know, to make this easier for you?'

She shook her head, and her own soft voice matched his. 'Just be here.' She reached for the packet, and he instinctively moved to sit next to her on the bed as she unwrapped it. One hand stole out and rested gently on her back, feeling the tension there, but also feeling her relax, just a little. She turned towards him, and, emboldened by the searching look in her eyes he leaned closer and touched his lips to hers.

'For luck,' he murmured, drawing back.

They continued, for a sweet, intense moment, to look into one another's eyes, saying nothing, but both understanding the new promise that blossomed invisibly between them. At length Nita turned away and placed the mushrooms on her tongue. Keeping her face averted, she began to chew, and Doron sat very still until she indicated she was ready to lie down. He moved to a stool on the

293

other side of the bed, and watched as she stretched out; Belle was still moving silently, barely noticed, around the room with her smudge stick, and after a few more minutes she took her place wordlessly in a seat by the window.

They both watched the young woman, her eyes closed, motionless on the bed, and after what felt like hours but the ticking clock told him was only twenty minutes, Doron heard her steady breathing deepen, and he glanced at Belle, who nodded. *It's started...*

A familiar pulling sensation, and then weightlessness... She floated inside the rainbows once more, but, instead of reaching out to touch them, she felt the need to taste them. She licked each colour, like a child tasting lollipops. Freedom and lightness of soul brought a burst of joyful laughter.

When the rainbows cleared she was high in the air, looking down at unfamiliar land filled with a thick mist. She had never before had any control over where a vision might take her, and it was so hard not to give in to it, but, with all the strength she could muster, she concentrated on Ruhi and Alima.

Suddenly, from nowhere, there was a blue horse, rearing and pawing the air. There were white tepees in the background but they were too high, and so many people, weaving in and out of the mist, wandering around in different directions. Original Coloradans, by their dress; ancestors of Native Americans, but their forms were indistinct, confusing.

She called out, 'Katzper-soodge-away... I don't understand!'

As if drawn by her desperate question she found herself pulled towards the tepees. The next thing she saw did not correspond with what she expected to see inside, yet she knew she was in some form of

294

dwelling. After passing through many layers her feet now felt solid ground. A tunnel? No, a corridor.

She passed people, unseen, and walked on until she saw what looked like a hospital, then she was inside it. As she passed through, she was pulled to another room at the end, and once inside she saw Ruhi and Alima in white coats. They were taking the blood pressure of a man who had removed his shirt for the examination, and as she moved closer she saw it.

The mark of the bear.

Doron had smiled at Nita's childish antics and laughter at the start of her vision, but the poked-out tongue, and the look of wonder, had soon faded into puzzlement, and now into something much more worrying. She began to shake, and Doron picked up a towel and gently touched it to the sweat that had appeared on her brow, but Belle shook her head and he reluctantly stopped. He'd never felt so helpless.

The shaking and sweating went on and on, for a good half an hour, and all the while he wanted nothing more than to wake her, and tell her she was safe, but he forced himself to sit still. And to watch her. Much as it tore at his soul and made him want to look away, he owed her, and so he watched. He saw a flash of white in her hair, and wondered how he'd never noticed it before among the shining jet, but his heart turned over as he realised the more he stared, the more he saw.

He looked up and beckoned Belle closer, and she gazed down at Nita with such compassion and sorrow that he could do nothing else but rise and draw her close, in an embrace that comforted them both. Over her head he kept his eyes firmly on Nita, until he at last pulled back, and then looked down, asking silently if Belle was alright.

She nodded and patted his face in wordless gratitude, and they resumed their vigils, each absorbed by their own thoughts, but unable to look away from the young woman who meant so much to them both. And whose hair gradually, strand by strand, turned white even as they watched.

Nita's eyes flew wide, and her harsh gasp brought answering cries from Doron and Belle. She raised herself on one elbow, shaking harder than ever, and Doron was unable to stop himself from seizing her and pulling her close. Belle uttered soothing words as Nita's breathing calmed, and Doron felt able to let go of her. Belle gave her the glass of water, and she took a sip before sinking back against her pillow.

'I'll tell you what I saw, before I lose the details,' she said, her voice hoarse, 'but then I must sleep.' She looked up at Doron and caught at his hand, speaking urgently now. 'The girls are safe, but you must take back to your people everything I've found out. I don't understand it, but it might help, so you must go right away.'

He nodded, and wrapped his other hand around hers, hoping the simple gesture told her how important she was to him. He thought she understood; she held his eyes with hers while she told him everything she'd seen, but they were becoming glassy, and her face and neck were bathed in sweat; she had barely reached the end of her tale before she pulled away from him and lurched to the edge of the bed. She leaned over the bucket and convulsed, and

Doron gently took hold of her now snowy hair and held it away from her face while she vomited.

When the shudders had died down, Belle gave her a towel and she sat back, smiling weakly and wiping her eyes. Doron, his heart filled with awe and gratitude, brushed strands of hair from her sweating face.

'Thank you,' he said quietly. 'I knew this wouldn't be easy on you, but... oh, what you've been through for us.' He shook his head. 'Sleep now, you've earned it.'

Nita lay down and curled onto her side, drawing her legs up to her chest. Her hair had fallen onto the pillow, and she looked at it, sighed, and closed her eyes. She murmured something, but he didn't understand it, it sounded like, '*Tsh-arr-toot-sib*, Dakayivani.'

Belle stroked Nita's head as she drifted off into sleep. 'Yes, my darling,' she said quietly, 'white hair, like your great grandfather. Rest easy.' She looked over at Doron, and her old eyes were rimmed with both sadness, and tired acceptance. 'These visions are gifts, Mr Malik; but sometimes a price must be paid for a stolen one.'

Chapter Sixteen
The Message

Doron pulled up at the perimeter parking area, and waited while Moki reached for the stunning wreath he had laid carefully on the back seat. They climbed down and, as he gave Moki the keys to Nita's truck, Doron looked over to see John approaching, followed by what looked like most of the inhabitants of Hope Meadows, eager for news.

'My people made this for the lady, Clare,' Moki said, passing John the wreath.

'Thank you,' John said, clearly touched, and examining it with real appreciation. 'This is beautiful, I can see how much care has gone into the making of it. I'll give it to Todd.'

Moki nodded, and shook his hand, then Doron's. 'Please tell me when you have a plan, I know we will all help where we can.'

As the townspeople crowded around, he melted back and took up a place beside Nita's truck, watching quietly. Doron turned to the group, at the front of which, naturally enough, Farrah and Ravi stood waiting, their eyes telling him they half-expected a miracle. He told them, as carefully and fully as he could, of the vision Nita had explained to him, but even as he spoke he could see confusion and disappointment rippling through the crowd. His heart sank as he realised no-one understood.

'Is that all she got?' Ravi demanded. 'It's not much help, is it?'

'Ravi,' Farrah urged, her own disappointment emerging as annoyance, 'don't be ungrateful.'

'He's wasting our time! He goes off on some pointless—'

'Look,' Doron sighed, 'you're pushing my patience now. You have no idea what Nita went through to force this vision to help find *your* girls.' He saw Farrah flinch, from the corner of his eye, and wished he hadn't said that; the twins belonged to them all now. 'We're doing our very best,' he added heavily, and Ravi opened his mouth to say more, but Doron had had enough. 'If you can't say anything helpful, Ravi, I suggest you keep your mouth shut.'

Ravi's expression darkened, and he backed away and turned to look over the crowd, seeking out those who had been ready to help. Within a few minutes, as everyone watched in silence, he had gathered a group and they had moved towards their cars.

John appeared at Doron's elbow. 'Shouldn't we stop them?'

Doron shook his head. 'Let them go. I've been hard on Ravi, he needs to feel he's doing something useful. And you never know, they might find something to help.' He gave his brother a brief, wry smile, and dropped his voice so Farrah couldn't hear. 'Besides, don't you think it'd be easier not to have him around for a while?' He spoke up again. 'Okay, guys, I see Hope Meadows residents, and some of you have come over from Carbondale to help. Are there any Coloradans?'

299

A man somewhere near the centre raised his hand, somewhat self-consciously, and looking around him to see if he was the only one. Sensing his hesitancy, Doron smiled and gestured him forward. 'Maybe you can help?' he said when the man had come to the front. He briefly explained the vision again, in case the man had missed anything, and the Coloradan blinked and nodded before he'd even finished.

'Sounds like Blucifer,' he said eagerly. In answer to Doron's questioning look, he went on, 'It's what we call the blue mustang statue out at Denver Airport. You must have seen it when you arrived in Colorado?'

Doron shook his head. 'We came via Eagle County. Go on,' he added, his hopes lifting again, but the man shrugged, a little deflated. 'That's all I've got, sorry.'

'He's right,' another voice called out, and Doron looked up to see Paul Morgan pushing his way excitedly to the front. 'And I think I know what those tepees you talked about are, too.'

'Okay, let's have it.'

'I think they're the roof of the Jeppeson terminal,' Morgan said. 'It's designed like snow-capped mountains, but they could look just as much like tepees. You said the whole place was in a thick mist, right? So Nita might not have seen the runways, or planes.' His excitement grew. 'That *must* be the place, Ron! It has six levels, too, so that'd account for her feeling of passing through so many, don't you think?'

Doron turned as Moki came back, his own expression hopeful, though twisted in thought. 'The airport was built on the site of a burial ground,' he said. 'Local Native

300

American spiritual leaders performed a ceremony to put to rest the spirits of their ancestors. Nita must have been witnessing their—'

'That's right!' Paul broke in. 'I remember now; before I took up office in the Senate, my predecessor met with the leaders. Sorry,' he said belatedly to Moki, to excuse his interruption, and the old man inclined his head in acceptance. Excitement was understandable. Doron looked at John, and saw his own slow, relieved smile reflected on his brother's face.

John took a deep breath. 'The prophecy says that the one with the mark of the bear—'

'Will rise from the burial grounds,' Doron finished. 'That's it!' He shook Moki's hand, then clapped Paul's shoulder in thanks before he raised his voice again.

'Okay, for those who might not have heard, we're now as sure as we can be that the girls are being held underground at Denver Airport.' As the cheers rose, he held up a cautionary hand. 'But we also know it's a military complex, with high security. The way Ruhi and Alima talked about it, it'd be impossible to get anywhere near without being seen, and even then we'd have to get through blast-proofed doors. We'll talk to the girls again tonight, to see if they've got any more information for us.'

He let the murmurs of disappointment and frustration ripple through the crowd, along with the inevitable suggestions of burrowing, explosives, and distraction, and when it had run its course he spoke again, letting them hear the determination in his voice. 'I get it, it's hard to sit by and do nothing, but this is going to take special planning. All I can suggest is that you go back home, go

301

on with your work, get some sleep if you can... and be ready in the morning.'

***

Denver International Airport

The coffee looked like shit, and tasted worse. Still Ian sipped at it, because what else was there? Learning that his time at Hope Meadows was not to be repeated, and realising it had put an end to his hopes of warning the people there, had been hard to take with a smile, but he'd managed it. Appearing unaffected, indifferent, he'd left the President and the colonel to their plans and headed for the gym, and then the barber, where he'd demanded a buzz cut – and although he had been ordered to do so, it suited his mood.

The ready-meal sat in front of him in its plastic tray, untouched; his stomach was a knot of anger anyway, despite half an hour on the punch bag. He'd have been unable to eat it even if it had been the best Aberdeen Angus – to which it bore as much resemblance as a sloe berry to a bottle of gin.

'On a diet, huh?' Steve pulled out the chair opposite and nodded at the congealing food. 'Nice haircut, by the way.'

'Thanks.' Ian glanced around, and lowered his voice. 'Rom's back, from the mission I should have had, and I've no idea what he's been up to.' He sighed. 'I should've come clean to the folks at Hope Meadows before I left, but I'd no idea what the colonel's plans were, then.'

302

Steve pursed his lips. 'I heard Rom brought back two kids. Indian girls. Twins, I guess, from Hope Meadows.'

Ian's blood chilled. 'Ruhi and Alima?'

Steve shrugged. 'No idea, but they've been locked away in the med centre. A couple of guys from maintenance saw Parker bring them in.'

'Shit!' Ian rubbed at his prickly scalp. 'The poor bairns must be petrified, taken from their parents and being cared for by that cold-hearted cow.'

'Rom's been bragging about disposing of another traitor, too. Woman called Clare something.'

'Not Clare Hampton?' Ian felt ill at the thought.

'Maybe.'

'She's the colonel's wife, a lovely woman.'

It was Steve's turn to look surprised. 'I didn't know he was married.'

'Aye, he was. And I've met his son, too. You'll remember me telling you about Todd and his family? They're the ones who took me in when I got there. Smashin' people, all of them.' He paused and looked around again. 'Everyone here's been told that the twins were a government experiment gone wrong, but it's all lies.'

'Seriously?'

'The colonel was sprung from an Israeli jail, he's nothing but a murderer.'

Steve looked uncomfortable. 'What can we do about it?'

Ian shook his head, but his voice was determined. 'All I know is we have to get the lassies out of here.' He thought for a moment, chewing his lip. 'I'm on guard duty

303

Thursday evening,' he said at length, 'that's the only time I'll have access to the outer doors. If I can get a message to the girls today, they might be able to do their dream thing, and tell the others.' He frowned. 'Failing that, I'll have to get them out myself, somehow.'

'Thursday, huh?' Steve sat forward, his eyes distant as he thought aloud. 'If we *can* get a message out, that'll give them, what? Three days to come up with a plan.'

'I'm listening.'

'Okay, so we can't get in to see the kids, but their meals are taken straight to the med centre by Parker. Maybe I can get your message to them that way.'

'How?'

Steve gave him a knowing look. 'I know the cook pretty well, she used to give me extra rations before we started getting low on them.'

'Oh, aye?' Ian couldn't help returning his friend's brief grin, despite his worry.

'Yeah. Looks like all that flattery might finally come in handy. Write your message,' Steve tapped the table between them and sat back, 'and I'll put it in some saran wrap and hide it in their food. I've seen it done in a film, way back.'

'Did it work?'

'No,' Steve confessed, 'but that was prison. They know the kids can't escape from here, so they're not so likely to be looking for anything suspicious.'

'Well, it's all we've got.' Ian nodded. 'Aye, that's what we'll do then. If no-one shows on Thursday I'll know the message didnae get through, and I'll do my best to get them out, myself.'

Steve studied him for a moment, and now his own voice was sombre, but determined. '*We'll* do our best.'

***

Ruhi and Alima were absorbed in their work when the door hissed open, and Julie came in, still in her theatre whites and with a surgical mask hanging from one ear. She peeled off her gloves and dropped them into the waste bin by the door.

'You'll be pleased to hear the colonel's doing well,' she said, in answer to their wordless query. 'The PICC line was inserted satisfactorily, and the injection has been given.' Her words were admiring, but her voice remained neutral. 'Whatever was in the solution you created is killing his stem cells at a remarkable rate. His blood count's falling, and if all goes to plan, he'll be ready for the transplant tomorrow.'

'Okay.'

Julie looked from one to the other, and went on briskly, 'So, who's the lucky donor?'

The girls exchanged a glance. 'We haven't decided yet,' Ruhi said.

'Well you've got until tomorrow to make up your minds.' Julie looked at the dinner trolley, frowning at the leftovers. 'I brought this in an hour ago, and I'm not leaving until you've finished it. Can't have you undernourished for your big day, can we?' She frowned, as they didn't move. 'Come on, pick up the pace! I don't have all day, it'll be suppertime at this rate.'

Ruhi waited until the woman had turned away, then pulled a face at the congealing plates, but Julie must have seen her reflection in the glass. 'What was that for?'

'It's not very nice,' Ruhi said, after a glance at her sister, who nodded agreement.

'I suppose it's all parties and picnics back at your cosy little homestead then, is it?' Julie gave a soft snort. 'Well don't go imagining you're going back to that anytime soon.'

'What?' Ruhi's breath stuck and she couldn't get any further words out.

'Just that. You two aren't going anywhere.' Julie shrugged. 'They won't miss you for long, anyway.'

'They will!' Alima put in, her eyes wide and horrified. 'They'll be looking for us!'

Julie eyed them with something close to pity, but it was a cold, distant type of pity. As if they were nothing more than a couple of flies stuck in a net curtain. 'You really think a couple of little brown girls more or less is going to affect the world? Once your work is done we'll be well on the way to ridding the population of *your* kind.' She gestured at the plates again, and now her expression was flat. 'Now eat.'

The twins removed their own gloves, and wordlessly took their meals through to their room. They sat down to eat while Julie watched over them, but it was hard; neither was particularly hungry, and they were both close to tears; Ruhi knew her sister was finding it as hard to swallow as she was, past the lump in her throat. It was a relief when they'd finally managed to finish, and even more so when Julie whisked the plates away and left them alone.

306

Ruhi reached across the table and took Alima's hand. 'You mustn't listen to her.'

'She was just being mean, wasn't she?' Alima said, hope kindling in her eyes. 'They'll let us go, they have to!'

'No, I don't think they will.' Ruhi faced her sister squarely. 'But the one thing she *was* lying about, was how our people feel about us. They won't give up on us, and we have to trust that.' She came to a decision, though her heart trembled as she spoke. 'I'll do it,' she said, with a bravery she didn't feel. 'I'll be the one they take.'

Alima looked at her with brimming eyes. 'But that's not fair on you, you're always taking the lead.'

'That's because I'm oldest.'

'Bossiest, you mean.' Alima sniffed, and found a smile. 'Let's take a bet instead.'

'Like what?'

'I don't know.' Alima thought hard. 'We could bet on... what Julie's going to moan about next. I reckon she'll complain about not getting enough time off.'

Ruhi couldn't help but laugh a little at that, and she nodded. 'You're on. I bet she whines about having to bring us those beastly meals all the time.'

At the end of the working day, they both took off their whites and put them in the laundry basket with sighs of relief. At the same time, there was a tension in the air as they waited for Julie to appear with their supper.

Right on time, she came in with their supper trolley and a familiar scowl. 'I hope you appreciate this,' she said, 'I'm a trained nurse, not a goddamn kitchen maid.'

307

'Yess!' Ruhi automatically made a fist of victory, then stopped in dismay as she realised what that victory meant for Alima. How could she have forgotten the seriousness behind it all? She blinked back tears of remorse. 'I'm sorry.'

Alima gave her a trembly little smile. 'It's okay,' she said. 'You'd be better at looking after me afterwards, than the other way around, anyway.'

Julie didn't stand over them this time, and Ruhi sent a silent raspberry after her as she left; it somehow made her feel a little bit better.

'What gooey mess have we got this time?' Alima asked.

Ruhi took the lid off one dish and poked at it. 'Macaroni cheese?' she ventured. She took a fork and tasted it. 'Actually it's not too bad this time.'

Neither one of them wanted to bring up the subject of what they now knew Alima would have to go through, and so they ate in silence for a little while, until Ruhi's fork tine snagged something in her bowl. She pulled a face, and peered closer, but her initial distaste changed to surprise. 'What's this?'

Alima leaned closer to look, as Ruhi pulled it from her bowl and wiped some of the sauce off it. 'Dunno, but it's not food, for sure. Go and wash off that stodge and we'll have a proper look.'

Ruhi ran the plastic under a tap, rubbing with her fingers to wash away the last of the creamy sauce. 'There's paper inside it!' She patted the plastic with a piece of paper towel and peeled back the edge, drawing the folded paper out carefully. She opened it, with trembling fingers. 'It's a message!'

They pored over it together.

Dear Ruhi and Alima,

Get this message to the others, and we'll get you out of here on Thursday. Send one person to meet me at 1800hrs, Level 1 maintenance stairwell, via the middle west parking garage at Denver Airport. I can get them in, but will need help getting out.

Mustang Sally.

They read the message over a few times, memorising it, then Alima took it and ripped it into the smallest pieces she could, before flushing it down the toilet as before. She met Ruhi's eyes as they walked back to finish their meal, and the sudden, heightened sense of excitement and hope was like electricity. Neither one mentioned it aloud, though each knew the other was puzzling over who had sent it, and knowing they had a friend inside their prison, even if they didn't know who it might be, was enough for now.

***

Nita and Doron found a welcoming committee the following morning as they arrived at the Milburns' cabin. John and Jen were waiting for them, along with Sinead, and as they exchanged greetings Holly and Hannah came into the sitting room, with Leon and Luca. Everyone was staring at Nita, wide-eyed, and she couldn't work out why; it was unnerving, and for a moment she reverted to feeling like the newcomer again.

Then Holly spoke up, her voice awed. 'What happened to your hair?'

309

Nita relaxed and smiled. 'A side-effect from the vision yesterday. It was a shock, for sure, but I don't know... I kinda like it.' She flicked it, for emphasis, and Holly looked delighted.

'So do I! It's really pretty.'

'I like it too,' Hannah put in. 'Sorry for staring, but it was such a surprise.'

The boys didn't know what the fuss was about, and amused themselves by calling to the dogs, so Jen gestured for them to take the sofa, while John pulled up the dining chairs.

'I'm so sorry you had to go through that ordeal needlessly,' Jen said to Nita. 'If we'd only known someone was going to contact us anyway, through the girls—'

'Nothing's wasted,' Nita assured her. 'We had to try, or feel as if we were, and in any case the vision helped to decipher another part of the prophecy.' She turned to Sinead. 'How's Todd doing?'

Sinead gave a tiny shrug. 'Not great, but he's doing the best he can. I thought it was a good idea for him to take care of the kids this morning. He's never angry around them. And a bit of normality might help them, too.'

'We saw the girls again last night,' Doron began, once they'd settled into their seats. 'The first thing we have to tell you, is that there's no way those guys at the compound are letting them go. The woman in charge of them is as much a racist pile of crap as anyone, and she's made no secret of the fact that the master plan is to eradicate all people of colour.' He glanced at Nita, who raised her chin but said nothing. This was nothing new to her, but it was likely the first time her new friends had met such blatant – and lethal – bigotry first-hand.

'This is... terrible.' Sinead stared at them all in horror. 'So it's not just about the vaccine then?'

'Seems it's much bigger than that.' Doron's face was grim. 'And the girls were told we'd never bother to come and find them. That they were worthless to us.'

'Those poor kids,' Jen murmured. 'It's a blessing you were able to put them straight on that, at least.'

'Everyone should be told about this,' Sinead said, 'it's important we know what we're up against. I'll make sure the word's passed around, so everyone's extra vigilant. Especially around the kids.'

The others nodded, and Nita saw Leon and Luca swap a look that gave her hope for all their futures; these kids weren't going to let any harm come to their friends.

'The girls were also worried about the procedure they're going to have to go through today. And who can blame them?' Doron rubbed his eyes hard, and shook his head. 'We felt pretty useless at not being able to stop it.'

'But,' John added, with his usual keen sense of when optimism was needed, 'they were glad to report they have a friend on the inside. They didn't know who it was, and I must admit it didn't twig with me either, until I talked to Jen this morning.'

'Go on,' Sinead prompted.

'The girls were given a note smuggled in with their food,' John said, 'with some instructions on how we can get in there. It was signed, *Mustang Sally*. I thought it must have something to do with the mustang at the airport, until Jen reminded me of the first time she and Sinead saw

311

that Scottish bloke, Ian. That's the song he was singing while he was waiting to register.'

'Yes, it was.' Sinead frowned. 'So he's in with Veritas then? That doesn't make sense, if he's willing to help. He left without saying goodbye though, so what was he doing? Spying on us?'

'Seems likely,' Nita said. 'Do you remember my first impression of him? I felt at the time that he wasn't to be trusted, but that he was a good man. Maybe he had no choice.'

'Everyone has a choice,' Sinead said bluntly. 'We all became fond of him, especially the kids. And now we find out it was all an act, to find out more about us?' She shook her head, her expression grim. 'To think we were worried something had happened to him. The children were devastated. It's despicable.'

Jen spoke reasonably. 'Well, we don't know the circumstances, and he's definitely trying to help now.'

'Could it be a trap?'

Doron shook his head. 'Unlikely. What advantage could it be to Veritas, for us to go to their complex? It's been kept secret until now, and they would run the risk of being contaminated. No, I believe he's trying to help.'

'We have to believe that,' John said, though he sounded as reluctant as Sinead, 'and we've got three days, now, to come up with a plan. It's not going to be easy to explain that to their parents, but it's all we've got.' He looked at his daughters, who gestured to the boys to leave the dogs alone and pay attention. 'The kids have an idea,' he said, 'and I'm going to help them. We don't have much time but they think they can do it.'

'Ian's implant will be an RFID tag,' Leon began, 'that's Radio Frequency ID,' he added, as Sinead raised an eyebrow. 'The tag stores an antenna and a microchip, and the chip stores the code ID. With the right parts, Luca and I are sure we can make a gadget that can copy the tag, and use it ourselves to gain entry.'

Doron sat forward, interested. 'Why not just use Ian's tag?'

'Because we're going to write a software programme, called a virus, that can be added to the copied tag,' Holly supplied, drawing all adult eyes onto her and Hannah, who took up the narrative.

'Then, when our tag is scanned to get inside, the information from the virus will travel to their access control server along with it, and basically...' she shrugged, 'open a backdoor for us to get inside the computer to get control.'

'What's this *us?*' John asked. 'I told you girls you're not going. I'll have to go, I'm the only one who'll be able to do it.'

'You'll have to get inside the complex first,' Holly argued. 'We don't know how near you'll have to be, for the wi-fi to work.'

Jen still looked unsure. 'Why do you need to get control of their computer?'

'Because it controls all the doors,' John said, 'both internal and external. We don't see a problem getting in that way, but once they know we're inside they can shut the whole place down, and we'll never get out.'

Nita saw Jen visibly shudder. 'But I thought only one person was to go. And I don't like the idea of you being there on your own, John.'

'He won't be going anywhere on his own,' Doron said, putting a hand on her arm. 'Don't worry. Everyone who can fight, or help in any way, should go too, and we already have a lot of people willing. We'll organise them all on the outskirts of the airport, just in case they're needed, and after an agreed period of time they can all move in.'

John nodded. 'While we're working on the gadget side of things, Ron, perhaps you could let the men know, and organise it?'

'Sure, and tonight we'll let Ruhi and Alima know—'

'Hold on, why only the men?' Nita chipped in, bristling a little. 'We may not be as physically strong as you, but we're just as capable of fighting.' She looked around at everyone in turn, gauging their reactions, and was glad to see both Jen and Sinead straighten their backs; they were both tough women, she already knew that, and might prove invaluable in any conflict they might face. 'Everyone should be given the opportunity to decide for themselves,' she said, her voice quiet but firm. 'There are women at the Springs, and maybe here too, like myself, who have learned to fight. I for one will be going with you.' She saw Ron's mouth open ready to speak, but held up a hand that brooked no argument. Her smile, however, kept pulling at her lips. 'Yes, Ron, you said you need anyone who can help, so I *am* going too. And unless you want another broken nose you won't try to stop me.'

314

Denver International Airport

The breakfast tray looked strangely bare, with only one bowl, but even that remained untouched; Ruhi couldn't bear the thought of eating in front of Alima, who had remained nil-by-mouth since last night's supper. Alima herself sat quietly, her fingers knotting and twisting around themselves as she stared at the door, waiting for the moment when Julie arrived to change her forever.

It had taken a lot of persuasion for Ruhi to convince Julie to allow her to accompany her sister to the theatre, but, perhaps sensing a mutiny of some kind, the woman had eventually acquiesced, and both girls were now dressed in gowns and scrub hats, as was Julie herself.

The sisters walked, hand-in-hand behind her, down the long corridor to where the complex surgeon waited – a corridor that seemed to stretch forever ahead of them, yet conversely end too soon at the door to the theatre suite. Ruhi and Julie washed their hands and put on gloves and masks, while Alima climbed onto the trolley and lay facedown, as instructed. Julie, with surprising gentleness now she was doing what she was trained to do, inserted a cannula into the back of Alima's left hand, and Ruhi squeezed her right one.

'Don't worry,' she whispered, 'I'll be with you the whole time, and you'll see me as soon as you wake, okay?' She gave her sister the brightest smile she could find, and, as Alima's eyes slipped closed she felt almost as if the anaesthetic were affecting her too, but snapped back to reality as the trolley was wheeled into the theatre itself.

315

Once everything had been prepared, the surgeon inserted a terrifyingly large needle into the back of Alima's hip. 'We'll need to carry out two extractions,' he told them distantly, his eyes narrowed as they focused on his work. 'One from each side.'

Ruhi winced, as he attached a syringe, and began withdrawing fluid. When he began the second extraction she looked at Alima's face, and her heart failed her to see the face of her sister's spirit form appear, the mouth wide open in a silent scream.

Chapter Seventeen
Sacrifice

Thursday, 5.55pm

John's flashlight played over the inside of the designated maintenance stairwell, showing him nothing but bare concrete walls. A momentary unease gripped him, and he checked his watch; still a few minutes before the appointed time, there was nothing to say he was in the wrong place despite evidence to the contrary. He put down his bag and turned off his torch, and made himself sit down on the bottom step, though every instinct in him fought against inaction.

After a few minutes a low clunk sounded, and he started to his feet as one of the walls slid aside, almost noiselessly, to let the light of another flashlight spill through. He could just make out the tall, burly shape of the man who'd moved among the Hope Meadows people as a friend... Despite the hope offered during the dream meeting with the twins, the sight of the man in person was a different matter, and John instinctively tightened. He reminded himself that the Scotsman was redeeming himself now, at least, he seemed to be... But what if this was just another betrayal?

'Did you come alone?' Ian said, his voice low.

The question alerted John's original suspicion, but when he peered more closely he saw nothing but concern on the man's face.

'Yeah, I did,' he said after a moment. 'The others will give us an hour, and if we're not out they'll come in nearer to provide backup.' Not only reassurance, but also a warning, and he could see Ian recognised it as such.

The Scotsman nodded. 'Good. Steve, a friend of mine, will have distracted the techies in the surveillance room... they get bored easily.' A brief grin lit his face, but vanished when John didn't return it. 'They won't have seen you drive in, alone,' he added, 'but it would have been impossible not to notice a whole fleet of cars.' He checked his own watch. 'Steve will have made sure they won't have noticed the extra door scans either, which will buy us some time.'

He gave John a searching look, and John recognised his need to convince him of his trustworthiness. 'Are the girls alright?' he asked, knowing he'd only have the man's word for it either way.

'They're well enough, considering what they've been through. But they recover fast.'

That rang true enough, though John flinched at the thought that they'd been mistreated, and he felt his muscles tense again. 'They trust you? Enough to go with you?'

'Aye. I'm not sure I deserve it, but they do.' Ian's face softened, and that, more than anything, convinced John he was genuine in his wish to help them. He gave a nod and a half-smile, and Ian visibly relaxed.

318

'Right, I'm supposed to be out here havin' a piss, so I'll take you down to the next level then go back in on my own. Give me a minute to disable the other duty guard, and I'll be waiting for you.' As John followed him through the door in the wall, Ian held up his wrist once more and the door closed.

'Hold on.' John squatted to open his bag, and withdrew the laptop and the scanner. 'Give me your wrist a minute. This'll make a copy of your tag, so we can use it when we enter the complex.'

'No need,' Ian said, 'mine will work there.'

'But this copy will send a virus to your computer, so I can hack the server.'

Ian raised an eyebrow. 'How the—'

'Tell you later,' John said, his patience slipping. 'No time now. Just hold up your wrist and aim your torch this way.' He aimed the scanner at Ian's tag, and hit 'copy.' The red light turned green, and John attached it to the laptop with the USB cable. When he was satisfied the data had transferred, he looked up at Ian and nodded.

Once they reached the bottom of the staircase John nodded. 'Okay, on you go. I'll give you a few minutes.'

He made himself count to two hundred, then pushed open the metal door and found himself in a wide corridor. He caught sight of movement; Ian was waving him over urgently, then he bent and retrieved the unconscious guard's hand gun.

'Here,' Ian said, passing it to John. 'Get changed, quick. This bloke's a bit bigger than you, but better a uniform that's too big than too small.'

319

He helped John strip the guard, and John pulled the uniform on over his own clothes. 'How many people are there here?'

Ian rolled the guard against the wall with his foot. 'A couple of hundred.'

John frowned. 'Well if the complex is as huge as the girls say it is, surely this can't be the only entrance?'

'No, there's an emergency exit somewhere below this level, along with the reservoirs. I've never seen it, and don't have access, but I do know they send maintenance crews through it. They keep a 737 on standby for a quick getaway, so it's got to be kept in top condition.'

'Okay,' John said, satisfied. 'Once we're inside, get me as close to the computer room as you can.'

'Right. Steve will be expecting us both, but he won't know about the change of plan. I'll have to go ahead, and tell him to hang on for a wee while, but I'll take you where you need to go first, and then come back for you.' He glanced around them again. 'With any luck we'll be into the medical centre, and out of here with the lassies, before anyone else needs to get involved.'

'Let's hope so.' John pointed his scanner at the door, and, once they were through, Ian used his own to close it behind them. They made their way to a room containing only a few chairs and a whiteboard, and Ian left to appraise his friend of the situation. John chose a chair at the back of the room, where he'd be out of the sightline of the door, then opened his laptop again and set to work on the security system. He couldn't help marvelling at the skill with which the children at Hope Meadows had prepared everything; he could only hope their efforts would be rewarded by the safe return of their friends.

He put the programme through its paces, shutting down the door controls, and as his fingers flew across the keyboard, his mind leapt ahead to the possible outcomes – with all the luck they needed behind them, the doors would be primed to fail-safe rather than secure, leaving the doors unlocked to allow personnel to escape in the event of a mass evacuation.

'How goes it?' Ian had returned, without John noticing, so deep was John's concentration.

'I'm in,' John muttered, only briefly raising his eyes before focusing once more on the screen. He dug into his pocket, and threw a set of keys across. 'You go and get the girls, and take them in my jeep to the others. By that time they'll be waiting in the open air car park. It'll only be a little while before everything's disabled.'

He was vaguely aware of Ian backing out of the room, and the soft click of the closing door, before his mind was once more absorbed by rows of numbers and symbols... numbers and symbols which would, in a matter of minutes, mean the difference between life and death.

***

Ian gestured to Steve to keep out of sight, and rang the buzzer at the door of the medical centre.

The tinny voice wafted out of the door-com. 'Who is it?'

'Sloan V-198.' Ian injected urgency into his voice. 'Turner V-197 needs help!'

'You're supposed to go through the correct channels, Sloan. You need authorisation.'

'No time!' Ian banged on the door. 'I think he's having a heart attack. *Open the door, man!*'

After an endless wait, when Ian felt sure it was all going to collapse here, because of a jobsworth with a fondness for red tape, the door buzzed and the latch clicked open. Without giving himself time to think, Ian pushed through, with Steve at his heels, and was aware of a dozen or so faces turned to him in astonishment.

Their surprise turned to alarm, as he levelled his hand gun at the nearest, and spoke in a brusque voice.

'Where are the girls?' No-one spoke, and he jabbed the gun sharply towards the nearest medic. 'The subjects! Where are they?'

'The twins?' the medic stammered. 'Only Parker V-30 knows, and has access to them.'

'Bullshit! You know where—'

'What's that?' Steve put a hand on his arm.

A faint hammering came from the far end, where, in a wall of mirrors, he saw a door. As he watched, the handle began to jerk frantically; someone was in there trying to attract attention, and it could only be Ruhi and Alima.

'In here!' The voice was faint, but unmistakeably that of a child.

'Go and get them,' Ian said, gesturing to Steve while he continued to hold the gun on the medic, who was white-faced and looked as if he were about to be sick. Ian couldn't help feeling sorry he was the cause of such distress; the man was just doing a job, like anyone else.

His attention was snagged by the door once more, but this time it was because it had suddenly been wrenched open from the inside. Steve stopped briefly in surprise, but had clearly seen the girls, and leaned in to pull them out of the lab and into the relative safety of the ward. They fell on him in relief, and he shoved them behind him; for a moment Ian was unsure why, then he saw what Steve had seen: Julie Parker advancing towards him, something small and bright clutched in her hand. A scalpel.

Julie swept the small but lethally sharp blade savagely from side to side, her face fixed in furious desperation. 'Hand them over!'

As the scalpel passed perilously close to Steve's raised arm, Ian's army training took over; before he had time to think he had swung the barrel of his gun, aimed at Julie's chest, and squeezed the trigger twice. Julie stopped in her tracks, and for a split second Ian thought he'd missed, but a sudden bloom of crimson on the front of her lab coat reassured him otherwise. Her knees unlocked and she tumbled gracelessly to the floor. Ian felt no remorse; he'd despised the woman for so long, and now the world was rid of her. At his hand.

The girls whimpered into the silence that descended as the crash of the gun faded, and Steve recovered enough to usher them away from their crumpled jailer.

'Get them out,' Ian called to him, throwing him John's keys. 'I'm going back for John.'

Even as he spoke, a harsh wailing sound tore through the room, echoing off the walls, and everyone flinched at the volume of it. Fire alarms. Raised, no doubt, by the tech guys who'd seen what was happening before their screens failed, and the one thing that wouldn't have been disabled during the otherwise comprehensive shutdown. Steve took the girls' hands, and the last Ian saw of them, as they joined the crowds making their escape into the corridor, was Steve nodding to him to go on, to do what had to be done.

***

Richard Hampton closed the door to the president's office, and put a box file on the desk before taking the seat Holloway indicated.

'You're looking well, Richard,' Holloway said. 'The transplant's taken years off you.'

'I feel great.' Hampton accepted the tumbler of whisky Holloway offered, and smiled across at the president. 'The stem cells have grown fast, my blood count's back to normal.' He indicated the file, which had the donors' names printed in large, bold letters on the label. 'Those are the details: stats, histories, possible complications, outcomes, surgical notes... Everything. Plus I ensured the twins' research was requisitioned.'

Holloway glanced at it, and shrugged. 'Why do I want that?'

'If anything should happen to the surgical team,' Hampton gave him a pointed look, 'the new one will have everything they need. Besides, it'll be your turn next, you might find it useful to know what's happening.' He swigged the whisky and let out a contented sigh. 'But according to Parker,' he added, 'the operation seems to have somehow weakened the donor subject, so it might be best if you get your treatment from the other one.'

'Weakened how?'

Hampton shrugged. 'She's... not what she was. Not to worry though, the other one'll be fine.'

Holloway waved a vague hand. 'Sure. Whatever.'

'Once we've inoculated all personnel,' Hampton went on, 'we can finally leave this place and head over to Peterson. We can't stay here much longer.'

'This is our only chance, Richard. We could've moved to the Cheyenne Mountain Complex if that bitch of a president hadn't changed all the entry codes before she died.'

'All is working out well, Max,' Hampton soothed him. He turned to the sanity screen to catch another glimpse of the outside world, and froze as the screen blinked out. Dead. He waited, with a rapidly-beating heart, for it to go live again, but it remained black, and before either he or Holloway could speak, the fire alarm blared through the corridors.

Hampton lurched to his feet, as the door flew open and Rom stood framed in the doorway.

'Sir, systems are down, and the complex has been compromised.' He moved aside, and Hampton saw a familiar face staring back at him, the barrel of a gun pressed to his temple.

'I've also been informed that the twins have been stolen.'

'What?' Holloway's bellow of fury seemed to amuse the prisoner, who gave him a tight smile which Holloway ignored. 'Is the place secured now?'

'Negative, sir. We've sent personnel to the front entrance, but all hell's broken loose. We can't close the doors, and we're being pushed back inside. All personnel have firepower, sir, but no one's willing to go hand-to-hand, in case of contamination.' Rom twisted to look behind him, as they heard voices and footsteps in the corridors, hurrying past the offices. 'There's a detail escorting senior members of staff to the emergency exit,' he said. 'They're waiting for you, and I suggest you leave now.'

'No,' Hampton said, after a brief glance at Holloway. 'We're staying.' He looked at the prisoner. 'I should have killed you and your brother years ago, Malik.'

'Probably.'

'What exactly have you managed to sabotage?'

The prisoner shrugged, and something about the way he spoke was momentarily distracting. 'I've only disabled your security systems, but as we speak, my men are on the way to your power source, with an electromagnetic pulse generator, which'll fry all your electrical equipment.' He grinned. 'You'll soon be in the dark, with no air.' The grin faded, and the man's eyes grew as hard as his voice, and as filled with loathing. 'You're finished, Hampton.'

Hampton's fury burned. One hand grasped the front of his prisoner's too-baggy uniform, and the other curled into a fist as if it belonged to someone else. He was unaccustomed to taking matters of violence into his own hands, so it was only when he felt the skin of his knuckles break, and the impact rocket up his arm, that he realised he'd actually struck a blow that sent the younger man staggering backwards, barely keeping his feet. For a split

326

second he felt a surge of triumph, but the prisoner shook off the droplets of blood that beaded his lower lip, and his smile returned, more insolent than ever.

It was only then that Hampton realised he wasn't looking at Doron Malik at all, and he belatedly recognised Todd's boyhood friend, John Milburn. No wonder he'd been distracted by the voice; Malik had been raised as an American, his brother as English as Hampton himself. But the words, rather than the accent, were what mattered now.

'Think it's true, what he said?' Hampton threw another worried look at Holloway, whose lips had thinned.

'We have no way of knowing, but *if* he's telling the truth, we have no choice. We have to leave, now.'

Hampton turned to Rom. 'Get the President out of here, and take *him* with you as insurance.' He grabbed Milburn and thrust him at Rom. 'I just need to collect some paperwork, and I'll be right behind you.'

***

Ian pushed open the door to the room where John had been working. Balanced between two seats near the back of the room was a laptop, its lid open and the USB blinking in the port, but John was nowhere to be seen. There was little likelihood he would have left Hope Meadows tech behind voluntarily, which meant he'd probably been seized by someone belonging to the complex.

Ian hissed a curse, and snatched up the laptop and shoved it inside his jacket. In the corridor once more, he turned towards the offices, then hesitated; there was a very small chance John might actually have headed out in search of his backup after all, once the work was done. He'd made no secret of the fact that he didn't entirely trust Ian's motives, and no way of knowing whether the girls had been rescued at all... It was entirely likely he'd play it safe.

Ian joined the crowd at the exit making its way towards the concourse, and scanned the distance beyond with a keen, practiced eye. Alongside the vehicles abandoned during the virus panic he saw the cleaner, familiar outlines of jeeps and at least one truck, and there was faint movement too, amongst the dull gleam of long-neglected chrome bumpers and wheel hubs; if he hadn't been looking for it he'd never have seen it.

With the cameras down, those forming the backup had safely moved from the perimeter to a position nearer the terminal. To the right he could see the base personnel gathering and awaiting orders, their attention entirely diverted towards the concourse.

Ian knew the drill, he'd have ordinarily been among them. He also knew he had limited time in which to find John, before the man was whisked away and held hostage until Hampton had his pet twins returned to him. Or worse. In all likelihood he wouldn't be freed at all. Ian started to walk backwards towards the parking lot, slowly at first, but increasing speed as soon as he dared, until he was sure no-one had spotted him. Then he turned and ran full pelt towards the waiting group.

He hadn't quite reached them before he heard the soft clunk of car doors opening, voices talking over one another, and then two groups of shadows merged into a single unit that came running towards him.

'We have the girls!' Doron's voice reached him first. 'Your friend delivered them safely and Ravi's taken them back—'

'I can't find John!' Ian rasped, breathless from stress and exertion. 'Last I saw he was using this.' He withdrew the laptop from his jacket and laid it on the ground between them. 'He did what he had to, but I had to leave him to it while Steve and I got the girls out.'

'Show us,' Doron said grimly, his expression betraying the deep fear he felt for his brother.

Ian nodded. 'Follow me, and keep close. Are you armed?'

'Most of us are.'

'I have a knife in my boot,' Nita added.

'Just don't be afraid to use whatever you have, these guys won't think twice.'

He scanned the little group: Doron, Nita and Todd had moved forward, and behind them he could see Steve, with a couple of others. One of them was Belle's son, Beau, and the other was the bloke who ran one of the main Hope Meadows supplies stores with his wife. Garcia? It wasn't important, and there was no time to waste on introductions; these people were his army now, and he needed them all.

'We have others,' Beau said, as if he'd read his mind. 'They're ready to follow, and they're armed too.'

'Tell them to wait,' Ian advised. 'It'll be hard enough for me to get you six in without being spotted, a bigger crowd will wreck our chances. But as long as some of us

329

are in,' he gave Doron an encouraging nod, 'John stands a chance.'

'Get us in, then,' Doron said bluntly. 'Now.'

Ian led them into the parking garage, where they remained out of sight, watching the crowd growing. The emergency exit was still crammed with personnel, but the entrance to level 1 was now unmanned, and accessible; Ian stood guard until the others had vanished into the stairwell and down to the dim, emergency-lit corridor beyond, then followed.

He led them swiftly towards the presidential offices, but before he turned into the corridor which led directly to Holloway's office he heard voices ahead, and halted, raising a cautionary hand to prevent questions. He leaned cautiously around the corner, and saw Max Holloway, and a few other members of the senior staff, shuffling out of the office suite. They must have been debating the wisdom of leaving, Ian realised, or they'd certainly have been among the first to seek safety – which meant they knew it was a major security breach rather than the genuine emergency that the fire alarm indicated. They'd be on their guard, then.

He watched the little group start down the corridor in the other direction, and straightened in relief as he saw John following them, wiping blood from his mouth but apparently otherwise unhurt. But before he could share this good news he let out a hissed curse instead; Rom was bringing up the rear, and as they turned to follow the others Ian saw he had a revolver pressed into the small of John's back. His own gun was cocked and ready to fire, but it was too risky a shot; he could either miss entirely, and simply alert Rom to their presence, or the bullet would pass straight through him from this distance, and do Rom's job for him. Either way, John would die.

'What's up?' Doron appeared at Ian's elbow, and Ian moved back to allow him to take his place. Doron peered around the corner and caught his breath. 'Where are they taking him?'

'To the other exit,' Ian said, grateful for once, for the blaring fire alarm. 'I don't know where that is; it's a private one. They'll be heading to the airfield.' He moved Doron aside again so he could check the rate at which their time was slipping away. 'Why doesn't he use his spirit to help him get away?' he asked Doron.

But Todd replied first, and his voice was grim. 'He's fast, but a bullet's faster.'

'If they wanted him dead they'd have shot him already, surely?'

'He's more useful to them alive, but if it's a straight choice he doesn't stand a chance.'

'Wait here,' Doron muttered, and doubled back to speak to Steve. 'Go back to the others, tell them to watch for people leaving. It's vital we don't lose them.'

By the time he re-joined Ian, their quarry had vanished around a corner, and Ian knew all too well that not far beyond that one lay any number of directions they might have taken. 'Come on, but keep as quiet as you can, we don't want to spook that Rom bloke into anything.'

'Let me go in front,' Doron said, edging past. 'John might get shot before he has a chance to release his spirit, but I won't.'

'Are you sure you know what you're doing?' Todd asked, and Doron flashed him a quick, tight grin. 'Nope. Come on.'

They ran, Ian praying no-one would shut down the alarm that was covering the sound of their feet on the corridor; they'd left the carpeted presidential suite behind, and emerged onto the sheet tile that characterised the rest of the facility.

He was relieved to see the tail end of the little party just passing through a door at the far end of the corridor, before it split into a four-way choice, and watched in fascination as something whizzed past him; a blur of movement without solid form, but with the suggestion of arms already outstretched as it reached the two remaining soldiers, and Rom and John. The wraith spun among them, knocking them away from John, and into the walls, and they fell, stunned and momentarily helpless, while John stared for a moment, astonished. Then he broke away and ran back down the corridor.

'The president's gone,' he shouted. 'Those soldiers are just escorts, so—'

'Watch out!' Todd cried, and lunged forward to seize John and drag him out of harm's way.

Ian followed his gaze, to see Rom struggling to a half-rise from where his fall had been cushioned slightly by his fallen colleagues. He raised his gun, but Rom had snatched up his own weapon, and, in the same movement, fired from his awkward position on the floor. As Ian watched, Doron's wraith shoved again, and the gun spun away from Rom's hand as the guard collapsed once more.

Ian turned to John, who remained unhurt but dazed at the near-miss. Todd, however was sheet-white and clutching at his thigh. He fell against the wall, his face blank with shock but his eyes bright with hatred. He made a grab for Ian's gun, and seemed as surprised as Ian when he was able to wrest it from his slackened grip. He aimed it with one hand while the other tried to staunch the flow of blood from his leg, and even as Rom began to rise again, and reach for his own gun, Todd squeezed the trigger.

Luck must surely have played a part, or something kinder... Todd's hand had been shaking, and his eyes blurred with furious tears as he cried out his mother's name, but the bullet found its mark. Struck directly in the heart, Rom was dead before he hit the floor again.

Todd dropped the gun and sagged back against the wall, and Doron and John both turned to him and eased him to the floor where he sat, hissing through gritted teeth, both hands clawing at the top of his left leg.

Doron squatted beside him, then raised his eyes to John. 'We need to stop this bleeding … now!' He stood up again and began to unbutton his jacket, but Ian had beaten him to it. His jacket lay on the floor and he was pulling his t-shirt over his head. As soon as he handed it over, Doron placed it over the wound pressing down firmly to staunch the bleeding.

'We don't have time to get him back to Hope Meadows, we need to do something now.'

'I'll help you get him to the med centre. It's well sign-posted but it'll be quicker if I show you.' Ian replaced his jacket and looked worriedly at Todd, who was breathing in short bursts. 'Can this other fella help me carry him?'

'Diego,' the man supplied. 'Yes, I'll help you.'

Doron gave them a grateful nod, then looked around. 'Where did Nita and Beau get to? They were right behind us.' His face was drawn and worried. 'Dammit...'

'Just go,' John urged. 'I'll find them. You get Todd to safety.'

Ian manoeuvred himself behind Todd and brought his arms up from underneath, grabbing Todd's hands and holding them over his chest. He nodded to Diego, who lifted Todd's legs while Doron kept the pressure on the wound. Todd slumped, and Doron drew a sharp breath.

'He's going into shock, 'let's go!'

A light popping sound came from beyond the doorway through which the president and his entourage had vanished, and it took Ian a moment to recognise it for what it was; distant gunfire.

'Who's shooting at who?'

'Nita's people are still out there, with some more of our lot,' John reminded him, wiping Todd's blood from his hands distractedly. 'They're only here as backup, but if the compound personnel have fired on them, they're going to fire back.'

'Christ, this could turn into a bloodbath.' Doron cast one desperate look back at John as they set off towards the med centre. 'Please, just find Nita...'

***

Nita had been about to follow the others, as they set off down the corridor in the wake of Doron's spirit, but as they passed the office a movement caught her eye. Not everyone had left, it seemed. She walked back, vaguely aware that Beau had also broken away from the main group and followed her, his gun drawn. He still had her back, even now, and she threw a grateful look over her shoulder. He returned it with a grin and a shake of his head, his gaze going briefly to the ceiling. *Only you…*

She smiled, and peered into the office. She couldn't see anyone; it had been just shadows playing tricks. But before she turned away she saw a box file sitting on the large desk. The label was facing outward, and on it was printed: *Ruhi Nasir – control. Alima Nasir – donor.*

Nita frowned and, without thinking, she started into the room, her hand already outstretched to seize the file. A moment later hard fingers clamped around her upper arm and dragged her aside, and at the same time she felt a bruising pain at her temple.

A British voice grunted in her ear. 'What do you think *you're* after, you little bitch?' She could only guess at who it was, but she assumed it must be Richard Hampton.

'Let her go!'

Nita twisted in her attacker's grasp to see Beau stepping into the room, gun in hand, his face tight with anger. A shot sounded somewhere in the hallways, and Nita jumped, her heart slithering in her chest.

'Drop that, or I'll shoot her,' Hampton said, driving the barrel of his gun harder against Nita's temple. She couldn't help crying out, and Beau's eyes went to her in an agony of indecision. She wanted to tell him not to cave in

335

to the threat against her, but before she could say anything he'd lowered his gun to the floor, and rose again, his hands raised to his shoulders to show he was no longer armed.

The roar of Hampton's gun was so loud, that Nita thought, for a split second, he'd shot her anyway, and that she was in her final, shocked moments. But even as she recovered from the instinctive, violent recoil from the sound, she saw Beau take a single, stumbling step before falling to the floor, a spreading stain covering the front of his t-shirt. She snatched a single, horrified breath, and then the gun was jammed against the back of her head, sending a shard of pain through it.

Another shot came from down the corridor, and as Hampton hesitated, she used his momentary distraction to reach back over her own shoulder and grasp the gun's barrel. She screamed in pain as the heat of it seared her palm, but she didn't let go; it was her life or Hampton's now, and all those long-ago sessions, when Joe had so earnestly made her rehearse the moves over and over again, merged into one desperate moment as her muscle-memory took over.

She ducked beneath her own arm, and turned at the same time, and the movement twisted Hampton's gun arm, pulling it upward; she'd hoped he would let go in shock, as Joe had been confident should happen, but she only heard him grunt in pain as his shoulder twisted at an unnatural angle, and he wrenched his wrist in his desperation to keep hold of his weapon.

The second bellow of the gun shocked her into stillness, for the length of time it took her to realise that

Hampton's own finger had convulsed on the trigger. The direction of her twist had brought the barrel down into direct contact with his chest, and she felt a spray of hot blood across her cheek as the man's heart pumped ferociously one final time. Her double-burned hand throbbed, and she let go of the gun, praying her skin would not remain stuck to the metal.

The instant Hampton's body fell away from her she was stumbling towards her stricken friend. She sank to her knees beside him, knowing he was gone, but crying his name over and over, still hopelessly praying for a miracle. She took his head into her lap, hating the empty, glazed look in those formerly laughing brown eyes, never more to tease her, or to smile at her temper tantrums... He'd been Billy for her, when Billy had left this world, and now she held his limp body in her arms, while his spirit travelled on without her.

She wasn't sure how long she sat, chanting his name over and over, but a commotion in the doorway finally dragged her eyes away and she saw John staring at her in horror as he took a tentative step forward.

'We heard shots...'

She realised she was covered in blood from her head to her shoulders. 'It's not mine.' She nodded at Hampton's still form, but returned her attention to Beau. 'He was unarmed,' she said, grief choking her. 'He'd put the gun down! He just—'

'I'm so sorry, Nita,' John said gently. He crouched next to her, and gently lifted Beau's head from her lap. 'We'll come back for him, I promise. We won't leave him here. But we have to go now.' He looked at her hand. 'You're hurt.'

'A burn,' she said, pulling away. 'It's nothing. It will heal. Where are the others?' She dazedly allowed him to help her to her feet. 'I heard shots, too.' She caught her breath again. 'Ron! Is he—'

'He's not hurt,' John said quickly. 'But Todd is. He killed Rom, but Rom got off a shot first, and hit Todd in the thigh.'

'Oh, no...'

'The others have him down in the medical centre. They need you, Nita. Can you do it?'

She nodded, and took one last look at her old friend. 'Farewell, courageous one,' she whispered, then looked at the others, her eyes stinging. She blinked away the tears. 'Take me to the medical centre.'

Diego remained on guard outside the door, while in the otherwise empty ward, Doron was bent over Todd, working on the wound in Todd's upper thigh. He looked up as Nita came in and his expression exactly mirrored that which had been on John's face when he'd seen her. She shook her head quickly, and repeated that the blood wasn't hers.

He closed his eyes briefly in relief, and looked beyond her for Beau, but when he looked back at her he read the answer to his unasked question. The shock and compassion on his face nearly brought her to tears again, until she felt John's hand, strong and steady, on her back.

'She could do with some salve on this burn.'

338

'I'll get it,' Nita managed. 'You go and help Ron.' She went to the glass cupboard on the wall, behind which lay an array of pharmaceutical supplies. It all seemed so calm and normal down here, a different world to the way things had been upstairs – it helped her to push the horror of Beau's needless death to the back of her mind.

'Where's Ian?' John asked, looking towards the door.

'He went to join the others outside,' Doron said. 'If things turn nasty again he's better off out there than anywhere, with his skills.'

Doron nodded and turned his attention back to Todd. 'The bullet travelled clean through a muscle, luckily it's missed the femoral artery. Nita, can you hold this while I try to close the wound? John, stand by his head and keep watch for any sign he's regaining consciousness.'

Nita tore a package open with her teeth, and began wrapping gauze around her hand as she and John crossed the room to take up their positions. Doron had begun to put a few stitches in place, just to see them through the journey, when the relative peace was shattered by a single gunshot out in the corridor.

Nita flinched as the memory of Hampton's horrific, self-inflicted wound flashed across her mind, enhanced by the hot, coppery smell of blood that was still all around. Then realisation hit. 'Diego!' She put down the instrument tray.

'Nita, don't! But Doron was mid-stitch, and couldn't stop what he was doing.

Nita's instinct took her at a run to the door, but there common sense took over and she drew back, her heart thudding painfully as she heard footsteps coming towards

339

the door; whoever had fired the shot then, it couldn't have been Diego.

Aware that, behind her, Doron was continuing his work on Todd and trying to remain silent at the same time, she took a slow, trembling breath, and reached down to her boot. The whisper of the blade as it slid free of the protective pocket sounded as loud, to her, as the gunshot, but she knew it would have been easily masked by the approaching footsteps.

She spared a glance over her shoulder at her friends by the operating table, and took a firmer grasp of the knife handle, knowing their lives now depended on her ability to deliberately inflict injury, or possibly death, on another human being. To her horror she saw Todd's uninjured foot jerk, and at the same time John raised panicked eyes to Ron, and clapped his hand over Todd's mouth, stifling the man's cry as he swam back to consciousness. Ron uttered an oath and worked faster, as John bent to whisper urgently in Todd's ear.

The footsteps halted at the door, and Nita's breath stopped. Whoever was outside knew that there was someone here, and curiosity at the sight of Diego standing guard must now have given way to training; this was the nerve-centre of the whole complex, after all, and was to be protected at any cost. She could picture the figure out there, raising his gun in readiness even as he pushed open the door, and the moment he stepped through and aimed at the twins she drove the knife forward.

The sharp blade pierced the soldier's flesh easily, sinking deep into the meat of his bicep and making the hand that held the gun spasm. The weapon clattered to the floor, and Nita pulled the blade free and snatched up the gun herself.

'Go!' She blinked away tears of shock and revulsion at what she'd done, and glanced beyond him to where Diego lay. She saw, with a surge of despair, that there was no question of trying to save him. 'Go,' she repeated, her voice now icy with rage. 'I'll shoot you if you don't, I swear I will.'

He gave her a look of fearful disgust before turning, his hand clamped to his bleeding arm, and stumbling away up the corridor. Nita shut the door and leaned on it for a moment.

'We've lost Diego,' she said, breathless and still shaken. For once wishing she wasn't medically trained; it was all too easy to picture exactly what that blade had done to the muscle and bone. 'We have to—'

'He's coming around,' John said sharply. 'What do I do?'

Doron looked at Nita, who shook her head helplessly, and he made his decision. 'Help me get him outside. We can put him in the back of one of the empty cars.' He tied off the suture, leaving only a small open wound which he finished with steri-strips, and Nita grabbed a compression bandage off the trolley and shoved it into her pocket. 'I'll put this on him when we get to the car. There isn't time now.'

Todd let out a low groan as John and Doron helped him first to sit, and then slide off the bed, but he put an arm around each of their necks and took a couple of deep breaths. Nita watched him anxiously, not sure he was up to this, and John and Doron hesitated too, but Todd

341

somehow found the ghost of his usual grin, and nodded at the door.

'What are we waiting for?'

Nita hurried ahead of them, finding her way out of the complex after only a few false turns, and they emerged inside Level 1. Through the large windows, at the far end, they could see the taxiway was packed with uniformed personnel, queuing to take their place on the waiting 737, and Nita and Doron stumbled to a halt, hissing in frustration.

'Where's your jeep, John?'

'I gave the keys to Ian, he'll have given them to his mate to get the girls away.'

'Can we make it to the other cars without being seen, d'you think?'

'No-one's looking,' Nita said. 'Too keen to get away.'

'They know they've already lost the girls,' Todd muttered, and took another careful breath as he shifted his arms across their shoulders. 'Nothing else matters now except their own safety. Come on, I'm feeling woozy as hell.'

John took a fresh grip on his friend and, keeping a wary eye on the gathering at the other end of the concourse, the three of them made their way as swiftly as they could towards the waiting cars.

Four people from Carbondale, who hadn't been involved in the skirmish as the president had escaped, were hovering, waiting to be sure they weren't needed after all. A couple of weapons snapped up at the sight of John's uniform, but they were quickly lowered again and, at John's signal of dismissal the four climbed into their car and pulled slowly out towards the main road.

'Let's go,' Doron said breathlessly, as he and John reached the remaining vehicles. 'John, leave that uniform here, we don't want some trigger happy idiot back at Hope Meadows thinking we've got a prisoner.'

John stripped off the uniform and dropped it onto the ground, as Nita took over helping Todd into the back of Doron's jeep. 'You go back with Ron,' she said, when he emerged again. 'I'll follow right behind.'   She glanced around. 'Where's Ian?'

'He and Steve have gone in to recover Beau's and Diego's bodies.'

'Already? Is it safe?'

'They know the complex,' John said. 'They'll be okay.'

'For all we know, part of the plan might be to burn the place to the ground once the president's away,' Doron added, closing the door carefully so as not to jar Todd. 'We can't risk leaving it too late to bring them out.' He came over to her and took her by the shoulders.

He looked closely at her for a moment, silent, but there was a look in his eyes that told her he understood what she'd given of herself today; how deeply she'd been affected by what she'd had to do, and by the loss of her close friend. He pressed a brief kiss to her brow and released her, and climbed into the passenger seat next to his brother.

She watched them pull slowly away, John behind the wheel visibly wincing as they drove over a drain cover and the jeep jolted; no doubt Todd had made his feelings clear about that… A tight, sorrowful little smile found its way

343

onto her face, painted there by relief that they had not only rescued the girls, but destroyed the racist enclave that had no place in this new world they were building. The lives of Diego and Beau had not been given in vain. But their loss was sharp, and her smile quickly faded.

She pulled out her own keys and flexed her burned hand as she walked over to her truck. Now she had time to think, she realised how lucky she'd been not to have lost a finger when that second shot had been squeezed off, in Hampton's desperate, final act. The slide had been pulling away from her grip as the shell casing was expelled, otherwise it might have been a very different story.

In the meantime her palm and fingers felt tight and painful, and the anaesthetic properties of the salve she had found would soon wear off. She would see to it properly when she got back to Hope Meadows. Or maybe Ron could do it for her... a feeling of peace crept through her at the thought of sitting quietly somewhere alone, letting him bathe her sore skin. Together. And safe.

A sound from behind brought her up short as she reached for the door handle of her truck. Her heart thudding, she peered in the direction from which it had come, and saw the unmistakeable outline of a uniform jacket, and she froze, trying to calculate how long it would take to pull open the door and jam the key into the ignition. There was no way she could do it silently, but if she could do it quickly enough she might still escape before the soldier brought his weapon to bear on the windshield of her car. Then she blinked.

344

'Ruth?' She took a step closer to the figure, and sure enough it *was* Ruth, swimming in John's discarded uniform jacket, which she was cinching about her waist with her own leather belt. The sleeves had already been rolled back, and she was a tall woman; at a quick glance she could easily pass for one of the compound staff. 'What are you doing?'

Ruth bent to pick up the uniform cap, and tugged it over her own hair. 'Making things right.'

'What do you mean? Things *are*—'

'You let them get away!' Ruth turned on her, her expression fierce. 'You should never have done that! They'll only come back again.'

'But we were outnumbered,' Nita said reasonably. 'If we'd shown ourselves and returned fire, beyond trying to stop the president and his group, we'd have lost our own people.'

'Well now you don't have to worry about it.' Ruth stooped again, to her own discarded jacket and dug into the pocket. 'I can stop them with this.' She held up a generously-sized hip flask.

'And what's that?'

'Whisky.' Ruth gave her a tight smile. 'My own personal stash. I'm sure plenty on that flight will be happy to share it with me.'

Nita frowned, still puzzled, but before she could ask anything further Ruth had unscrewed the cap of the flask, and her mouth was working. Nita suddenly realised what she was doing, and why.

Nita had seen that look of despair, when Ruth had realised the full horror of what had happened to her best friends. She had seemed, on the surface, to accept everyone's assurances that she was not to blame, but deep down she must have been carrying the guilt like her own personal contamination. It seemed the distraught woman had finally hit on a way of finding a use for the very thing that had poisoned her life.

Ruth lifted the flask to her mouth, and spat, clearly making sure she had transferred every last drop of moisture from her mouth. 'I'm making things right,' she said again, in answer to the despairing look Nita gave her. 'Don't try to stop me.' She backed away, her face determined beneath the layer of fear.

'But when they find out—'

'It'll be too late by then.' Ruth's eyes shone with sudden tears, and she blinked them furiously away. 'I can't live with it, Nita. I killed the two people I loved most. The two people who—'

'But it wasn't your fault,' Nita pleaded, her own eyes stinging. 'Come back with me, we'll talk. You'll see—'

'No.' Ruth looked a little calmer now, and she lifted her chin and straightened her shoulders. 'Let me do this for my friends. I owe them this at least.' She reached into her pocket and took out a short-bladed penknife, and to Nita's dismay she drew the blade over her exposed wrist. She hissed in pain, then let out a harsh breath and shook her hand, sending tiny droplets of blood onto the sun-baked tarmac.

Nita instinctively moved forward, but Ruth took another step back. 'My war wound.' She gave Nita one last look, and then the underlying fear was gone, replaced by a strange kind of peace. 'No regrets, Nita. Make sure they

346

know that.' Then she turned, and broke into a run towards the dwindling group still boarding the plane.

'Ruth!'

But it was hopeless to try and stop her now. Nita watched her join the last few soldiers, and as the staircase retracted the plane's engines fired. The whole planeful of personnel was doomed, and not one of them knew it.

Chapter Eighteen
Returning Home

The long drive back to Hope Meadows had been difficult, and painful, and Nita had had to make a stop when she had become overwhelmed with her grief for Beau, but finally the welcoming lights of her new home town came into view. She parked her truck and sat for a moment, just breathing in the pre-dawn air that wafted through the open window, and looking at the lights and lanterns that had been placed all along the town's perimeter.

She glimpsed a movement near the fence, and looked more closely to see Jen and Sinead. Her throat tightened in gratitude as she realised they must have been waiting just for her, since almost everyone else would have been home by now.

She climbed down slowly and shut the truck door, using the time to compose herself against the waves of mixed emotions that rolled over her; gratitude for the simple but unbreakable friendships she had made, among her own people and the good people of this town; grief for those who had not returned; relief that it was all over. The two women drew her into a silent embrace, while she swallowed the words which couldn't be spoken.

When she had herself a little more under control, she pulled back, and over Jen's shoulder she saw Moki walking towards them, and beside him, Belle, supported by Rena who had an arm about the older woman's shoulder. Nita gave Jen and Sinead another grateful look, and broke away to meet the little group. Belle knew already, that her son had gone, and Nita clasped her tightly as they both wept for the loss.

'We are blessed that you have returned, at least,' Belle said after a moment, wiping her eyes. 'We have heard much, but no-one has been able to tell me what happened to Beau.

Nita told her, in a tight and cracked voice, how Beau had given his own life in the saving of hers. 'He held no weapon when he was cut down,' she finished. 'It was an act of courage and honour for him to give it up, and I will never forget his sacrifice.'

'It's late,' Jen said, coming over but keeping a respectful distance and speaking in a low voice. 'Nita, will you come to our home for a few hours sleep?'

'Where will you stay?' Nita asked Belle.

'With us,' Rena said. 'Moki has been offered a bed for the night too. He'll take Belle back to the Springs when it gets light.' She touched Nita's arm. 'You've been through a lot, you should rest now.'

'The dogs?' Nita mumbled, suddenly bone-tired at the thought of sleep. 'What about them?'

'They're being cared for. A nice Canadian lady and her husband, and their little girl, said they'd keep them until you're ready.'

'That must be Wavun,' Nita said. 'That was kind of her.'

'There is one other thing,' Moki said. 'Ruth's guard has said she's managed to get away from him. When you all left, he locked her cabin door and windows but forgot about the skylight.'

'Many cars have the keys left in them,' Jen said, 'so none of our people are without transport if they need it. We think she took one.'

Moki nodded. 'We don't know where she went.'

Nita gave him a tired, half-smile. 'She's probably the bravest of all of us.' She told the little group what Ruth had done, and what she planned to do now, and there were murmurs of admiration that she wished Ruth could have heard. 'I'll be back to take you up on your offer,' she told Jen, 'but I'll go to the surgery first and see if Ron needs any help with Todd.' She caught sight of Sinead's expression, and touched her hand. 'He's going to be fine. Go back to your children, I'll come and tell you as soon as he's ready to see anyone.'

She settled a groggy and grateful Todd, after the wound had been re-stitched and re-dressed, and was just washing her hands when she heard a jeep pull up outside the surgery.

'It's Ian and Steve,' Doron said, peering out of the window. His face was grave. 'I think we'll have to ask them to put Diego and Beau in the hall for now, until Todd's on his feet and we have room here for them.'

Nita swallowed past a lump in her throat, and nodded. 'I'll go. I'll make sure they're... that they look...' She broke off, unable to say it.

'I'll go and see Ana and Belle,' Doron said quietly, 'and let them know.'

Nita carried blankets and sheets over to the hall, while Ian and Steve brought their two fallen friends in, and for a while, to her relief, the doctor in her took over. She found she was able to put aside her grief for a while and look on the dead with gratitude and respect, and as she arranged the stiffening bodies into postures that looked more peaceful, and cleaned blood from their faces, she was glad their loved ones were at least spared the sight of a head wound.

She was pulling a blanket up to Diego's chest when Ana arrived, and after a few murmured words she left the woman to grieve alone. She went back outside to find Ian rooting in the back of his jeep, and stopped to see if he needed help.

'The girls left this behind,' he said, drawing out the vaccine porter that Ruhi and Alima had left in the lab. 'And this,' he added. 'We found it in the office when we went in for Beau.' He handed her the folder she'd seen on the desk, with the girls' names on the spine, and once inside the surgery he placed the vaccine porter in the freezer and spun the combination lock. It was chilling to think that there could still be enemies out there, but foolish not to consider it, even now.

Nita looked out of the window a few minutes later, to see Ana coming out of the hall, her hands pressed to her mouth to stifle her sobs. She was stumbling a little; no doubt her eyes were blurred by tears as she made her way back to her cabin. And now that she had seen Diego for herself, she had the devastating task of confirming to Rosa and Sofia that it was true; their father was never coming home. Nita's own tears burned as she watched the

351

hunched shape dwindling into the distance as the sun rose on this, the Garcias' bleakest day.

She was about to turn away from the window when another movement caught her eye, and she adjusted her line of sight to where Sinead had come out of her cabin, and was half-running towards the jeep. Ian had his hand on the door handle, and he turned towards her, his expression of greeting fading into one of surprise as Sinead shoved at him, catching him off-balance, and jabbed her finger at him in furious counterpoint to whatever she was saying. She knuckled betrayed tears from her eyes and hit him again, both hands shoving savagely at his chest, and Ian stood calm while she purged herself of her anger.

Then he spoke, and Sinead, now breathless, listened. Nita had no way of knowing what he said, but a moment later Sinead sagged and wrapped her arms about his waist. Ian let her weep against him for a moment, and Nita, watching from her window and feeling every complicated emotion, felt another tear slide down her own cheek.

When Sinead drew back she was composed enough to accept Ian's hand as he drew her around to meet Steve, and after a brief conversation she gestured towards her cabin, and the two men nodded. The three of them, worry-worn, exhausted, but clearly overwhelmed with relief, made their way down the road to the cabin, hard-won safety, and the warmth of companionship.

Belle had been waiting in the shadows, and Nita watched her move to stand by the hall door, one hand on the jamb but unable to make herself step forward into the hall. Her breath caught at this stark reminder of who was in there; not just some patient, or a sad casualty of the war in which they'd found themselves, but Beau. Her friend. This woman's son.

Belle at last crossed the threshold, and went to face the cold truth of her loss. As Nita drew near the door she heard soft singing, and her throat locked up until she had to open her mouth to gasp in air past the tightness. Belle was sitting cross-legged at Beau's head, her hand moving across his hair with the tenderness only a mother knows. Nita's own fingers felt the the thick, soft texture in sympathy, but she knew the pain in the woman's heart was something she would never understand until she had felt the love that had birthed it.

Still, the soft singing and the rhythmic, unthinking movement, brought a great wave of grief crashing down on Nita, and she let out a choked sob. Belle looked up and saw her, and held out her free hand. She didn't speak, but her meaning was clear: *come. Sit. Remember with me.*

Nita took up a place at Beau's left shoulder, and laid her hand over his heart. Big as the sky, still as stone. He had placed his faith in the goodness of man, and had lost his life because of it; now he ran with the wolves and flew with the eagles, and she and the others he had left behind could only sit. And remember.

***

Ruhi and Alima had stood together in the dark last night, as the ragged, exhausted rescuers returned from the compound. Their own safe return had been greeted with so much joy, from the whole town, that any lingering

353

suspicion that Julie had been right was instantly dismissed. Their mother had seized them and their father in one enormous hug, squeezing them so hard Ruhi had thought she'd never breathe again. She had caught Alima's eye in the midst of it all, but her own joyful laughter had not been mirrored on her sister's face. Alima had smiled, and subjected herself to the embrace, but her eyes had looked... empty. Nothing had changed.

Ruhi had swallowed the fear, and told her mum everything she had told her dad in the car, and all the while her father had gushed gratitude, and apologies for the way he had behaved. Ruhi briefly wondered what he had done, or said, that he felt he must apologise so desperately, but it seemed no-one minded anyway, and then all her attention was on Alima as they waited for the return of the others. What had those people done to her during that operation?

Alima's health was perfect, and her intelligence unchanged; during their escape she'd responded as quickly as Ruhi when Ian's friend Steve had told them to stop, to hide, or to run like a cheetah. She'd easily kept up with both of them as they'd crossed the compound to where John Milburn had left his car, while Ian had kept the soldiers at bay and given them time to reach it, and had scrambled in without hesitation, keeping low as instructed.

But she hadn't said a word on the long drive back to Hope Meadows, and had avoided Ruhi's questioning gaze by staring out of the window. Her hands lay limp in her lap, and her shoulders slumped... Ruhi's heart ached to see it, and her hatred for that horrible Hampton man burned inside her. She hoped he'd died a nasty death, and that

354

he'd known he was dying. Her own thoughts frightened her, but she held on to that fierce hatred; it made her feel stronger.

Most of the volunteers had driven straight home, to either Carbondale or the Springs, but the others had begun to arrive at Hope Meadows now. There was desperately sad news of Diego Garcia, from the supplies store, and his wife Ana and their daughters had been led away numb and disbelieving, comforted by her closest friends.

But nothing had prepared them for the shock of learning that Beau, the forever-smiling young friend of Nita's, had also been killed. Ruhi had clutched at Alima, guilt tearing through her at the thought that both men had died saving them, but Alima had remained wooden in her arms, offering no comfort.

Not long afterwards, Doron and John had arrived, and taken a white-faced Todd straight to the small surgery next to the main hall. Word came back that he'd shot the man who'd killed his mother and taken Ruhi and Alima away from Otto's lab, but that his own wound was serious. Ruhi felt tears prickling again. She turned once more to Alima, hoping that now she was home some of the shock would be eased by familiarity, and the closeness of their parents and friends, but Alima had merely given her a faint smile that again left her eyes untouched, and accompanied her home without a word.

Now Ruhi knocked at the door of the Milburn's cabin, and after a moment Jen opened the door, but her smile of

355

welcome faded as Ruhi looked up at her. 'What's wrong, love?'

'Can the twins come over to ours?'

Jen looked doubtful. 'I'd have thought it's a bit too soon for—'

'It's Alima,' Ruhi broke in. 'It's like all her feelings have... gone dull. I've tried to help, but I'm not, I'm not...' She stifled a sob, and Jen drew her into her arms.

'It's okay,' she murmured. 'We've all been worried about her, none of us like seeing her like this. So lost.'

'I'm not *strong* enough,' Ruhi managed to gasp out between hitching breaths, and felt Jen's embrace tighten. 'Holly and Hannah have always been stronger than us,' she mumbled against Jen's shoulder. 'Can they come? I'm so worried.'

'Of course they'll come.' Jen moved away and was about to call to the twins, but they must have heard Ruhi's voice, and they appeared in the front room already pulling jackets on.

'What can we do?' Holly asked as they clattered down the steps and set off to Ruhi's cabin.

'I don't know. Maybe you'll just feel what to do, somehow, when we get there.'

'But she's your sister,' Hannah put in, 'why would we be able to help any better than you? Or anyone else?'

Ruhi shrugged. 'We think you're different, stronger, because your dad is a *pure* Nephilim. I mean, the Fathers helped us all get born at the same time, but our dads don't have the same genes as him and Doron.'

Holly and Hannah glanced at one another. 'I hadn't really thought of it like that,' Hannah confessed. 'I hope you're right, and that we'll know what to do, because I don't have a clue yet.'

Thankfully Ruhi's parents understood something was going on in which they could play no part. The worry for their daughter was clear on their faces, and they looked on the arrival of the Milburn girls with a brightening hope, and withdrew to the kitchen to give them space and peace to do what needed to be done. Ruhi still had no idea what that would be, but even as they led Alima to the bedroom she sensed something unspoken had passed between Holly and Hannah, and she felt her own tension ease a little.

'Just lie down and relax,' Hannah said, squeezing Alima's hand.

Ruhi thought her sister looked hopeful too; she'd known she hadn't felt right, had said so even as her physical health had recovered, but had been unable to put it into words. Hampton had stolen part of her, and had taken it with him into his own darkness when he'd shot himself. Ruhi didn't want to think what would happen if they couldn't restore her, but she knew she'd never stop trying, no matter what it took.

She sat on her own bed, and Holly and Hannah sat either side of her, holding a hand each. Nothing happened, and after a while Alima's eyes slipped closed in the quiet of the room; she was as exhausted as Ruhi after everything that had happened. Holly and Hannah remained motionless, their hands still clasping Ruhi's, giving her some of their strength as she fought against a growing helplessness, but she felt tears slip down her cheeks. *It should have been her!* And, but for that stupid bet, it would have been.

She was about to beg them to try harder, but a glance at Holly showed her the girl's eyes had gone white. She looked at Hannah and saw the same thing, and her breath stopped in sudden excitement. The girls' spirits lifted away from their bodies, forming recognisable shapes in the air between the beds, and then slipped across to where Alima lay, asleep or unconscious, it was impossible to tell which. They lay down either side of the motionless girl, wrapping their misty arms across her body and holding her tightly.

As Ruhi watched, the cloudy-white of the wraiths flared into the colour of leaping flames, and their movement as they enveloped Alima appeared to cover the girl in a cloak of warmth. Alima's own spirit began to show, pale and sickly, lying flat upon her still form like a sheet. Lifeless. Ruhi's heart twisted; was this the last time she would see her sister's spirit? Was this the expelling of the last part of her, leaving only the limp shadow of a girl with a broken soul?

The colour of Holly's and Hannah's wraiths deepened from bright flame to a warmer, richer orange, and they remained with their arms wrapped across Alima, giving everything of themselves until their own colours began to fade. Ruhi wanted to jump to her feet, to beg them, no matter how much it took from them, to give Alima a little longer. Just a little...

Then it happened. The pasty-white fingers of Alima's spirit began to glow faintly, and then the colour crept up the pale arms, infusing them with light. Holly's and Hannah's spirit arms linked across Alima's body, boosting

358

one another now, as much as they pushed their strength into their fallen friend.

Alima's spirit became three-dimensional, and glowed a deep orange, tinted with the heat of yellow flame. It rose away from Alima's corporeal body, reaching for her saviours, and the three wraiths clung to one another, their foreheads touching, while Alima's colour steadied.

Then the three of them withdrew slowly, and Ruhi felt the twins' hands pull away from hers as the girls fell, exhausted, across the bed. Alima pulled herself to a sitting position, her eyes immediately seeking her sister, and Ruhi slowly moved away from the sleeping Milburn girls, and sat next to her. Her questioning look was met with a smile and a nod, but this time when she looked into Alima's eyes they were bright once more, and filled with life. She was whole again.

Part Four
Fruition

The organisation known as Eagle was set up thousands of years ago to protect all Nephilim twins born throughout history. The original name is not known and until recent times was known as Eegool, the Hebrew word meaning circle. The circle, being a universal symbol for eternity and oneness, also has a protective magical element.

Native Americans believe the Eagle to be the creature closest to the Creator as it flies the highest and has a sacred connection to visions. The modern day council of Eagle members consisted of five powerful people, one from each continent and each with a different belief system.

'We can reject everything else: religion, ideology, all received wisdom. But we cannot escape the necessity of love and compassion.... This, then, is my true religion, my simple faith. In this sense, there is no need for temple or church, for mosque or synagogue, no need for complicated philosophy, doctrine or dogma. Our own heart, our own mind, is the temple. The doctrine is compassion. Love for others and respect for their rights and dignity, no matter who or what they are: ultimately these are all we need.'

Dalai Lama XIV

'Between October 23 and 24, 2007, another "hairy star" named Comet 17P/Holmes literally exploded from a magnitude of 17 to a magnitude of 2.8. (The lower the magnitude, the brighter the star.) In other words, it increased in brightness by a factor of a nearly a million in just a few hours. Sky and Telescope magazine has called it "the weirdest new object to appear in the sky in memory."

The comet's core made of rock and ice is only about 3.5 kilometers in diameter, but its coma formed by the gas and dust given off is massive. This greenish-blue ball coldly blazing in an inclined and elliptical solar orbit unexpectedly has become the largest object in our solar system -- even bigger than our sun.'

jedisimon.com

Chapter Nineteen
The Blanket

August 4PV (2007), Palisade

'So, Odina,' Nita smiled at the child sitting on the bed in the surgery she shared with Doron, 'how's your finger?'

The little girl waggled it, a serious look on her face. 'It's stopped crying,' she said at last.

'Well that's good, then.' Nita gave a stern expression. 'And no more playing with glass, okay?' The girl nodded, and Nita smiled again. 'Okay, let's take a look; I think your stitches can probably come out now.'

'Will it cry again?' the girl asked, worried, as Nita peered closely at the finger.

'No, honey. It might feel a little weird when I pull the stitches out, but it'll be fine. Now, are you ready?'

Wapun, Odina's mother, came to sit next to Odina and put a comforting arm around her shoulder. 'Brave girl,' she murmured.

Nita kept up a light chatter as she carefully pulled up the knots of the three stitches, and snipped them, feeling the child flinch slightly as she pulled the stitches free of the healed skin.

Odina chanted softly in Hally, under her breath, as each one came free. '*Dani, kah—*'

'Tren!' Nita said with her, as the last one came free. 'There we are, all done. Your mama's right, you *are* a brave girl.'

'Thank you, Hania Nita,' Wapun said, hugging her daughter closer.

'My pleasure.' It had taken some time to get used to the new name Moki had bestowed on her; Spirit Warrior, in the Hopi tongue, but it reminded her of those days with Billy, when she had taken on that role for herself, and it helped ease the ever-present ache of missing her old family.

'Do you want to keep the stitches as a souvenir?' she asked Odina, who pulled a face and shook her head. She laughed. 'It might help you remember to stay away from broken glass.'

'I'll remember.'

'Good.' Nita arched her back, rubbing at the base of her spine, and sat down with a little sigh of relief.

'Are you off home now?' Wapun asked, looking at Nita's swollen belly. 'You've only got a couple of months to go haven't you?'

Nita nodded. 'I'll work a little while longer though, and anyway the pregnancy's only part of the reason I'm only part-time. Now everyone has the same immunity as the twins, our workload's a lot lower. No real illness, just accidents.' She poked out her tongue at Odina, who giggled.

'How does it feel?' Wapun asked.

'Fine,' Nita said, a little puzzled at the question from someone who was a mother herself. 'Apart from the odd craving, of course, but the pregnancy's gone well, thanks.'

363

Wapun gave her a little smile. 'That's good, but what I meant was, how does it feel knowing that, thanks to you, we're all enjoying such good health? I mean, inside all of *us,* is a part of *you.*'

Nita gave a surprised laugh. 'I never really thought of it like that. It it is kind of weird now you mention it, but it's Otto and the girls who deserve the thanks, for understanding what they could do with my unusual genetic make-up.'

Wapun sobered. 'Of course, and I understand the little ones had nightmares for a while. And what their parents must have gone through too...' She shook her head. 'I can't imagine.'

'It was bad,' Nita agreed. 'Thankfully they've made a full recovery, but of course we're all keeping our eye on them for any relapse; trauma like that can hide and resurface, we know that too well, after all we've been through.'

They were silent for a while, thinking about it, but Odina's impatient fidgeting brought Wapun back. 'So, have you decided on a name yet?' She nodded at Nita's bump again.

'If it's a girl, I've decided—'

'Odina! Odina!' the girl sang out, giving a little wriggle on the bed.

'Well, that *is* a lovely name,' Nita allowed, 'but if there were two Odinas we'd be sure to get muddled, wouldn't we? So, I've chosen Rose, instead.'

'Wasn't that your Kuku's name?' Wapun asked.

'It was. And if it's a boy, Ron wants Daniel.'

'Fine names.' Wapun nodded her approval. 'Well, we've taken up enough of your time, I'd better get Odina and her finger back home.' She lifted her daughter down off the bed, and took her hand. At the door, she turned back and gestured to a bag she'd left on the desk. 'Some peaches for you there, fresh off the tree.'

'Wonderful, thanks!' Nita waved them off, then spent the next half an hour tidying things away before finally slipping Wapun's very welcome gift into her bag. She locked up for the day with a little sigh of relief, and, since she had arranged to visit Moki's house just a street away before she went home to Hope Meadows, she decided a walk would do her good.

She never tired of seeing the Rocky mountains in the distance, nor the meadows around her, now bursting with wildflowers whose scent she breathed in as she walked slowly up the street. Nestled between Grand Junction and the Grand Mesa National Forest, Palisade was a beautiful place, and she always marvelled over the dun-coloured bluffs for which it was named, as she drove in.

But there was more to the town than the natural beauty of it; the Council of Elders had chosen it both for the quality of the soil, and because it was the nearest town to the small hydroelectric plant, and irrigation system, from the Grand Valley Diversion Dam. Now, by working together with those in Hope Meadows and Carbondale, everyone had access to power and clean water, and had cultivated an abundance of crops; families were settled, and babies were being born... Nita smiled to herself as she rubbed her belly and thought of Doron and their baby. No life was without its problems, and the hard work had not stopped once the communities had begun to thrive, but it was all good.

But, as appealing as Palisade undoubtedly was, she had quickly come to realise that her true home was wherever Doron Malik waited. Since he and John were the twins' protectors, there was no question of either of them moving away from Hope Meadows, and, after Todd had generously gifted him his mother's cabin, it had not taken Doron long to ask Nita to move in with him. She hadn't thought twice, and they had agreed to split their time between the surgery there, and this one in Palisade. She was finally at peace for the first time in what felt like forever.

The afternoon heat was oppressive, but the avenue of trees provided blissful pockets of shade, and Nita walked slowly between them, looking around at the huge, detached homes that sat in their sprawling grounds... Didn't people ever feel lonely in those vast spaces? She thought of the small cabin she shared with Doron, of the little annoyances of close-living domestic life that made her click her tongue, or roll her eyes, and knew she would have it no other way.

Moki's home, however, unlike some of these sprawling houses, was a bungalow. It had a neat garden at the front, dominated by a large, leafy Cimmaron Ash that cast a wide patch of shade in which he now sat on a bench, the inevitable book in his hands.

He heard her step on the path and looked up. 'Hania Nita!' He rose and took her hands, guiding her to the bench. 'Was that a good idea, to walk here in your condition?'

'The exercise is good for me, you know that.' Nita sat down gratefully. 'But I have to admit I didn't factor in the heat.'

'Sit there then, I've made some mint tea, it'll cool you down.'

Nita obeyed, closing her eyes and enjoying the flickering shadows as the leaves above her dipped and swayed in the faint breeze. After a moment Moki returned with a large tumbler, and a footstool which he placed before her. He sat quietly, waiting for her to speak, and she sipped at the deliciously cool tea.

'How're things with you?' she asked after minute or two of companionable silence.

'Good.'

'Crops going well?'

'As expected. The soil here is blessed, and with the additional newcomers over the last few years, we can now extend into Montrose County and increase the corn production.'

'That's good news.'

'I understand you have recently met survivors from Africa?'

Nita nodded. 'They sailed to Brazil, and made their way from there to Colorado. It might not be long before we see the first plane.'

Moki grunted; she wasn't sure if he was pleased about that or not, but it was an inevitable part of life, and she herself was quietly excited at the prospect. 'We also have some doctors and nurses now,' she went on, 'so we can finally open a section of the hospital in Glenwood

Springs. And some more teachers, too, which has taken the pressure off Jen and the others.'

'And how is Jen? And her mother of course. I was sorry to hear the news of her father's death.'

'They're doing alright. Sue's moved back to Hope Meadows which has been good for them both. Tony was a good man. A heart attack is something our immunity doesn't protect us against unfortunately.'

'Indeed.' He gave her a sidelong look. 'Though I feel you didn't visit today to talk of such things.'

Nita smiled. 'No, you're right. I do have something else on my mind.'

'Then speak it.'

'It's Rose's blanket.' She shifted slightly on the bench. 'I told Sinead about the Ute tradition, for each generation to copy the design.'

'Go on.'

'Well, Rose's grandmother made the blanket, and it hasn't been copied since. I felt I ought to carry on the tradition, but have no idea how to weave. When Sinead asked for a pattern, so she could knit a copy of it to make a baby blanket, I made her one.'

Moki waited expectantly, but Nita was chewing her lip as she thought it through once again, still bemused. 'As I copied the stripes, the lines somehow reminded me of the Hopi tablet, so I compared it to the photo I have of it. I know the photo is only of half the tablet but, Moki, the lines are identical!'

'Of course.' Moki sounded so matter-of-fact, that Nita couldn't help staring at him.

'What do you mean, *of course?*'

368

'A long time ago I told you that the Hopi's *Man of Sin* was the old man that you saw in your vision, remember? And that he was also the Ute's *Sinawav*.'

'Yes,' Nita said slowly, 'and I meant to ask you about that, but so many things have happened since, it slipped my mind. I still don't see the connection though.'

'You will remember that two of his sons were taken in by my people, and two taken in by your own people. So two became Hopi, and two became Ute.'

She nodded. 'I remember that.'

'Each community took care of their half of the sacred tablet that came from… well, we now know it came from Moses' brother, Maor. The Ute brothers, for reasons we were never told, decided to take one half of the tablet to their Hopi brothers, without their Chief's permission. It broke on the journey. All the pieces fell out through a hole in the old, worn bag that contained it, and when they arrived at the home of the Fire Clan, all that was left was the bag, stained with the lines of the tablet.'

Nita's eyes widened, and the tumbler was lowered, forgotten. 'Sinawav gave his bag of sticks to Coyote, to take to the Ute mountains,' she said in quiet awe, as the connection became clear, 'but all the pieces fell out on the journey. The lines on the tablet look like sticks.'

Moki went on, 'The wives of the Hopi brothers wove a blanket for the Ute brothers to take home with them, so they had a record of the sacred lines that the Man of Sin had travelled so far to give to them. Their chief was furious of course, and the brothers were cast out, leaving their home and their families behind them. But the blanket became a sacred item, and to ensure its message was not lost, each generation had to copy it exactly.'

'I was told the blanket was a copy of the line marks of Sinawav's bag,' Nita said. 'Like the stories passed down through all cultures, this one has changed into something almost completely different. I wonder what became of the Ute brothers.'

'No-one knows. I would guess they went to live with another tribe; they would find it difficult to survive on their own, and with no women.'

'And if they had more children it could explain why the immunity gene was so widespread among our peoples.' Nita smiled at him and touched his arm. 'Thank you, Moki.'

He nodded, and fell into his more usual silence again, but his words still resonated as Nita finished her tea and left him alone once more in his shady haven.

Back at Hope Meadows she turned off the engine and sat for a moment, enjoying the quiet. Even before she got out of the truck she saw three dogs pelting towards it, their grinning faces making her wonder, not for the first time, how they could recognise such things. Despite almost every house in the compound being open and welcoming to them, and being fussed over like a queen and her princes, they would break down walls to be at Nita's side; she climbed from the truck and sat down to receive them, as she usually did now, since bending at the waist had become more difficult.

They snuffled and murmured their greetings, and succumbed happily to her attentions, and after a while

Nita pulled herself to her feet again, using the door handle to help, grunting as she did so. The birth of this baby couldn't come soon enough, not only for the joy of meeting hers and Doron's child at last, but for the simple pleasure of thoughtless, easy movement.

The town was, as always, alive with purposeful activity and a sense of routine. At this time of year the storing of harvested crops took up a great deal of time, and no-one was exempt from doing their part, nor did they wish to be; from the moment a child could walk they were given something to do that brought them some satisfaction and sense of being part of the machine that kept everyone fed and warm.

Sinead waved at her from her porch, and Nita waved back, before taking her bags out of the truck and accompanying the eager dogs over to where Karl and Emily sat sorting carrots into crates. She went indoors to find Sinead, still dressed in a dirty apron, washing her hands at the sink.

'Sit yourself down, I'll get the kids to clean up and then they can go and play for a while. They deserve a break as much as anyone.' She called out of the front door, then put water on to boil while Nita settled down at the table. As soon as the children had gone out again, to find sticks to throw for the dogs, she sat down and listened, with ever-widening eyes, as Nita told her everything Moki had said.

'What a wonderful story, and you're right, they're identical. It does tie in a lot of information.'

'And now that you know the story,' Nita said, 'you'll understand why your offer to make the blanket means so

371

much to me.' She felt the sting of tears and told herself it was her stupid hormones playing up again, but the sense of peace and release she felt, deep down, was undeniable.

Sinead seemed to understand, and she smiled. 'Well I wanted to give you something special, and now I have a pattern I'll get cracking. I'm so glad you like my idea, it's going to be...' She trailed away, and kept looking at the photograph and the pattern.

'What? What is it?'

Sinead frowned. 'Look at this, Nita.' She indicated the pattern. 'The lines are different sizes, and so are the spaces. It's quite unusual, don't you think? It's almost like they were randomly made, but I don't think they were.'

Nita still looked at her blankly. 'They must be.'

'I'd never noticed it before, not until I'd seen it on paper.' Her face had taken on a new light, she looked cautiously excited.

'What do you mean?'

'Well... No. You'll think I'm nuts.'

'Try me.'

'It's just... Oh whatever. Here goes.' Sinead shrugged. 'Don't you think it looks a bit like a... a barcode?'

Nita's first instinct was to laugh, but when Sinead didn't join in, she looked closer. 'I guess it does, a bit,' she conceded doubtfully. 'But really, a five-thousand-year-old *barcode*? I thought those were invented by some guy drawing lines in the sand, back in the '50s.'

'I've no idea about that,' Sinead said, 'but stranger things have happened these last few years, so why not? It might have been the only way the Fathers could get a message to us through Maor. He couldn't write, after all.'

372

Nita remained unconvinced, it was just too crazy for words. But, she told herself, Sinead was right; stranger, equally unaccountable things *had* happened, and hadn't she learned by now that nothing could be ruled out? What if that guy on Miami beach hadn't been there by accident? Had simply been a conduit? What if the Fathers had been working through him?

'I'll take it over to John,' she said at last, feeling the stirrings of the same excitement she could still see on Sinead's face. 'If our resident computer man can't figure it out, no-one can.'

Two days later, she found herself sitting outside the same cabin, but this time all six of them were there, and, as she sipped her tea, she found herself eyeing the bottles of beer they were drinking with more than a little envy. She and Doron had hurried over to Todd and Sinead's cabin at the news that John had something to tell them; and now she was hot and bothered, and the baby was pushing inside her almost as if he or she knew something was happening and wanted a closer look. A foot or hand was wedged beneath her ribcage, and Nita worked at it to push it back down, and blew irritably at her snow-white fringe. Jen threw her a look of sympathy, but John tapped his beer bottle with his pen, and halted the different conversations that had sprung up while they settled.

'Right, I hope you're sitting comfortably,' he began, his eyes alight as he looked at them in turn. 'This is going to blow your teeny tiny minds.'

Nita and Doron exchanged glances of mingled amusement and anticipation. 'Speak up, O wise one,' Doron said dryly, and when the ripple of laughter died away John grinned.

'I took the pattern you gave me, Nita, and Sinead was right. It *is* a barcode.'

The murmur of interest around the table grew, then quickly faded as they realised this wasn't the revelation for which John had called them together. Having discussed it among themselves over the past couple of days they'd been in two minds; there was nothing to say that the man who'd been credited with the invention hadn't been subject to intervention from a supernatural source, just as Nita had said; no-one knew better than they did that it was entirely possible.

'I wasn't sure if it was anything,' John went on, settling into his stride, 'or even if the pattern was still accurate after being copied over millennia, and by so many people. You know how these things can warp even a tiny bit, and then a bit more. I had to re-draw the thirty-one lines, and set up different scanners to read it.'

'And?' Todd rolled his eyes and looked around at the others. 'Likes to milk the moment, this bloke, doesn't he?'

John swatted at him, still smiling. 'For the first few attempts, nothing.' He held up a hand to stem the good-natured protests. 'There are so many different one-dimensional linear barcodes,' he pointed out. 'Eventually I worked out that it was what's known as a *code 128*.' He paused, clearly enjoying the moment. 'Are you ready for this? It includes letters. It's actually two words!'

'What?' Doron sat upright in his chair.

'What are they?' Sinead asked, her eyes huge.

'Spit it out, man!' This from Todd, of course, who nevertheless looked impressed and excited.

'We thought it might be numbers,' Doron said, 'that they might be co-ordinates of some kind.'

'Or a code,' Nita added.

John waited for the buzz to die down. 'El dani,' he said.

Sinead blinked. 'That's Hally, isn't it? Dani, kah, tren...'

'It is, yes,' Jen supplied. 'It reads The One.'

They all spoke over one another again. 'What one?' Todd wanted to know.

'The one what?' Doron asked.

'That's what we don't know,' Jen confessed. 'Hally's not a written language, so it's even more surprising to find the words in a language we understand.'

'So, the message sent by the Fathers, five thousand years ago, and presumably what all this has been leading to, is... The One. Bit of a let down, isn't it?'

'I don't know,' Todd mused, 'I always enjoyed The Matrix.' But he still looked disappointed. 'Still, it's a bit better than 42, I suppose.'

'Huh?' Doron looked confused.

'The answer to the ultimate question? Hitch Hiker's Guide?' Todd raised an eyebrow, but shrugged. 'Never mind.'

'Honey, it's got to mean something,' Nita said, putting her hand on Doron's arm. She could sense the disappointment coming off him in waves. 'Why would they bother otherwise?'

'I agree,' John said, optimistic as ever. 'We just have to work out what it is.'

'Hmm.' Sinead took a long swallow of her beer, and closed her eyes. 'El dani. El dani. El dani—'

'Wait!' Nita caught her breath, just as Doron had, when he'd urged John towards the *father, son* connection. 'Say it again, Sinead, keep saying it!'

Sinead cracked one eye open and obeyed. 'El dani – el dani-el...' She stopped, and now it was Doron's turn to look shocked, while Todd spluttered on his beer.

'Daniel!' Doron turned to Nita, who nodded, unable to speak. He looked back at the others. 'That's the name we've chosen for a baby boy.' His voice broke. 'Daniel's *The One*?'

'No way,' Todd said, his voice soft, disbelieving, as he wiped his mouth on his sleeve.

'We still don't know what it means by that though,' John reminded them. 'I think we should look at Dakayivani's prophecy again.'

'I have it by heart,' Nita said. 'We already know about the sickness, and that Hampton was the skinwalker that rose from the burial grounds at the airport.' She shot Todd a quick glance and then looked away, her heart sore at the look on his face. 'My great-grandfather wouldn't have understood what a marrow transplant was, so that part was confusing. But Hampton was walking around with Alima's DNA inside him, so it's understandable.'

'And you are Hania Nita,' Doron said with unmistakeable pride in his voice. 'The spirit warrior who defeated him.'

376

'A two-spirit will re-unite the scattered tribes, and you will know him by his name,' Nita went on, feeling Doron's hand close over hers. She returned the pressure, her heart swelling with gratitude for having found these people who had helped her as much as she had helped them.

'That might be it,' Jen said. '*You will know him by his name*, and we've just been given his name. Daniel will be the one to reunite the people.'

Todd spoke up. 'Wasn't there a bit about the two-spirit being part bear blood, and part eagle? The blood of brothers?'

Nita's own voice sounded distant and quiet to her own ears, but she heard the truth of her words as if it were being shouted from the mountain tops. 'Our child will have both mine and Ron's blood. Ron is part of Eagle, and is descended from Moses; my name means *bear,* and I'm descended from Maor. He will have the blood of both of those brothers.'

'Someone once told me that prophetic visions only give a glimpse of a possible future,' Todd said, 'but so far those we have been given have been accurate.'

'If our child is destined to be the one to unite people,' Doron mused, 'do you think this will be enough to convince Moki to sway his vote on the council of Elders? To bring our people together for good?'

'No,' Nita said with a little sigh. 'He's a stubborn old man, it'll take more than that. We'll have to wait and see about the two-spirit part. But...' She looked at Doron, and everything else seemed to diminish around them both, as, for the moment at least, they became no more or less than two people with a child in their future. 'It looks like we're going to have a baby boy.'

Chapter Twenty
Daniel

October

If Nita had been uncomfortable and impatient two months before, now she had convinced herself that nothing was ever going to change; she was going to stay the size of an elephant forever. She was clearly going to make history as the first woman to stay pregnant for—

'Hey, how's it going?' Sinead sauntered in through the open door, carrying a package wrapped in tissue paper.

'Nothing doing,' Nita grumbled. 'This baby won't budge. I've tried pelvic tilts, moxibustion... Even belly dancing,'

Sinead laughed. 'I'll bet *that* was awful good to behold!'

'Laugh away,' Nita said darkly, though she couldn't help smiling, 'it'll be your turn next.'

'Oh, I think not, we're happy as we are, thanks.' Sinead handed her the package. 'Looks like I've finished this just in time.'

Nita pulled at the blue bow, and the tissue paper fell away to reveal the hand-knitted blanket. She lifted it out and unfolded it, and her smile lost its rueful edge and became one of appreciation and gratitude.

'I know you like bright colours,' Sinead said, watching her almost anxiously. 'That's why I used red for the background, like Rose's blanket, but different colours for the stripes.'

'It's beautiful, I love it.' Nita pressed it to her face and breathed in the smell. 'And it's so soft too!' She hugged her friend, a little awkwardly as her belly seemed to get in the way of everything now. 'Thank you so much.'

A voice called hesitantly from the doorway. 'Okay to come in?'

'Maya! Of course, please do.'

Maya had brought a woman with her who Nita recognised from her check-ups; one of the best of Maya's trainee midwives, and, as much as she respected her, her unexpected appearance told Nita what was in store. She gave an inward shudder.

'It's nice to see you, Bo,' she said, nevertheless, and the shy little woman gave her an apologetic smile.

'You too. You're looking very well.'

'How are you doing?' Maya asked. 'Still breech I take it.'

Nita nodded. 'Afraid so.'

'He *has* to be a male then,' Sinead put in, 'they do everything arseways.'

The women smiled, and Nita was grateful for the moment of levity. 'I really don't want a Caesarean,' she said, 'but nothing's shifting him. I guess we're going to have to go with manoeuvring him.'

'You've not long to go,' Maya agreed, 'ECV is probably going to be the only thing to do now. My hands won't let me anymore, but Bo's very capable, as you know. And I'll be here to supervise. It won't take long, but, as you know, it'll be—'

'Uncomfortable.' Nita grimaced. 'I know. Medical speak for damned painful. Okay, let's get it done.'

'Just a sec,' Sinead put in. 'Maya, do you mind if we try one more thing first?'

'Anything,' Nita said, and had to smile at the desperation she heard in her own voice. 'What do you have in mind?'

'Well, when my ma was pregnant with our Pat, he was breech too. She got into a warm bath, and put a packet of frozen peas on her belly.'

'And that worked?'

'Little bugger soon turned. Worth a go, anyway, right?'

Maya nodded. 'That's a great idea. It can do no harm, that's for sure, and if you're lucky Bo and I won't be needed, but we'll drop back in a couple of hours anyway, to see how you got on.'

A short while later Nita lowered herself carefully into the bath, feeling the warm water lap at her skin, and hoping Sinead's idea wasn't as nuts as it sounded; she didn't relish the idea of someone, however careful and professional, manipulating her tight and aching belly with the force that would be needed to turn this baby head-down. She rested her head back against the the bath and closed her eyes, while Sinead went off in search of something suitable from the freezer.

After a moment Sinead returned. 'I couldn't find any peas,' she said, 'but there's this frozen... looks like... porridge?'

Nita peered through the steam. 'It's cooked quinoa. That'll do fine. Come on, then.'

Sinead leaned over to balance the bag, and Nita jumped as the ice-cold packet touched her warm skin. She almost snatched if off again as the cold spread across her body, but the thought of the alternative stayed her hand, and instead she clutched at the handles on the side of the bath and gritted her teeth until her skin became numb.

Sinead perched herself on the closed lid of the toilet, and began to chatter about nothing in particular, providing a friendly background hum as Nita half-dozed, enjoying this rare moment of relaxation. She told herself she would soon crave chances like this, and would look on them as a luxury.

Abruptly she sat up straight, with a sharp gasp, and the frozen quinoa tumbled off her and into the water, with a barely noticeable splash. The bath water rippled, and as Nita stared down at her belly she saw it change shape in front of her eyes. There was a disorientating twisting feeling that made her feel a little sick, followed by a powerful, dragging sensation, and a sharp pain in her groin made her grunt. But it all stopped as quickly as it had begun, and was followed by a feeling of euphoria that she knew must be shining out of her eyes, as she raised them to meet Sinead's.

Sinead had been equally transfixed by the miracle. Her mouth hung open as if she were trying to say *wow*, but couldn't quite manage it, and then she broke into a grin and raised her hand to high-five the stunned and relieved Nita.

'*Yes!*'

***

23 October

Doron had been at Nita's side since the contractions had started, but her initial gratitude had quickly turned to irritation when he gave one piece of advice too many. Thankfully he wasn't the only one to find themselves on the sharp end of Nita's tongue, or he'd have thought he was back at the spa where they had first met, with the glare of her torch full in his face. Even Maya, supervising Bo and giving Nita gentle encouragement to push, was not spared.

'I *am* pushing!' Nita snarled between puffing. 'If I push any more I'll turn inside out!' She rolled onto her side. 'This is useless. Help me off here so I can squat.'

Doron hovered at the other side of the room and wished he could do something useful; Nita was exhausted, her hair lay flat, plastered to her face with sweat, and her limbs visibly trembled as Maya and Bo eased her off the bed and into a more natural squatting position. She held onto the tailboard of the bed, while the two women placed towels beneath her, and Doron had to force himself not to kneel beside her; she needed freedom and space to move, and she did, shifting from side to side and giving gutteral moans deep in her throat as she rode each new contraction.

Before too long she began to pant again, and Doron's heartbeat picked up. Maya and Bo moved into position either side of Nita as she raised her chin and pushed again; Maya had told her not to scream, but to push all the energy down inside instead. To use it, instead of releasing

383

it into the room. She did so, and Doron watched in some alarm as her face turned puce with the effort, but with a shocking suddenness her eyes shot wide, and her mouth dropped open in a soundless cry of release and astonishment. The head was out, and with one more, almost nonchalent push, Nita delivered the child into the waiting hands of her midwives.

Bo eased the boy onto the towels, and a couple of minutes later, while Doron was still staring at him in mute awe, Nita grunted again and the afterbirth came slithering out, to be whisked away by Maya. Bo cut the baby's cord and wrapped him securely, then placed him reverently in his mother's eager arms.

Nita's eyes were fixed on the child as she was helped carefully back onto the bed, but she looked up at Doron as he came over, and the tears were standing in her eyes even as Maya went about the business of cleaning her and examining to see if any stitches were needed. It all seemed to be happening in another world, even for Nita.

'Look what we've made,' she whispered. 'Look at our son.'

Doron's own eyes were stinging, and he blinked away the blur so he could see his child more clearly. 'Hello, Daniel,' he said softly, and his voice caught on the words as he touched one finger to the perfect, smooth cheek. He looked back at Nita; hot, sweaty, exhausted, and felt the surge of love for them both like a physical ache. He couldn't speak, but managed to mouth the words, *I love you*.

She nodded, and there was no need for her to say it back; the proof lay there in her arms. Her eyes kept slipping closed, and after a few minutes Bo took Daniel gently from her and gave him to Doron, while Maya finished her ministrations and helped Nita change into clean nightclothes.

Doron was aware of the bustle going on around him as he sat in the chair with his son, but his attention was on the sweep of dark eyelashes against the curve of an infant cheek, and the dimpled, starfishing fingers that clutched with instinctive strength around his own. He looked across to draw Nita's attention to it, but she was sleeping so he reluctantly gave Daniel over to the midwives, to carry out their tests, checks and weighings, and went outside.

He could hear low voices and quiet laughs; the hiss of a cap being twisted off a bottle of beer; the muted remonstrations to an overactive child... all the familiar sounds of a small crowd waiting for news. It was dark now, but he pulled the door shut behind him and raised a finger to his lips, and he could still see familiar, friendly faces in the light that spilled from the surrounding cabins. His smile was soon mirrored on them all as they looked expectantly at him.

'We have a boy,' he called quietly, and the few rousing cheers were quickly hushed, but there was joy in the words of congratulations that drifted up to him from the group. A few people climbed the steps and patted him on the back, but as Doron turned to go back inside, he saw the lights of a jeep come sweeping along the perimeter fence, and turned back. The vehicle parked haphazardly in the parking area, and those who remained muttered to one another, perturbed to see someone in such a hurry, especially at this time of night. Doron's joy was further shadowed by trepidation as he saw Moki climb down from the jeep and come hurrying over, but as the elder drew closer Doron realised the urgency was caused by excitement rather than worry. He'd never seen Moki so animated.

He half-ran to meet him. 'Moki? What's going on?'

'I need to see Nita.'

'She won't be able to help, she's sleeping and I'm not going to disturb her.'

'But I must see her,' Moki insisted, pushing past him. 'I have wonderful news!'

'So do I.' Doron smiled as he followed. 'She's just given birth to our son.'

Moki stopped in surprise. 'But he wasn't due for another week.'

'You know how babies are.' Doron shrugged, suddenly the expert, he thought with a little grin.

'Of course, of course!' Moki beamed. 'That's wonderful news indeed. And are they both well?'

'They are. Although she's very—'

'Oh, but that changes everything,' Moki interrupted, his eyes widening as he realised something.

'What?'

'I must see him!'

'That's not a great idea,' Doron said firmly. 'I'd be happy for you to stop by tomorrow and—'

'No, it must be now. Please! I'll explain later.' Moki was becoming agitated now, and Doron hesitated. This was so unlike the elder that he was torn between duty and curiosity.

386

'Okay, but I still don't want to disturb Nita. Tell you what, you wait here on the porch. I'll bring him to you...*if* Maya's finished checking him over.'

Moki nodded, a little impatiently, and Doron threw him another curious look as he went back inside. Maya had laid Daniel in the crib next to the bed, and in response to Doron's raised eyebrow she nodded.

'He's perfect,' she whispered.

'I need to take him outside for a minute, is that okay?'

'Keep him wrapped up warm.' Maya handed him the blanket Sinead had knitted, and showed him how to swaddle the baby securely, but not too tight. 'Be quick. Nita will not sleep long, and we need to get them skin to skin, and feeding, soon.'

Doron carried Daniel out to the porch, wondering at how light he was, and suddenly terrified he would trip on a loose carpet and drop him. Moki was sitting on the bench beneath the porch roof, and as Doron appeared he stood up to take closer look, and drew a sharp breath.

'He has come!' he said, his voice barely audible, but filled with reverence.

'What do you mean?'

'The blue star, Kachina, appeared in the sky tonight.'

'The what?'

'The sign that the lost white brother of the Hopi has come.' Moki sat back down, as if his legs would no longer hold him up. 'It is said that he will have pale skin and black hair, and will come wearing red.' He pointed to the blanket. 'And he will bring the missing piece of the tablet with him.' His gaze shifted from the blanket to the baby's serene, sleeping face, and Doron saw there were tears in his eyes. 'Welcome, Pahana,' he said quietly.

Then he looked up at Doron. 'Thank you. I'll leave you now, and will return at a more convenient time.' As he descended the porch steps he called back, without looking. 'I'll be calling a meeting of the Council of Elders tomorrow.' At the bottom of the steps he turned back to Doron, and there was resolve written into the lined features. 'This time our vote, to accept this new way of life, will be unanimous.'

Maya had helped Daniel latch on for his first, brief feed last night, and this morning Nita had struggled a little doing it alone, but finally got him settled, and Doron went to prepare breakfast. It was definitely a morning to push the boat out, so he used some of the last wild strawberries to garnish a stack of warm pancakes, and took them, with a glass of cold milk, through to where Nita was propped up against her pillows with Daniel at her breast. Her milk hadn't come in properly yet, but the boy had taken the nourishment he needed, and had fallen asleep, a yellow-ish milky residue spilling from the rosebud lips. Doron lifted him gently away from his mother and wrapped him firmly the way Maya had shown him, before laying him back in the crib.

Nita was already tucking into the pancakes as if she hadn't eaten for days. It must feel like that, Doron thought, remembering last night; they surely didn't call it labor for nothing. He climbed onto the bed beside her, and told her about Moki's visit. When he reiterated the elder's parting words, Nita lost all interest in the berries, and her face lit in a smile that made him wish she hadn't just given birth.

'We can all be one people now,' she enthused, unaware of the sudden longing that held him. Her eyes were bright as she pushed her hair away from her face. 'It's the most wonderful news.'

'Explain to me again about the prophecies,' he said, tearing off a piece of pancake, and channelling his thoughts determinedly away from the way her lips closed over the strawberry in her fingers. 'Such a lot has happened I want to be sure I have it right.'

'Well, the Hopi and the Navajo both believe we are currently living in the fourth world.' Nita shifted back against her pillows, and winced at the unthinking movement. 'The first three were destroyed by fire, ice and flood. The fourth was to be destroyed by earth changes and sickness, we've already seen this.'

'Damned right.' He took a slug of her milk. 'Go on.'

'The Anishinaabe prophecies are described as *Fires*, and we're currently living in the Sixth Fire, a time of sickness. The time of the Seventh Fire will be the time of a new people, a united people, and peace. It's believed that Pahana,' she stole a glance at their slumbering son, 'will lead us into the fifth world and the Seventh Fire. Only then will we become closer to our creator.'

He followed her gaze. 'That's a lot of responsibility for a new born child.'

'Well he doesn't have to do it right now,' Nita pointed out with a laugh, but Doron remained troubled.

'Yeah, I know, but still. It's a lot for anyone. And I guess we have to wait and see if he's going to be the *tainna wai'ppe* your great-grandfather spoke of.'

'A *tainna wai'ppe* is a two-spirit,' Nita said, 'but their spirit part was not like the ones you and the twins have.' She ate quietly for a moment, and he saw she was searching for the best way to explain. 'My great-grandfather was a third gender,' she said at length, 'highly respected for his differences. As were others, until homophobic Christians forced them to conform. It was a terrible time for them, and remained so for hundreds of years.'

'I wouldn't want that for our son.'

'Of course not. Who would?' Nita eyed him carefully. 'Would it bother you if he was a different gender?'

'No! No, of course not. That's not what I meant. I just know what it's like to be different, and I want nothing but good things for him.' He watched her finish her breakfast, and tried to explain what he meant.

'The Fathers manipulated both the timing of our births, and our becoming aware of our spirits, to coincide with us being able to communicate with them.' He took her now-empty plate and slipped it on top of his own. 'Uri told me it takes 375 years for a solar eclipse to happen again in the same place, so that was their one and only chance to communicate with us. Will they do the same with Daniel?'

Nita put a hand on his arm. 'He'll be growing up in a different world, Ron,' she said gently. 'A better, kinder world. He's not even a day old, and you're already worrying about his future.'

'I've been worrying about his future since you told me you were pregnant,' he pointed out dryly. 'You can't pretend you haven't been doing the same. It's what all parents do.'

'Well he's going to be fine, so let's just concentrate on getting him fed, changed, and burped for now.' She gave him a little smile. 'One day I may worry that he'll be as handsome as his father, and that women will take advantage of him.'

'Oh yeah?' Doron felt a faint flush on his cheeks, but he hid his own smile and raised an eyebrow. 'Did you take advantage of me?'

Nita grinned and leaned over to kiss him. 'Of course I did, and I intend to do so for the rest of my life.'

Chapter Twenty One
The Weddings

1st August 5 PV (2008)

'There's still time to back out, you know.'

Doron and Todd both turned to glare at John, who was wearing the easy grin of one who has already walked this particular path, and whose role is now to simply enjoy watching others do the same.

'You're supposed to be putting us at our ease,' Todd grumbled, running his finger around the collar of his shirt, 'not making it worse.'

'Sorry. I admit, I was nervous as hell when I married Jen.'

They waited outside Doron and Nita's cabin, the grooms fidgeting with ties and straightening blue linen jackets that didn't need straightening, and staring at the door as if they could force it to open by willpower alone.

To distract himself, Doron kept twisting around to look at the area that had been set up in the field adjacent. A large space had been cordoned off, with rope adorned with ribbons, and two volunteer guards stood at the rear corners watching for any wildlife that might cause a problem. A small stage had been built for the evening entertainment, with more lights adorning the edges, with speakers and a microphone set in place ready. There were to be no gifts, but each person had brought a donation of food and drink, and placed it in the large marquee that had been erected nearby and decorated with lights. It was strange to think that, the next time he and Nita danced together, they would be married.

'What's taking them so long?' he muttered, turning back. 'What time is it?'

'They've got five minutes yet,' John said, 'and girls take longer to get ready than we do. You know darn well you'll appreciate the result,' he added with another grin. He turned, as the door to Rena and Alex's cabin opened. 'Here come the flower bearers, right on time.'

Five of the joint towns' youngest children came down the steps, looking equally self-conscious and highly excited; both brides had agreed to dispense with the tradition of flower girls only, so all of them carried small buckets they'd decorated themselves and filled with flower petals. The boys, Karl and Paco, wore the same blue suits as the grooms, but topped off with cowboy hats, into which Paco had stuck two large eagle feathers he had collected.

Two of the three girls, Emily, and Meiying had wanted to be princesses, so were dressed in identical long party dresses in different pastel shades, with flower tiaras for their hair. Odina, however, had insisted on jeans, but bowing to Wapun's compromise she sported a smart white pair, with a blue lace shirt. She too had a cowboy hat, but Paco only had two eagle feathers, so she had hunted about until she found a brilliant blue tail feather from a steller's jay, and wore that with every bit as much pride.

She and the princesses were skipping along behind the boys, careful not to spill any petals from their buckets, and Rena watched from the top of the steps with a warm smile, as the men crouched down to acknowledge them. The boys dutifully reciprocated high fives, and Odina stepped forward to receive one as well. Her tiny hand almost disappeared in theirs, but she beamed in delight as she rejoined the girls.

'You look so cool!' Doron said with approval, as he surveyed the group. 'Girls, you look beautiful. You all ready?'

'Yessir!' the boys chorused.

'Well it won't be long now, we just have to wait for the ladies to come out.'

'Will they be princesses too?' Emily asked Todd.

'I really don't know,' Todd said. 'It's a big secret. We'll see soon though...Aha!'

As he spoke, the cabin door opened and Sinead emerged, dressed in a long summer dress of green chiffon, and with her red hair piled high and decorated with flowers.

For once Todd was struck speechless, except for a whispered, 'Wow,' as she joined him and took his arm. He kissed her, and Doron was touched to see his eyes glisten as he pulled back and looked down at her again.

But his own attention was drawn back to the doorway again as Nita stepped out and into the bright afternoon sun. All he'd known was that Belle had wanted her to wear traditional white, but Nita had been worried that, with her white hair, she would look more ghostly than glowing. So, while Farrah had made adjustments and alterations to existing clothes for everyone else, she had made Nita's from scratch, from a glorious red faux suede. It reached the floor and was fastened by small straps, with long fringes stitched to the waist, and shorter ones hanging from the bodice.

Half of Nita's hair was plaited, and entwined with feathers and beads, and encircling her waist was a beaded belt Belle had made for her. She wore a small, matching pouch around her neck, that Doron knew contained her treasured possessions: a braid made from blended locks of hair from Rose and Joe, and the car-stone that Billy had loved. Rena and Belle had attached small beads to the ends of each fringe, and it warmed Doron to the soul as he realised how much care these women, as Nita's surrogate mothers, had taken.

Todd and John whistled their appreciation again, but he could do little else but stare; it hit him all over again how lucky he was, as he realised that this vision of natural beauty was walking towards *him*. He even found himself glancing around as if there had been some cosmic mistake, but no. Her dark eyes smiled up at him, and she took his hands when he held them out to her.

'You're so beautiful,' he murmured. It was like telling the sky it was blue; no words could do justice to the purity of her beauty.

'You're not half bad yourself.' Nita squeezed his hands, then let go to take his arm instead, and they joined Todd and Sinead as John walked ahead, whistling to the milling guests to let them know they were coming.

It seemed everyone had come today, to witness the first weddings to take place since the merging of the neighbouring communities. Two rows of chairs had been placed in the field, for the elderly and anyone else who might have trouble standing, but the remainder of the guests were quite happy to stand. It gave the event an informal atmosphere, and there was much laughter and chatter as they shuffled into place to watch the small procession.

At John's signal, the crowd parted to make a human aisle to lead the brides and grooms towards the front. The children walked down the aisle, scattering their petals in the couples' path, and Doron and Nita both turned to wave at Daniel, who was sitting on Rena's lap at the back. He waved his chubby arms at them and bounced in excitement, and this time when they exchanged smiles the nerves had gone, replaced by familiarity and contentment.

The three freshly-bathed dogs sat quietly around Rena's chair, watching the parade with great solemnity, but a moment later Nita gave a little squeak of surprise as Kimi, belatedly recognising her mistress beneath all the finery, appeared at her side. The dog walked perkily alongside her all the way to the front, much to the amusement of everyone else, and for once Boss and Echo were the sedate ones, taking their role seriously and staying behind to protect their new young master.

Todd and Sinead walked in front, with Doron and Nita behind to accommodate Todd's slower pace; although his leg had healed well, he would always have a noticeable limp. Alex, nominated for the role of celebrant, waited for them at the front, with an air of nervous pride at the importance of today's ceremony. Uri and Maya were standing at the edge of their row, and as Ron passed them

Maya reached out and hand and grasped his. She squeezed briefly, and gave him a smile that recalled everything they'd been through together, from the very start. It made his heart clench a little, to remember it all, and he smiled back, hoping his feelings showed as deeply as he felt them.

John moved to the left to stand next to Jen and her mother, with the girls behind them, and Belle stood to the right with Moki. Both Jen and Belle held two flower garlands each, and John and Moki were the keepers of the rings. The children had moved away to be with their respective parents, their roles now fulfilled, except Karl and Emily who stood with the Milburns.

'*Sannu* and good afternoon to you all,' Alex began. 'Honoured guests, family, friends, and neighbours, it's a wonderful thing to see everyone here as one people. We have all come a long way together, through hard work and compromise. We honour the Fathers and our ancestors, remember our past, and look forward to our future together, for we all are Children of Sinai.'

He paused to let his words echo, and then settle. Then he smiled around at everyone, the formal introduction over. 'Although not the first wedding ceremony I have had the honour to preside over, this is the first to be held at Hope Meadows,' he said, 'and after consultations with all of you, we have done our best to amalgamate all your traditions. I think you'll agree it's worked out quite well.'

There were murmurs of approval, and Doron squeezed Nita's hand. She smiled up at him.

'It's a beautiful day,' Alex went on, 'and I thank you all for your help, and for coming to witness these marriages.

I would like to thank the flower girls and boys, so thank you, children you did a wonderful job.'

'I know!' rang out a high voice Doron recognised as Odina's, and a murmur of affectionate laughter ran around the crowd.

Alex smiled too. 'The ceremony will be brief, but no less meaningful for that. However a ceremony is performed, the joining of two people was, and always will be, a spiritual occasion, where promises are made and love is declared.'

He turned to Doron and Nita first. 'Do you, Doron Malik and Nita Rogers, both promise to love and honour one another other, above all others, and stand together through the good times and the bad times? Do you promise to love, not only the person who stands beside you today, but the person they will inevitably become? And do you declare to these people here that you will do whatever you can to make that person happy?'

Doron and Nita answered, 'We do'

'Which of you wishes to change their name, and for what reason?'

'I wish to change my name to Malik,' Nita said firmly. 'The name Rogers was forced upon my ancestors, and holds no meaning for me.' She glanced up at Doron, and then back to Alex. 'The Maliks are proud and honourable people, and I'm happy to be known by this name.'

Alex's smile warmed further at this endorsement of his son's family's name. Then he turned to Todd and Sinead and repeated the vows. Once they had responded he said again, 'Which of you wishes to change their name, and for what reason?'

Todd replied, his voice low but carrying clearly nevertheless. 'I wish to change my name to Gallagher. My father brought shame to the name Hampton. The Gallaghers were a strong, loving family, and I am happy to be known by this name.'

Jen and Belle rose, and brought over four flower garlands. Todd took his and placed it over Sinead's head. 'With this jaimala I accept you as my life partner.'

The other three did the same, and Doron heard his own voice shaking with emotion, as he was sure the others heard theirs. John and Moki came over with their rings, and they placed them on each other's fingers. *With this ring I give you my eternal love.*

Alex then turned to the congregation. 'Please welcome Doron and Nita Malik as husband and wife!' When the clapping had died down he gestured to the other couple. 'And please also welcome Sinead and Todd Gallagher as husband and wife.'

Doron, his heart singing, took Nita's hand in the crook of his elbow, and stood back to allow Todd and Sinead to precede them once again down the aisle between the chairs. As he did so he saw Karl tugging at Alex's sleeve.

'What is it?' Alex bent down, and the boy whispered something in his ear. He straightened again, his face serious, but his voice kind. 'Well now, children, this is a very serious matter. Have you both given it a lot of thought?'

They nodded, and Alex hurried after Todd and Sinead. Exchanging faintly worried glances they went into a little huddle, but when they parted Todd was wearing a look of immense pride, and Sinead patted a tear from her eye and nodded.

Alex walked back to the children, took their hands and turned to the guests once more. 'Valued friends, I wish to inform you that, from this day hence, these two children will be known as Karl and Emily Gallagher.' He turned to where the Milburn family were standing. 'Holly, Hannah, perhaps you would be so kind as to amend these records as well, when you record the name changes?' The girls grinned and nodded, and the newest Gallaghers joined the newlyweds, and were gathered into the embrace of the first true family they had known for four years.

The guests once again moved to make a human aisle directing the newlyweds to the marquee. Here, Moki presented the couples with traditional two-spouted wedding vases, from which each couple took a drink together, to signify that they now shared everything. Finally the buffet-style feast began, and everyone was given a glass of wine to toast the couples' health.

Rena brought Daniel over to Nita, and she placed him on her hip where he promptly seized her jaimala and pulled out some of the flowers. Doron managed to take them off him before they reached his mouth, and Nita swung the garland so it lay across her back and handed him a hard biscuit instead.

'He will be an inquisitive one,' Otto said, smiling at the boy as he came up to shake Ron's and Todd's hands. 'Perhaps a scientist, yes?'

'Let's hope his approach to science is bit more discerning, if so,' Ron said, pulling a face at the child, who grinned at him around his mangled biscuit.

At around six o'clock, as people gathered around outside chatting and telling stories, they heard a tapping on the microphone, then Ian's voice came over the speakers as he set up the backing tracks he had found.

'Get your dancing shoes on, folks!'

The music began, and Doron was glad to see the Scotsman's manner relax, clearly revelling in the guests' reactions to his music. Ian had moved back into the small cabin on his return to Hope Meadows, but had spent a lot of his time helping the widowed Ana Garcia. Their relationship had evolved naturally, from close friends to settled couple, and Ian had recently moved in with Ana; the happiness of having a family once again showed in his face, and in hers as she watched him with undeniable pride. He, in turn, was giving a not-very-discreet thumbs up to Steve, who seemed to be getting along very well with Meiying's widowed mother.

Doron and Nita handed Daniel back to Rena so they could relax and enjoy their evening together, and they looked around for John and Jen; it seemed an age since they'd had a proper chat about anything except the wedding. Doron saw a group of girls, eyeing some teenaged boys who were showing off for their benefit, and was a little startled to recognise Holly and Hannah, with Ruhi and Alima. They were growing up fast...

'There they are, look,' Nita said, breaking into his thoughts. 'What on earth...?'

Doron looked where she'd pointed, and saw his brother and sister-in-law, their faces wearing identical looks of mingled laughter and horror as they started towards the dance floor. He followed their trajectory, and

401

saw Moki standing at the edge of the floor talking to Jen's mother.

Moki let out a great guffaw, surprising everyone within earshot. He stepped away from Sue, holding his belly as he laughed, and everyone around him started to smile as well; for such a serious man, his laughter was utterly infectious. Sue was laughing too, but there was a puzzled tilt to her head, as if she had no idea what she was laughing about, but was powerless to stop it.

To Doron's further surprise, Moki held out his arm to Sue, and gestured to the dance floor, where they vanished among the crowds, still laughing.

'I've never seen Moki laugh before,' Nita said as they joined John and Jen. 'What just happened?'

Jen rolled her eyes. 'My mother, who, incidentally, was partly the reason I became interested in speech problems, just called him Monkey.'

'No!' Nita's shocked laughter joined Doron's, and they all turned to look at where Moki and Sue were dancing and chatting.

'She compounded the issue by saying his actual name was just like the boy from Jungle Book,' John added, grinning.

'He was lovely about it,' Jen went on, 'told her not to apologise, and that he couldn't remember the last time something made him laugh like that!'

'Well hooray for Sue,' Nita raised her glass in the direction of the dance floor. 'May she never change.'

The sun started to go down behind the distant mountains; the sky turned a beautiful burnt orange, and soon all the trees would become silhouettes, stark against the skyline. Babysitters had been organised for Karl, Emily and Daniel, at Hope Meadows, so the newlyweds had one child-free evening before family life resumed once again. Parents were gathering up the other younger children and taking them to the hall, where mattresses had been placed on the floor and a babysitting rota had been organised.

Ian switched off the microphone, and was now playing recorded songs so he could spend some time with Ana. The songs he'd chosen for this part of the evening were slower, quieter, and although the party still went on, there was more talking now, and people had dragged chairs into little groups and were laughing amongst themselves.

On the dance floor, couples had moved closer together and were rotating slowly, smiling at one another or, in some cases, their faces buried in the necks of their partners, caught up in the romance of the night.

Doron clasped Nita around the waist and she looped her hands around his neck; he suddenly felt like a lovesick teen, and bent to kiss her smiling mouth. She responded eagerly, and just as he felt himself falling into the happy place where nothing mattered except the taste of her lips and the scent of her skin, he jerked back.

Nita looked at him blankly as he stared around. 'What's up?'

'My mom *has* taken Daniel home to bed, hasn't she?'

'Yes, why?'

'I could've sworn I heard him call me, you know his funny way of saying *Dada*. It was like he was next to—

403

There it is again!' The voice echoed in his head as clearly as if he held the boy in his arms.

She frowned. 'I heard nothing.'

'I'm sorry, Nita, I have to go and check on him.'

'I'm sure he's—'

'I'll be right back.'

Rena opened the front door to his quiet knock. 'What on earth are you doing here? You should be at your reception.'

He stepped inside. 'Is Daniel okay?'

'He's fine! He's not asleep yet, too much excitement I guess, but he's such a good quiet boy there didn't seem any need to try and force him.'

'I need to see him.'

'Of course, but what's up?'

'I don't know. I just need to see him.'

He went directly to the bedroom that used to be his, and pushed open the door. Daniel was sitting quietly in his cot, reaching for his toes, his face set with concentration. He smiled when he saw his father, and reached out his arms, his little fingers clasping and unclasping in his usual *pick me up* gesture.

Dada!

His lips hadn't moved.

Rena was standing behind Doron, her arms folded. 'See, I told you he's fine.'

'Yeah, he is.' Doron lifted his son out of the cot, and as soon as he touched him he felt an old, familiar feeling come over him. He moved to the bed and lay down, with Daniel still in his arms. 'Something's happening here,

404

Mom,' he murmured. He took a deep, steadying breath and let it out slowly. 'Just don't worry, okay?'

He was on a mountain, and couldn't see far, yet he knew it wasn't Mount Sinai. There was little light, and when Doron looked up he could see the moon passing over the sun; full dark would descend any second, as the eclipse became total. Stone steps in front of him led up to the entrance of a cave, and he looked instinctively around for his brother, but there was no sign of him so he climbed to the cave alone.

Alone?

For a second his breath stopped in sheer panic as he realised Daniel wasn't with him either, but when he could see clearly again he found he was back at Hope Meadows, sitting at one end of his old bed. At the other end were the Fathers, holding two babies on their lap, one in each arm.

'Welcome again, Doron.'

Doron nodded a greeting, then looked around. 'We're not really at Hope Meadows are we? Where's Daniel?'

The Fathers gave a slow nod, and looked down at the babies. 'Do you not recognise your son? This boy and girl is *El Dani* in his spirit forms.'

Doron felt the tension in his limbs ease as he looked again. 'This is the first time I've seen them.' He rubbed his face. 'Where are we?'

'Once there were four of us,' the Fathers said, as if he hadn't spoken. 'The others did not survive, but we each had a bridge between your existence and ours. One that we can only take you to when the moon is between the sun and the earth. Our bridge was through the sacred Mount Sinai, and that is the only place we could communicate with you. *This* bridge is through one of the sacred peaks of the *Sōngshān*, the Song Mountains, in China. This cave is named for Bodhidharma, a Buddhist monk.'

'So... How is this possible?'

'We have waited so long for El Dani,' the Fathers said softly, looking down at the infants in their arms. 'He is a precious gift to all, not just to you. Not only will your son be a great leader, but he will be able to communicate with us, on any of the four bridges, during a total eclipse. We called to him, and he brought you here.'

'But why? Why is all this happening?'

'We came here so long ago, and have existed longer than man can imagine, but to enable us to remain here we need the spirits of the twins.' The Fathers' voice was quiet, yet powerful; measured, but irrefutable. 'The Mother was dying, Doron. Her soil and waters were polluted; she was forced to give too much. If she died, we would all cease to exist, and that is the reason she gave birth to the virus. To protect herself and us. We created the immunity gene so that *we* may continue, and that *you* may have a chance to prove you can care for her. You must not make the same mistakes, considering yourselves separate from the rest of life. We are all linked, and depend on each other.'

Doron felt shame creeping through him. 'I understand,' he murmured. 'I swear we will do all we can to ensure it doesn't happen again.'

406

'The Fathers are pleased.' The atmosphere changed subtly, the message delivered. 'We have little time now, Doron, do you have any questions?'

'Yes!' He sat forward eagerly. 'Who are you? What are the Fathers?' After a heartbeat, he added, 'And what am I?'

'We are An,' the Fathers said. 'Ki, the Mother, or Mother Earth, existed before all else and it was She who created life. When the An first came here we made adjustments to Her creations. Only one species survived, therefore only one An survived. We donated some of our DNA to a select few, and they were named Anunnaki.'

Doron repeated the word in a murmur, and it sounded unexpectedly comfortable and familiar. The Fathers seemed to sense this, and nodded.

We gave the Anunnaki knowledge and powers, but our gifts were abused, and Ki suffered greatly. Over time She brought forth fire, ice, flood and now sickness to destroy you. But, as you know, some survive.'

'And me?'

'You are Anunnaki, also known as Nephilim. You are of An and Ki. The knowledge and powers bestowed upon you come with conditions that we have set within your DNA, so they cannot be abused again. We cannot communicate with Ki, but we feel Her presence and She is also pleased.'

Doron absorbed this, before another question arose. 'You know that, because of Nita, we've been able to give everyone the double immunity. Will the next generation inherit the same immunity? And will any of them be different in other ways?

407

The Fathers smiled. 'Everything is happening as it should. Evolution takes time.'

It was frustrating, but it was all he was going to get. 'One more question then,' he said, 'one a lot of people have asked us. The old belief in heaven gave many people comfort, but now they ask if they will be reunited with lost loved ones.'

'They will, but not as they have been told, nor in a way they can imagine. Your creation began with the Mother and the Fathers. All that has been returns to the Mother, so you see that, by harming her, you harm yourselves and those who have already left the physical world.' There was a brief pause, then, 'Before we go, know that El Dani is to lead you to a future that is acceptable to all, but that there will be those who will endeavour to return to the old ways. This cannot be allowed to transpire.'

The Fathers passed the baby's spirits over to Doron, and as his arms rose to receive them they merged into one, and it was then that he truly recognised Daniel as a father would. At sight of him, the most important question of all burst up through him and he cursed that he had not asked it first. 'Wait! Is my son in danger? Will his destiny make him a target, either for... for mortal enemies, or some higher... Come back!'

But the Fathers had already begun to fade. He saw their lips move, even as the image became one with the background, and he tried desperately to read the words he couldn't hear, but it was too late.

He awoke with a heart-thumping start, to find his mother and Nita watching.

408

'Your eyes,' Nita began, and he nodded and put a finger to his lips. He rolled carefully onto his side with Daniel, who was fast asleep with his thumb in his mouth, and stood up with Nita's help.

He looked down at his son for a long, searching moment, wondering what the world had in store for him, and how he might somehow make the boy's life any easier. But he knew he couldn't. No parent could, but most parents weren't cursed, with the knowledge that their child would play such a massive part in the future of mankind; his heart hurt, knowing that this little scrap of humanity would someday bear such a burden. He kissed his fingertips and pressed them to the soft, warm cheek, and laid Daniel gently down in his cot. Nita covered him up, and they left the child still sleeping, unaware of the enormity of his very existence.

'How long was I out?'

'Less than a minute,' Rena said, her eyes worried. 'Ron, are you both okay?'

'We're fine.'

'What happened?' Nita asked.

Doron told them everything. Almost. The only thing he left out was that sudden, agonising certainty that their child was destined to walk a strange and dangerous path through life, and that there was so little they could do to ease it for him. There was no doubt that Nita would come to ask that question herself, before too long, but today was not the day for it. They would talk, and they would make plans and try to prepare, but not today.

Unknowingly echoing that thought, Rena spoke decisively. 'Right then, this news can be passed on to everyone another time. This is still your wedding day, and as it's the only one you'll have, you'd better go back and enjoy yourselves.' She held up a hand to forestall argument. 'Daniel's settled, and there's no cause for concern. Go on, off you go.'

Both Doron and Nita were surprised no-one had noticed their hasty departure.

'I'm kind of insulted, actually,' Doron said with mock hurt, but feeling some of his earlier good cheer return at the sight of their friends. 'Want to dance? The music's picked up again.'

They took to the floor next to where John and Jen, and Todd and Sinead had formed a small circle. Doron was gratified to notice at least someone had marked their absence, but it seemed the wrong reason had been unquestioningly applied.

'Where did you two sneak off to then?' Todd asked, and winked at them before resuming his moves.

Jen raised her eyebrow and nodded at him. 'I never knew he could dance.'

'He can't,' Sinead laughed, and as an aggrieved Todd made a big show of proving her wrong, John moved alongside Doron and spoke beneath the beat of the music. 'You went off somewhere without me, didn't you? I felt it.'

Doron nodded. 'Yeah, I'll tell you all tomorrow. It's not the time.' He looked searchingly at John, to check he wasn't hurt by it, but John gave him a brief grin and punched his arm to absolve him, before moving back to wrap his arms around Jen from behind and nuzzle her neck.

Sinead's voice cut across a quiet section of the music. 'I *said*, we're not really married until the marriage is consummated!' She looked mortified as several faces swung around to look at her, then started to laugh helplessly.

'I think we've already accomplished that,' Todd pointed out, chuckling at her embarrassment. 'We just did it the other way round.'

'That doesn't count!'

'No-one's going to know when and where our marriage is consummated, Mrs Gallagher.'

'I will, *Mr* Gallagher! The children are being watched, and I'd sort of like to make it official before I have any more wine.'

'Oh you would, would you?'

Todd took a step closer to her, and she shrieked as he hoisted her into a fireman's lift and walked off the dance floor. Sinead waved goodbye to everyone upside down, still helpless with laughter and beating Todd half-heartedly about the shoulder blades.

Doron and Nita joined in as the other guests cheered their departure, then they resumed their dancing. The music abruptly switched to a slow number, and Doron gave her a pointed look as he gathered her into his arms.

'Don't even think about it!' Nita said.

'You enjoyed the caveman thing the other night,' he reminded her.

She smiled. 'A momentary lapse.' Then she changed the subject. 'I still can't believe what happened tonight.'

'It's not every day your son meets with the Fathers.'

'Oh, well, that too. But...Ron, I heard Moki *laugh*. It's made my day.'

'I thought marrying me would've made your day.'

She considered him carefully, her head on one side. 'It's a close second.'

'Mrs Malik, there has to be *something* I can do to make your day.'

She stretched up, her mouth tantalisingly close to his, but without touching. Her breath made his skin tingle. 'Take me home, and maybe we'll work something out.'

Doron put one arm around her back and bent to slip the other beneath her knees, and she put her arms around his neck and kissed him as he lifted her into his arms and carried her home.

Acknowledgements

After publishing Children of Sinai, I felt that there should be more to the story and it simply wouldn't leave me alone; I was compelled to get it down onto paper. The sequel has taken longer than I imagined due to (thankfully successful) treatment for breast cancer.

The amazingly talented author **Terri Nixon** and I worked together so incredibly well on Children of Sinai that we have also co-authored the sequel Children of Sinai II:The Sixth Fire. Once the research and writing was done, I handed my draft to Terri who advised, edited, mentored, and added her own wonderful style of writing and magic to my story, and here we are with another book.

I would like to thank my husband **Kev**, for thinking I'm clever and giving me permission to base Ian Sloan on him (with the proviso that I didn't kill him off); my beautiful step-granddaughter **Poppy Anning** for being the perfect model for the twins and my father **Milburn Elliott** for the song that Ian Sloan sang to Emily: Dad wrote '*Awaken Little Dreamer*' for me when I was a little girl.
Shelley Clarke

Both Terri and I would like to thank beta readers **Todd Jones** (Shelley's wonderful son and super veterinary nurse)**, Lori Hockey, Sheeba Atkinson** and **Jane Clements**, for giving up their time to check through the first draft; **Chris Bloodworth Photography** for his patience, super photographic talents and work on cover designs; **Zoe O'Farrell** of **Zooloo's Book Tours** and her book bloggers for their hard work in achieving hugely successful book blog tours for both Children of Sinai and The Sixth Fire; **Ant Hockey** for his help in finalising the original book trailer; super authors **Lex Allen, Bryan Quinn**, **Suzanne Rogerson** and **Jessica Belmont**, our wonderful families, dear friends and fans for their support, including the grey flannel knicker brigade from 1970's Rochester Grammar School: **Lori Hockey, Sheena Cunningham, Veronica Odhams and Deborah Brown**; **Stuart Whyte**, Studio Head of Playstation London Studio for his invaluable advice on RFID tags and cloning, and Terri's brilliant and lovely son **Dominic Pine,** for his willingness to share his expert advice on security systems.

Finally, acknowledgements go to the following works and their authors, for without them it would have been incredibly difficulty to find the information needed to write the sequel:

Dictionary of Ute Indian Language - compiled by Mormon V Selman, who was a missionary and teacher among the Ute Indians in Thistle Valley, Utah from 1849 to 1880

The Southern Ute and Ute Mountain Ute Tribes In The Twentieth Century - a thesis by Richard Keith Young

The Ute Creation Story – as told by Alden Naranjo

Southern Ute Indian Tribe website

The Hopi Prophecies - Ross Bishop

Crystalinks for details of the prophecies

Peoples of the Mesa Verde Region - Crow Canyon Archaeological Center

Legends of The Star People – David S Lewis

Carbondale explores generating hydropower from Nettle Creek - article by John C Volson, Post Independent, Aspen, CO Colorado

Indian Child Welfare Act – Wikipedia

Glenwood The Early Days - Yampah Spa, The Hot Springs Vapor Caves

Glenwood Springs Hydroelectric Plant - Colorado Encyclopaedia

Heathrow Airport Fire and Rescue Service for their advice on aeroplane fires

MedlinePlus Medical Encyclopedia – Bone marrow transplants

About The Authors

Clarke Nixon is author duo Shelley Clarke and Terri Nixon, who first met while working together in the Faculty of Arts at the University of Plymouth. They quickly became friends, and when Shelley had an idea for a story, Terri, already an established author, helped her to shape it into a novel and get it into print. Not only were they compatible colleagues, but they discovered they were a great writing team too

Shelley Clarke was born into a naval family in Kent in 1958, and consequently moved house a lot as a child. She had ambitions to follow in her father's footsteps and join the Royal Navy, and to become a carpenter, but these were not female occupations at that time. So she learned to type… which has come in jolly handy for putting her stories first onto paper, and now onto screen.

Shelley is a keen painter, poet, and karaoke enthusiast; she loves mad family get-togethers, hates olives, ironing and gardening, and currently lives in Devon with her husband Kev, and their two Tibetan Terriers Nena and Pepi, who make them smile every day.

Shelley often forgets she is a grown-up.

Terri Nixon was born in Devon, but grew up on the edge of Bodmin Moor, Cornwall, where she discovered a love of writing that has stayed with her ever since.

She also discovered apple-scrumping, and how to jump out of a hayloft without breaking any bones, but no-one's ever offered to pay her for doing those.

Terri writes family sagas for Piatkus (Little, Brown,) and crime thrillers for Hobeck Books, as R.D. Nixon. She has also written horror, as T Nixon, and contributed to several multi-author anthologies using a number of variations on her name/s. She might be forgiven for not knowing who she is on any given day.

www.terrinixon.com

Printed in Great Britain
by Amazon